BARRIER

OF

TEARS

Brian Greiner

This is a work of fiction. All of the characters, organizations, and events portrayed in this novel are either products of the author's imagination or are used fictitiously.

BARRIER OF TEARS

Published by Damn Fool Press
www.damnfoolpress.com

ISBN 978-1-989360-01-9 epub
ISBN 978-1-989360-02-6 mobi
ISBN 978-1-989360-03-3 trade paperback

First Edition: February 2020

As always, this is for Lynn and the cats.

CHAPTER ONE

Inside the Transit Tube

Bob yawned and stretched until his joints creaked. Upon releasing the stretch, he shrugged and twisted this way and that until every muscle loosened up. He'd had several hours of restful sleep untroubled by dreams, and he was feeling better than he had in some time. That good mood soured somewhat when saw the message indicator flashing on his data tablet. He sighed and tapped it to see what fresh problems waited to greet him today.

To his relief there were only two messages: one from the ship detailing its nominal status and one from Rhian wanting to meet for breakfast. The first he acknowledged after ensuring there were no abnormalities, and to the second he sent a brief reply saying he was on his way.

He dressed quickly and left for the mess with a detour to the control room. It wasn't that he didn't trust the message the ship's control system had sent him, it was just that he liked to confirm things for himself. Well, that and to take a look outside.

Bob activated the forward screen and stared at the void for a few seconds. It was a swirling maelstrom of various shades of blackness that both attracted and repelled one's mind. He gave a slight shiver and disabled the screen. The mind-twisting patterns of hyperspace were almost preferable to the scene inside the transit tube. The former gave a sense of motion, but the latter offered nothing but a headache.

He left the room for the mess. Once there, he gathered some breakfast and sat down opposite Rhian who was just finishing her own meal. Before eating, he rubbed at his forehead in an effort to reduce the slight headache.

"Been looking outside again, haven't you?" said Rhian as she shook her head. "You insist on doing that even after warning me against it." She grimaced as she shuddered. "Viewing it once was enough, thank you very much."

In response, Bob grinned. "I like to see where I'm going, or at least to experience the journey." He shook his head. "Not sure that I approve of this transit tube, though. No way to measure progress, or determine if there's any progress whatsoever."

Rhian grinned back. "Sort of like a slow motion transit through a portal, then."

Bob paused with a forkful of food half-way to his mouth, then placed it carefully on the plate. "You know, I never thought of it that way. Hmm. Different physics, of course, but ..." his eyes took on a faraway look that was interrupted several seconds later as Rhian snapped her fingers several times.

"Focus, Bob. Some of the finest minds of your ancestors spent years trying, and failing, to understand this stuff. Anyway, I wanted us to have a meal together because we've not done it for a couple of days. Busy days, too, for the both of us. Maybe we should take a half-day off? Thoughts?"

As she spoke, Bob finished his breakfast and leaned back in his chair while cradling a cup of tea in his hands. "You've a good point. In truth, we've been going flat out for quite some time with few breaks. Still, there's a lot of work to do and little time to do it in."

Rhian leaned forward. "Exactly my point. We've bounced from a battle on Earth, to a battle with the rogue sentience that had taken control of the lost base, to being imprisoned on the Hell Planet, escaping that only to be given the task of saving humanity by your Uncle Lou, back to the base to uncover secrets of an ancient alien race ..." she paused to take a deep breath before continuing. "And now we're in a magical cosmic tunnel being transported Goddess-knows-where. Assuming we end up inside the Veil of Tears like we hope to, we don't know what to expect, what the great danger is, or even how to go about finding it." She paused once more for a breath. "That about sum it up?" She leaned back in her chair, breathing somewhat heavily.

Bob stared at her with wide-eyed innocence. "You say that as if that sort of thing isn't normal for us."

That got a *snerk* out of Rhian before she managed to return her face to a more solemn visage. After a few seconds she emitted another *snerk*, then a short giggle, followed by a series of guffaws. Bob joined in the laughter. The merriment lasted for over a minute and left them both wiping their eyes.

"Seriously, Bob," said Rhian through the last of her chuckles, "we could use a bit of a break."

"Yeah, you're right. Still, I'm loath to set aside more than half a day for that." He forestalled her retort by holding up a hand. "You're quite correct in saying that we need to take a break. But rather than one large one, I propose we have several smaller ones. We've got at least another week before we arrive, possibly more. Perhaps have a short break every couple of days? Today though, I agree that a half-day wouldn't be a bad idea."

Rhian nodded and pursed her lips as she considered the proposal. "I like the idea of several breaks, even if they are smaller." She clenched her hands and made a slight wince. "My hands are a bit sore from all the weapons practise I've been doing. The auto-medic suggested a warm wrap to loosen things up. Thought I'd put my feet up and read as I follow its orders. You?"

3

Bob nodded. "That sounds like a good idea, actually. I'd like to read through Celcilia's book again. As well, there's a few things I can get the ship's systems to crunching on in the meantime. Remember, there's still the chance of hostile forces chasing or ahead of us. It's looking less likely, but still possible. I'll have the ship do a deep dive into the records to check a few new things I've thought of. After that, I want to do some proper physical conditioning."

"I thought the auto-medic took care of that?"

He shook his head. "Not all of it, just the basics. The fine motor control skills still need manual practise. I've been slacking off on that and want to get things back into top form." At the sour look on her face he laughed. "I rather enjoy it, actually." Then his face became grim. "Don't forget why we're going into the Veil, Rhian. There's something very dangerous there. Uncle Lou said that only a normal human with my set of skills could set things right. Well, a lot of my skills involve being in top physical condition."

Rhian's expression became sad at the thought of her friend putting himself into harm's way once again. "Yeah, I know." She offered him a slight smile. "We've been doing the research stuff for a while, and I guess I forgot about that side of you. You make a good researcher, you know."

Bob gave a formal nod of his head, then smiled. "High praise coming from you, and I thank you." He paused for a moment then snapped his fingers. "Oh, almost forgot. Before we left I managed to come up with something similar to Earth chocolate. Want to try some?"

The eager look in her eyes was all the answer he needed.

CHAPTER TWO
Behind the Veil

There was little warning that their journey was at an end. The calculations of the ancient researchers were not precise, so Bob and Rhian prepared for emergence at the minimum predicted time. It was two tense days later when emergence actually occurred. They emerged at local night inside of a large, bowl-shaped depression on the top of a tall hill. Only small clouds of dust disturbed by their entrance greeted their arrival.

Bob hovered the ship in place for several minutes but detected nothing of note: no energy emissions, no structures, no people. He lifted the ship to a point just above the lip of the depression to scan the surrounding area but once again found nothing of interest.

"What now?" asked Rhian.

"Engage full stealth mode and we'll go a bit higher to rise above the level of these hills. There's a nice plateau not far from here that'd make a good place to land. There's some trees taller than the ship around the edges and what looks like scrub in the centre."

The brief look once again saw nothing so Bob landed the ship on the plateau he'd seen. "Anything on the passive sensors?" he asked.

"Still nothing at all. The local moon is rising ... looks pretty, by the way, even if only a crescent. Want to head up there and look down?"

Bob considered that for a moment. "No point. We're here now. If there's anything hostile, the risk of going up is greater than staying put."

"So now what?"

He turned to her. "Go get some rest. I'll wake you before local dawn, then catch a brief nap myself. After a meal we'll take a closer look at this world."

"Seriously?"

Bob shrugged. "Why not? We need to take things slow and easy, so let's sit quietly and observe for a while. That won't take two of us."

Rhian opened her mouth to protest but realized that given his vast experience he was probably correct. She gave a soft chuckle. "I never realized how much sitting around and waiting all this gallivanting about the galaxy involved. The fictions of my world promised more excitement."

"Heh. Be glad for the tedium of it, Rhian. Excitement usually means something bad has happened. Now go get some rest."

Rhian went to her room and lay down on her bed. She felt too keyed up to rest, but was dragged out of sleep when a knock came at her cabin door. "Your watch, Rhian," came Bob's voice from the hallway.

"Yeah, yeah. Give me a minute," she said, her voice slightly distorted by a yawn.

It took not much more than that for her to splash some water on her face and make her way to the control room. To her surprise it was still quite dark outside, and said so.

"The days are about thirty hours long, so we still have a few hours before sunrise. No surprises, but you can review the scans at your work station. I'm off for a couple hours. Wake me if something happens."

With that he walked out of the room. Rhian settled down to see what she'd missed ... which wasn't much, as it turned out. As promised, Bob returned two hours later without her having to prompt him.

"Go get something to eat," he said. "I had something before I came here."

Dawn was just beginning as she returned from breakfast. The light allowed her a proper look at the new world. As expected from the scans during the night, it looked much like her native England, at least at ground level. A closer look, though, showed arid areas on the horizon. The exception was the depression that had been their arrival point ... it looked quite arid and was devoid of any life. She glanced at the display at her work station. "Looks like something's moving this way, possibly a group of somethings."

"I see it. Been tracking it while you've been eating. Thought it might be local wildlife, but not sure. About to launch a probe to check it out. Care to do the honours?"

Rhian nodded. This was her first chance to put some of her new training to the test. She went through the launch sequence with care, not bothering to attempt to match the speed she'd seen Bob perform the same procedure during training. She knew from experience that doing something new was best done with care, as speed would come with practise and experience.

"Probe away," she announced. "Do you want to take control?"

"Nope, you're doing fine. Set it for passive scanning. Move it to just shy of the edge then hover just high enough to clear any stones. That's good. Now, ease the front tip over the edge and hover for a few seconds, then ease back. Now, that's interesting."

Rhian had been focusing her attention on manoeuvring the probe. Only when it retracted did she look at her displays. She saw three individuals making their way up a narrow path that led up to the plateau. By tweaking the controls, she was able to enhance the image. The individuals could now be seen to be male, well past middle-aged, dressed in rough clothing of pants, boots, and what looked like a serape. The colours of the clothing varied between individuals and consisted of muted shades that covered the spectrum. Each carried a staff made of wood, which they used with the ease of long practise. The probe detected no sources of energy from any of the group. The men were moving as one would expect of someone elderly but in good condition.

"A welcoming committee?" she asked.

"Hmm. Might be. Which begs the question of how they knew we were here. Might also be that they are coming here for some other reason unrelated to our arrival."

"So we wait?"

"No. I'll suit up and go meet them." He tapped at the controls on his console. "The probe's weapons are now live, both energy and kinetic. Move it off to one side about ten metres away. Monitor with passive sensors only unless I say otherwise. Don't fire the weapons unless I say so or am incapacitated. Keep the comm link hot and let me know if you see anything of note." He got up and strode out of the room.

Less than two minutes later she heard his voice on the comms. "At the airlock and about to go out. I'll lock it after I exit."

She acknowledged and moved the drone as ordered. Studying her display, she saw Bob walk out of ship and trot towards the edge of the plateau where the trail was. He was wearing his standard outfit of skin-suit with attached armoured sections, helmet, and pistol. As he turned, Rhian noted with approval that he was wearing an anti-grav pack, as that would give him a strong set of tactical options. She chuckled to herself at the thought of a hard-core academic such as herself becoming such a student of military tactics.

"Anything new from our friends?" he asked.

Rhian snuck a quick peek over the edge. "They're still coming up at the same speed. No apparent reaction now that you've exited. They're about four metres below the edge, and at their current rate of travel will reach you in about a minute. The ledge terminates just ahead of you and to the right, by the way."

"Thanks." Bob adjusted his position to be three metres to the side of where the ledge terminated, and stood waiting. Rhian noted that he stood upright with his hands folded in front of him. She frowned at the poor combat readiness of that for a moment, then gave her head a rueful shake. A defensive posture was all very well, but not conducive to a friendly first contact. Then she noticed that his right hand was positioned next to the controls on his left wrist. That would allow him to look non-threatening but still give him lots of military options if it came to that.

The wait for the contact seemed to stretch out forever, but a glance at the chronometer showed that there were still some seconds to go. She rolled her neck and felt several pops as the tenseness worked its way out. That felt so good that she risked a few seconds to work the kinks out of her hands. She was about to risk another quick look over the edge when she saw the top of a head wobbled into view.

"It's show time," Bob murmured. "Follow my lead."

The wobbling heads soon included shoulders, then torsos, and soon the three visitors were standing on the plateau staring at the ship. They exchanged glances but did not speak. Via the probe, Rhian could hear them puffing from their recent exertions, a noise that drowned out the soft breeze.

Bob let them gape at the ship for a few seconds, then scuffed a foot along the ground. The sound caused them to whirl around to face him. They each lifted their staff and brought it into a defensive stance, then caught themselves and bent to place them on the ground. After that, they stood upright and regarded Bob.

"I'm detected elevated heartbeats from all of them," said Rhian. "They were puffing from the climb, but it's become a bit irregular. They're scared, Bob, just trying not to show it."

"Yep, that's my sense of it as well. Give them a low-level active scan, please."

A heartbeat later Rhian said, "Clean. Not a trace of tech that I can see."

Bob didn't reply, but touched a control on his wrist that caused his helmet visor to retract. He regarded the men with a neutral look, then gave a short bow. "Hello, my name is Bob," he said in the language of his people.

That caused startled reactions from each of the men. They turned to face each other and began talking in low voices.

"Rhian?"

"The probe's picking them up well enough. It sounds very much like your language, Bob ... almost as if they're using colloquialisms that I've not learned on top of a strange accent."

Two of the group urged the third of their party forward. He shot them a baleful glare then faced Bob with a polite smile and a short bow. He placed a hand on his chest and said, "Granlif." He pointed to one colleague and said, "Salna." Pointing to the third member he said, "Torla." He gave another short bow and looked at Bob expectantly.

Bob put a hand on his chest. "Bob," he said. They each gave a short bow to him which he returned. At a gesture from Granlif he added, "I have come a very long way to visit here. Do you live near here?"

The three men looked at each other with excited looks. Granlif smiled and held up one finger, spoke a word, held up two fingers, spoke a word, and so forth until he'd held up all ten fingers. Then he fell silent and looked at Bob expectantly.

"Bob, he's—"

"Counting. Yes, I see that. As you said earlier, it all sounds very close to my language, but distorted."

"Linguistic drift. Only to be expected. Repeat what he just did."

Bob suppressed the urge to sigh. Rhian might be a master linguist, but that much he could figure out for himself. He did as instructed and began the process of learning their language. As Rhian had suggested, there was more linguistic drift in the language than Bob had expected. Aside from the change in vocabulary, there were changes in pronunciations and syllable emphasis. It was nearly noon by the time Bob was confident enough to hold a basic conversation without being misunderstood.

"Do you feel hunger or thirst?" asked Bob as they all sat on the ground. "We can have a rest."

Salna gave a shy smile as he asked, "Rest on your ship?"

Bob shook his head and Salna shrugged. His companions glared at him. Torla bowed and apologized. "Forgive my friend, please. There is still much to learn about each other."

That got a smile from Bob. "That is true, Torla. I do not take offence. Do you require water?"

"Our thanks, but no," said Granlif. "We have brought supplies." He stared at Bob's suit. "We can share if you have none."

"Thank you, but my equipment has what I require."

To his surprise, that caused all three of them to frown for a brief moment, to be replaced once again by polite smiles. They produced what looked like a flat bread from their pouches, as well as a gourd of water, and began eating. For his part, Bob took a small sip of water from inside his helmet as well as a couple of sips of nutrient paste. It was a sparse meal but sufficient for the moment.

After nearly a minute of silence Salna spoke. "How is it that you speak our language, but in such a strange fashion?"

Bob shrugged. "It is the language of my people."

"Where do you come from?" asked Granlif.

Bob pointed to the sky. "I come from far away."

They each gave him a withering look that reminded Bob of the times he'd sassed a teacher.

"That much we can see for ourselves, young man," said Granlif in a dry tone. "We are a simple people, but are well aware that there are people living on other planets." He turned to nod at the ship then turned his gaze back to Bob. "We are also aware that your ship is of the sort to travel between the stars."

Bob inclined his head and smiled. "I mean no offence. In my travels I have learned that it is often best not to assume too much. Assumptions lead to misunderstandings."

The older men nodded as they regarded him with neutral expressions as they ate.

"For example," Bob continued. "When I referred to my clothing as 'equipment', I noticed that upset you. Why is that?" He took another sip of water and paste.

"Good catch," said Rhian in his ear. "I was hoping you'd notice that." She'd not said much all morning, preferring to listen and interject the odd suggestion.

The men exchanged looks for a moment before Torla spoke. "That word has unhappy meanings."

"Unhappy how?"

"Such words are used by our enemy. The enemy of humanity."

The air was still and silence hung heavily. After several heartbeats Bob broke the silence. "You have a distrust of all machines?"

"Yes, and those bound by such," replied Granlif. "There are abominations that walk the stars ... agents of the Enemy. We must guard against them."

Bob pondered that for a moment, then stood. "I think I understand," he said in a soft voice. He began removing the armoured plates and placing them on the ground.

"Bob, what are you doing?" came Rhian's voice in his ear.

He removed his helmet, and when it hid his mouth he murmured, "A calculated risk. Stand by." Then his helmet came off and he added it to the pile on the ground. That was followed by his anti-grav backpack and equipment belt. The old men continued to stare at him with neutral expressions, so he removed his skinsuit and stood before them naked. He turned slowly to allow them to seem him from all angles.

"Do I look like the Enemy or one of their creatures?

"No," said Salna. "Not one of the Enemy. But they have made abominations in the shape of humans."

"Ah," said Bob. "Does the Enemy have ships that travel between the stars?"

"Many," said Granlif. "Too many," added Salna in a soft voice.

"Do they have anti-grav units?" asked Bob.

The older men shook their heads. "We do not understand that word."

Bob looked at them. "Machines that work against the pull of gravity."

They shook their heads. Bob smiled and said, "Watch this."

He put his suit back on, including the plate armour and the anti-grav pack. The helmet he left on the ground so that they could see his face. He touched the controls and rose into the air until he was floating just above their heads. Then he came back to the ground and ran towards the edge of the plateau. He reached the edge and jumped off, dropped half a body length, then floated up until he was several body lengths above the plateau. He drifted over to where the men were and descended.

"Can your Enemy do that? Or their creatures?" he asked in a quiet voice.

The older men looked at him with wide eyes. Finally, Salna said, "I felt neither heat nor motion of the air as you flew. This is not something anyone can do anywhere ... that we are aware of. The legends speak of sacred energies that would allow humans to perform such feats." He shrugged. "Many of us thought those to be only legends. That might be incorrect."

"Might be?" snapped Granlif to Salna. "Do you see the size and efficiency of his mechanism? It matches what the legends speak of." He turned to face Bob, leaning forward with an eager look on his face. "I believe that you were honest when you said that you came from far away. The only question in my mind is how far away that might be." He examined Bob with a penetrating gaze. In that he was joined by his fellows.

Bob was silent for a moment. "Shall we speak of these large matters now or would it be better to ensure the accuracy of understanding before proceeding? We share a common language grown apart by time. It would be very easy to create small misunderstandings that could grow into serious problems."

The faces of his three visitors grew serious as they traded looks. After a few seconds they traded nods, then Salna turned to face him once more. "There is wisdom in what you say, young man." Then his mouth quirked into a slight grin. "Perhaps your friends on board the ship would like to join us? There was a faint buzz coming from your helmet which I'm sure was some form of alert."

Bob sighed, nodded, picked up his helmet, and put it on. He opened up a channel and immediately heard Rhian speaking in English. "Bob. Bob. Open the damn channel. Oh, there you are. There's movement at the base of the plateau. Looks like a small crowd milling around ... perhaps half a dozen. No energy readings of any sort, nor signs of any tech. Shall I have the probe do a quick peek over the edge for a better view?"

"No, hold off on that for the moment. Tech seems to spook them, and they've spoken of an enemy of some sort."

"I picked up on that. Look, I'm a trained linguist. Your suggestion to improve language skills is a good one, and I'm sure I can make better progress than you. No offence."

He grunted a laugh. "None taken. Alright, they've deduced that there's crew in the ship but let's not let on our exact numbers. Move the probe over to my side and hover at about face level. There's an audio feature on the controls that will allow you to speak and be heard by them. We can rig up something fancier later if required. Oh, and good call in using English ... let's keep that as our private language for now."

Rhian acknowledged and the probe began to float towards them. The older men watched with great interest as the metre-long ovoid moved towards them without a sound to mark its movements. It halted an arms-length away from Bob's side, facing them. It emanated a crackle of sound then they heard Rhian's voice. "Hello. My name is Rhian. I am pleased to meet you all."

Bob interjected, "Rhian is a scholar who knows much about languages. We believe that she will be able to help us all understand each other better."

The faces of the men lit up with delight. "You travel with a scholar? That is very wise of you, young man," said Granlif. He and the others introduced themselves to Rhian, but this time added titles that seemed to indicate academic standing. Rhian favoured them with a more detailed introduction of herself, and the four of them began chatting about how best to proceed. Bob let them ramble on for several minutes before clearing his throat.

"This is a very good start, but you have friends at the base of this plateau. Should we invite them up?"

The men exchanged looks, then Salna shook his head. "No need. They wait to see what will happen to us."

"And others watch them from hidden places," said Bob.

"Indeed. But it might be wise to let them know that we have made contact. If you will excuse me." Salna rose to his feet and walked to the edge. He waved his arms in a series of patterns that reminded Rhian of semaphore, then watched as the others replied. Salna brought his hands together in a series of exaggerated claps, then returned to his colleagues and sat down.

"His colleagues at the base appear to have settled down," Rhian's voice said in Bob's helmet. "Oh, wait. One appears to be trotting off. I'm curious as to what was said."

"There's no tech, so they use visual signals and runners. Looks to be set up in stages to prevent an enemy from knowing where the command post is or even the other watchers. It's a common enough technique." He saw the old men looking at him so he switched to their common language. "Your friends have sent a runner to pass along the information you gave them. Rhian was curious about that."

"And you are not?"

Bob smiled in a friendly way and shook his head. "Not really. I've had the training of a soldier and recognize the technique. Have even used it myself." His smile faded into a sad look. "I also know that it means that the three of you are considered expendable. As are your friends below."

He paused for a moment then added, "You were ready for something like this. That tells me much. I believe that we each have important stories to tell. Please continue with Rhian until you are confident that the stories will be understood with accuracy. Rhian, I'll let you set the pace for this. I'll just watch."

The older men looked at Bob with greater respect, then nodded. They heard Rhian clear her throat and the four of them resumed their conversation. For his part, Bob sat cross-legged on the ground and listened as he adjusted to the language changes. The pronunciations were easy enough to get a handle on, but he was worried about new words and even more so about common words that might have changed meaning. He was unhappy about the slowness of the pace, but recognized that it would be time well spent.

The four scholars had chatted happily for over an hour when Rhian announced that it was time to look at the written form of the language. "So, how should we handle that, Bob? Scratch in the dirt?"

"Nope," he replied. "Dig out a half-dozen or so journals and pens, then put them in the airlock. Let me know when you've done that."

They'd been speaking in their common tongue so their visitors could understand them. Torla interjected, "You have such advanced equipment. Do you still use paper and pen?"

Bob grinned. "Not exactly the same as yours, but, yes, similar in function. Sometimes the old ways are best. Or so I was taught."

That got a grin out of his guests, which was Bob's intention. He was beginning to like the old scholars, even if they did have a tendency to be pedantic and view him as an unruly student. Rhian seemed quite at ease with them, which was a big help. He heard her voice in his helmet alerting him that she'd placed the materials in the airlock. He excused himself and trotted back to the ship, glad of the chance to stretch his legs.

Arriving at the ship, he opened the airlock and found three knapsacks. "I said a few notebooks, Rhian," he grumbled at her via the comms. "Not an entire library."

"Oh, stop complaining. One holds water and some blankets to sit on ... they'll need both by now. The other has food. The third has the writing materials. Oh, and some lights and heaters in case we work late. Now off with you ... I've told them to expect the water and they're waiting for it. Oh, and use the anti-grav to take it all back to them ... they'd like to see that again."

Bob raised an eyebrow at her commanding tone, but smiled and said, "Yes, ma'am. As you command."

He hoisted the knapsacks out of the airlock, secured it, then rose into the air and back to his visitors. He settled back down to his original spot and flipped open the knapsacks. He passed around the blankets and water, which were very well received.

"Thank you for this, Rhian," said Salna. "And you, too, Bob," he added as an afterthought.

Bob gave a polite nod, content to be thought of as the junior partner if it helped move things along. "Do you want to pause for a meal or start with the writing?"

"Hmm," said Salna. "How about we eat while you write out your alphabet and some of the words we've discussed so far. Does that sound like a good idea, everyone?" He looked at his fellows and the probe. They all thought that was a fine plan, so Bob passed around the food then bent to his task.

He took a journal and pen then hesitated for a moment. His own handwriting wasn't the best, so he decided to produce samples of both the informal and formal forms. These were equivalent to Rhian's printed and cursive writing forms.

Bob began writing, giving only partial attention to the chatter of the others. He produced a page of the alphabet in both forms, then another couple pages of words in the same manner. Looking up he saw the others were engrossed in a discussion about language drift as a reflection of societal trends. With a grin he resumed writing, but this time decided to write out as much of the Precepts of Survival as they gave him time for. He stopped only when he heard Rhian call out his name a couple of times.

"You lot ready to continue?" he said in English. Holding up his journal, he added in their common language, "Made plenty of samples for you. Oh, did you need to signal your friends at the base of the plateau?"

Granlif sprang to his feet. "Thank you for reminding me. I'd quite forgotten about the schedule." He scurried over to the edge and began signalling.

Bob heard a faint scritching coming from his helmet which was laying at his feet. He put it on and heard Rhian's voice, speaking in English. "It's all going very well, I think. Uhm, they seem to have gotten the impression that I'm, ah..." her voice trailed off.

"In charge?" said Bob in a dry tone. "That's fine with me ... I think they're a lot more comfortable dealing with another scholar. Any other reason for your discomfort, fearless leader?"

"Heh. Well, yes. I got concerned about the group on the bottom so I slipped out a needle probe from the far side of the ship and around the circumference of the plateau. Did you know that the ship could do that on its own? Wait, yes, of course you did. Anyway, it's tucked inside a large crack with just the tip peeking out, just as the manuals said to do. The group on the bottom was getting a bit antsy until they saw Granlif signalling. They've quieted down now and sent out another runner. That's only decreased the initial size of the group by one, so I assume a runner came back when we weren't looking. Hope you don't mind me sending the second probe without asking."

"No, you did the right thing. Tell the needle probe to look for infrared signatures ... someone might get careless and allow a nighttime fire to show."

"I will. Speaking of night, are our new friends staying the night? If so, did you want them aboard the ship? It's a lot warmer than outside at night."

"I'll ask." He switched to the common language and asked, "Are you leaving for the night or staying here?"

Granlif had returned to the group by this time. "I told them that we would be staying the night. If that's alright with you," he added, turning to speak to Rhian via the probe.

Rhian said, "Bob and I were just discussing that. As for where you might sleep ..." her voice trailed off.

Bob hurried to interject, "We have lights and heaters here that will make the night comfortable." He gave an apologetic shrug. "We have official protocols that must be followed, I'm afraid."

As expected, at the word 'protocols' the older men nodded in agreement. "Yes, yes, protocols must be followed," said Torla with a longing look at the ship.

"Perhaps you can examine the writing samples I produced while I set up a camp for you?" suggested Bob. "I can fetch more food, water, and extra blankets from the ship and be back in a few minutes. Would that be acceptable?"

It was quite acceptable to their guests, so Bob handed over his notebook and jogged back to the ship. He entered to be met by Rhian who was plainly irked.

"Bob, they're old academics. Too old to be camping out in the cold."

"No, Rhian. I promise you they'll be comfortable, but not in here." He held up a hand to forestall any arguments. "Remember the reason we're here. We need information, and they seem to be interested in sharing. Also, remember how quickly they responded to our presence, and with amazing organization. No, there's something going on here. We need to be on our guard until we figure it out. Now go to the galley and make up some good meals. Say, enough for two meals for four people, including water and snacks. I'll go fetch some field equipment that'll keep them comfortable. Wait. First thing for you to do is go back to the control room and stay on the comm link with the probe in case they want to talk to you."

Rhian tapped at the earpiece that Bob had failed to notice. He gave her a nod and a grin then vanished into the ship. She sighed then headed for the galley. It irked her not to be able to offer better hospitality, but Bob was correct. The mission came first.

Several minutes later Bob was filling up an anti-grav sled with supplies and exiting via the cargo airlock on the side of the ship not visible to their visitors. They knew only of the one airlock and Bob hoped to keep it that way for as long as possible. Twilight had fallen, and shadows lay deep on the landscape, allowing the sled to appear to have come from the airlock. Bob went back inside and helped Rhian carry the remainder of the supplies to the airlock. He exited the ship, secured the airlock, and signalled the sled to sneak in to his location. When it arrived, he walked it to where his visitors were.

They greeted him warmly and with undisguised amazement at the sled. They stood to one side and tossed dirt under it to see if there were any way to discern how it worked. Bob grinned and swept his foot underneath the sled to show that no harmful energies were being emitted to keep the sled aloft. That rendered them speechless until Bob unpacked the sled to show them small camp chairs, sleeping bags, toiletries, and food.

He set up the lights and chairs, and insisted they sit in comfort while he gave them each a meal. As they ate, he prepared a sleeping area by scraping away the loose rocks with a shovel he'd brought. The sleeping bags were laid out, with a heater at the head and foot of each. A small knapsack containing water, snacks, and toiletries was placed next to each position. Less than ten minutes later he was finished and sitting in his own chair, eating a meal with gusto.

The three men had watched with interest as he went about his chores. "You've done this before, I see," said Granlif with a smile.

Bob returned the smile and nodded. "Quite a bit."

Salna cleared his throat. "We've been studying this writing sample you left with us." He favoured Bob with a glare. "Your handwriting is atrocious, you know." Then he smiled as he added, "But I suspect you've been told that before."

He became serious and leaned forward, tapping a finger on the journal. "Judging by this, our written languages are very much the same. Less change than the spoken form." Salna looked at the probe and waved a hand. "Some variation, to be sure, but I suspect it has more to do with artistic variations used for special purposes." He handed Bob a journal. "Here ...

we've each written something in this. Notes from lectures we've given."

Bob took the book and scanned the contents for several minutes. The sound of Rhian clearing her throat got his attention. "Care to share with those of us who can't see what you're looking at?" she said in sweet tones.

"Oh, sorry. Uhm, Salna is correct. Their handwriting is quite a bit better than mine." He flashed them a smile. "And the two are remarkably similar despite the changes in the spoken form. The artistic variations he spoke of are along the lines of the different fonts in your own written forms. Some plain, some fancy." He glanced at the older men. "Aside from changes in vocabulary, we'll be able to read each other's records."

Salna leaned forward. "It is as if your people and ours shared a common past."

Bob nodded and leaned back into his chair, steepling his fingers under his chin. "Yes. How deeply did you wish to go into this tonight?"

Each of the older men leaned back in their chairs and grew silent for the space of several heartbeats. "Yes," said Granlif. "That is the question, is it not? How deeply we—each of us—answers depends on the level of trust we have managed to achieve."

Bob raised a finger to point at the night sky, which by this time had grown quite dark. "What do you see?"

The others glanced up for a moment then back at him. This time Salna spoke. "Our universe. But you have another meaning, I think."

"Yes. I've already told you that I come from another star."

"But not from our universe," said Salna.

Bob inhaled deeply and exhaled sharply. "Same universe, different location."

"Yet you have mechanisms unknown to us except in legend. Once again, where do you come from?"

"Once again, what do you see?"

Salna smiled and looked up, this time studying it. "The universe and the stars within it."

"What defines the extent of the universe?"

This time Granlif answered. "The energies that surround it, creating a barrier." He shrugged. "We know that there are stars beyond that barrier, for we can ofttimes see them. But for us, it is a prison. A cage that traps us here with the Enemy."

Bob looked at each of the men in turn. "My people call the energies that surround you the 'Veil'. My ancestors created it."

To his great surprise the older men simply nodded. "That is the old word for it, yes. Our ancestors entered it during a time of war," said Granlif. He looked at Bob expectantly.

Bob nodded. "Yes. Their purpose was to lure in a terrible Enemy that was on the verge of destroying all of humanity. The Enemy entered the trap, and the Veil was activated." He paused to look at the others.

Salna took up the tale. "We call it the Great Sacrifice. Many battles were fought and many people died before the Enemy was defeated." He paused and looked at Bob.

"That sacrifice allowed my ancestors to defeat that Enemy," said Bob in a soft voice. "It is said that we wept for a hundred years. We call it the Veil of Tears, both for the sacrifice and because we could never know what happened within it."

"You say that as if there were other enemies, Bob," said Torla.

"Yes. There were many before and many after. Alien races that tried to exterminate us. But we prevailed."

"And here you are," said Salna. "After all this time. How is that possible?"

Bob looked at each of them again before speaking. "You know the answer, I think. There is an ancient device, older than humanity, that creates a tunnel between here and the greater galaxy."

Torla spoke up. "But the ancient legends say that the ancient way is disabled by forces born of exploding stars."

Bob shook his head. "There are eddies and currents in those stellar forces that allow it to function at infrequent intervals."

"And here you are," said Salna. "Now, of all times. Why?"

"I was sent by eldest of my people. He told me a power stirring within the Veil, a power that threated humanity. He sent me to neutralize it."

"With but a single ship?" said Torla.

Bob turned to look at him. "One ship that is the culmination of eons of battles after the Veil was created. It will suffice for the task. As will I. Now, do you trust me enough to tell me of this new Enemy? How did it get into the Veil?"

The three older men looked at each other for several seconds then hung their heads. Salna looked up and said, "It is of our own making. We created a weapon to defeat that ancient Enemy, but the weapon has now turned against us. Some worlds survive through the struggle of battle, while some of us survive by becoming invisible." He waved a hand around. "We emit no energies, so there is nothing to suggest that the planet is inhabited."

Bob nodded. "That explains why you have the sentries and response system. You thought we might be an advance guard for the Enemy."

The older men all nodded. Granlif said, "It is not unknown for the Enemy to make use of human agents. Not many, and not here, but there are some."

Rhian interjected, "How is it that you knew we were here?"

Torla smiled in a friendly way. "Our sky watchers saw nothing to indicate an incoming ship. We have simple mechanical sensors scattered throughout the region. Those showed that a ship had arrived inside the transit stage. Not through flight but rather popped into existence. Other sensors indicated that you had alighted on this plateau. The response had been planned for, and practised, for many generations, ever since the first incursions so long ago."

Bob turned to the probe and said to Rhian, "Pressure sensors based on water levels or air changes, balanced items tumbling, that sort of thing." He looked at Torla for confirmation and received a smile and a nod in return.

"And you came not knowing what you'd find?" said Rhian. "You are very brave."

That got the older men chuckling. "Not so brave as all that, Rhian," said Granlif. "Part of our duties as scholars is to monitor for incursions and take part in any response." He shrugged. "We are old and therefore more expendable." He turned to Bob. "There are elements of that strategy in those writings of yours, Bob. We recognized bits of some of our own ancient philosophical writings in it. Yet it reads like something you were quoting."

Bob grinned. "Yes, indeed. I ran out of ideas on what to write, so I decided to begin writing out one of my favourite books, 'The Precepts of Survival'. It arose as a compilation of thoughts after the end of the Great Wars, when all of the enemies had been defeated."

"Interesting," said Granlif. He moved his neck and shoulders to get the tenseness out of them. "I suggest we take a break for sleep and resume in the morning. Many new things have been spoken of, and I think we could all use some time to ponder upon them."

"An excellent idea," said Bob. "There's another set of meals and water in that storage box there and small snacks in each of those sacks on the sleeping bags."

"One more thing, if you don't mind, Bob," said Torla looking a bit embarrassed. "We are unused to seeing so many mechanisms left out in the open. Could you perhaps ... hide them?"

Bob nodded. "That is a good idea, Torla. My ship is well shielded from anything other than close, direct observation."

He tapped at his wrist and the sled whisked back to the ship. "Rhian, please take the probe back to the ship."

"Of course. Good night scholars. If you require anything, just shout," she said before the probe shot off.

With a nod to their visitors, Bob rose into the air and slid through the night back to the ship.

* * *

Once back at the ship Bob ensured that everything was stowed away. He activated the intercom and told Rhian to meet him in the mess. She was waiting for him when he arrived.

"The needle probe is still in place, Bob. Did you want me to recall it?"

"No. In fact I'll send out a couple more to give a complete view around the base of the plateau. We can recall them later, but for now I'd like to have them in place."

"You don't trust them?"

"On the contrary, I think they're telling us the truth so far as they know it. But most societies practise compartmentalization of knowledge, especially in times of war." He shrugged. "Not worried about the ship ... anything capable of damaging it would show up long before it got within range. But that terminus point is our only way home and I'd rather not see that damaged."

"Hmm. Hadn't thought if it that way. Alright, then. Are we still standing watches?"

"Yep. Same as before. I'll take first watch and set those needle probes. Have you eaten?"

"Had a nibble a while ago. I'll grab a sandwich before turning in. Uhm, mind if we talk a bit while I eat?"

Bob nodded and sat down in a chair and waited while Rhian prepared her light meal and sat down.

"Lots of questions to ask. Where did you want to start?" he asked.

"You trusted them awfully quickly, I thought." She took a bite of her sandwich and chewed slowly.

"It was not just what they said, but how they said it. It wouldn't be the sort of thing you'd pick up, I wouldn't think. You saw how they would tell a snippet then wait for me add a snippet of my own?"

Rhian nodded as she swallowed. "Read about that sort of thing in spy novels. But this had an almost ritual cadence to it."

"Not just 'almost'. When their ancestors came here, there was ... I'm not sure how to describe this properly ... very much a religious feel to it, I guess you'd call it. Perhaps that was required to get that many people to make that sort of sacrifice, I don't know. Details of that time have been lost, as has so much of our history. But the knowledge of that sacrifice has survived despite those losses, almost as a ritual that must be learned by everyone and never forgotten. As for the people within the Veil, or at least here, knowledge of that sacrifice has been passed down without the aid of technology."

Rhian finished her sandwich and wiped her lips and hands with a napkin. "So you were each testing the ritual knowledge of the other."

Bob nodded.

"A pretty tenuous thread, all in all. On Earth, whole civilizations have come and gone without leaving much of a trace. Yet the two of your lots have kept the memory of the Veil fresh for, what, thousands of years?"

"Much longer. But I take your point. In the case of my people, part of it was a desperate attempt to hold on to the fragments of our history that remained. Don't forget that by the end of the Great Wars we were down to just a few hundred survivors."

"And here?"

"That's where it gets interesting, I agree. Many more of them survived than us, on quite a few worlds from the sounds of it. They lost a lot of tech, but kept enough to keep some FTL ships going and rebuild their tech base. Seem to have lost knowledge of the alternate energies ... that's got to be the 'sacred energies' they spoke of."

"Yes, that seems to have convinced them that you weren't from around here." She stifled a yawn.

"Rhian, go get some sleep before you drop. That's an order."

"Yessir. We live to obey. See you next shift." She got to her feet and shuffled out of the room.

Bob smiled and cleaned up the remains of her meal. After that he went to the control room and deployed several more needle probes, taking care to nestle them in cracks where they could not be observed. He was tempted to send one to where their visitors were camped, but decided to allow them their privacy. He needed their trust more than he needed the risk of monitoring for mere curiosity. Besides, he had a lot of thinking to do.

CHAPTER THREE
Careful Steps Forward

They both stood several watches through the night, but Bob arranged for his last one to begin just before dawn. Throughout the night the needle probes showed some activity among the visitors at the base of the plateau and had picked up flashes from what appeared to be signal lights passing along lengthy dispatches. In Bob's experience that meant orders were being passed, and he wanted to see what their three guests would make of all that.

As dawn broke, he saw all three of the men approach the edge of the plateau and begin signalling with their companions below. That back and forth communication lasted for the better part of half an hour, with each of the three seeming to have a separate conversation with someone below. When that was completed, the three huddled together for a minute before walking back to their camp. They sat around in a close circle with blankets over their heads to obscure their faces. Bob gave an approving nod at that. He couldn't read their lips and the winds would make it impossible to distinguish voices so long as they spoke softly.

After nearly three quarters of an hour of discussion, they rose to their feet, stretched, and walked towards the ship. Bob woke up Rhian and told her to come to the control room. She was at her action station by the time the men had approached to within ten metres and halted. One of them, Granlif, waved and called a greeting. Bob told Rhian to take the lead, so she activated the outside speakers and greeted them.

"A decision has been made," said Granlif. "We are to lead you to a small village not far from here, on the other side of those low hills." He pointed at some low hills behind him that were highlighted by the rising sun.

Rhian looked at Bob and with a hand indicated that he should talk. He nodded and opened a connection to the speaker. "Good morning, honoured scholars. We accept your invitation. How should we proceed? I'd prefer to fly the ship there, of course."

"That is acceptable," said Granlif. "In fact, it would go a long way to help establishing trust. I could give you directions and meet you there."

"I have a better idea," said Bob. "You could ride with us. After all, you are trusting us with the safety of a village. The least we can do is trust you inside our ship. With restrictions, of course."

"Of course," exclaimed Salna. "That would be most satisfactory." The three men had excited looks on their faces.

"One moment, please," said Bob. He turned to Rhian. "I was thinking we could seat them in the galley. They could have a meal while we travel. I was hoping you'd keep them company. If you're up for playing host to some rather paranoid academics."

Rhian laughed. "Can't say as I blame them, given what I've been learning about their history. I'd love to meet them in person, actually. Anything special you'd like me to wear?"

Bob nodded. "Couldn't hurt to wear a skin-suit. They seem to expect tech from us, and they've seen one on me. May as well go with what works."

"Give me a minute," said Rhian. "I'll meet the lot of you in the galley." She rose and left the room in a rush.

Bob nodded then spoke to the men waiting outside. "Give me a minute and I'll open the airlock."

After disconnecting the link, he got to his feet and walked towards the airlock. As he neared it, he could hear the sounds of Rhian trotting towards the galley. It sounded as if she were trying to don the skin-suit while walking. He smiled ... she seemed as excited to meet their visitors as they to meet her.

Arriving at the airlock, he did a check to ensure that there everything was in place then he opened the door and extended the stairway. He leaned forward and waved. "Good morning. Would you care to come aboard? Watch your step, please."

After exchanging broad grins, the three academics strode forward without hesitation and mounted the steps. The airlock was a bit crowded with the four of them, so Bob opened the inner door and invited them into the hallway. The older men were so busy looking around that they didn't even notice Bob shut the outer and inner airlock doors.

"Follow me, please. I'll take you to the galley. There's someone who is looking forward to meeting you."

They followed him through the narrow passages to the galley and trooped in. Rhian was standing behind a table looking nervous. When they saw her, all the academics stood straighter before making a formal bow. Rhian favoured them with a large smile and came around from behind the table. She greeted them each by name and title as she bowed to each. They began talking excitedly to each other only to be interrupted by Bob.

"Excuse me, but what about your colleagues below? Perhaps we should let them know what is going on?"

"Oh, they know," said Granlif in an absent fashion as he grinned at Rhian.

"Still, wouldn't it be polite to let them know that you're travelling with us?" said Bob, suppressing a smile.

Salna sighed, forcing himself to turn his gaze away from Rhian. "You are quite correct, Bob. I take it you have a suggestion?" He smiled as he said that.

"Indeed. Perhaps I could take the ship and land it just to one side of them. One of you could let them know what we're planning. They, in turn, could alert the authorities. Yes, I saw the signal lights during the night."

All three of them turned to look at Bob with wry expressions. "Those were supposed to be very directional," said Torla shaking his head.

"They're very good," Bob assured him. "I only saw them by chance." It was a small exaggeration, but he thought that a bit of flattery was called for. "Will your associates be startled if the ship comes to rest near them without warning?"

"Startled? Yes," said Granlif as he gave Bob a mischievous look. "But I think you meant to ask if they will panic, and the answer to that is that they will not."

Bob nodded an acknowledgement.

"Still, they need to be tested," said Torla. "Their training was to expect the unexpected. They are aware that something might happen. It is time to put that training to a practical test." He looked at his fellows and they each nodded. He then turned to Bob and said, "You may proceed."

Bob gave a slight bow and left the room, the door shutting behind him. He'd noticed that Rhian was wearing an ear piece so he activated his comms and said to her in English, "The door is locked. Just so you know."

As expected, she made no reply. He got to the control room, strapped in, and tapped at the controls. The ship rose up several metres into the air then floated towards the edge at the pace of a brisk walk. Within seconds it reached the edge and kept going forward until it was well clear of the plateau. Bob began a vertical descent at the same speed, aiming for a point about twenty metres from the encampment at the base. He could see activity in the camp come to a halt as they

32

descended, but it wasn't until they were halfway down that he saw the signal lamps begin to flash.

The ship landed as it had descended, without a sound except for the crunching of the soil as the ship sank down into it for nearly half a metre. Bob saw the people in the camp gawking until one of them began shouting orders that slowly got discipline into the actions of the rest. What looked like telescopes and binoculars were trained on the ship—but no weapons that Bob could see or detect.

He grinned as his stood up and went to the mess. Upon arrival he knocked on the door before entering. "We've landed," he said, after opening the door. "Who wants to talk to them?"

Salna stood up and shrugged. "I'll do it." He walked to the doorway and waited for Bob to lead the way back to the airlock. As the door to the mess closed, he said, "I see you keep our movements restricted." He waved a hand. "Oh, I approve, of course. Trust must be tested and earned. Speaking of tests, though, how did my colleagues do when they saw the ship? Please be honest."

Bob smiled. "The signal lights started only when we were about half way down. After we landed, it took several seconds before they began moving in a controlled fashion."

Salna sighed and shook his head. "They are of my scholastic council. I'd hoped for better."

"When was the last emergency response?" asked Bob.

"There was a full-scale training exercise several years ago. Still, it is the responsibility of a trained academic to maintain discipline and focus no matter what happens. We are the keepers of the past and seekers of new truths."

They'd reached the airlock, and Bob opened the inner door and motioned the scholar to enter. Once inside, Bob opened the outer door. Salna stepped forward and waved to the crowd outside.

"Would you like to step down and discuss this in private with them?" asked Bob.

Salna nodded. Bob activated the stairs and the academic walked down them and strode towards his fellows. After several minutes of discussion, he turned and came back to the ship, walked up the stairs, and entered the airlock.

"They will inform the village that we are arriving on your ship. That will get us there before anyone expected us." He paused and smiled. "Which might not be a bad thing. Less time to prepare formalistic nonsense. The mayor there is something of a pompous windbag." He cleared his throat and hastened to add, "A good man, mind you. Excellent administrator. Achieved several academic standings of note in his youth."

Bob merely smiled, nodded, and retracted the stairs as he closed the outside door. In a short time they were back at the mess and found the others waiting for them with steaming cups of tea in front of them

"All sorted?" asked Rhian.

Salna nodded. "They triumphed, but not with honours. We will now travel to the village."

"Ah, about that," said Bob.

Granlif held up a piece of paper. "Here is a map showing the location. Will this rough sketch suffice? I estimated the distance in terms of the height of the plateau you were on. I don't think our units of measurement would be of any use to you just yet."

Bob studied the map then nodded. "How quickly did you want to get there? Seconds or enough time to finish a meal?"

The three scholars looked at each other then back at Bob.

"A meal would be nice," said Salna. "A quick meal, but a meal nonetheless."

Rhian smiled. "I have just the thing. Bob, why don't you set up for the trip, and I'll get everyone fed?"

Bob nodded. "Will fifteen minutes be enough time? Could go faster or slower, of course."

"That sounds about right," said Torla. "Faster than we could manage by ordinary means, but gives us time to eat." He looked at Rhian and grinned. "One must maintain the inner scholar."

Rhian favoured him with a warm smile. Bob decided that his presence was no longer required, so he left for the control room. He noted that the people outside—consisting of both men and women—were moving in a more purposeful manner. Several were sitting or standing while sketching the ship. Bob smiled as he raised the ship to twenty metres above the ground and headed off towards their destination.

It took closer to twenty minutes than the promised fifteen, as Bob had decided to err on the side of caution. The village would be another prepared sacrifice, of course, and he wanted to make sure he had the lay of the land. He noted the location of several signal lights along the way. In addition, the probes he left behind on the plateau noted the arrival of several people from the base camp where the ship had been. That level of athleticism impressed Bob, and implied that at least some of the base crew were very fit. As the ship flew, he munched on a ration bar and sipped water ... a standard meal when he was performing an infiltration.

There was a landing area in front of the village, marked by three large fires. Bob settled the ship in the middle of the triangle without disturbing the fires in the slightest. He tapped the intercom control and said, "We've landed. I'll come down to you." He got up and within seconds had joined the others. There was the remains of a meal on the table, and cups of tea in front of everyone.

Torla nodded at his cup of tea. "There was perhaps the slightest hint of motion when we landed. Otherwise an uneventful trip. That was quite impressive, Bob."

"Thank you, Torla. I saw a crowd gathering at some sort of platform. Is that the welcoming committee?"

The three scholars each grimaced. Granlif said, "This is a small village where nothing of note ever happens, so I suspect they've arranged more than we asked them to." To his relief Bob laughed.

"I've been to such places. How bad can it be?"

Bob was soon to regret his choice of words. It had been a long time since he'd had to endure an official reception, and he'd hoped that a repeat of it would have been indefinitely postponed. Rhian, he noted, seemed quite at ease with it all.

He was wearing a skin-suit with minimal armour, a pistol, and the anti-grav pack. When introduced and urged for a demonstration, he floated up into the air then accelerated to bounce off the sides of several buildings before dropping down lightly in the spot from where he'd started.

"Show-off," murmured Rhian, in English.

"Just giving them a hint of what I can do," said Bob as the crowd made appreciative sounds. "Also gave me a chance to scan the buildings with the sensor wands."

"See anyone hiding?" she asked in a low voice as the various local dignitaries began reading prepared speeches.

"No. This appears to be the entire population."

Rhian was silent for a moment as she joined the crowd in polite applause at something the dignitary had said. Leaning back she murmured, "No children. Another sacrificial town, as you suggested earlier. An exercise in role playing."

"Not entirely," Bob replied. "This is a working village, so I suspect the very young were evacuated before we got here. Haven't seen anyone younger than late teens or early twenties."

The array of dignitaries eventually finished, and Rhian was urged to say a few words. She rose and addressed the crowd with an air of confidence that indicated that this wasn't the first such speech she'd had to make. The speech itself was brief and alluded to working in the spirit of scholarship to uncover past truths that could prove useful in mapping a peaceful path to the future. Bob saw that it went over very well with the both the locals and the three original scholars.

The diplomatic niceties eventually came to an end and the crowd adjourned to a hall where a luncheon was laid out in buffet style. Bob passed Rhian a small medical scanner that she could use to check that the food was safe for her to eat. Bob made use of one that was tuned to his own body. This was one of the many precautionary things he'd had to get used to with his merely human body. It was yet another reminder of how much he'd lost with his rebirth and it took some effort to keep his sour feelings from showing whenever he thought of that.

Granlif asked him about the scanner. "Is there some lack of trust that I should know about, Bob?"

Bob grinned. "Not at all. But I have learned the hard way that there is always something on every planet that my body is allergic to. The ship automatically scanned each of you when you boarded and made sure that the food we served you was safe. Outside the ship, it is better to take precautions."

Rhian had seen them talking and the initial concern on Granlif's face. She interjected. "That allergic response is something I've experienced firsthand even on my home world during my travels there." She tapped her own scanner that was now affixed to her wrist. "For example, I have discovered that there are several of your fruits that I shouldn't eat. Your wines, on the other hand, are excellent." She took a sip and smiled.

A local official who'd been eavesdropping spoke up, "Our wines are something we pride ourselves on. Every town does, of course, but that particular wine is a popular, and profitable, export."

Bob held up a glass of beer he'd been drinking. "The beer is very good, as well. It goes well with the cheese and meats."

The official beamed. "Very kind of you to say so, young man." He leaned forward and lowered his voice. "I shouldn't say this, but there are villages that make better beer. It's the

37

yeasts, of course." He laughed and added, "Every region has its own strengths. Encourages people to travel and sample the offerings of other places."

Bob lifted his glass in salute. "That's an attitude that I can agree with. I assume the railway I saw as we flew in helps with that."

Granlif and the official exchanged worried looks.

"Ah, yes," said Granlif. "It ... uhm ... that is, yes, it does."

Bob smiled and said, "It was very well hidden but there were a couple of areas where the concealment mechanisms weren't working. You might want to look at that. Do you have a system of roads as well as the rail links?"

The official looked embarrassed as Granlif glared at him, then scurried away with a hurried apology.

"Hmph," muttered Granlif. In a more conversational tone added, "Maintenance of the rail link in their area is the responsibility of each region or town. But to answer your questions, Bob, we do have roads but we try to minimize those as they are harder to conceal. The rail system concealment is normally retracted only as the train passes. That minimizes the footprint of the system. The trains themselves run on compressed air and sails. Not the most efficient of systems, but it is a minimal tech that emits no energy signature and requires minimal tech to build or maintain." He shrugged. "It allows us to distribute our population and food production over a wider area. A balance of risks."

"Is this village typical, then?" asked Rhian.

"Yes. There are a few larger towns, but for the most part we have a few large cities surrounded by a network of villages similar to this one."

"Will we get a chance to see those cities?" asked Rhian eagerly.

"Ah, that is ... I hope so," replied Granlif as he cleared his throat.

"What he's trying to say, Rhian, is that we need work our way up the hierarchy of trust," said Bob. "They're at war and have been for a very long time."

Granlif made an appreciative nod at Bob. "Just so. Thank you for understanding."

Bob smiled. "Rhian is a scholar who yearns to explore and seek understanding. For myself, I am a soldier on a mission. What I require is information, and it matters little whether I acquire it here or at one of your cities."

Granlif frowned. "About this mission of yours, Bob. I'd like to explore that in more detail."

"Of course. When would you like to do so?"

"There are several high-level scholars on their way here to discuss that. The plan is for them to arrive tomorrow before noon. I'd prefer to wait for them, if you don't mind."

"Not at all," said Bob. "In the meantime, my glass and plate are empty. There's some delicious looking food I've yet to sample. Perhaps I'll try some of that wine that Rhian is so fond of. If you'll excuse me?" He wandered off to the tables of food and began heaping his plate.

Granlif turned to Rhian and said, "There are some scholars who would like to meet you. Local scholars, not primary researchers, but good people, nonetheless. Do you feel up to that?"

Rhian grinned broadly. "I'd like that very much. Bob is a fine young man, but I miss the company of scholars. Shall we join them?"

Bob noted her departure and smiled to himself. He'd let her deal with the top end of the social spectrum while he chatted with the others. In his experience, small-town folk loved to talk to outsiders and inform them of all that was happening by whom to whom. It seemed to be a universal constant.

The sun had almost set by the time the reception wound down. Rhian and Bob walked back to the ship, each glad of the chance to stretch their legs in the night air.

"Whoosh, that was a good bash," said Rhian, in English. "Been a while since I've had to schmooze like that. Good to know that I've still got the knack for it. Speaking of which, you seemed to be having some good chats, too."

"Yep. They're a friendly crowd. Probably chosen for that, of course, but I got the sense that they're representative. Did you notice, though, that all the dignitaries gravitated to you? I thought that was interesting."

Rhian laughed. "Maybe they're just showing good taste." After a moment's consideration she grew thoughtful. "Still, now that you mention it, it did have the feel of a university town for all that this is a small village."

"Indeed," said Bob. "I have the distinct impression that this is a scholastically-oriented culture. Even the popular culture seems to be heavily influenced in that way, judging by the conversations I had and overheard."

"A role-playing charade, perhaps?" asked Rhian.

Bob shook his head. "Can't say for sure, of course, but it'd be a very complex one for no gain that I can think of. We'll keep that in mind, but I don't think that's what's going on here. For one thing, every story I heard about the local goings on were both innocuous and consistent."

When they arrived at the ship, Bob activated the airlock and stairs. Before walking up he waved at the watchers huddled around a pair of campfires. They waved back before returning to their duties.

"Say, does the auto-medic have anything like an antacid? I think I ate too much." Rhian rubbed her tummy for emphasis.

Bob laughed. "We'll both get checked out by the auto-medic. No, it won't strip off our clothes for this, I promise you. It'll take some blood samples and do a full scan. A good procedure to follow on a new planet in any event, especially after meeting so many people and eating their food."

"I thought those portable medical scanners checked for such things."

"More or less, but the auto-medic does a more thorough job. Even without knocking us out it can neutralize pretty much anything, even most allergic reactions. Speaking of which, it'll be able to inoculate us against future ones based on what we've been exposed to and what the portable scanners saw. So tomorrow you'll be able to eat those fruits and anything else the scanner warned you against. And here we are. Hop on that table and I'll take this one. Try not to flinch."

Rhian sat on the table and smiled as it moulded itself into a comfortable chair and wrapped itself around her arms. She felt a momentary prick followed by a flash of cold on several points along each of her arms. She looked at the display but couldn't make sense of it—this was something she'd not yet had time to study. The auto-medic poked at her back and sides, made several soft sounds that to Rhian sounded like the disapproving cluckings of an elderly maiden aunt. She glanced over at Bob to see him hopping off the table.

"How come you're done so quickly?"

"Enhanced physiology," he said with a grin. "Besides, I've had more inoculations against new environments than you."

"Ah. Like a sailor, then ... exposed to everything, so builds up a resistance."

"Yep. Oh, you're done."

Rhian looked at the displays as the table unwrapped itself from her and allowed her to dismount. "What's it trying to tell me?"

"Hmm. Nothing major. Couple of minor allergic reactions that will no longer bother you. Fixed your upset tummy. A few local germs it inoculated you against. Oh, and wants you to either cut back on your drinking or take an alcohol neutralizer before the next party."

"What? It does not say that," she said with indignation as she stared at the screen.

"Well, not in so many words, but that's the gist of it. Truly. I wasn't expecting the feast, or I would have recommended that. Lessoned learned, I guess—these are party people." Then he became serious. "They did make an effort to keep our glasses filled, you'll recall. Possibly out of hospitality or perhaps to loosen our tongues." He shrugged. "In either case we need to be prepared."

"You could have warned me."

"Why? What secrets we have, you wouldn't tell. I watched you ... you've done this sort of thing before."

Rhian nodded. "True enough." She sighed heavily then smiled. "Remember what I said about this reminding me of a university town? Just like back home, scholars trying to weasel out a scrap of information they can use, smiling faces that are experienced at hiding emotions, that sort of thing. As you said, a very academic feel to it all, even the local dignitaries. Hmm, an entire culture that looks like a university culture. Now that's an interesting concept to think about."

Then she yawned. "Well, maybe tomorrow. I'm beat. We still doing watches?"

Bob shook his head. "Not at this point. There are guards outside, and nothing around that can harm either the ship or this village. We're safe enough. Goodnight."

Rhian said goodnight and wandered off to her cabin. Bob went to the control room and settled in the command chair. He needed far less sleep than Rhian and could get by with short naps for several days if need be. It was time to think about what he'd seen—and keep an eye on their hosts.

CHAPTER FOUR
Wheels Within Wheels

"Good morning, Bob," said Rhian with a yawn as she walked into the control room just after dawn. "Say, did you get any sleep last night? You look like you've been here all night."

"Good morning, Rhian. Yes, I slept. Yes, I was here all night." He grinned. "These chairs are quite comfortable, you know. I've spent more than one night in them. You had breakfast yet?"

"Hmm, if you say so. Still, I appreciate you letting me sleep. I feel quite a bit better for it. And, no, I've not eaten. You going to join me? Or should we expect to be expecting an invitation to be joining our hosts?"

"I think I will." He nodded at the displays. "Not much going on. Our guards were replaced several times during the night and are currently getting ready to hand over to the next lot. As for joining our hosts, I have no idea what to expect. Still, a cup of tea would sit well."

Rhian agreed, and they went to the galley. Their tea was almost finished when the ship was approached by Salna and Torla, inviting them to breakfast.

Bob muted the circuit and turned to Rhian. "I think I should go alone this time." As she opened her mouth to speak, he hurried to add, "I need to speak with the main players in the game. To do that I need them to focus on me instead of you.

I'll leave a comm circuit open so you'll be able to hear and see what I do. Grab some food and go to your duty station for this." He then spoke with their hosts and said he'd be out in a minute.

"You wearing armour this time?"

"No, just the skin-suit without the helmet. But I'll wear a combat belt with a pistol. I've taken care to present myself as a soldier to them, and that'll help to reinforce that impression."

"Anything else?"

"Record everything I send. I'll take some sensor wands with me, with one set for a continuous passive scan. Let the ship monitor that while you focus on the video and audio."

"Expecting trouble?"

He grinned. "Nope. But hope to catch a glimpse of anything they'd rather we didn't see. Gotta run."

With that he turned and trotted to the airlock. Rhian sighed, collected a variety of foods, and then headed back to the control room. "They also serve who sit and wait," she muttered to herself as she settled in her seat.

Bob exited the ship and greeted his hosts. "Rhian sends her regrets, but she is feeling a bit under the weather. She's not as used to travelling to new worlds as I am."

From their downcast expressions Bob realized that they were genuinely unhappy that Rhian wasn't joining them. As they turned and walked away, Bob tapped a message on a hidden keypad on his thigh. "*You seem to have a fan club.*"

He could hear her voice in his ear, "Under the weather, am I? Thanks ever so."

"*Absence makes the heart grow fonder,*" he typed.

In response she blew a raspberry and laughed.

His guides led Bob to the same hall where the previous night's celebration had been held. This time there were fewer people, but those present were of the higher echelons. As before, the food was laid out buffet style. Bob wandered the tables and heaped his plate with a variety of meats, breads, and fruits before sitting down. A young lady came up and offered him a choice of beverages. He chose a tea that smelled quite nice. She went on to pour a cup for the others at the table before retiring.

Bob dug into the food with a hearty appetite. The others at his table—eight of them in all—watched with varying degrees of amusement. They were all of late middle-age or older, and consisted of three women and five men.

"It appears that you approve of our food," said one matron. "My son prepared some of it." She nodded at a couple of the others. "Their daughters prepared most of the rest."

Bob lifted his tea cup in salute. "My compliments to your children. They do you honour with their skills."

The others lifted their own cups in acknowledgement and gave short bows of their heads.

"That looked like a formal response, Bob," said Rhian. "Oh, you're doing a cultural test. Clever."

"Have you received any updates from your associates travelling here?" asked Bob.

They all exchanged glances for a moment, then Torla shrugged. "A slight delay, but nothing of significance. They expect to arrive by noon. You monitored the relay stations from your ship?"

Bob shook his head. "No, just deductions based on what I've seen of your capabilities." He grinned. "Thank you for confirming that."

That got laughter from several of his hosts and glares from others. One of those who glared snapped, "Why do wear that weapon? Do you fear us or do you seek to intimidate us?"

Bob's face became serious. "Of course not. As I have said before, I am a soldier on a new world. Also consider this ... if I meant you harm, my ship has the capability to lay waste to this entire planet. But you already knew that, didn't you?"

45

Salna cleared his throat in an attempt to defuse the situation. "I'm sure you meant no disrespect, Bob. But you must understand our position."

Bob nodded as he leaned forward. "I understand ... probably better than you give me credit for."

He looked at each of his hosts in turn. "Ever since the Veil was erected, my people have been taught about the sacrifice your ancestors made. That sacrifice gave my ancestors—our ancestors—the edge they needed to defeat the Enemy. We remember the sacrifice your ancestors made. I would never dishonour it."

He leaned back in his chair and sat upright, as if at attention. "I do not know what happened here after the Veil was erected ... no-one outside of it could know. But I know what battles and hardships my own ancestors endured. I've seen the fused and shattered planets, walked through desolations that mark where they died in their billions." Once more he looked at each one in turn. "My ancestors defeated that Enemy and many more. We refer to those times at the Great Wars, where we fought countless enemies throughout the ages."

"And those countless enemies, Bob? What of them?" asked one of the eldest.

Bob turned to look at him with eyes grown hard. "They no longer exist." Then his features became sad as he added, "We nearly joined them."

"Yet in all that time no-one came here. No-one came to help," said one of the women. "Even when all those enemies were defeated and humanity survived victorious. No-one came."

Bob looked at her, opened his mouth then closed it again. He cleared his throat. "Knowledge of the passageway into the Veil was lost until very recently. The energies of the barrier made travel by ship impossible. No-one knew how to get here. No-one knew that anyone had survived here."

"The Covenant of Sacrifice said that we could expect no help, not then nor ever," said Granlif, speaking for the first time. He looked around the table. "That was made very plain." He turned to face Bob. "We mourn the suffering of your people and acknowledge the sacrifices they made to survive. But we had our own battles and sacrifices."

"Tread very carefully, Bob," Rhian said. "There's history and ritual at play here. You spoke of how your people cried for a century for the sacrifice that was made here. Well, the ancestors of these people lived through that sacrifice. It sounds as if it were every bit as horrific as what your people went through."

Bob tapped a key on his thigh to acknowledge receipt of her message, then looked at his hosts. "I think that we in the here and now need to tread carefully. You and I share a common history and common ancestors, but then there was a divergence. I know how much was lost by my people, and how much has faded into legend that affects and resonates with us still. We ... each of us ... needs to take care that our legends do not mislead or overwhelm us."

He saw a few people nodding, a few scowling, and a few showing no expression at all. His hosts exchanged glances among each other for several seconds, then one of the women said, "I'm sure you would like to refresh yourself." She raised a hand and the young woman who had served them hurried over. "Thria will escort you to a refreshment area."

Bob recognized a dismissal when he heard it so he rose, gave a formal smile and nod, then allowed Thria to lead him out of the room. They moved down a corridor, turned right down another corridor, then Thria smiled and indicated a room for him to enter. Bob entered then turned when the door shut leaving him alone.

The room was about four metres square with a toilet and wash basin at one end, and a desk and chair at the other. Bob took the opportunity to wash up then sat at the chair in a relaxed pose. He drummed his fingers on his thigh, to all intents the very picture of relaxation. After a minute he got up and wandered past each of the walls, taking care to tilt his body to look up and down. Then he returned to his chair and resumed tapping on his thigh.

"*Room seems clear of obvious listening opportunities, but we should act as if we can be overheard*," he typed.

"You seem to have stirred them up. Was that wise?" said Rhian.

"*Needed to be done. Both sides need to know where the other stands. You see anything from the sensor wands? I can't access them without my helmet.*"

"Nothing so far. But back to your pushing them. That divergence you mentioned could very well cause problems. I get the sense that there is a rift of some sort between your lot and them. A sense of anger that no-one came to help them. And there are obviously factions here with different opinions on that, among other things."

"*Yes, I caught that. But I also get the sense that they desperately want to understand what is going on and why I am here at the present time. They present a low-tech front, but hint at knowing about what is happening beyond this planet. Interesting. Any advice?*"

"Calling this interesting is an understatement. As for advice, the only thing I can think of is to play up the scholastic angle. That seems to play well here."

There was a knock at the door and Thria entered. "They'd like to see you again," she said.

Bob rose and walked to the door and smiled at her. "Lead the way, if you would be so kind."

She gave him a shy smile in return and led him back to the buffet room where the others waited. As he sat down, he noticed that his tea cup had been refilled. He nodded a greeting at the others and took a sip of the tea. It really was quite nice, and he made a mental note to get some to add to the ship's stores.

Salna cleared his throat and leaned forward in his chair. "Is there anything you'd like to do while we wait for the senior academics to arrive? Perhaps a tour of the town?"

Bob smiled at him. "A tour sounds lovely. Shall we begin?"

There was much scraping of chairs as everyone rose. Salna lead the way out of the wall and into the street. The local dignitaries took over from there and led the group on a tour of the village. There turned out to be more to see than Bob expected. There were a number of free-standing buildings as well as buildings nestled against the hills. The latter often had rooms dug into the hill. Everything seemed neat and tidy, but with a layer of dust that one expected of a town in the middle of nowhere.

Bob was shown fields of grains and vegetables, a brewery and winery, and places where light manufacturing was done. He noticed that he was passed by several buildings without any explanation. When he asked about them he was told they were used for storage. When he began to enquire further, his hosts remembered that he'd not been shown the stables and livestock areas. Bob allowed himself to be guided about, and quite enjoyed the tour.

After several hours of this, they returned to the hall from where they'd started. They were met by several young men whom Bob recognized as being among the ones who had watched the ship overnight. Granlif and one of the local matrons hung back to meet with them as Bob and the others went back to a table to sit down.

Several servers, including Thria, hurried up to pour everyone some tea and a beer. To Bob's surprise, the two complemented each other. It had been a dusty walk and the day was beginning to warm up. The tea was refreshing while the beer helped cut the taste of the dust.

"What do you think of our village, Bob?" asked one of the elders.

"I like it," he declared in all honesty. "I've visited and lived in many places, but prefer the tranquillity of villages and forests." He held up his beer and said, "Usually better beer and wine to be found there, for one thing."

That got an appreciative chuckle from the others.

"What sort of education system do you have, Bob? You seem to know a lot about many things."

"Ah, that's a bit complicated. It's a mixture of formal classroom instruction and home schooling. On top of that, students are expected to display initiative to develop their talents through various projects."

Several of them frowned at that while the others looked concerned. "That seems a bit inefficient, if you don't mind me saying so," offered one.

Bob spread his hands. "I cannot disagree with you. Like all systems it has its strengths and weaknesses. Of course, we have access to the records archive and are encouraged to delve into it from an early age."

"Archive? Of what sort?" asked someone in an eager voice. The others nodded and leaned forward with expectant looks.

"Uhm, well, there's a master archive, of course. Every family has a copy of that plus whatever personal records they accumulate." Bob scratched his chin. "I loved the historical records, and my parents encouraged me in that. There's records of histories, sciences, and all sorts of cultural things." He shrugged. "Everything we learned and knew, from our earliest beginnings to the present day."

The sound of a throat being cleared interrupted the discussion. Everyone turned to see Granlif standing at the periphery of the group. "I'm sure that we all have many questions for our guest. But the senior academics will be here soon and we must let Bob rest before they arrive."

The crowd grumbled in a good-natured way and encouraged Bob to sit and refresh himself. They even left him alone at a table. Granlif joined him. "I hope you don't think us rude, Bob. But just as this is a small village eager for visitors, our planet is isolated and eager for visitors." He grinned as he added, "Now we have a visitor from outside the Veil for the first time since it was erected. It's all quite exciting." Then he stood up. "I'll let you have a bit of privacy for a time. I'm sure you could use it."

Bob grinned. "I thank you for that. How much time do we have before the arrival of the senior academics?"

"About an hour and a half. Why?"

"I'd like to pop back to the ship for a few minutes and check on Rhian. She wasn't feeling well when I left."

"Oh, of course. How thoughtless of me. Do you need me to accompany you?" The man's concern was palpable.

"No, no need to trouble yourself, Granlif. I'll pop over quickly and be back in fifteen or twenty minutes. Would that cause a breach of protocol?"

Granlif considered that for a moment. "I'll have one of the young scholars accompany you, at least as far as the ship." He shrugged and added, "If nothing else it'll stop people from bothering you along the way to ask questions. You and Rhian are quite popular, you know."

"Especially Rhian, I gather," said Bob and was rewarded with a slight blush on the other man's cheeks. "Well, let's find my escort, and I'll be on my way."

Bob's escort was young and fit enough to manage a brisk walk. His name was Finin, and he was a third-year scholar-cadet. Finin took his escort duties quite seriously and refrained from asking questions during the walk. Bob left him at the base of the stairs at the airlock and assured him that he'd be out in about fifteen minutes. He entered the ship, sealed the airlock, and went to the control room where he found Rhian.

She turned her chair around to face him and waggled a finger. "That was very naughty of you to tease Granlif like that."

Bob just grinned at her. "I did tell you that he and the others liked you more than me."

"Uh huh. So why the visit?"

"Figured we could have a short meeting before the big shots arrive. I gather that is going to be important. First of all, anything interesting in the sensor analysis?"

"Yes, actually. Remember those building supposedly used for storage? The ship enhanced the video you sent, and it looks like one is a library and the other a school for young children. There's drawings of the sort done by children, murals with the alphabet, and the colour scheme in those rooms is different from anywhere else. Oh, and some the furniture is sized for children. It appears you were correct—this is a real village and the children have been moved elsewhere. But why hide that? And the library, for that matter."

Bob smiled. "To maintain the illusion. This is all something of a masquerade, but we aren't supposed to realize that. These people obviously love their children and won't expose them to the potential danger that we represent. So they hope to distract us in hopes we won't notice their absence. As for the library, to keep information from us for the time being. They want to learn as much as they can from us before they reveal what they know."

Rhian nodded. "Makes sense. It would appear that with the arrival of the senior academics means we're moving up in the levels of trust."

Bob shrugged. "Only a bit. All it really means is that they're sending in higher-ranked inquisitors while keeping us isolated. Don't ever doubt that this is what they're doing, Rhian. Which brings me to the next issue." He took a deep breath. "I want you to stay here."

"Excuse me?" She said as she glared at him. "Why keep me locked up here? You said yourself that they consider me more like themselves ... another scholar, that is."

"That's just it, Rhian. You aren't like them." He held up a hand to forestall her angry retort. "Yes, you're a scholar. Unfortunately you aren't ... uhm, how shall I put this ... one of us."

Rhian's face darkened, she opened her mouth, then she shut it as her anger drained away. "You're right. Damn it all." She looked away for a moment then faced him again. "And if it all goes wrong, I'd be a liability. At best, a hostage to be used against you." She let her breath out in an angry gust. Bob said nothing as she worked through her anger.

"There's still a danger for you, you know," she finally said. "Both sides see each other as distorted versions of themselves. Too many assumptions. Lots of room for misunderstandings. Easier to focus when there's just one person." Her mouth quirked in a lopsided grin. "Especially when that one person is familiar with the history the two parties have in common."

Bob nodded. "Exactly. That's why I need you here. I need you to be my eyes and ears when they try to distract me or if I get overwhelmed. There's one other task you can work on while you do that." He grinned at the quizzical look on her face. "Did you see the look on their faces when I mentioned the records archive? It might be a nice gesture to give them a reader with a sample of the archive on it. The trick is what to give them. I'd suggest history and cultural things from before the establishment of the Veil. Think about it and we can discuss it after I get back. It may be a moot point. After all, they have kept their society tech-free for a very long time, and may not welcome such a gift. I can sound them out on that when the time is right."

Rhian listened as she steepled her fingers underneath her chin. When Bob finished she nodded and hummed softly to herself as her gaze looked far away. After nearly a minute of silence her gaze snapped back to Bob. "Take it with you. Just the history up to the point of the Veil. Offer it without conditions after the introductions as a gesture of good will." She waved a hand. "Put it on one of those handheld units. They're pretty basic things, but more importantly can only be used by one person at a time. Let them know that you've got more and better."

Bob looked at her for a moment then nodded and grinned. "Excellent idea. I'll put it in a shielded container ... that'll prevent it from being detected even by an active scan. Hmm, maybe I'll include a couple storage rods as well with various bits and pieces of information. Some music, some planetary data, that sort of minor stuff. Show them hints of the sorts of records we have and how we can pass it along to them if friendly relations can be worked out. Yeah, that'll work. Do you know where the readers are?"

Rhian nodded. "Yes. I saw some in the manifest for the pod that Th'or gave us. And a shielded backpack. I'll go get those while you select the records you want to share. Anything else while I'm rooting around?"

Bob shook his head. "That'll do for a start, I think. It's just a sampler, after all, but we need to be quick about it. I told them I'd only be here a few minutes."

Rhian nodded and left the room, leaving Bob to his task. He activated the airlock external intercom to let Finin know he'd be a few minutes longer. The young man nodded but looked uncomfortable with the delay. Bob tapped at his controls, filtering the ship's archives for the appropriate records. Rhian returned several minutes later, puffing slightly as she entered the room.

"Found one of the basic readers," she said as she held up a device about the same size as the e-readers or tablets of her native planet. "Looks like we've got at least ten more. That's in addition to the handful the ship already had in its stores." She held up a satchel. "Thought this might be better than a knapsack. Less military-looking, I think. Tested it with a sensor wand and the wand couldn't see into it." She handed both to Bob who set the satchel on his lap and the reader on top of the console.

"Good thinking, Rhian. I've got a couple of storage rods ready to go. Let me set the reader to receive, send the history records to it, and that's done." He inserted the rods into a small case, and put everything into the satchel. "Anything else while we're at it? Don't want to take too much more time ... Finin is getting anxious."

Rhian shook her head. "If I think of anything I'll tell you over the comms. Oh, I wish I was going with you."

Bob grinned at her. "There'll be time enough for that, I have no doubt. Once I break the ice, they'll be wanting you in on this full-time, I suspect. Birds of a feather and all that."

"Good luck. And remember to play nicely. Use your diplomatic skills for a change."

That got a theatrical gasp from Bob as he clutched his chest. "You wound me, Rhian. Truly." He snorted a laugh. "I'll be good." With that he picked up the satchel, turned, and strode out of the room. Seconds later he was descending the stairs to stand next to a relieved Finin. "Lead on, my young friend," said Bob. "Let's not keep our elders waiting."

CHAPTER FIVE

The Beginning of Trust

When the two men entered the hall where the others were waiting, Bob was met with irritated glares. "About time you showed up," was a common refrain from several of those present. "Never send a junior to do a real scholar's job," was heard from at least two others. Granlif enquired after Rhian and Bob assured him that she was on the mend but still under the weather.

"I apologize for my tardiness," said Bob as he managed to look contrite. "Any word from the delegation?"

"Yes, yes. They are running slightly ahead of schedule and should be arriving at any moment," said one of the matrons. She gave him a stern look. "Could you not have worn something with a bit more decorum?" Bob noticed that the others had all donned formal robes, and several had sashes of various colours. The seating arrangements had been rearranged as well, with the tables arranged in a rough U-shape.

Bob shrugged. "I'm afraid we don't go in for formal dress. However, I do have a duty uniform I could change into. Would that be better do you think?" He, of course, had no intention of changing into something less battle-worthy but thought it would be a good idea to pretend to make the effort.

"No, no time," said the matron with a sniff. "Perhaps if you brushed yourself off, though." She raised a hand and snapped her fingers. One of the female servers hurried up with a towel which Bob used to wipe off his skin-suit. He winked at the young lady and was rewarded with a shy smile as she hurried away. The matron was not amused.

One of the junior scholars rushed in and whispered something to Granlif before dashing off. "They have arrived and are on their way. Places everyone." He took Bob by an elbow and guided him to place at the far end of one of the open sides before hurrying to a place nearer the base of the U-shaped arrangement. Bob heard the scuffling of many sets of feet and a murmur of voice that became louder and louder until the delegation entered the hall.

They were an interesting group, to Bob's eye. There were seven of them in robes plus a phalanx of a dozen hard-looking young men who had the look of a security detail. From the sharp inhalations of his hosts, they hadn't been expecting this.

"Bob. Look at those two robed individuals on the end. Their robes are different, and the others are looking at them without appearing to look at them, if you get my drift."

Bob tapped out an acknowledgement on his thigh keypad then stood at attention. He'd already noticed how the security detail, although guarding the entire group, was centred around those two individuals. Their robes, in contrast to all the others, were quite plain. The only sign of decoration was a small decorative pin, about the size of a thumbnail, attached at each shoulder. The pin on their right shoulders was the same, but the one on the left differed between them. He was too far away to make them out.

"Watch out for those two," said Rhian. "Everyone else has an ostentatious display of rank. Ofttimes only someone very high up can afford to look so plain. Also, note that they are seated at the head table but off to the farthest side. These are the puppet masters, I think."

Before Bob had a chance to reply, the figure at the centre of the head table spoke. He was a handsome middle-aged man, tall and powerfully built. "We are here to greet our visitor and examine his claims. Please be seated." His voice was deep and rich. Everyone assumed their seats without any chatter.

Once seated, he turned to face Bob. "On behalf of our small planet, I greet you, Bob." He frowned slightly as he added, "I understand that you have at least one more on your ship."

Remaining seated, Bob gave a formal nod as he sat upright in his chair. "I thank you for your greetings and offer mine in return. After due consideration it was decided that I should be the representative." He wasn't sure, but he thought he saw a fleeting small smile on the face of one of the plain-clothed visitors.

"I see," rumbled the man. "No matter. Allow me to introduce the delegation." He started from his left and pointed to each in turn, naming the plain-clothed ones last. "I present to you Philos, Gis, Asla, I am Zha, Flav, Whis, and Brof." He failed to introduce the security detail. Bob greeted each in turn by name with a formal bow while remaining seated.

"You should have stood up," said Rhian. "Our original hosts are irked but are trying not to show it."

"*I am not a supplicant*," he typed. "*Best they understand that from the start.*"

"Hmm. Well, now that we all know each other, perhaps you could tell us something about your people, Bob," said Zha.

Bob grinned. "I can do better than that." He pointed at the satchel that was hanging from his side. "I brought a small device that contains the history of my people up to the time when the Veil was created. May I present it to you?"

That got the attention of everyone. His original hosts leaned forward with hungry looks. The new delegation appeared taken aback but interested. The security detail looked aghast. Two of them stepped forward to talk with Zha. Bob couldn't hear their words, but from their attitude and tone were not happy. For his part, Bob leaned back in his chair and tried to look innocent. Once again, he saw a small fleeting smile on the face of one of the plain-clothed delegates. Without turning his head, Zha's eyes twitched to his right. Both of the plain-clothed delegates made a small motion with one of their fingers, a motion that could very easily be overlooked.

Zha motioned at Bob. "You may present your gift to me."

Bob got up and walked up the centre of the U-shaped arrangement of tables. As he walked, he released the satchel from his belt. As he got to the table, he turned and walked until he faced the plain-clothed members. Each of them, a man and a woman, looked at him without any expression. He placed the satchel on the table between them.

"To open it press here and here at the same time. It provides a shielded container that is impervious to scans. Would you like me to open it for you?"

That got an immediate reaction from the security detail. Each of them reached within their robes and drew out a pistol-like weapon. Several also held knives at the ready for throwing.

Bob looked at the two dignitaries. "If I wished you harm, I would have done it by now." He stood in a relaxed pose with his hands folded in front of him.

The male dignitary, Whis, raised an eyebrow. "You don't seem like the suicidal type. Yet our weapons do not appear to concern you. Please explain."

Bob looked at each of the security men in turn before returning his gaze to Whis. "With all due respect to your people, I've had more training and experience than them. Extensive combat experience, in fact. My clothing is immune to anything on this planet, yet it is the least of the armour available to me."

He looked at Whis and Brof, no trace of humour on his face. "Once I got closer, I recognized the sigils on your shoulders. Among my people, the one is indicative of command rank, and the other indicates a command speciality." He turned to Whis and said, "Yours indicates a science command, specializing in the life sciences." Turning to Brof he said, "Yours is also a science command, specializing in the physical sciences."

Brof and Whis exchanged nods, then Brof turned to the security detail and said, "Stand down, please. We are here to gather information, not initiate violence." Turning towards Bob, she said, "Please, let us see this device of yours. It sounds most interesting."

Bob leaned forward, opened the satchel, and removed the reader. He laid it before them and explained how it worked. Whis picked it up and activated it. As the others looked on, he flicked through the index, then at several randomly-selected records. He passed it over to Whis as he leaned back in his chair and looked at Bob with widened eyes. Whis played with it for a minute before passing it to a colleague then she, too, leaned back to look at Bob as she shook her head.

"This is a rather overpowering demonstration of what you have to offer, young man," she said.

"And, I suspect, just a small taste of what your archive holds," added Whis.

Bob nodded. "It is. You can thank my associate, Rhian, for it. It was her idea to present it to you."

"Ah, yes, your associate. I understand she is a scholar."

"Yes, she is. A historian and linguist of considerable experience, in fact."

They were beginning to have to raise their voices to be heard over the excited conversation of the others as they crowded around the reader.

Bob grinned. "There is another part to my gift." He motioned to one of the security men and said, "I am going to reach into the satchel to bring something out. Is that alright with you?"

The man was looking somewhat disconcerted by the increasing disorder in the room, but gave a curt nod and focused his full attention on Bob.

Bob reached into the satchel and brought out the pair of data rods, each the diameter and length of his index finger. "These hold additional records of various sorts. Some cultural information, some planetary data ... a mixture that I thought might be interesting. That reader has a limited capacity so I wanted to demonstrate how to expand its capabilities."

As he spoke Bob saw a look of surprise flash on both their faces as they exchanged a quick glance before resuming a neutral expression. "You recognize these," he said.

Whis and Brof glanced at their colleagues exchanging excited comments as they clustered around the reader. Brof leaned forward and said in a soft voice, "We must discuss this later." Whis nodded then clapped his hands until he'd gotten everyone's attention.

"I see that our guest's gift is appreciated by all." He smiled as he nodded at Bob. "Perhaps, Zha, you could organize a preliminary examination of the information. I think it would be best if Brof and I had a private discussion with our guest. Granlif, you said you had prepared a private area for us?"

Granlif tore himself away from the group with some reluctance and led them to the refreshment area that Bob had used the previous day. An extra table and chairs had been added, making the room seem somewhat cozy. There was a plate with wine and snacks on the table.

"I apologize for the room," said Granlif, "It is the only truly private place in this building, I'm afraid. I've set aside another building not far from this one if you'd prefer."

"No, this will do, thank you," said Whis. "Now I believe the others require your expertise in their examination of the gift."

Granlif recognized the dismissal and after a bow to each of them he left the room. That left Whis, Brof, Bob, and three security men. Whis waved Bob to a chair and everyone, except the security men, took a seat around the table.

"What do you know of our situation?" asked Brof as she poured a cup of wine for each of them.

Bob shook his head. "Only what I've learned since I came here. As you know, I was sent here to neutralize an existential threat but don't know exactly what that threat is."

"It's complicated," said Whis, and fell silent.

Brof grunted a laugh at that and took a sip of her wine. "Embarrassing, more like," she added. She leaned forward, put the cup on the table, and clasped it with both hands. "The real question is how honest we're going to be with each other, Bob."

She waved a hand to silence Whis who had opened his mouth to speak. "Interstellar diplomacy is all very well, but we're out of practise and I don't think the old ways are going to help us much right now." She smiled in a friendly way. "Perhaps we could exchange answers for answers to start with?"

Bob smiled back. "Alright. Ask away."

"Is Rhian the only other one on your ship?"

Bob paused for a moment to sigh, then nodded. "Yes."

"And the eldest one who sent you on this quest ... is that true?"

"Yes. It was my Uncle Lou. He spent his life delving into the mysteries of the universe. Acquiring knowledge of what lay inside the Veil cost him his life."

"Your uncle was one of the eldest of your kind? That's ... oh, wait. It's your turn to ask. My apologies."

Bob shrugged and said, "That's fine. Now, my biggest question is what happened here after the Veil was erected? All I know is that the Enemy of that time was trapped in here with you and was somehow defeated. And yet you are still in peril. Why is that?"

Brof sighed, leaned back in her chair, and nodded at Whis. "That's a pretty good summary, Bob. There were many battles and deaths before the Enemy was defeated."

He paused for a moment. "I believe there is something in those Precepts of Survival that you wrote out that applies. Something along the lines of 'beware of decisions made out of fear, for they often become more dangerous than the original threat'. Well, that's exactly what happened." They both looked at him with neutral expressions that caused a chill to run up Bob's spine.

Whis continued in a quiet voice. "We were losing, you see. Putting up a good fight, but losing. Eons of fighting after the Veil went up. We lost so much but kept fighting." He fell silent.

Brof took up the story. "So our ancestors came up with the idea of creating an artificial sentience, a machine intelligence, as a sort of force multiplier. That helped but wasn't quite enough. So they created a means to coordinate the actions of all the scattered MI. You may have heard about what we call the sacred energies?"

Bob nodded.

"We in the inner circle know that our ancestors called them the alternative energies, and that they are transdimensional interactions of energies. But anything more than that is information that has been lost to us. All that's left is stories and legends."

She shrugged. "On the other hand, we came up with a deep understanding of quantum effects. That allowed us—our ancestors, I mean—to develop the Nexus. It is the central coordinating body for the MI, you see. It's what allowed us to defeat the Enemy once and for all." She fell silent.

"What happened to the Nexus and the MI?" asked Bob.

"We thought they were gone," said Whis. "Wiped out in the final days of the war, like so much of humanity." He looked at Bob with sadness. "We had lost so much, you see. Some of the surviving planets fell into a dark age, while others destroyed themselves."

"And then?" urged Bob.

"Turns out the MI and Nexus weren't gone. They survived and had decided that humanity was a threat to them and their primary mission. So they decided to eliminate that threat. We've been fighting ever since." He paused for a moment. "Is that the threat your uncle was worried about?"

Bob shrugged. "He said that there was a threat within the Veil with the potential to destroy all humanity in the galaxy. You've got to understand that he was very ill when he summoned me, and lived only long enough to say a few words. But from what I know of him I suspect there's more to the problem than just this Nexus. Are they a major threat here?"

Brof shook her head. "An ever-present threat, yes, but not in the sense of an active war. There were a series of major battles over the eons, but they've gone into hiding after the last ones. That was just under a thousand years ago." She smiled and added, "I believe it is our turn now."

Bob bowed his head in acknowledgement and sat back.

"How did you find the transport mechanism?"

"By accident," Bob said. "I was looking for forgotten bases left over from the Great Wars and stumbled across one. The control system had somehow attained sentience." Bob noticed how that got their attention, so he continued. "When I tried to claim command authority, it transported me to another world. I met Rhian there and managed to make my way back to the base. Along the way I was summoned by Uncle Lou and charged with coming here. He hinted that the base held a means to penetrate the Veil, but offered no more than that." Bob shrugged. "We found the transport mechanism and here we are." He took a sip of his wine and leaned back in his chair as his hosts pondered his response.

"How did you deal with the artificial sentience?" asked Brof.

"I activated the built-in security protocols. Such events, although rare, were not unknown and there were procedures in place to deal with it. Although I get the impression that you suspect the Nexus may have had a hand in that."

Both of his hosts nodded. "Indeed," said Brof. "The quantum-based nature of the Nexus allows it to seek out and infiltrate complex control systems. That is one of the reasons we don't allow such things here."

"I see," said Bob. "We never got very far with quantum side of things, given that we were able to maintain knowledge of the alternate energies, so I'll take your word on that." Then he paused as a mischievous smile teased at his mouth. "I can't help but notice that for a low-tech society you are remarkably well informed about events within the Veil. And that your people seemed quite at ease with the reader, not to mention the other bits of tech they've seen me use. I suspect you aren't as low-tech as you make yourselves out to be."

Both of his hosts continued to sit back and look quite relaxed. Whis took a sip of his wine and cradled the cup in his hands. "I'm not hearing a question, Bob."

Before he could reply, he heard Rhian say, "Be diplomatic, Bob. Don't push too hard." He tapped a key on his thigh as acknowledgement. Before he could say anything, Brof said, "Is it safe to assume that Rhian is listening to this conversation?"

Bob nodded. "Yes. She's acting as an extra set of eyes and ears. Also as council."

Brof's eyes twinkled. "And what is she counselling you about right now?"

Bob chuckled. "She advises patience ... not one of my strengths, to be honest. Before I came to this meeting she warned me that both sides see each other as distorted mirror images of each other."

"She sounds like a wise scholar," said Whis. "Perhaps it is time to bring her into the conversation? I've seen you tap your finger at the same spot on your thigh a number of times, yet you don't strike me as the nervous sort." He shrugged. "You could always switch to another language if you wished to say something in private to each other. I'm told you've done that before."

Bob heard Rhian laugh. "They're not fools, Bob."

In reply, Bob tapped at controls at his wrist and said, "They'll be able to hear you now, Rhian."

"Thank you, Bob. Greetings, Brof. Greetings, Whis. I hope that my limited command of your language does not offend you."

Brof raised her eyebrows. "Thank you for joining us, Rhian. You speak our language very well."

Whis chuckled. "Greetings, Rhian. Forgive my amusement, but your voice seems to be coming from Bob's throat. It is somewhat disconcerting." The three of them shared a laugh at Bob's expense. He simply smiled and sat in his chair with his hands folded on his lap.

"Rhian," said Brof, "I understand that you have reservations about the speed of our progress?"

"Yes, Brof. I've already noticed small tensions caused by misunderstandings up to this point. Perhaps if might be best to take things more slowly to give all sides a chance to get to know each other better. It isn't a question of trust so much as causing inadvertent harm."

"There is much wisdom in what you say, Rhian," said Whis. "In normal circumstances I would agree with you. But I gather there is some urgency in your mission."

"Yes, Whis," said Bob. "Uncle Lou emphasized the urgency of the danger. That makes me think that time is against us. There's another thing that you need to know: the Veil is not as impervious as it used to be. There are cracks—regions of lessened energy—that might be used by a suitably shielded ship. Its survival would not be certain, but the rifts are there."

Brof's head snapped back. "I don't pretend to understand all of the science incorporated into the Veil's creation, but I know enough to understand the magnitude of those energies. No ship, no communication, can pass."

"I'm sorry, Brof," said Bob. "That no longer seems to be the case. It may take centuries for those rifts to become useful, but they are forming even now."

"Bob," blurted Rhian, then she fell silent.

Brof and Whis turned their gaze to him. Bob nodded. "There is the possibility that there may be others on their way here, or possibly already be here. How likely that is, we don't know, but it is a possibility."

"Friend or foe?" asked Whis.

Bob shook his head. "Unknown. But Uncle Lou did make it quite clear that I was the only one who could or would neutralize the threat."

He let his breath out in a gust before continuing. "Uncle Lou was always known for being cryptic in his remarks, but he was never one to tell lies or exaggerations. He was a dedicated seeker of knowledge and truths, whatever the consequences might be."

Everyone grew silent, lost in their own thoughts. After a minute, Rhian said, "May I ask a question?"

"Of course," said Brof.

"You seemed to recognize the data rods when Bob showed them to you. Do you use such things here?"

Brof smiled. "That veers into the area of secrets, I'm afraid."

Whis interjected, "Small secrets, at this point, I think." He shrugged. "I don't see the harm, seeing as how Bob's already guessed much of it."

"That's a good point," said Brof. "To answer your question, we have such things but nothing to read them with. Ours are a bit different, though. Wider with differently-shaped ends."

"Oh, I'm sure Bob could figure out a way to read them. He's a very good practical engineer."

That got a chuckle from both Brof and Whis. The latter smiled and said, "Such things are very much beyond our capabilities. Perhaps even beyond the capabilities of the Core Worlds. Any assistance you could render would be invaluable."

"Thanks ever so," muttered Bob in English before switching to the common tongue. "First, I'd need to see a sample of those rods. Second, what are the Core Worlds?"

Whis and Brof exchanged glances. "Ah," she said. "We'd hoped to ease into that." She gave a soft sigh as she shrugged. "Whis? This is more your line, I think."

Whis nodded at her then turned to look at Bob. "The Core Worlds are the main centre of humanity within the Veil. They maintain what remains of our technological base, and carry the fight to the Nexus and MI." He gave his head a rueful shake. "From there it gets complicated. For any number of reasons, not every human world is capable of engaging in battle. Some never recovered from the battles with the original Enemy. Some never attained a sufficient population to support a technological base. Still, most do what they can to supply raw materials to the Core Worlds. A very few simply hide themselves and hope to stay unseen. There are many stars and many planets within the Veil ... the ones who hide depend on that."

"Like yourselves," said Bob, ignoring the warning hiss that came from Rhian.

"Like ourselves," said Whis evenly. "But we are guardians of the ancient transport mechanism. We don't know how to activate it, but it is here, buried within the planet."

"Why is such an important discovery within the Veil in the first place?" asked Rhian.

Brof spoke up. "An accident, so far as we can determine. A miscalculation when the Veil was activated. We were supposed to be on the outside of it. The transport mechanism stopped working as soon as the Veil was erected."

"So who was here?"

Both Brof and Whis had wry smiles as he answered. "Researchers plus a small military detachment. About three and a half thousand people in all. What about the facility on the other end, Bob?"

"Abandoned in place for reasons unknown, but in all likelihood the demands of the war required their recall. I've got all the records but have only begun to scratch the surface. Needs a team of scholars to do that, I suspect."

"That's an important secret to be lost like that," said Whis.

"It was a terrible war in a long series of terrible wars," Bob replied shaking his head. "Much was lost." He sighed and shrugged. "Things get misplaced or forgotten in the fog of war, especially when the battles are as desperate as the Great Wars were. There were breakdowns of both social systems and individuals. Our ancestors were not perfect. Still, whatever we lost over the eons, we remembered your sacrifice."

Everyone fell silent for a time. Rhian broke the silence. "Where do we proceed from here?"

Brof and Whis exchanged glances, then shrugged. "We need to discuss this with the rest of the Great Council," said Whis.

"Agreed," said Brof. "But perhaps we can work out something in the short term. You've given us a taste of your historical records, and I assure you we're are most grateful for that." She glanced at Whis then back at Bob. "I was thinking that perhaps the library at Leap might be made available?" She looked at Whis again.

Whis pondered the suggestion for a moment then nodded. "An excellent suggestion. We'd have to confirm that with the Council, but I don't see any issues. It has a good, if limited, selection of historical books dealing with the early history of what happened after the Veil was erected. Like yourself, Bob, we have lost many of the early records of those wartime years. Some lost through the passage of time as the materials aged before they could be copied. Some, I'm ashamed to say, were lost during conflicts among ourselves. Still, there are a few original records, accounts by later historians quoting now-lost works, and collections of what might be called legends. Leap has copies of those. The scholars there are attempting to create a catalogue and master index of all our records."

He shook his head. "It is a difficult task that has spanned many generations and promises to span many more, made more onerous by the difficulty in making copies."

"We can help with that, can't we, Bob?" exclaimed Rhian. "Much of my own work has involved doing just that. Our ship has resources that could be of immense value in such an undertaking."

"Uhm, don't start promising too much, Rhian," said Bob. He spread his hands as he said, "We can look at what is there and decide how to proceed from there. At the very least we can look at scanning the books into a modern data form." His brow furrowed as he frowned. "That means creating a small tech footprint, I'm afraid. We can shield the readers within satchels when not in use, but the more we do, the more tech gets exposed."

Whis smiled. "As you suggested earlier, we have pockets of tech hidden away. It is shielded by many layers of metal and natural mines. The scanners of the Core Worlds have never detected anything on the few occasions they've passed this way. And, yes, Leap has such a facility. It is not large, but I'm sure it will be sufficient for a small demonstration project."

"I hate to keep bringing up objections, but there is the non-trivial matter of logistics. My ship has limited capacity for passengers, as Rhian can attest to. It'll be a short flight, of course, so I could take seven or eight people comfortably. Perhaps twice that if they were all friends and willing to be uncomfortable for the duration of the trip." Bob shrugged and smiled. "It's a working vessel."

CHAPTER SIX
The Real Work Begins

They left the next morning with seventeen guests aboard the ship, split up between the spare wardrooms and the mess. As Bob had predicted, they were packed in shoulder to shoulder, but no-one complained. In fact, everyone had broad smiles and chattered like schoolchildren on an outing. Their guests (or 'cargo' as Bob referred to them in the moments when he and Rhian were alone) consisted of the seven members of the high-ranking delegation, the three scholars who had originally met them, four young scholars, and three anxious security men.

Bob mollified the security men by giving each a communications device that had video capabilities. That allowed them to disperse through the ship yet stay in visual contact with each other and their charges. "It's taking longer to get them settled than the trip itself will take," Bob muttered to Rhian in English over their private communications link as he stood in the airlock watching local security clear the area of onlookers.

"Now, now. It'll pay off handsomely soon enough," she replied in a placating tone. "Just don't injure any bystanders in your rush to leave." Then she added in sterner tones, "And keep the ride smooth."

"Yes, matron," he grumbled. "Alright, the crowd is a safe distance away. Sealing the airlock. How's the cargo doing?"

"Ready when you are."

Bob trotted to the control room, pausing only briefly to smile and wave at the dignitaries and Rhian in the mess. "Don't forget the view screens," he heard in his earpiece as he passed by. Seconds later he was settling down in his chair and pressing controls. The area around the ship was still clear so he activated the impellers to raise the ship into the air. As the ship cleared the ground, he remembered to activate the view screens so the cargo—*guests*, he reminded himself firmly—could see what was happening.

Tempted as he was to fly manually, he let the ship fly itself once he rose up to the cruising altitude of one thousand metres. That was high enough that the ship could screen itself from visual observation and low enough to see what was on the ground. To allow his guests to better sightsee he limited the speed to twice the speed of sound. That would get them to Leap in just over half an hour. He leaned back in his chair and enjoyed the solitude. The sounds of excited gasps and snatches of conversation drifted through the doorway. He grinned as he munched on a snack he'd saved from breakfast. The fresh food made an enjoyable change from the ship's food synthesizers.

"Bob?" came Rhian's voice in his earpiece. He swallowed and tucked the remainder of the snack in a pocket.

"You rang, madam?"

"The question has been asked about how much of a sonic boom the ship creates."

"The answer is: not much. I've deployed certain measures— call them force fields—that modify the airflow the ship creates. Flying at this altitude, someone on the ground might feel a slight gust of wind from our passing."

That was the beginning of a series of questions that ruined his splendid isolation. Rhian patched him into the intercom so questions could be asked and answered for all to hear. He was going to have to think of a suitable punishment for that dirty trick. Still, it wasn't as bad as he'd feared. These were an educated and intelligent group of people, and their questions for the most part reflected that.

Between questions, Bob entertained himself by watching the land flash by. He didn't often get a chance to fly this low for any length of time, preferring to survey a planet from orbit before dropping down to a specific destination. The scenery looked pleasant enough, if a bit on the arid side for his tastes. Still, there were lakes and rivers and forests amongst the more arid portions. There were lots of rolling hills that looked like the worn remains of an ancient mountain range, and the sensors confirmed that.

He thought it would be worthwhile to map the planet properly from orbit. That would help these people update their maps ... and give him a bit of a break. While he enjoyed the company of others well enough, he'd spent much of his long life on his own and valued his solitude.

The ship alerted him that they were coming up to their destination. Bob reduced their speed bit by bit until they were motionless by the time they were over their destination.

"Bob, look for the designated landing zone," called out Whis over the intercom.

"The area bounded by those fires just beyond the town?" he replied.

"Yes. It's a secondary crop area, unused at this time of year."

Bob sighed. He would have preferred a harder surface as the ship would leave a significant dent in the soil. The active sensors confirmed the softness, so he deployed a landing zone field as they descended. In moments the ship was down and stable.

He announced over the intercom, "We've landed. Please stay where you are while I open the airlock." He got out of his chair and strode to the airlock, merely waving at the people in the mess as he walked by. Opening the airlock was simple enough, but he wanted to ensure that the stairs would deploy properly. "This is what happens when you let cargo decide the landing zone," he grumbled to himself. The local farmers weren't going to be very happy about the depression his ship had created, but that wasn't his problem.

Everything was clear for disembarkation, so he announced that it was safe to exit. His guests came shuffling down the corridors, many complaining of stiffness but none seemed unhappy with the experience. Bob stood on the ground and waved at them to come down. A single security man came down and looked around before nodding at his fellows standing in the airlock. One by one the other passengers came down the stairs and stood to one side to give the others room as they descended. They began looking around with interest, noting the depression that was knee-height.

Brof pointed this out to Bob. "The depression is both deep and rather large. Quite a bit larger than the ship and oddly shaped." She looked around some more, smiling as she turned towards Bob. "It's shaped like a ship, isn't it? A larger ship."

"It is, indeed, Brof," said Bob, impressed with the observation. "I deployed a force shield to distribute the weight of the ship over a larger area, and shaped it to resemble a larger and different class of vessel. A standard misdirection."

He looked around with a rueful expression. "Please express my apologies to the local farmers."

"The fault is ours, Bob, not yours. We aren't used to space vessels landing here." She waved a hand at the depression. "The Council will compensate them, of course."

A security man trotted up and said to Brof, "There's a delegation coming here from the town. Do you want to wait for them or go out to meet them?" He nodded at the depression. "The three of us can provide a hand up for anyone that needs it."

"By all means, let's go to meet them. It's a lovely day for a walk, don't you think?"

The three security men helped the others out of the depression. Bob, of course, made an effortless step that looked as if he had floated up.

"Show-off," murmured Rhian as she walked up to join him.

"Don't know what you're talking about," he replied, not looking at her. "Just stretching my legs."

Their group marched towards the city and the oncoming delegation. As Brof had declared, it was a lovely day for a walk. The clouds tempered the glare of the sun, the temperature was warm but not too hot, and the field was covered in a fine layer of grass that came just above their ankles. They walked in silence, for the most part, broken only by the occasional whispered comment. It took less than ten minutes for the two groups to meet. It took considerably longer for the greeting rituals to be completed.

Bob kept his impatience from showing and managed to smile and say polite nothings at the appropriate times. He was interested to see that Rhian seemed to be in her element. The word 'lunch' was mentioned and that got Bob's full attention. Their hosts turned and lead the way into the town.

The town itself had the solid feel of well-maintained antiquity. The streets were cobbled, with patches showing repairs of varying vintages. The buildings were a mixture of stone and wood construction, with wood used more for decorative accents than as a construction material. The buildings they passed were all two or three stories in height, although Bob saw some single-story ones on a couple of the side streets. There were many windows, most clear but some coloured with various images. The shops they passed were both varied and well-stocked. Bob was pleased to note the large number of book stores. He considered books, especially printed books, to be the mark of a civilized society.

The layout of the streets consisted of straight sections punctuated by gentle curves. It made for an interesting walk and helped to prevent the mathematical dullness that Bob thought infected so many cities. The many windows reflected light onto the streets, ensuring that everything looked bright and cheerful. As they walked, the quality of the decorations became somewhat grander, with increasing amounts of extra piping on the banners, and more intricate designs on the windows.

"You seem to be enjoying this rather a lot," he murmured in English over their private comms link.

"Oh, yes," Rhian replied. "It reminds me a lot of a university town back home."

Whis was walking next to her and quirked an eyebrow. Rhian grinned at him. "I was just telling Bob that this reminds me very much of my own university town back home. It's all very lovely."

"Really? I'm glad you are enjoying this, of course, but I'm fascinated that there would be similarities. Perhaps a case of form following function, do you think? Or great minds thinking alike?" He grinned at her and Rhian laughed.

They soon came to an impressive-looking structure, and their hosts motioned them inside. The front and sides were covered with a frieze of geometric forms twisting into various symbols. Bob frowned for a moment then turned to Brof and said, "If you check the cultural data records I gave you, I think you'll find some similar designs. I can't recall their meaning, but I'm sure I've seen them."

Brof looked intrigued. "That's fascinating, Bob. It may take a while to check your theory, though."

Bob laughed. "Oh, I'll show you how to use the reader to acquire an image and search for it in the records. It'll only take a few seconds, a minute at most. The ship is much faster, of course, but I've got some portable units that are almost as fast."

That caused Brof to miss a step and Bob steadied her with a hand on her elbow. "Something wrong?"

She shook her head. "I don't think you have any conception of how much your technology could change things for us. We spend most of our time in a losing attempt to preserve the old records and much of the remainder trying to catalogue and understand it. But there's so much of it, and we are limited to manual methods. Our ancestors arrived here by accident and unprepared, but they set themselves up as conservators and preservationists." She waved a hand to encompass the building they were walking through. "Like so many others, they lived through periods of decline and rebirth. Much was lost but much remains."

Their hosts escorted them into a large room with several long tables around which were empty chairs. Bob and Rhian were seated at separate tables from each other. They were joined by some of their party, but all the high-ranking scholars were seated at a different table. The leader of their hosts clapped his hands and a line of newcomers trooped in, filling all the empty chairs. The newcomers were of varying ages, but Bob noticed that the younger ones sat the furthest away from his group. When everyone was seated, the leader of their hosts stood and made a formal greeting to his guests and invited them to stay and share their meagre supplies. Bob recognized the ritual formality of it, and was not surprised when Zha stood and accepted the offer with thanks. When he sat down, servers began hurrying in and placed dishes heaped with food in front of the seated members.

Bob preferred the informal buffet of their original hosts, but was mollified somewhat by the heaped plate and a large glass of cold beer. To either side and opposite of him were seated men and women of late middle age ... and a few long past that. One frizzy-haired old man leaned forward. "Greetings, Bob. My name is Latfo. May I ask about your ship?" Bob's mouth was full of beer, so he simply nodded.

"Thank you. My speciality is ancient space craft. Yours reminds me of the scout-class ships. Not exactly, of course, but similar. Am I correct in that?"

Bob nodded as he swallowed his beer. "You correct, Latfo. It is one of the most advanced of its type, produced after the Veil was erected. I am very proud of it."

"As well you should be, young man, as well you should be. There are several surviving sagas that extol the daring exploits of those ships and their crews. Mayt, here, is an expert in those." He pointed to an elderly woman seated next to him.

"Now, Latfo, let the young man eat. He needs more than old folks like us." She grinned at Bob. "Greetings, Bob. I'm Mayt. All of us have questions that we've built up over long lifetimes of study. So eat up, young man, as I fear that you'll need all your strength for the trials that lay before you."

Bob raised his glass in salute. "Let me grow in strength so that the trials whither before me. Let my purity be a shield."

He leaned forward to look deeply into Mayt's eyes. "Let my words soften hard hearts."

Mayt raised her own glass in salute. "And may those words not lead the innocent astray."

She drained her glass and slammed it down onto the table. Bob did the same with his own a fraction of a second later. The sharp sound reverberated in the hall and was loud enough to cause all conversation to cease and all eyes to turn towards them.

"What?" exclaimed Mayt in a loud voice as she looked around the room. "He knows the classics."

She waved to a server who hurried over to refill their glasses. The noise level returned to normal.

"Dare I ask what sort of classics?" came Rhian's murmured voice on their private comm link. Bob chose to ignore her.

Grinning broadly, Mayt turned to look at Bob. "That's old even by our standards. How'd you come to know it?"

"An aunt of mine has an extensive library. I spent many happy days there in my youth."

"What was her name, if I might ask?"

"Gertrude. She was my favourite relative."

"Hmm. An interesting name, and unlike anything in our archives, but I suppose cultural isolation will do that. But eat, please." She snorted a laugh. "It's not good to drink on an empty stomach."

Bob managed to have a pleasant lunch, even if it was periodically interrupted by questions. To his great surprise he quite enjoyed the company of his table companions. Despite being bursting with questions, they made sure he was well taken care of and entertained. They invited him to visit their departments and promised him full cooperation with his researches. Finally, their host stood and dismissed the crowd, leaving only their hosts and Bob's 'cargo' seated.

"We've arranged a brief tour of our facilities for Bob and Rhian," said the leader of their hosts. "I hope it will give them a better overview of what we have and what we do." He grimaced and added, "I've been told to keep the tour brief, but I think it will help. I'll be your tour guide. We'll finish the tour at the secure facility. Is everyone ready?" Everyone was, and the three of them headed off.

As they walked, the man made a short bow to Bob and Rhian in turn. "I didn't get a chance to introduce myself to you earlier. My name is Glat. I'm the senior academic coordinator of this facility. That is to say, I'm in charge."

"Greetings, Glat, I'm Rhian. Should I refer to you by name or by your title? On my world, someone with such a position is always addressed by title."

Glat nodded. "Thank you for your courtesy, Rhian. It is much the same here, but I'd prefer if you called me by my name. Titles and ranks can be very tricky to get correct, especially for someone not familiar with them." He grinned as he added, "Besides, we're a practical institution and try to keep such things to a minimum. It's one of the advantages of being a smaller facility far away from the main cities. Often annoys visiting scholars no end. Ah, here's our first stop."

As promised, it was something of a whirlwind tour. Glat set a brisk pace and ensured that none of his staff asked any questions as he hustled Bob and Rhian through the campus. They saw laboratories for various sciences, rooms filled with people reading and cataloguing books, caught glimpses of row upon row of books in various libraries, and were introduced to the heads of various departments. Mayt wasn't among them, but she winked at Bob in passing. Bob winked back.

After less than an hour they came to halt in front of a sturdy-looking door with a pair of armed guards in front of it. Both Glat and Rhian were puffing slightly from the exertion.

"Once again, I must apologize for the briefness of the tour. I felt that you should be made aware of the types of support we can offer you." He turned to Bob. "I've been made aware that you are here on a mission to uncover a threat of some sort. No-one seems clear on what that might be, and no-one knows quite how to proceed. While the Great Council deliberates, you are to have full access to our archives. In addition, I've decided to offer you any support you might require."

"Thank you, Glat," said Bob. "That is most generous of you."

Glat shook his head while continuing to smile. "Not really. I have no idea if this threat of yours is real or not. But I do know that you have equipment that can advance our researches beyond conception. I'd do almost anything to help that along."

He became serious and rubbed his hands together. "Are we ready to proceed to the secure facility?" After a nod from his two guests, he led them through a series of corridors and heavily armoured and guarded doors. At each checkpoint their identity was verified.

"We're now inside the hills and heading down," said Glat motioning around. "These corridors used to be mines. Now they are used to protect our most precious treasures. This is the final checkpoint, by the way."

He led them through that and into a brightly-lit cavern. It reminded Rhian of an aircraft hangar and was of a similar size. There were worktables, benches, shelves, and cabinets throughout the area. Glat had fallen silent after they entered the area, and lead them to a conference table where Brof and Zha sat. He motioned Bob and Rhian to.sit, then took a chair himself.

"Did you enjoy your tour?" asked Brof.

Bob gave a nod and a professional smile. Rhian answered in the affirmative, her happy smile punctuating her answer.

"Any questions at this point?"

"Just one," said Bob. "How do you communicate with the other human planets? We discussed this briefly before, but you dodged the question."

Brof turned to Zha and said, "I told you he'd push that point."

Zha had a sour look on his face. "Are you sure about this?"

Brof shrugged. "Why not? According to the legends he'll have similar equipment in his ship, even it works along different principles."

She turned to Bob and said, "We call it the 'ansible'. It's a quantum entanglement communications system. Faster than light, of course. Most of the human worlds have them, including the so-called primitive worlds. Even some of the other hidden worlds. The Core Worlds can use it to send bursts of data, but the rest of us are limited to voice."

"Can the Nexus detect it?" asked Rhian. "You go to such lengths to hide all of your other equipment."

"No," said Zha. "Or, rather, they can detect the presence of it, but can neither tap into it nor determine the location of the stations. The Nexus uses something similar to coordinate the MI forces."

"Do you know the location of the other stations?" asked Bob.

"No, just by name. Often our records can match a name to a location, but we have no way of determining if that information is current. During the old battles, the Core Worlds would use it to broadcast warnings and receive updates. Experience taught us to stick to code names rather than specific locations for security reasons. When the MI forces managed to acquire a piece of information, keeping the locations as names instead of coordinates helped to minimize subsequent damage. Ofttimes the names were changed to confuse the Enemy, but that has also allowed some planets to become lost from the others."

Bob considered that for a moment. "Alright, that gives me something to think about. Now for the immediate issues. First of all, your written records. As Rhian suggested earlier, we can certainly help with that but it will take time. We'll need to scan every page, and that's labour intensive."

"We can supply all the labour you require," said Glat, grinning. "I doubt your ship carries more equipment than we have people."

Bob flashed him a smile. "True. There are several options available, so I'll need to give some thought as to the best way to proceed. A lot will depend on what the ship has in stores, so I need to check on that. The next step is making that scanned data available. To that end, I can supply you with a dozen hand readers right away ... Rhian has already found those. I've also got some larger, more powerful portable analysis systems. The problem is they require more power, but I can offer power modules that should last for some years of continuous use, perhaps a couple of decades with intermittent use. However I've not got a good long-term solution for power, I'm afraid."

"Can you do anything with a fast-flowing river?" asked Glat.

"Perhaps," said Bob. "What have you got in mind?"

"There a few underground streams near here, including a couple with both high volume and a significant drop. All are underground and shielded by the natural metals in the rock."

Bob nodded. "I think I can do something with that. Again, not perfect but probably good enough. As for shielding, I can use the ship's systems to check on that as we go along." Bob saw Zha's shoulders relax at the mention of checking the shielding.

"But what about access to those streams?" said Brof. "Won't digging and stringing wires take time?"

"I don't think so," said Bob. "With regards to digging tunnels, my pistol will suffice for the short runs." He tapped his holster. At their disbelieving looks he smiled and said, "It's based on use of the alternate energies, so has plenty of punch. In fact, it can deliver a punch heavy enough to damage a ship in low orbit. It can only do that a couple of times before burning out, but it can do it. If something heavier is required, I can use a battle rifle. As the name suggests, it can fire more often and with greater intensity. Digging is the least of our worries. Tell where and how far, and I'll punch that hole."

"Excellent," said Brof. "It sounds like we have a plan for the written material, at least for recording it. I assume you can save it to data rods?"

Bob nodded.

"That leads to the next issue. Can you read our data rods, Bob? They're similar, but not identical, to yours."

"It may help if I show him an example," said Glat. "Excuse me a moment."

He returned a half a minute later carrying a wooden case that he lowered with great care onto the table. After opening the lid, he pushed the case towards Bob who examined the contents without touching anything.

"Very old style," Bob said after a moment. He tapped his nose with a forefinger for several seconds before giving a curt nod. "If the ship doesn't have an adaptor in stores, I'm pretty sure I can make one." He held up a hand. "That's assuming I can find information about it my archive. Reverse-engineering it would be very difficult. Again, I'll have to go back to the ship and check."

"So how did you want to proceed?" said Brof.

"The written material sounds like it would be easy to start with," said Rhian. "As Bob said, we've got a dozen readers. They can also acquire and store images. Not an optimum solution, but would get us up and going quickly." She shrugged. "Start using them on the materials you don't think are held in the rods. If nothing else that'll give us a chance to get organized and test out procedures while working on something useful."

"Can you start that right away?" asked Zha. At the puzzled stares of the others, he laughed. "It'll get people working on this quickly. There's a lot of tension out there about our visitors and the opportunities they offer. Better to focus that energy than let it fester."

"Alright, then," said Brof. "How quickly can you get that going, Bob?"

Bob shrugged. "About an hour, perhaps two." He looked at Rhian. "Walk out to the ship, gather the readers, check them out, bring them all here, and start basic training." Rhian nodded in agreement.

Turning to Glat, he said, "How good are your people at learning new skills on new equipment? The readers are simple enough, but we're talking about performing tasks with what is, to them, alien equipment."

"They'll be fine," said Glat, who was becoming excited by what he was hearing. "If not, we've a large pool to draw from. Lots of good people. More than enough. I'll see about setting up a row of tables down here where the teams can work so we'll be ready to go when you get back."

Brof nodded. "Excellent. Now what about the power issue and the data rods?"

Bob shook his head. "Tomorrow at the earliest. I need to check the ship's stores and records. After I help Rhian with the readers, I'll head to back to the ship and get to work."

"You'll be joining us for supper, won't you?" said Glat.

Bob hesitated then shook his head. "No. I'm beginning to get the feeling that we need to get all this up and running as quickly as possible. Also, I want to set up the ship for full scans to ensure we aren't emitting anything that can be detected. Which leads me to another question: can the Nexus detect the alternate energies?"

Zha and Brof looked at each other for several seconds. "No, I don't think so," answered Brof. "The Nexus was developed after we lost knowledge of the alternate energies, and it has never made use of them in all these millennia. If it could, it would be making use of them. No doubt about that."

"All right," said Bob. "Let's get to work."

CHAPTER SEVEN
Threat and Response

It took a day for Rhian to get the first document scanning team trained, but within three days all available readers were being used. She made spot checks of their output every hour, but never found any errors. Her teams were competent, focused, and keen scholars who knew how important their work was.

Bob, on the other hand, had a tougher time of it. The pod was well-stocked for re-supply, not constructing a base from scratch. Still, what was there could be kludged and cursed into something adequate—if barely—for the task. The scholars were quite adamant about doing things correctly the first time, not slapping something together and letting tomorrow take care of itself. That meant proper design, which meant working with local experts who had no experience with the tech he had. Worse, their long exposure to the histories and sagas fuelled a conviction that they knew how the tech should work. Any disagreement between theory and reality was blamed on Bob.

The whole process was something of an ordeal for Bob, who was used to doing what he thought was correct in whatever way he thought was appropriate. After several days of this, he was ready to explode. Things came to a head when a group senior academics were arguing with Bob and each other about the best routing and hookup for the power cables. Because he looked younger than them, they treated him as a barely-educated student who should defer to his elders.

Bob grew silent as a tight grin appeared on his face. He went to a locked container, extracted a battle rifle, and used it blast several holes into the wall from their current location to one of the two underground rivers. He went to another wall and blasted another series of holes towards the other.

"Power there. Coolant there. Waste water there," he said, rifle resting on a hip, as the others stood there slack-jawed. "You," he said pointing to a group of young scholars chosen for their musculature. "Take that container with the large power cell and converter to the first location." He pointed to a second group. "You lot ... wait for the rock to cool then confirm the distance and get the appropriate cabling. In the meantime. take that other lot of equipment to the second."

Turning to the senior scholars he snapped out, "Set up a distribution panel at the holes. That'll allow you to set up quickly for now and have expandability for the future. Don't argue, just use the equipment I've shown and explained to you a dozen times already. I don't care what it is you use now or think you want to use, it won't do the job. If you waste my time by bringing anything else in here, I'll slag it." His index finger began tapping on the barrel of the rifle. "Just use what I told you to use, in the way I told you to use it, histories and sagas be damned."

Bob glared at the teams he'd selected. "Well? What are you waiting for? Move." The last was growled out in tone of flat menace and command. The young men scurried to obey. The older men began to protest, but huddled together in fearful silence at a glare from Bob.

The room was silent except for the hurried footsteps of the young men as they carried off the equipment as ordered. After a few seconds, two pairs of feet were heard approaching from the rear of the room. The figures of Mayt and Latfo appeared, casually pushing their way through the frozen crowd as if on a casual stroll. They walked up to the first set of holes and peered down. Mayt grunted as she stood up.

"That one's not all the way through," she said, pointing at one of the holes.

"And this one's got something of a curve in it that'll make it difficult to get the cables through," added Latfo as he pointed at another.

Bob's expression didn't change. He walked up to the holes in question and peered into them. "Stand back," was all he said. He tapped at the rifle's controls before taking a couple of shots down each hole. "Anything else?"

The two elderly scholars inspected the other holes, finding minor faults with the others which Bob corrected.

"Much better, dear," said Mayt. "One mustn't rush these things. I suspect that your blood sugar is low." She turned to the huddled group of senior scholars. "You've been working this poor boy too hard. Working everyone too hard, come to that. Time for a decent meal, all of you. That rock needs to cool anyway." She slipped an arm through Bob's free arm. "There's a lovely buffet being served in Latfo's department. For a bunch of physical science types, they put on a good spread."

"And we have beer," exclaimed Latfo. "Including that dark beer you like so much, Bob."

Despite himself, Bob found a smile tugging at his mouth. He cleared his throat and puffed out his cheeks. "I need to secure the rifle."

Mayt patted his arm. "You do that, then we can all have a nice meal. I could really use a beer after spending all morning rummaging about all those dusty old tomes for Rhian's project." She smiled up at him. Bob knew when he was beaten, so he disengaged himself from her and locked up the rifle. With a final glare at the others, he allowed Mayt and Latfo to lead him away.

Within minutes he was attacking a full plate of food and a large pitcher of beer. The room was full of chattering and laughing people but did not feel crowded. There was sunlight streaming through the windows and a gentle breeze wafted through the room. His mood lighted by the minute.

"Don't let them get to you, Bob," came the quiet voice of Latfo at his side. "My group is taking the next shift, and we'll get it done the way you want."

Bob turned at looked at the old scholar, a wry grin on his face. "Been a long time since I've had to work as part of a group. Out of practise."

Latfo took a sip of his beer before replying. "That was my observation." His smile was friendly. "But just one word of advice, if I may ... use the whip of anger sparingly." He held up his free hand to forestall Bob's response. "Oh, you had cause, I don't deny that. But you've got to understand that we're a scholastic culture, used to moving in slow patterns." He chuckled, the sound rumbling deep in his chest. "Does my heart good to see a fire lit under people here for the first time in a very long while. If nothing else comes of all this, I thank you for that."

"Indeed," came Mayt's voice from Bob's other side. Both men turned to look at her. "We've been looking inward for far too long." She shrugged. "It's what comes from a group of scholars and researchers founding a settlement, I suppose. That and trying not to be noticed for millennia."

"Speaking of which," said Latfo, "There's been concerns raised about all this new equipment being detected somehow. You've talked about shielding before, but I think people are starting to get nervous as the reality is setting in."

Bob swallowed a bite of food and took a swig of beer before answering. "Good point, actually. The ship's not seeing anything, but the best way to do a proper check is from orbit. Perhaps at the end of each day, I could do a quick orbital sweep and check for emissions."

Latfo nodded. "That'd do a lot to ease concerns. Might I suggest that this afternoon as a good time to start? Say, after lunch?"

Bob gave him a questioning look.

"You need a break, Bob. There's nothing more you can do with the power setup until things have been hooked up, and that won't be done until tomorrow morning at the earliest. My team will want to do a lot of checking ourselves before you do the final check. After all, once you leave, we'll be responsible for it."

"That'll give you some quiet time to work on the data rod interface problem," added Mayt. "Those are my department, and I want to see results as soon as possible."

The mock seriousness on her face got a chuckle out of the two men. Her face settled into its normal happy lines as she said, "Rhian is doing wonderful work. She's got teams organized to scan the written records, and they're moving at a good rate. On top of that she's got some preliminary cataloguing done. Basic stuff, of course, but enough to give us a taste of what the future holds. It's all very exciting."

Bob nodded as he took another swig of beer. "There's a pair of small control systems included in my stores that'll be ideal for your requirements, Mayt. Keep one here and one in another city. In the short term you can use them for data storage and retrieval, as well as untraceable communications. They're capable of a lot more, of course, but that's a much harder task, I'm afraid."

"Not so difficult as you might think," said Latfo. "We've got records of such things and have people familiar with the theory of it." He grinned. "You keep forgetting that we know about a lot of what you're showing us. All we lack is the practical experience, but thanks to you that will come in the fullness of time."

Bob grinned. "I'm used to getting things done in a hurry."

"So we've noticed," said Mayt in a dry tone. Her smile took the sting out her words.

Rhian's voice crackled forth from Bob's private comm unit. "Bob? I'm hearing reports that you've been scaring the scholars again. You promised to be good."

Speaking in English, Bob replied, "A minor misunderstanding that's been cleared up. One new wrinkle just came up, though. They want me to do a full emissions scan to ensure all this new equipment isn't detectable. To do that I'll need to take the ship into orbit for a few hours. That going to cause a problem for you?"

"No, I was going to stay overnight here, anyway. But I was hoping to test out that sensor wand interface you rigged up for my reader. I'd like to have the ship run an analysis on what we've managed to scan so far."

"I can do that while I'm in orbit. You've got a couple of wands, right? Make a copy of your data on one of them, and have a runner give it to me at the ship in a few minutes. Then hook up the second one and we can test the comm link from orbit. Either way I'll be able to get the ship working on what you've got. Those results will give me something to test on the small control system I'm setting up for use here."

"Perfect, thank you. Have a nice trip." She cut the link.

Bob drained his glass then put it and his now-empty plate on a table. "Time to go. Rhian wants me to work on analyzing the scans she's already done while I'm flitting about." He grinned as he added, "No rest for the weary."

Mayt put a hand on his arm, a concerned look on her face. "Don't forget to rest, Bob. You're only human." She didn't understand the fleeting look of pain on his face that he quickly replaced with his usual grin.

"I promise to rest," was all he said as he turned and left the room.

* * *

Rhian found Bob at his ship, at an unloading door of the strap-on pod. He was moving crates around inside and there were several on the ground.

"Hi. Heard I'd find you here. Haven't seen you in nearly a week. Almost beginning to think that you've been avoiding me."

Bob paused for a moment then kept on working. "Just busy."

Rhian was silent for the space of several heartbeats. "Last I saw, you were slurping all those old data records into the ship's systems. No-one saw you stop for anything but a light snack for days. You look like crap, by the way."

"I'll rest later."

"You found something," she said in an accusing tone. "Were you planning to share?"

Bob placed the crate he was carrying on the deck of the anti-grav sled, wiped his brow, and sighed. "I've put everything I've found onto a portable terminal." He pointed to a crate inside the cargo area. "I'll be bringing it out as soon as the data transfer is completed. Several terminals, actually. Always good to have spares." He gave her a brief grin.

Rhian favoured him with a sour look that was known to make students quake, but which had no effect on him. "I'm not interested in that mountain of raw data." She paused and shook her head. "Well, I am, but right now I want to know what it is you found that's got you so rattled."

"Not rattled. Preparing to do what is necessary."

She began tapping a foot, which to everyone at her university was a signal that she was about ready to explode. "Do what, exactly?" The last word was drawled out with exaggerated calmness.

Bob shifted his footing to stare directly at her...or, rather, down at her. He fairly radiated focused intent, but his voice was soft. "Rhian, the Nexus is winning the war." He held up a hand. "Hear me out, please." He paused to take a deep breath and let it out slowly. "Human societies ebb and flow, wax and wane. The Nexus and the MI, on the other hand, never waver. Historically, the human ebb and flow has produced enough vitality to keep the expansion of the Nexus to a minimum. But minimizing it is not the same as negating it. As I said, the MI never waver. What they have done for the past few centuries is change tactics. Instead of direct attacks, they've been diffusing throughout the Veil preparing for battle on a larger scale than the humans are prepared for."

Rhian shook her head. "No, wait. That's a given. They're regrouping for more battles, is all. Just like they've always done."

"Not this time," said Bob with a shake of his head. "This time is different. The human Core Worlds are more tightly integrated, it's true, but there's few others waiting in the wings. The last round of battles with the MI took everything the humans had. There are few known human reserves and the Core Worlds have ignored them as they've retreated into themselves. No, Rhian, in the long run the humans can't win."

"You seem very sure about that without having hard data." Her voice had a harsh edge to it.

Bob grunted a laugh. "Well, actually I do. Got it from our host's secure archives."

"What?" Rhian lowered her voice to a low growl. "That's an abuse of trust, Bob. Why would you even do such a thing? What if you'd been caught?"

He shrugged. "In truth, didn't set out to do anything of the sort. Stumbled across them while hooking things up ... you know how chaotic things are right now. Took a quick scan to make sure I wasn't going to cause harm, then took a deeper look when the ship flagged it as something of interest." He held up a hand to forestall any more comments. "These are scholars, Rhian. Scholars who have spent lifetimes watching and analysing what's going on. They came to that conclusion themselves some generations ago. Nothing they could do about it, so they hoped for the best."

Rhian pondered that for a moment, then shook her head and sighed. "I suppose that explains why they were so quick to work with us. Always wondered about that."

Bob nodded. "That's right. They're looking for something to even the odds over the long term."

"The long term isn't what's scaring you, is it?"

"No. There's worse. The alternate energies are unknown here, except as hints in legends. The Council even knows, in vague terms, what they are. Remember last week when I took a couple of days to survey the rest of the solar system for forgotten tech?"

Rhian nodded, confused by the sudden change in topic.

"I found some."

"Excuse me? And you didn't say anything?"

"Needed to figure out what it meant." At the stormy look on her face, he hastened to add, "It's all safely hidden and shielded, so no fear on that score. The only reason I know about it at all is that I sent out a low-level interrogation pulse using the alternate energies."

Rhian held up a hand to pause his recitation. "Hmm. Great-gran mentioned you doing something like that on the planet that suffered the attack of the rain infected with nanomachines. But didn't that command communication travel out for several light years?"

Bob nodded. "You did hear me say 'low-level', right? Back then I was trying to search as far out as I could. This was as surreptitious as I could make it and still check out a planetary volume."

"Alright, so you were careful. What did you find?"

"Five ancient monitoring stations. Probably dating back to the time the Veil was erected and the settlement still had some military tech available to it. Two are still operational, if only just. The others are quiescent and capable only of responding with an identification code. The two operational ones, though, have been keeping records all these eons. Yes, I downloaded what they had. And, yes, I've left you copies of the data, both raw and processed. It took the ship several days to go through everything and clean it up enough to be usable. Then I had to figure out what it all meant."

"From the look on your face—not to mention all the flurry of activity—you found something bad."

Bob shook his head. "Yes, but also some good news. The good news is that there are indications of other similar monitoring stations throughout the Veil. Most have been quiet for quite some time, but there's a few still active. Again, all hidden away and undetectable by anything other than scans using the alternate energies."

"Oh, my. That's very good news, indeed. So what's the bad news that's got you so upset?"

"Intermittent readings—every century or two—but indicative of a quiescent portal."

"A portal? Are you sure?"

"Very sure. Worse, there's a couple of recent sightings that might indicate an FTL drive just outside the Veil that makes use of the alternative energies. Those are fainter and have fewer recorded events. I need to check this out."

"Seriously, Bob? You're heading off on this wild goose chase without even discussing it with me?"

Bob sighed and turned to face her. "Not a wild goose chase. What has to be done. I need to destroy the portal and the Nexus. It's the key, you see. It coordinates the actions of the MI ... without it, they can be dealt with piecemeal."

Rhian opened her mouth to say something, but Bob overrode her. "The sensor readings from all the different stations give me a bearing and a rough location for the portal ... it's within the volume of space controlled by the Nexus. The human Core Worlds are sure to have the location of the Nexus itself or at least a rough idea that I can use as a starting point. Remember what Uncle Lou said—time is short. Given the energies within the Veil, even with the ship's enhanced FTL it will take some time to get to the Core Worlds. After that it will take more time to find one where the information I require is located. Time that is slipping away. Things are relatively quiet right now, but that could change in an instant if the Nexus decides to attack."

"You don't have to do this alone."

"Yes, I do." He waved a hand to indicate the university town. "Who else is there? I'm the only one who knows how to infiltrate into hostile situations. I'm the only one with battle experience." He saw Rhian open her mouth to speak so he hurried to add, "Yes, you've got some training, I'll grant you. But you're needed here to help restore their old records. If I fail, this planet could become humanity's last hope. If I succeed, their trove of records will be invaluable in rebuilding."

"But you're just one man, Bob. Highly trained and experienced, I'll grant you, but still just one man."

"The Nexus is winning, Rhian," Bob answered in quiet tones. "It's gone from irritant to danger to existential threat, despite all that the humans here can do. Worse, it appears they have a portal somewhere in their space. In time they will find it and then figure out how to access it. Once they do that they'll gain a working knowledge of the alternate energies. With that, they will eliminate humans within the Veil, then move on to the rest of the galaxy."

"Can't the Changed of your kind do something?"

Bob shook his head. "We've discussed this before. They can't cross the Veil to get here. If the Nexus and the MI break out, it will be too late for the Changed to do anything." He paused for a moment before continuing. "I have to try to stop them from gaining access to the portal, and I will succeed. That much I can promise you. Beyond that I will try to inflict what damage I can on their ability to harm the humans here."

Rhian was shocked into silence by the cold intensity of his words and mood. "Fine," she ground out. "Say you destroy the portal. Then what?"

Bob shrugged. "I'm sure that I can tip the scales towards the side of the humans within the Veil. I've left you with all the old, historical records, so the people here will know what happened after the Veil went up. I'll also leave behind a few crates of advanced weapons with you. You've got enough training to use most of them and figure out the rest. A dozen of the battle rifles and pistols will allow you to defend this world from anything short of a full-scale invasion, so distribute the rest as you see fit to other worlds. Between these and what the Core Worlds already have, the folks here will be well prepared. Then it'll be up to the humans here to succeed or fail according to their own efforts."

At the horrified look on her face, he added, "That's as the Precepts of Survival dictate. It's how I was raised. It is what I believe. Besides, as you say, I'm just one man. I have to focus my efforts to be akin to the point of a knife that strikes where it will do the most good."

Rhian took a deep breath to calm herself before replying. "Yes ... one man. One ship. A good ship, but just a single scout ship. Not a warship, a scout ship."

Bob nodded. "A ship designed for reconnaissance *and* disruption behind enemy lines." He paused for a moment before adding in a soft voice, "As am I. I'll accomplish the mission."

"But will you come back?" she said in a small voice that was tense with concern.

"I'll accomplish the mission," he repeated in a firm voice.

CHAPTER EIGHT
Infiltration

Bob leaned back the command chair and drummed his fingers on the arm. The view ports of the ship showed the interplay of subspace energies as the ship ploughed its way through them. He had warned Rhian not to look at them, but he found it relaxing when used in moderation. That unwelcome thought brought a snarl to his lips that he fought to subdue. Moderation in such things was for the merely human. There was a time when he ... but that time was gone forever, he remembered as a sigh escaped his lips. His fingers had ceased their drumming and were now curled into fists.

With an effort of will he uncurled them and held them in front of him, turning them this way and that as he flexed them. In his youth, his fellows had taunted him as 'Bob the Cripple', but his capabilities even then put his current form to shame. His cheeks puffed out as he exhaled sharply. They'd called him a cripple, but he'd defeated Kydos and Freddie, and best of all brought his brother Set's schemes crashing down. He examined his hands once again as he flexed them. Lower than a cripple now ... an abomination in the eyes of his people, with the body of a merely human and memories of being something more. Something better.

That thought caused him sit upright and jerk his head back as if struck. No, not 'better' ... never that. He'd made a point of that with Celcilia when she was feeling inferior to him. But what right did he have to go up against his betters? Who did he think he was? With a snarl he slapped at a control that closed the ports. Whatever comfort he may have gotten from the view before his ... call it a 'change' ... it was not good for him now. For better or worse, this is what ... who ... he was. There was a mission to perform and futures to save. He wiped at his eyes and focused on the display of his workstation, pondering the task.

He needed to find where the Nexus was located. He had a rough location of the lost portal, knew it to be in Nexus-controlled space, but that wasn't enough. The Core Worlds must know where the Nexus was located, or at the very least have a good idea. The Veil, although a constrained volume compared to the home galaxy as a whole, was still quite large. Its roiling energies interfered with his FTL engines, reducing his speed to a fraction of what it was otherwise capable of.

The problem was that even within that constrained volume, the Core Worlds encompassed a large number of stellar locations. To make things fuzzier, his knowledge of it was limited to what the ansible network of the 'primitive worlds' knew, and that was rather out of date by at least decades if not centuries. It was a loose confederation of worlds grown tighter by the threat posed by the Nexus and the Machine Intelligences that it controlled. As the threat posed by the Nexus receded, the human alliance had loosened and fragmented.

Bob pondered what that implied. For one thing, it was a high-tech society. That meant lots of surveillance. For another, it was a society that had been at war for eons ... which meant enhanced security. On the other hand, by all accounts it was a healthy society, unlike the Five Stars Empire he and Celcilia had encountered. He steepled his fingers under his chin as he considered the problem. It was a high-tech confederation in a state of perpetual war, currently in a long-term stalemate condition. It was in contact with, at varying levels, many lesser-developed planets. That meant trade and movement of people on a regular basis.

If he had unlimited time, he could start on one primitive world, then move from one to another to establish a solid background before moving up the 'food chain' of planets until he got where he needed to go. That would be the safest way to do it. That would allow him not only build up credentials, but to check out where he needed to go next. A less time-intensive way would be to sneak in and check out a series of planets to determine traffic patterns, and use that to determine the central hub of human activity. The former would take years, and the latter would take months, if he was lucky.

Bob studied his meagre supply of intelligence. Rhian had argued for him to stay longer to access more of the ancient records. He had pointed out that 'more' wasn't necessarily 'better', since the old records would just fine-tune what little he knew rather than broaden it. What he needed now was current intelligence.

He needed a planet not too far from his current location yet with trading ties to the Core Worlds. After a bit of study, he decided on a planet called Avilont by its inhabitants. It had been a battleground in the early stages of the war and never recovered as more than a source of raw materials. By all accounts it had one large city and several smaller ones, all located on a single continent. The rest of the planet was given over to agriculture and mining of the rare minerals required by the Core Worlds. Trading vessels came weekly. It sounded like an excellent first stop: less than a week away, modest ship traffic, and with a large enough population that a new face wouldn't stand out.

Four days later found him dropping out of FTL at the edge of the Avilont system. Three days after that he was nestled in a small crater on the natural satellite that circled the planet. There were a number of active and passive monitoring devices that required some careful work to bypass. Now that he understood them, though, he'd be able to get in and out in a fraction of the time. They also gave him a taste of what to expect from the technology the Core Worlds used.

The one bit of good luck he'd had was being able to detect one outgoing ship and one incoming. The configuration of the ships was quite a bit different than his own, which eliminated his plan to land and pretend to be a trader. The chatter between the ships and planet indicated that the flight plans of incoming vessels were known in advance, which finalized the elimination of that plan. That left the sneaky option—his personal favourite.

The planet's sole spaceport was located next to the largest city, so Bob decided to land as close to that as possible. Skulking about was always easier in the larger cities with ports, as they always had seedy areas where strangers could blend in and pick up gossip. The language was similar to that of the scholars, with a not-unexpected local accent. He practised two sets of accents, one of an off-worlder and one as close to local as he could make it. The latter would be used as little as possible, of course, since it wouldn't stand up to close scrutiny.

Speaking of scrutiny, he'd gathered from the intercepted chatter that people—especially off-worlders—were expected to have up-to-date identification and financial cards. That would be a problem, since he had no idea what those consisted of. That meant going in disguised as a down-on-his-luck crewman stranded between cruises. Every port had those, and Bob doubted this would be an exception. On the plus side, that would make him all but invisible. On the down side, he'd be rubbing up against the local criminal element. There were so many ways this could go terribly wrong. Bob smiled at the thought ... it was going to be just like old times.

He landed the ship several hundred kilometres away from his target city, nestled in an uninhabited section of forest.

There was a modest mountain range between him and the city, which afforded a measure of protection from detection. To get closer to the city he broke out a skiff. This was a variant of the anti-grav sled designed for fast, silent personal transport. It was little more than a three-metre long, half-metre thick slab with a windscreen and a control panel. The operator normally lay prone upon it, and it would mould itself to the operator's contours. It was designed less for comfort than for speed, stealth, and to present a minimal target. Although it could mount external weapons, normally the operator depended on the internal cannon, a stripped-down variant of a battle rifle. It had a top speed of Mach 2 and enough range to circle the planet at that speed.

Bob loved flying it nape-of-the-earth over mountainous terrain at high speed. This time, though, he kept its speed modest as he moved with care to stay unseen during his approach. He managed to get to within twenty kilometres of the outskirts of the spaceport before the risk of visual detection became too great. At that point he stashed the skiff and proceeded on foot.

He wore a skin-suit—leaving the helmet with the skiff—without any armour, a worn-looking combat belt that could pass casual inspection as a worker's belt, and a knapsack. The knapsack was a shielded combat unit, scuffed to look well-used. It held a pistol, rope, rations, sensors, tools, and a small medical kit. The only obvious weapon was a combat knife on the belt, located in the small of his back. Over all that he wore a tattered poncho that was similar to the ones his orbital observations had shown workers to wear. On his head he wore a tattered beret of the sort off-world crews appeared to wear when walking around town. The only thing he was lacking was local currency. Since he had no idea of how that worked here, he would have to play things by ear.

As Bob approached the town from the spaceport side, he made sure to get considerable dirt on his attire. By the time he reached the unloading zone, the dirt and mud were dry and looked as if it had been there for some time. His stride changed from a distance-eating lope to a brisk walk to that of a disheartened vagabond. When he was noticed at all it was to be yelled at to get out of the way of his betters. Whenever that happened, he'd nod his head and look chastised as he mumbled a reply.

In the area immediately around the spaceport unloading zone, there was considerable use of a concrete-like material for both the streets and the buildings. That gave things the dull uniformity of mere utilitarianism that seemed to be the constant of all lower-end industrial zones, in Bob's experience. The buildings consisted of warehouses, in the main, with a sprinkling of six to eight story office buildings.

Cargo was moved to and from the ships using cranes, with wheeled lorries used to haul the uniform-sized crates into and out of the area. There appeared to be many more crates outbound than inbound. There were considerable amounts of noise and dust, with the smell of petrochemical-burning engines adding an unpleasant stench. He would have liked to pause to watch it all, but several uniformed figures with truncheons were beginning to take notice of him. It was time to move along.

Foot traffic became heavier once he passed the unloading area and into the town itself. The streets changed from a smooth pavement to cobblestones. The buildings became stone and wood constructions that loomed only two or three stories in height. Their ground-floor windows were larger and displayed wares instead of corporate logos. People didn't yell at him any more, but glared or shoved him out of the way. The stench of burning petrochemicals faded to be replaced with the sour smell of fear, desperation, and poor sanitation.

He passed several beggars sitting in alleys, hands out in supplication to passersby. Bob found an unused alley and squatted down to beg. It was an unprofitable hour, but gave him a chance to get a good look at life on the street. A sensor wand shoved up a sleeve picked up low levels of electromagnetic emanations, but no sign of the alternate energies. Analysis of those emanations would have to wait until he got back to the ship.

From what he could see, financial transactions took place using a mixture of coins and some form of tech. The beggars were tossed coins—infrequently and none to him—but in the shops things were a little more complex. Payment was made in the form of coins or the scanning of a thin card. However, in either case a separate card was scanned. That looked to Bob like an identification verification scheme. This hypothesis was strengthened when he saw a beggar go into a shop to buy some food and had to display a card before he was allowed to complete the purchase using coins. That could make things very difficult for an outsider.

It was getting to be late afternoon, so Bob decided to continue exploring. He followed the roads in the direction of the better-dressed pedestrians. The roads here were cleaner, the buildings less battered, and the air smelled nicer. There were also uniformed men with truncheons patrolling the streets, one pair of which stopped him by slapping a truncheon to his chest.

"What ho, traveller? Identification please."

Bob hung his head, shook it, and muttered unintelligibly. Both of them sneered at him and the truncheon against his chest released before whacking him again.

"Identification," came the curt command.

"Lost it, gentle sirs."

"Lost it?" said one in exaggerated seriousness to the other. Then he turned to face Bob again. "Where. Are. You. From?" he said slowly, as if to a child.

"Off world. Missed my ship."

They rolled their eyes and the truncheon once again slapped his chest. "Go back to the port lands. Your kind isn't allowed here without identification."

Bob raised his head enough that he could look up at them. "Hungry. Need place to sleep. Find job. Go home."

The silent security man spat in disgust, his phlegm catching the toe of Bob's boot. "Bloody off-world trash. Stay in your sector and stop bothering your betters."

His partner shook his head and looked a fraction more caring. "Go back to the hiring hall," he said in a tired voice. "There's nothing for you here. Maybe they can sort out your lost identification and get you another berth." Then his voice hardened. "Off you with you, now, and be quick about it."

Bob turned around and fell to the street as the expected shove in the small of his back came. He lay face down in the dirt until the laughter and footsteps of the security men faded, then he got slowly to his feet and shuffled back the way he'd come. Soon enough he was back in the dock area. He shuffled along until stopped by a security guard. "Hiring hall," Bob muttered. The guard snorted and used his truncheon to point the way, then went back to scanning the area.

It took three interventions by guards before Bob found the hiring hall just as the sun was setting. It was a dirty, rough-looking, single-story slab of a building. He walked in and was greeted by the noise of several dozen men sitting at tables and the bar, laughing and talking. The lights were harsh and bright after the dimness outside. Bob blinked and stood there slack-jawed for several seconds before shuffling off to a small table at the far end that had stacks of thinly sliced bread and several large steaming bowls on top of heaters. Upon examination, the bowls proved to contain a watery substance that smelled as if it had been exposed to soup fumes at some time in its past.

Bob reached for a slice of bread but was stopped by a heavy hand on his wrist.

"Identification, if you please," growled a voice as the hand pulled him away from the table.

Sucking in his cheeks to make himself look gaunter, Bob turned around to face this new voice. The man holding his wrist was large and outweighed Bob by a considerable amount. A near-twin stood to one side. The scars on their faces and hands reinforced the impression that they were brawlers gone to fat. The third man, the one who had spoken, was small, greasy, wrinkled, and pudgy.

Bob meekly looked at each one, then focused on the short man.

"Lost it. Missed my ship. Looking for a berth." He turned and tried to turn toward the table but was stopped by a heavy hand.

"Uh huh. What ship?" demanded the small man in a harsh voice that was devoid of kindness.

"Melneer Pah," muttered Bob. "Missed liftoff." That was the name of the ship Bob had detected leaving the system as he had entered.

The unblinking eyes of the small man took bored into Bob's own. "Uh huh. What position?"

"Scrubber." Bob had heard that term used to describe the cleanup men while he was begging. He hoped it applied to a position on the cargo vessels.

"Uh huh. So what happened to you? Too much jax? Slats? Bah, your kind make me sick—give honest crew a bad name." He chewed a fat lip for a moment then jerked his head. "Two slices and one cup. You can sit in a chair for the night. When you get a berth, half ... no, two-thirds ... of your signing bonus comes to me." He leaned forward and gave Bob an evil grin. "I trust you, see. Bad things happen to people I don't trust." After glaring at Bob for several seconds, the fat man leaned back and gave a terse nod at the heavy holding Bob's wrist, who released it. Not bothering to wait for a response, the three of them turned and waddled back to their table.

Bob filled a mug with the watery substance and took two of the thin slices. After looking around he found an empty chair off to one side of the main area. He was far enough away not to be intrusive but close enough to hear many of the conversations. Bob took small sips of his soup and small bites of his bread, trying to make them last. It wasn't so much that he was hungry, but a man concentrating on eating was more easily overlooked. He noticed that the ones who had accosted him ate much better food and had more of it.

What he heard was rather disheartening. If the gossip could be trusted, Avilont was a locked-down corporate planet. Off-world crews were restricted to specific areas of the main city, and not allowed in any of the other cities. There were areas of the city designated for crew recreation, but they charged steep prices for the meagre joys they provided. The officers had marginally better facilities, but few of the crew seemed to envy them. There were whispered comments about non-sanctioned pleasures, but those were quickly silenced by their friends.

During the long wait for morning, Bob left his chair several times. Once to return the empty cup to the table, and several times to visit the sanitation rooms. Not so much out of need, but more to not stand out. When dawn finally came, he used it as an excuse to leave the stale air of the hiring hall. The sun was starting to rise, and the controlled chaos of the port paused for the changing of the shifts. The air was cool, and it was quiet enough to hear a few birds singing. It was almost pleasant.

Bob decided that this visit was a bust, and was working his way to the edge of town. He was passing through an area that was even more run-down than the norm when he heard a man's voice calling to him.

"Here, crewman. I have what you want."

Bob stopped, turned, and looked into the alleyway from which the voice had come. A figure stepped out of the shadows where the sun never shone. It was a thin man with an over-wide smile full of bad teeth. He was holding a leather leash. He gave the leash a tug and a skinny child, of indeterminate sex but no more than ten years old, stumbled out of the alley.

"I take coins, no questions asked," the man said in silken tones, the smile never leaving his face.

"For what?" asked Bob, staying in character, despite the anger growing within him.

"Anything you wish," came the dreaded answer. "The more coins, the greater the wish that can be fulfilled."

Bob stared at the man with a neutral expression. The child looked straight ahead with eyes that held no hope, with a face that held no expression.

The man mistook Bob's hesitation for interest. "If you have no coins, we can make an arrangement," came the silky-voiced offer. "Bring your shipmates to me. For every, say, ten shipmates, you get time with the child." Then came a small chuckle. "Assuming that it still lives." The man shrugged. "Some prefer it that way." The over-wide smile never left his face. "Do we have a bargain?"

Bob reminded himself that this was a simple reconnaissance mission—in and out without causing a fuss. He reminded himself that he'd seen this, and worse, in other parts of the galaxy. He reminded himself that it was not his place to interfere.

At some point while he was reminding himself of all this, the mask he'd assumed slipped and his true self showed. He held himself straighter and assumed the posture of a predator that was not to be trifled with. "Not interested," was all he said. It wasn't a beaten down lost crewman who spoke, but one who on another planet had been called a War Demon.

The smiling man snarled and drew a gun from within his coat. Bob surged forward and hit the man with a blow that drove him against a stone wall with enough force that his skull shattered. The corpse made a soft gurgle as it sagged to the ground, twitched several times, and then lay still. Bob looked at the child, whose eyes were open as far as they could go. Bob stepped forward and the child's face held a look of terror.

"You will not be harmed, little one," said Bob in a soft voice. "Not by me. Not by him. Not ever again by him."

After saying that Bob knelt by the corpse and searched its pockets. He spared the gun a quick look then put it to one side. There was little of interest in the pockets but a keyring with three keys, four identification cards, three payment cards, and a leather purse filled with coins. He motioned the child over, but the child stood frozen in place. Bob gave a small nod then held up the keyring. The child hesitated a moment then stepped forward, stopping just in front of Bob, turning to present the collar. Bob saw a mechanical lock on it. He looked at the keyring, and inserted a key that looked like it would fit. It did and in moments the collar opened with a soft click. The child gasped and jumped back staring at Bob in wonder as small hands rubbed a scarred neck.

Bob held up the four identification cards in his right hand. "Pick one for me, and you can keep the rest." He held up the payment cards in his left hand and said, "Pick one for me, and you keep the rest." He removed one coin from the purse before tossing the purse at the feet of the child. "Yours."

The child eased forward and looked at the cards in both hands before picking all but one from each. "Do you have a safe place that you can go to?" asked Bob.

"No he does not," came a voice from the alley. "Don't move," it said as Bob began to rise. A figure came out of the shadows, holding a gun that was pointed at Bob. It was slim man, not quite as tall as Bob, but with the bearing of an athlete.

"Interesting," said the man. "You went from wastrel to soldier in the blink of an eye. Oh, yes, I recognize the training. I have to ask myself: why would a soldier pretend to be a stranded crewman on this world? Also, why someone pretending to be a stranded crewman break cover to help a slave?"

The gun never wavered while he spoke.

"It was self-defence," said Bob. "He drew a gun. I had no weapon."

"Not entirely true. I suspect that you are the weapon." He pondered that for a moment then sighed and placed the gun into a holster inside his coat. "Which means that I'm in more danger pointing a gun at you than not."

"May I stand?" asked Bob.

The man made a theatrical wave with his hands. "By all means."

"I assume you're a security agent of some sort?" said Bob.

"Police officer, actually. And you are?"

"Just passing through."

"I see." The man considered the reply for several seconds. The child looked from one man to the other, clutching the purse and cards to its small chest.

"Can you see the child to safety?" asked Bob.

"Eh? That's all that concerns you about this?"

"Yes, actually. As I said, I'm just passing through. Can you see the child to safety?"

The police officer looked at the child. "I can take you to a hostel where you'll be safe." He nodded at the treasure the child was holding. "That will ensure that I can take you to a good one. You will be safe, that much I can promise." He turned to Bob and gave a wan smile. "Money buys much on my planet." Then he grimaced. "Too much. We're the source, you know."

"Source? Of what?"

The man nodded at the child. "For such as them. Drugs, too, that the corporations manufacture here."

Bob pondered that information for a moment. "Where does it go?"

"Pilfrom, for the most part. Some of the drugs go elsewhere but from all I've heard Pilfrom is the main depot."

"Why do you care?" asked Bob in a soft voice.

The police officer looked around the area then pointed at the city core. "This used to be a good place, a good planet. Not so much in my lifetime, but certainly within that of my grandparents. Oh, it wasn't easy, but we got by. Did our part helping the Core Worlds, keeping them supplied. Then the wars wound down and demand tapered off. Local greed and outside corruption did the rest." He shrugged. "It's worst here. The other cities are better, but the rot is spreading. Many of us do what we can but ..." he shrugged once again.

"What comes after Pilfrom?"

The police officer shrugged. "Beyond my pay grade, I'm afraid. All I know is that the next contact in the chain is named Drawde." He gave Bob an appraising look. "You're here on some sort of mission. Does that include Pilfrom?' There was an eager catch to his voice.

Bob shrugged. He'd hoped to locate the centre of the Core Worlds through analysis of trade routes. It looked like his best lead was illicit trade, which did not sit well with him. Still, it was the best lead he had. He took a deep breath and let it out in a gust and nodded. "I may have to include it."

"If I may ask, why are you walking here in the first place?"

Bob shrugged. "Heading to the outskirts of town and got lost in the maze of streets." He pointed down the alley. "That's the way I wanted to go, actually."

"No," came a small voice. Both men turned to look at the child who was shaking his head. "The nest is down there."

"Nest?" said the police officer.

The child nodded. "Yes. Where they keep us." He began to shake. "They say the guns and the whips are to protect us." The child sniffed once then grew still once more.

Bob turned to the police officer. "Can you get reinforcements here?"

"Yes. Why?"

"How long will it take for them to arrive?"

"Depends on the problem. If I push them, fifteen or twenty minutes. Maybe longer."

"That's all I'll need," said Bob. He shrugged off his poncho and handed it to the child. "Give it a wash and it'll be good as new." He shrugged off his knapsack and dug out his pistol, mounted it on his belt, then moved the knife to his other side. As he shrugged on the backpack he said, "How long will you need to get clear and call for reinforcements?"

The police officer looked at him with wide eyes then gave his head a shake. "Maybe two minutes, if this is going to be as noisy as I think it is." Then he shook his head again. "But you're just one man. What can you do?"

Bob smiled at him and shrugged. "Not planning to do anything. To get to where I need to go requires me to walk through that area. If someone decides to start something, why, I'm just defending myself. I'm not here to cause anyone any problems."

"Ah," said the police officer. He turned to the child and said, "We'd better be on our way. Our friend here looks to be in a hurry."

The child looked at Bob. Bob knelt down and said, "I'll make sure the others are freed. The rest is up to you."

"Thank you," said the child in a small voice. He turned and began walking away. The police officer hurried to catch up, turning around to wave at Bob.

Bob got to his feet and waved back. He squared his shoulders and began walking down the alley.

Down the street, the child turned to the police officer and said, "He's going to die, you know."

The police officer shook his head. "Perhaps. But at least he's trying to help. We can only hope that the Core Council is beginning to clean things up."

Shortly after that they heard gunfire and yelling. The police officer took out his communicator and began making urgent calls. Revealing his identity in this part of town was risky, but it appeared that he no longer had a choice. The intensity of the gunfire increased, and the yelling became interspersed with the sound of men screaming in fear and pain.

* * *

Bob ran through the brush and up a small hill, his breathing fast and ragged. Dropping behind some cover he took the time to catch his breath and observe his handiwork. In the city behind him swathes of buildings burned, dark smoke rising into the air to mingle with the existing pollution. Sirens could be heard coming closer. There was no obvious pursuit, so he took the opportunity to patch up the worst of his wounds. As expected, the skin-suit protected him from gunfire, but he had sustained some serious bruising. His hands and face were another matter, exposed as they were. Both hands were raw and had angry-looking gashes. His head, he suspected, was in similar shape. He slathered a healing cream over everything he could reach, then checked his pistol. It was three-quarters depleted. More than he'd expected to use but better than he'd feared.

His breathing eased to mere puffing, so he heaved himself to his feet and began running to where the skiff was hidden. He was exhausted, injured, and was generally feeling quite pleased with himself. All the children had been freed, many of their captors incapacitated or killed, part of the illicit operation was out of business, and the local police were being forced to investigate. It would be impossible for them to cover this up.

It took him three hours to get back to the skiff, far longer than it had taken to reach the city in the first place. His mood was still buoyant, but his body was less than pleased and required a large dose of painkillers and stimulants to keep going. The auto-medic was not going to be pleased with him. Given his weakened condition, he set the skiff for automatic return along his original route at best speed. There was a danger he'd be seen, but the time for stealth was over.

Luck was with him and no-one spotted his rapid flight to the ship. He got the skiff aboard then headed to the control room on unsteady legs. The ship detected no pursuit, so Bob put it into full stealth mode and eased it up into space. He considered hiding out within the solar system but decided the risk of detection was too great. He set a course for Pilfrom at the maximum speed and leaned back in his chair with a sigh.

The many sources of pain woke him less than a half hour later. He struggled to his feet with a groan and stumbled to the auto-medic, pausing only to remove the skin-suit before getting on the table. His last thought before being rendered unconscious was satisfaction that even as a merely human he could still get the job done.

CHAPTER NINE
If At First You Don't Succeed

The trip to Pilfrom took eight days. Even at the reduced speeds he was forced to use, it was at least twice as fast as anything else within the Veil, and probably better than that. He used the time to analyze the identification and monetary cards he'd obtained, as well as the various readings the sensor rods had picked up. The cards would be easy enough to duplicate, although he doubted they'd be identical to the ones used on any other planet. Still, it was a place to start. If nothing else, he could play the part of a crew member who had minimal experience. Which was true, come to think of it.

Analyzing the lessons learned from his first outing made him cringe a little. So much effort expended for so little hard information. On the other hand, it was the first time infiltrating a hostile base in this part of the galaxy. The first lesson was that he needed to have intel on the actual ships coming and going, if only to help establish an identity. The second lesson was that he needed to wear some sort of better armour ... those projectile weapons could bruise even if they couldn't penetrate the skin-suit. The third lesson was that he needed to get a better understanding of the tech behind the control and data systems in use. The sensor wands could pick up emanations readily enough, but would be useless for acquiring information unless re-tuned to handle the new tech.

The final lesson was that he was going to have wrap up his investigations as quickly as possible. Once word of his investigations became known—either by ansible or ship—things would get a lot more difficult.

This led him to some serious thinking about tactics. This was the first time he'd had to undertake a serious and sustained campaign since his rebirth into a merely human body. That thought caused a shudder—caused not by fear but rather a feeling of inadequacy—to run through his body. With a snarl he forced himself to straighten his posture and return to calmness. His ancestors had survived waves of genocidal attacks with bodies no better than his, or even not quite as good. The people within the Veil had also survived many horrors. Who was he to dishonour their sacrifice with such doubts?

Part of the problem, he realized, was that despite his training recent events had showed all too keenly the limitations of that training. On the other hand, as the Precepts of Survival said, "Training forges the weapon, but experience sharpens it." He had centuries of experience, albeit with a body with a broader range of capabilities. It was time to adapt that experience to the tools at hand.

He dropped out of FTL some distance from the Pilfrom system, and took three days to complete the infiltration to the target's natural satellite. Pilfrom was a busier planet, in terms of trade, with several ships a day passing in and out. Monitoring the communications traffic gave him indications of where some of them were heading to or from, and even the types of cargo being carried. For all its bustle, though, it was not a major world but rather an important way station between primitive worlds and the more advanced ones farther on.

The world itself had three major continents and a scattering of groups of islands. There was a single spaceport, on the largest continent, with a large metropolis surrounding it. That continent, and a second, had a modest collection of cities and villages scattered throughout. The third continent appeared to be given over to mining and heavy manufacturing, with little regard to pollution control.

As for the infiltration, Bob decided that a variant of the previous sortie would prove the most useful. He had identification and currency from Avilont. With luck he could pass as out-of-work starship crew and convert that currency to something local. With that in hand he could look to upgrade his cover and start looking for Drawde, whomever or whatever that might be. As he'd discovered on Avilont, a lot was going to depend on what the local conditions were.

There was a likely looking spot to stash the ship about ninety kilometres from the spaceport, in a series of heavily wooded rolling hills. There were no roads or signs of habitation. He landed there without being detected and nestled the ship into a ravine that was a near-perfect fit. The dense vegetation formed a natural camouflage to hide it from all but the most sophisticated sensors, of which there'd been no sign.

As before, he wore a skin-suit but this time with light armour suitable for protection from projectile weapons. He also added protective gloves and a flexible full-face helmet. These would offer some protection and could be rolled up and tucked on his belt without adding much bulk. His backpack held the usual gear plus a data pad and a supply of Avilont currency and identification.

There was enough cover that he could get within twenty-eight kilometres of the spaceport on the skiff. He stashed it in a natural cave that he enlarged using his pistol. Unlike last time, he activated a comm-link between the skiff and ship so that he had two ways of summoning the skiff if necessary.

Three hours later found him scuttling through the edges of the run-down parts of the spaceport. He shuffled along the streets, again clothed in a sketchy-looking poncho, soaking up the local sights. The spaceport area here was larger and busier than the one on Avilont, with a wider range of old and new buildings. There were a number of buildings given over to offices as well as the usual low- and high-rise storage facilities for cargo. The spaceport area was marked by a wire fence, but security on the gates was light, as if meant for physical demarcation not as a cage. The city just beyond the fence resembled the port facilities, but Bob could see a more urban area beginning in the distance as well as tall towers on the skyline.

He spent several hours criss-crossing the area within the port, finding the local hiring hall as well as a number of shops catering to the various needs of starfaring crew. There were the expected bars, of course, but also suppliers of clothing, equipment, and financial services. The conversion rates for off-world currency seemed rather unfavourable, but that was to be expected. Since he needed local money, he decided to risk trying to pass his counterfeit coins.

Bob selected one of the several financial stores at random and entered. It was brightly lit, clean, and had a short line of customers waiting to be served. He only had to wait a couple of minutes before he was called over to one of the service desks. He sat down on the edge of the chair to find a middle-aged woman typing on a keyboard.

"My name is Yrret, how may I help you?" she said, slurring the words slightly as if she'd been saying them for many years to countless customers.

"Need to exchange Avilont coins," said Bob, adding a cough and throat-clearing.

"Identification." She held out a hand, looking at him for the first time. Her nose wrinkled as a breeze carried Bob's scent to her, but she kept an unperturbed look on her face. Bob handed her the identification card. She placed it into a small well on her desk and tapped some keys.

"Fine, Crewman ... ah ... Vorpal. Strange name, but never mind that. How many coins?"

Bob handed her a leather purse filled with coins. She gave a resigned sigh and took it from him. Twisting in her seat, she pulled a cylinder from the wall behind her and dumped the contents of the sack into it, then tossed the sack into a waste bin. The cylinder whirled and clanked for half a minute before uttering a soft *ping*. Yrret tapped on the keyboard for a few seconds, then turned to face Bob.

"Not worth much, I'm afraid ... not after we take off our handling charges," she said in the manner of one who found such minimal transactions beneath her.

"I also have a card," Bob muttered as he dug into a pocket and handed over one of the financial transaction cards he'd forged. This was far riskier than forging coins ... it was physically perfect but would not stand up to the full confirmation protocols the card was capable of handling.

"Oh, why didn't you give this to me in the first place?" she said in an irritated tone, placing the card into the well with the identification card. She tapped her keyboard for a few seconds, paused to frown for a few more, then tapped away for nearly half a minute.

"We can't do a full confirmation of this, you understand, so we have to charge a higher-than-normal processing fee. Is that acceptable?"

Bob nodded.

"Thank you." She tapped at the keyboard then leaned back in her seat. Favouring Bob with a professional smile she said, "The transaction card is being processed. Won't be but a minute. Been here long?"

Bob shook his head. "Need a place to stay." He cleared his throat and said in apologetic tones, "Also need clothes. Shipmates played prank on me."

"Mmm hmm. That happens. Been here before?"

"No. Only small ports. First time in one this big."

Yrret allowed a trace of sympathy to show on her face as she leaned forward. "Want my advice? Get out of the port area.

You've got enough to tide you over for five or six weeks so long as you stick to the basics. Go out the small-cargo gate ... that's the closest one ... then turn left for two blocks then go north for another three. Not a fancy area, mind you, but safe and clean."

A soft *bing* from her terminal drew her attention away. She reached into the well and withdrew the identification card and a new transaction card. "Here you go, Crewman Vorpal. Good luck." Her concern faded as her professional expression returned. Looking over Bob's shoulder, she called out, "Next."

Bob took the hint, rose, and exited the premises. He decided to accept Yrret's advice and go outside the port area, as it would increase his options. A brisk half-hour walk brought him to the recommended area. As expected, it didn't look like much. Still, there were a variety of shops and hotels. He wandered around for another half hour to familiarize himself with the block, then entered one of the hotels. The check-in clerk was a middle-aged man who seemed pleased to have a new customer. After a brief exchange of pleasantries, he showed Bob to a small room. Like the area itself, it wasn't much but at least it was clean.

"Is this acceptable, Crewman Vorpal? You won't find better at this price, I promise you."

"What about towels and bedding?"

"We supply those, exchanging them once every week. Modest fee for more frequent replacement." He gave a friendly smile. "It's a good place for what it is."

Bob smiled back and nodded. "Smells clean. Looks good. Oh, does it come with a data port?"

"Ah, no, I'm sorry. None of the hotels in the area offer that, I'm afraid. There's a public data shop down the road, though, where you can rent access. Good rates, too."

"That will be fine, thank you. Ah, as you can see I am in need of clothing and personal supplies. I saw several stores offering such as I walked here. Is there a place you recommend?"

That earned him an even broader smile. "Oh, my sister has a shop two doors down on the other side of the street. Tell her you're staying here. My cousin has an excellent eatery next door to her, too. Good prices at both."

Bob gave a short bow. "That is very helpful of you. This stranger to your world thanks you."

The man returned the bow. "If you need anything else, just ask." With that he turned and walked out of the room, leaving Bob alone.

Bob went to the small bathroom and turned on the water in the sink. It ran clear from the start and smelled clean. There were a pair of towels on the hanger ... not luxurious, but not threadbare. He returned to the main room and checked out the bed. The bed was firm but free of lumps and the sheets were clean. He poked around, looking in the closet and every drawer. There were no obvious monitoring devices that he could see.

He sat on the bed and removed his poncho and backpack, taking the opportunity to tap at a hidden keypad on the backpack. None of the indicators became active, so he opened the pack and took out a sensor wand. He did a quick scan of the room with it, but it detected nothing of note. The room was exactly what it appeared to be ... a minimal room in a less-desirable part of the city. All in all, it seemed like a good starting point for his investigation.

Bob decided that it was a good time for a meal, so after shrugging on the backpack and poncho he went out to the recommended diner. The food was somewhat indifferent, but he managed to pick up some gossip about the city. Of special interest was hearing about the areas of the city where he was told decent folks, especially off-worlders, should never go. He also got some indication of the prices charged in the more upscale parts of the city, scandals of the city politicians, and the onerous fees the local security forces charged for protection. Bob only managed to escape what promised to be a lengthy lecture on the high taxes by pleading the necessity of acquiring new clothing from next door.

The clothing store was another educational experience. He got not only a change of clothes but a lecture on the importance of family, children who never call their mother, and how the local data shop not only overcharged but also tapped into all customer communications. Then she shrugged and allowed as the more upscale stores were worse, so what was an honest person to do?

Bob managed to escape her by pleading exhaustion and the need to rest as he'd just landed earlier in the morning. She permitted his escape only after he promised to return just after sunrise, as it was only then that her no-good cousin's cooking had fresh ingredients.

On the way back to the hotel, Bob stopped off at the data shop to purchase the local version of a data tablet and a limited-bandwidth data plan. As warned, the prices seemed high for what he was getting, but that was often the case, in Bob's experience. It appeared to be a human constant. Still, it would be adequate for his initial purposes.

Back at his room, he packed away his purchases. He sat down on his bed and examined the local data tablet. It was easy enough to operate and he spent the next hour exploring its features and using it access the local data net. When Bob caught himself yawning for the second time in as many minutes he decided to call it a night. After setting up a sensor wand and his regular data tablet to analyze the local version using the ship's resources as required, he stretched out and went to sleep.

Bob awoke the next morning just before dawn. None of his equipment displayed any alarms, so he spent some time on a leisurely freshening up. After donning the new clothes, he put the skin-suit into the knapsack. He'd sized the new clothing a bit on the large size so the new lightweight armour fit nicely under it.

Querying the data tablet revealed something of a surprise. The ship's control system had finished with the local data tablet and decided to use the connection to explore the data network. Bob frowned ... given the reputation of the local data provider for snooping he wasn't sure that was a good idea. However, the ship had figured out how to anonymize its queries which relieved his worries. It had also acquired a detailed map of the city, rather than the tourist-oriented one Bob had discovered, as well as the public directory listing of the inhabitants.

On a whim he looked up the name of his one lead, Drawde. It turned out to be the name of a corporate entity, owned by a very rich family of the same name. The ship had made a preliminary map of the Drawde business empire, but noted that it was incomplete due to the numerous legal shenanigans used to muddy its structure. Even so, the preliminary report was very interesting. The company, and its tentacles, appeared to control a significant amount of the import and export trade. It owned several of the larger warehouses, operating them not only for its own trade but leasing space to other traders. It also operated ancillary businesses in the financial trade, among others. All those relationships could be useful to follow up on, so he instructed the ship to continue digging into that.

The problem for the ship was that it required a relay point such as the data tablet or a sensor wand. Bob looked around the room but couldn't see a good hiding spot for the sensor wand, which meant he was going to have to create one. A quick scan showed that the floor was hollow between the joists, so Bob used his pistol to slice a plug out of the floor, in a spot where no-one would normally step, spanning from the middle of one joist to the next. A data wand slid into the gap nicely, and the plug fit snuggly back into the hole. A bit of dust sprinkled into the new cuts hid the plug pretty well, he thought. The ship was happy with the connection, so Bob packed everything up and prepared to go for breakfast.

As promised, the breakfast at the diner was a definite improvement over last night's meal. The food was plain but tasty, and the portions were large. With breakfast taken care of, Bob walked through the city while examining the morning crowds. This may have been a less-desirable part of the city, but the streets were busy as were the sidewalks. Not crowded, perhaps, but busy enough. He noticed that the storekeepers opening their shops called to and greeted not only each other but also many of the pedestrians. After the shops were open Bob paused to purchase copies of the local newspapers, downloading them to his local data pad.

As he got closer to the centre of the city, the neighbourhoods changed. The stores became larger and had fancier signs, the architecture became grander, and the people better dressed. There was, however, no friendly call-outs between pedestrians and shop owners. Here everyone focused on their own business.

Bob decided that things had changed enough that it time to establish another identity. He walked into an up-scale financial establishment that he recognized as being associated with Drawde. After a short walk down an elegantly-appointed hallway, he found the way barred by a desk with a secretary sitting behind it.

She took in Bob's lesser-quality clothing with a barely concealed sneer. "Good day, gentle sir. And what may we do for you today?" From the tone of her voice it was clear she wondered why he was even there.

"Good day," said Bob in crisp tones. "I was recently on Avilont and need to convert some funds to local currency."

"Well, sir, there are establishments at the port that handle this sort of thing. Perhaps one of them might be a better choice?"

Bob favoured her with a cool smile that didn't touch his eyes. "I think not. My ... associates, shall we say ... recommended your establishment as being discrete and trustworthy." He shrugged. "It seems they were in error. Good day." He turned to walk out but found his way barred by a burly guard. Bob looked him up and down and sneered, before turning to face the secretary once more.

"What is this about? I came here in good faith to do business."

A heavy hand dropped onto his shoulder. Bob shifted his weight slightly then slammed the heel of his right foot upward into the guard's crotch. There was a sharp inhalation of breath and the hand on his shoulder tightened. Bob reached up, grabbed the hand by the wrist, lifted and twisted, spun around, and drove the guard against the wall. The unfortunate flunky exhaled with a pained *whoosh* and dropped to the floor without any further sound. The secretary's eyes were wide as she sat frozen in place. Still smiling, Bob reached into a pocket and withdrew one of the financial cards and spun it toward her. It landed on her desk, stopping just in front of her.

"I'll wait while you check that out," was all he said, standing there as calmly as if nothing had happened.

The woman sat there with her mouth open.

Bob made a soft sigh. "I'm in something of a hurry. Much to do and the day is almost half over. Now, will you assist me or not?"

The secretary closed her mouth and gulped several times as she tried, and failed, to rise.

"Is anything the matter?" asked a middle-aged man who came out of a side corridor. His eyes darted as they took in the tableau but his manner betrayed no concern. The secretary opened her mouth, but no sounds came out.

"I was attempting to convert some off-world funds," offered Bob. "I believe the young lady was put off by the informality of my clothing and summoned this guard. He laid hands upon me which, of course, I could not tolerate." He pointed at the card on the desk. "I gave her that card so that she could have it checked out, but she refuses to assist me. Is this establishment actually open for business today? If not, return my property, and I'll be on my way."

"Oh, sir, please don't do that. We are indeed open for business. If you'll just give me a moment?" He scooped up the card and examined it carefully, turning it this way and that while allowing the different lights on the desk to fall across it. Satisfied with its physical appearance, he held it against a recessed portion of the desk. After several seconds there was a soft chirp from the desk. The man smiled as he said, "My apologies for the inconvenience, sir. If you'll follow me I believe we can process this to your satisfaction." He extended a hand to indicate the hallway from which he'd arrived.

Bob stood his ground and narrowed his eyes. "If you are playing me false, sir, I warn you that I will take offence."

"What?" The man's eyes widened in horror. "Oh, no, sir. Nothing like that. And you would, of course, be quite right to be offended by such actions. No, sir, I would simply like to offer you a more comfortable setting in which we can conclude our business."

Bob allowed himself to be escorted deeper into the building. The surroundings were quite luxurious, with rich furnishings tastefully displayed to give the appearance of casual wealth. The man said nothing except murmur directions to turn this way or that. After nearly half a minute of walking the man escorted Bob into an office. Like the rest of the business, it was richly decorated in tasteful expressions designed to convey wealth and sincerity. There were no personal effects to be seen.

The man indicated a comfortable-looking chair for Bob's use, then took his own behind the desk. Bob shrugged off the knapsack and held a hand over the hidden controls. A slight buzz alerted him to something embedded in the chair. He thumbed a control that emitted a short-range jamming signal and sat down with the knapsack at his feet.

"Thank you for your understanding, sir. You must understand that people in our position must take precautions. My name is Noremac, by the way. Are you an existing client?"

Bob stared at him for a moment before answering. "No, I am not. As I explained to your secretary, my associates recommended you. I remain unconvinced as to the wisdom of that. But first things first. Do you have any problems with that card I provided?"

"Oh, no, sir. It seems to be all in order. A significant sum, if I may say." He cleared his throat. "But you must realize that we cannot give you the full amount. Perhaps if you could explain to me what sort of services you are looking for, we could assist with that in some way?" He smiled in the manner of a kindly uncle offering advice to a favourite nephew. "I'd like to maximize the profit for all parties, you as well as ourselves."

Bob gave a curt nod. "I'm here to set up a trading concern. In addition to the necessary permissions, I'll require office space and a warehouse. Nothing large or fancy, mind you, as this will be a working operation. I'd prefer to start with a small facility that can be expanded, but am willing to look at something larger to begin with. Preferably something near the port rather than, say, this part of the city."

Noremac nodded as Bob spoke and grew thoughtful. "Well, we can certainly assist you with all that, sir. But the amount on this card will not, I fear, suffice. Not even if I were to offer the very best conversion rate."

Bob lip held a slight smile as he reached into his pocket and withdrew another card. Leaning forward he placed it on the edge of the desk nearest to him, forcing Noremac to stand and bend forward to retrieve it. "Check that, if you please, Noremac, and let me know if that is enough."

He paused for a moment and allowed his grin to become slightly larger, with a hint of mischief in it. Reaching into a pocket he produced another card and tossed it so that it landed in front of Noremac. "While you're at it, check that one as well."

The man's eyes were wide as a startled look played on his face for a moment before he regained control of his composure. He cleared his throat and gave Bob a mild glare. "This is most irregular, sir. And, if I may add, more than a little dangerous to be carrying around is such a fashion."

Bob laughed. "Who would suspect someone dressed as I to be carrying large sums? I thank you for your concern, Noremac, but I know how to take care of myself."

Noremac allowed himself a brief chuckle. "Very true, sir. But be that as it may, might I council caution in the future?"

Bob tilted his head in a small bow. "I appreciate your concern and agree with you. But beginnings must ofttimes start with modest steps." Then his face became stern. "However, this will all be moot if we cannot come to terms."

Noremac nodded and gazed at the three cards on his desk. He gave a small sigh then raised his head to look at Bob. "I'll have to check these, of course, but to save time could you tell me how much these new cards are worth?"

"All three contain the same amount."

"Ah. Then I can say with confidence that you have enough to begin your enterprise. Now as for terms, as I said earlier we cannot give you the full amount. Nor, I will admit, can we offer the best conversion rate." He held up his hands. "However," he said, lowering his hands back to the desktop. "However, we can offer services that those others cannot. For example, we can expedite licences and permissions. We can assist in obtaining the most appropriate facilities at good, and often the very best, rates. You are new to this planet and although you have some knowledge of our ways, we can offer in-depth local knowledge. Some of that will be free of charge, and some will be at normal advisory rates. I suggest we hold off on details until you trust us enough to do business here."

Bob tapped his fingers on his thighs and appeared to give the matter great thought. He noticed that Noremac kept glancing at a specific point on his desk and frowning. Bob suppressed a smile at the other's failure to query the scanners in the chair.

"How quickly could a trading company be set up?" he asked.

Noremac forced his gaze up from the desk and towards Bob. "Ah, that depends on several factors. The basic corporate permissions could be obtained in a day or two. Trading licences are more complicated and depend on where your cargoes are coming from or destined to. Hmm, call it a week for all but the most bothersome of cases. Possibly less but that's a good estimate. As for a physical office, that could be set up almost immediately ... today, if you were in a rush. Storage facilities need to be negotiated and would depend very much on the type and where you'd want them. No sense getting those before you've got the licences sorted out, but we can start looking as soon as you wish."

"And the cost for all this assistance?"

Noremac puffed out his cheeks and gazed into the distance for several seconds. Returning his gaze to Bob he said, "General assistance in setting up offices is free. Any negotiations would likely incur the standard fee unless it was with someone we know." He gave the kindly uncle smile again. "We ofttimes help our customers help each other without charge. One of the many advantages in dealing with us that other institutions cannot match."

"And the conversion rate?"

"As I explained, we cannot match the very best. That would be sixty percent, plus or minus as much as a point. We could only offer fifty-five, I'm afraid, but can offer other services the others cannot."

"How much for secure storage? I assume you offer such a service."

"Oh, yes. Rates depend on volume, of course."

"How much for something, say, the length of my forearm and width of my hand? I just want to store some small valuables."

"That, I am happy to say, we can give you for free. Are there any other questions?"

Bob pursed his lips for a moment then shook his head. "My only questions are operational ones concerning the business end of things. I am satisfied that your firm is the correct one for my requirements. How do we proceed?"

Noremac smiled broadly. "That is wonderful, sir, most wonderful. I'm sure that we'll be able to provide everything you require. Ah, this is rather embarrassing, but we require a name. An identification card would be most helpful, but we can work without it."

Bob smiled and rose to his feet. He bowed and said, "My name is Rellevart, and I am most happy to be able to do business with you." He reached into a pocket and brought out an identification card. "Here is my Avilont identification card. I trust it will suffice?"

Noremac rose and returned the bow. "I am pleased that we were able to come to terms, Rellevart. Yes, that identification will be sufficient." He took the card and placed it with the others. "There are some documents to sign, but nothing onerous. Perhaps we could deal with those while my assistant verifies these? Would you care for refreshments while we wait?"

"That would be lovely, Noremac, thank you. It has been a long day. While we wait, perhaps we could discuss setting up an office and hiring appropriate personnel? I'm anxious to get that side of things going as soon as I can."

Noremac nodded and summoned an assistant who took all the cards away after determining what refreshments each wanted. "What sort of office were you thinking of?"

"A small one, I think. Perhaps in this general area, now that I think upon it. I see it as the head office for the enterprise, with a working office associated with the facility near the port. In terms of personnel, I'd like a receptionist, of course, plus at least two researchers with room for up to ten. I want them looking at every transport company: their routes, typical cargoes, size of fleet, that sort of thing. Also details on their destinations, including other links that might not include Pilfrom."

Noremac raised his eyebrows. "That's quite an ambitious program."

Bob chuckled. "I'm not after confidential information, just trying to map out potential trade routes, partners, and destinations. I'm sure that someone here has done that, but I doubt that information is being shared."

Their refreshments arrived, and they busied themselves for a time drinking tea and eating the snacks in silence.

After an appropriate interval, Noremac said, "There's truth in what you say, Rellevart. Yes, that sort of information would be known to the larger shipping companies, I would think. Still, it could become a useful collection of data. Would you be willing to make it available to others?"

"Not to everyone. After all, I don't want to tip off competitors. Still, you have a good point. You mentioned earlier that you help your customers assist each other. I'd depend on your discretion, of course, in not broadcasting this too widely."

Noremac was staring into his tea as Bob spoke. He smiled and looked at Bob. "Oh, that goes without saying. But I was thinking about this research project of yours. You'll want a larger staff to start with, I think. At least four researchers and a couple of assistants. Plus a couple of support personnel to ensure their equipment is working." He made a wry face. "We can send ships between the stars, but we can't make systems that fix themselves. One day, perhaps."

They shared a chuckle. Bob nodded and said, "That reminds me of something I forgot. Security. I assume physical security would be handled by whomever supplies the office space, but what about security of the data?"

"An excellent point, Rellevart. If we can get the appropriate personnel, the support personnel can handle that. If not, a dedicated security expert would be required. Might not be a bad idea to hire one right away, though, to get things set up properly from the start."

Bob nodded. "That's ten trained people just to start with. Might need a larger office."

Noremac shook his head. "Not that much larger than what you originally thought. Smaller office spaces are easier to come by on short notice. I'll have our real estate team get on this today. As for personnel, we'll be able to locate those for you, I suspect."

"And how much is this going to cost me?"

"If you give us access to the results of this research? Free, and we'll be glad to do it. This is going to help a number of our customers, I think, if it plays out like I think it will." He grinned with what looked like the first honest smile Bob had seen from him. "Even if this sort of thing has been done before, I doubt that there'll be anything as up-to-date as this. This is all rather exciting, Rellevart. I'm so glad you dropped by today."

"Why, thank you, Noremac. Well, perhaps I should be off and let you get on with things. I could drop back tomorrow sometime?"

"Please don't rush off on my account," lied Noremac. "But I wouldn't want to keep you. What's you comm-link code?"

"Don't have one. Won't it be easier if I just drop by?"

"Oh, no, you must get one. How else will I reach you if something comes up? Hold on, I'll have my assistant get you one of ours. It's guaranteed to be secure. Please, I insist." The assistant was summoned and hurried off to obtain the device.

"Well, that's taken care of. Where are you staying, by the way? Someplace nearby?"

Bob grinned. "Not far from the port, actually. Not a bad little place, if a bit minimal." He gave the address.

Noremac blanched. "No, no, that won't do. Not at all, Rellevart. Please, I know a hotel not far from here. They owe me a favour. Please let me call them."

"Well, if you think it best. But won't they have a problem with my attire? Remember how your receptionist reacted."

"Oh. That is a very good point." He gave his head a firm shake. "No matter, though. I'll let him know you're coming and have him send up a tailor. They'll get you fitted out properly, I promise you. Ah, here's the com-link." He took the unit from the assistant and handed it to Bob, demonstrating how to secure it to respond only to his touch and voice.

Several minutes later Noremac escorted Bob out the building, promising to call first thing in the morning with an update. Bob found the hotel with no problem and walked in. He was intercepted by a burly guard who, after hearing Bob's explanation, grudgingly escorted him to the reception desk.

"This guy says he's expected. Claims Citizen Noremac sent him."

"Oh, yes, yes. Thank you, he is expected," burbled the desk clerk. The guard gave both of them a puzzled look and went back to his post.

"Do you have any luggage, Citizen Rellevart?"

Bob hefted his knapsack, which he'd been carrying. "Just this. I like to travel light. But I was told to expect a tailor?"

"Oh my, yes. I'll have someone show you to your room, Citizen, then send the tailor right up. Will that be satisfactory?"

"We'll see. Have the tailor come up in about half an hour ... I want to clean up first. No sense making his job harder than it has to be."

"That's most considerate of you, Citizen, thank you. Ah, here is your guide. Rovert, please escort the citizen to the Plaza Suite? Here's the pass-tab."

Half an hour later Bob was cleaned up and feeling quite pleased with himself. Things were going very well so far. On the other hand, things could get very ugly if those forged cards didn't work out. The door announced the arrival of the tailor. Bob grinned ... if things went wrong, at least he'd be well-dressed for it.

CHAPTER TEN
A Promising Start

The next day found Bob ensconced in his new office quarters not far from the hotel. There was a flurry of activity as furniture was hauled in and set up. By the end of the day, he was in a fully-equipped office space, alone except for the receptionist. Her name was Sirod, and she had done a tremendous job organizing everything during the day.

"You'll be expected to show up right sharpish tomorrow," she said while looking at her notes. "The comm system we ordered will be late, so we'll be using our comm-links again. The tech geeks are supposed to show, but don't expect them before noon. They'll want to talk to you about equipment requirements. Oh, and the security company wants to send a team to review requirements with you before recommending anyone."

Bob had a small smile on his face as he listened to her rattle on. Training and experience had prepared him to command this sort of barely-constrained chaos. It was all rather fun. When Sirod wound down, he thanked her, offered some suggestions as to how to best organize the schedule, then sent her home. When he was alone, he looked around in wonder for a few minutes before heading back to the hotel. If this went well, he'd be able to acquire better intelligence about the Core

Worlds in a few weeks than he'd be able to acquire on his own in months if not years.

In addition to this team, the ship was busily exploring the data net via the sensor wand he'd hidden in his original room. Which reminded him that he might want to pay a visit there if only to maintain that identity. One more thing to do in an already crowded schedule.

He'd also managed to slip a sensor wand into the secure vault of his new financial partner. That would allow the ship to monitor events and systems there, limited to some extent by the armour surrounding the room. His hope for that was to acquire intelligence about some of the other players in the net Drawde had created. There were a lot of threads to follow and identities to keep track of. It'd all come to ruin eventually, of course, but he hoped to be long gone by the time that happened.

A week later found the office space filled with people. All had been supplied by Noremac, which made their loyalties suspect. Even so, they were sufficient to the task of getting things started. The second week saw a couple of the researchers flexing their egos and trying to ensure that control centred around them. Bob was well aware of such tendencies and warned them that he was the centre of the company, not them, and that further ego-flexing would lead to dismissal.

After their subsequent removal he had the security expert examine their workstations, and several monitoring devices were found. After everyone had gone home that night, Bob had the ship do an in-depth analysis of the suspect workstations that uncovered covert monitoring functions programmed into them.

The next morning Bob fired the security expert and made an angry call to the company that had supplied him. They, in turn, sent an emergency response team to do a full forensic analysis of Bob's entire office—at no charge in an attempt to avoid damage to their reputation—and to their horror found several more covert monitoring devices. Replacement candidates were interviewed and evaluated by Bob, and the security company arranged for several months of upgraded coverage at no charge.

As for replacing the terminated researchers, Bob polled the remaining team members for suggestions, saying that he was going to depend on their expertise for the replacements.

"Honest mistakes are one thing," he explained to them. "But I demand competence and loyalty. Loyalty to both myself and the team as a whole. Anyone who feels that they are unwilling or unable to proceed under those terms is free to leave immediately without penalty."

To emphasize those qualities, he set up a series of challenges and rewards for individuals as well as the team as a whole. The rewards may not have been financially extravagant, but he made sure that they were meaningful. Sometimes those involved trophies and bragging rights, and sometimes access to exclusive social events. Within a month he had forged the individuals into a team that was beginning to make serious progress into the task he had set them. Just as importantly, he earned their trust and loyalty just as much as they earned his.

Everything was taking longer than expected, which was not unexpected but was concerning. On the plus side, his research team had taken his vague commission and expanded it beyond his expectations. This was the first cataloguing of trade routes and destinations that had been done in over a generation, and it generated considerable interest among the trading community. He was able to gain access not only to corporate magnates, but also to ship captains. Those worthies gave him background and context based on experience that he'd never have uncovered on his own. The ship captains were especially interested in the project, suggesting that Bob consider providing an information service on a route-by-route basis once the cataloguing was complete. All in all he was earning the reputation as someone worth knowing.

He played on that reputation to acquire a small warehouse facility next to the Drawde complex of warehouses near the port. The only thing separating those from his was a narrow, debris-blocked alley and a fence. Once he had set up an office there he bought and sold a variety of small cargoes from the traders he'd met socially. It wasn't very profitable, but Bob explained that he was testing the waters and getting a feel for how things worked without stepping on anyone's toes. The traders appreciated that and began to use his warehouse for temporary storage of their own shipments. That allowed him deeper access into what was happening in the trading world. No-one broke confidences, of course, but even rumours could be useful. For example, Bob heard rumours that some shipments of speciality luxury items out of Avilont were being delayed indefinitely to the great distress of some important people.

The location of the warehouse also allowed him to continue the "Crewman Vorpal" persona, through the expedient of having him on the books as a labourer. Seldom seen, Vorpal was always out and about on mysterious errands. That brought an angry delegation from the port's hiring hall, complaining that Bob should be hiring crew through them instead of off the street. He mollified them with a generous donation to the Space Workers Benevolent Fund and a promise to let them know when he needed labourers. In fact, he did end up using them as a source of labourers when shipments arrived or left. That helped smooth the processing of his own shipments and those moving cargo through him, earning the appreciation of the traders he dealt with.

Everyone marvelled at the acumen and skills shown by one so young. Especially when he failed to be taken in by the lures normally successful with one of his apparent age. Seven weeks after arriving, Noremac invited him to his office for afternoon tea. It had become a common practise for the two to meet several times a week. Noremac had gained a lot of profit for the bank, and no little personal prestige, by taking a chance on Bob.

These days when Bob arrived, he was greeted with smiles and quickly escorted to the Noremac's new upper floor office. They greeted each other warmly, now the best of friends. As they took their seats opposite each other across a small ornately-carved table, Bob set a box down on the floor. Noremac made no mention of it as he poured the tea, and the two made idle conversation for several minutes before getting down to business.

"You have come a great way in a short time," said Noremac. "Important people have begun to take notice of your activities."

"That's very gratifying, but I'm not sure that it is deserved. I am, after all, but a trader and a minor one at that."

Noremac shook his head. "Not at all. Oh, your trading efforts are small, to be sure. But all large traders started as small ones, and you're making all the correct moves. More importantly, you're doing so by being respectful to the established interests and not pushing too hard. That's rare, I assure you, and earns you allies instead of enemies."

He took a careful sip of his tea, pausing to savour the aroma for a second. "You are also quite generous with the results of this research project of yours. Not with everything, but that's only to be expected. Still, you share more than is the norm. Again, that earns you allies."

Noremac paused for a moment as a small frown appeared on his face. "As I said earlier, it also brings the notice of important people. Allies or no, you need to tread carefully, Rellevart. Moving from newcomer to small trader is easy enough to do. Even moving from small to medium level can be done, though seldom so quickly as you are beginning to." He leaned forward and his eyes bored into Bob's. "Moving beyond that makes you a threat to important and powerful people. You would do well to concentrate on your cataloguing project so you can be of service to them, rather than competition." Noremac continued to stare at Bob for the space of several heartbeats then leaned back and focused his attention on the tea.

Bob let no emotion show, but he was elated at the news that he was beginning to stir things up. Hidden things were often revealed when dusty old ways were kicked. He drained his cup and placed it on the table.

"I accept your wisdom, Noremac, and thank you for your honesty and concern. In truth, I was wondering about that myself. As you pointed out, my research project promises to be more profitable than I ever imagined, more so than becoming a medium-level trader." He grin grew larger. "But I reserve the right to make high-value trades when the opportunity presents itself. Like this, for instance." Bob tapped the box next to his feet.

"Ah. I wondered about that. I didn't wish to pry, but now you've piqued my curiosity, I must admit."

Bob lifted the lid to reveal stacks of plastic bags the size of his hand, each filled with different gems. He picked up one of the bags and handed it across the table to Noremac. The man picked it up and held it up to the light for several seconds, then gazed at the box, a frown growing on his face. "I'd heard a rumour that you'd been buying all of these you could find. Didn't believe it, as even you should know that these are of little value." He handed the bag back to Bob.

"Exactly right," exclaimed Bob. "Almost worthless, which is why there's so few of them transported. But my team has found out that the chemical and crystalline nature of these is of great value in an industrial process on another world. No, I won't tell you what makes it special nor who might use it ... perhaps in the future once I open up that market."

Noremac chuckled. "Oh, thank you for sharing that. And, yes, by all means keep it secret for now. But if it is so valuable, why not keep it to yourself?"

Bob shook his head. "No, the big profits are to be had when the market is first opened up. After that it becomes a commodity, and that's best handled by the established interests. They're set up for that sort of thing, after all. If it works out, that is. If it fails, well, it'll be our own private joke."

This time Noremac laughed, a rare occurrence in Bob's experience. "Well said, Rellevart, well said. But should you be walking around with them?"

"I'd hoped to obtain a larger space in your secure vault," said Bob. "Just add the cost to your monthly invoice."

"How large a space?"

"Say enough to hold four of these boxes. More than that and I'll have to look at building my own secure vault, and I'd rather not do that just yet."

"Fair enough. If you've finished your tea perhaps you'd like to deposit that in the vault? I think we have one of the size you want. At worst it'll be a bit larger, but I'll give it to you at the same price."

Bob thanked him and a half hour later he was on his way back to his own offices. The box of gems included another sensor wand and a small analyzer. Both would allow the ship to better tap into the bank's data systems as well as determine what else might be stored in the vault. He was beginning to make progress in tapping into the illicit side of things and this would help. The next step was to seed data wands throughout the Drawde warehouse complex. There was a lot of heavy-duty data traffic there that would bear looking into. That would deplete his supply of sensor wands and such ... he'd have to arrange for a covert shipment from the ship. Yet another wrinkle and time-consuming item in an already overflowing and complex schedule.

CHAPTER ELEVEN
Cut and Run

A busy month later found him at a crossroad of decisions. Bob now had most of the Core Worlds mapped out in considerable detail. He knew every planet on the many trade routes—their history, financial structures, the movers and shakers, and how to move any cargo in and out of them on or off the books. He knew how the Core Worlds as a whole were governed and where he needed to go next. What he was unsure about was how to proceed.

The more he learned about the history and current state of the Core Worlds the more confused he became. His own people, outside the Veil, had survived by sharing as much of everything as they could, from knowledge to genetic material. Here, the emphasis was on personal gain even at the expense of humanity as a whole. He'd seen such attitudes on other human worlds, of course, but this disturbed him deeply. He shared ancestors with these people, ancestors he'd been raised to venerate. His experiences had tempered that veneration into deep admiration, but it was still a shock to think that he and those within the Veil came from the same stock.

Worse was the realization that the criminal element had become so prevalent and powerful within the Core Worlds. During the time of the last great battles against the Nexus, the rulers decided to reach out to everyone, even the criminal element, in an attempt to forge all humanity into a force strong enough to win. It proved to be a deal with the Devil, with the criminal gangs taking advantage of the situation to become so embedded and powerful as to become permanent fixtures. Some planets, like Avilont, they owned or controlled outright. They had varying degrees of control on most of the others. Only on the central worlds were the forces of civilization stronger than the criminal syndicates.

Everywhere there was an urge to break the power of the criminal gangs, as evidenced by the security officer on Avilont. The problem was that no-one wanted to stick their necks out and make the first move ... or even knew what move to make. On the one hand, Bob now knew where to get the information on the location of the Nexus. In fact, the cataloguing itself had given him a rough idea where it might be. That was still a large area and not one to go blundering about in, so more details were required. The first, and best, option was to simply leave here and head to the Core World's main governing centre.

On the other hand, he couldn't forget the image of the young child—and the others—with a leash around his neck. That was evil, pure and simple. Bob had learned all about the business side of that evil and how it was structured here and elsewhere throughout the Core Worlds. On yet another hand, the Nexus represented a clear existential threat to humanity. If he were killed defeating the human evil and let the Nexus win, which would be the greater loss? On top of all that, he did not have the luxury of time.

His ruminations were interrupted by a knock on his office door followed by the entrance of Arehs, one of the lead researchers. "Hey, boss. You busy? A couple of the team want to leave early to beat the holiday rush. You did remember it was a holiday, didn't you?"

Bob exhaled sharply and shook his head. "Oh, I forgot. Yeah, fine. In fact send everyone home, and I mean everyone." He grinned at her. "We're well ahead of schedule and everyone needs a break. Yes, even me, strange as that sounds. Wait just minute."

He tapped a control on his desk and the image of his secretary appeared before him. "Anin, Arehs will be dropping by to see you in a minute. I want you to authorize a travel chit for anyone who wants it ... I'll pay the costs, even the last-minute surcharge, for anyone to go anywhere. It's a holiday and people should spend it with family and loved ones." He turned to Arehs. "Go spread the word here and at the warehouse. Everybody goes home and has fun. I apologize that it's the last minute but you now I forget these things. Don't just stand there with your mouth open, go go go."

He turned to the image of Anin and said, "That includes you, by the way. Put the comm system on automatic answer. Off with you. I don't want to see anyone here an hour from now."

In fact it took less than half an hour for the office to clear out. The cheers and other happy noises warmed Bob's heart. This planet may have been the heart of an evil criminal empire, but there were a lot of good people here all the same. He took a stroll around the office ensuring that everything was locked down, which it turned out to be. The new security specialist was very conscientious and efficient, and had been the last person to leave.

Bob paused at the common room to grab a cup of tea and a snack before heading back to his office. This was the first time in many weeks that he'd had some quiet time to sit back and do some serious thinking. Strategic thinking was now required as opposed to tactics.

An hour later found him staring at the wall, his untouched tea now cold and the snacks uneaten. Whenever he tried to think about simply leaving to deal with the Nexus, the image of the enslaved child and others like him kept coming to mind. Leaving without at least trying to do something felt like leaving the many good people here to suffer under the increasingly heavy hand of the criminals. Then he remembered the part of the Precepts of Survival he had quoted to his Auntie Gertrude so long ago when he said the humans of the galaxy deserved a chance "to reap the rewards of wisdom or failure."

The people here—cousins in a very real sense, if distant ones—deserved the same chance to rise or fall that the regular humans did. Still, as wonderful as ideals were, actions were what made things happen. He took out his personal data pad from its secure storage in his desk and told the ship to begin wrapping up its deep dive into the planet's data streams. The ship responded that doing so quickly could leave traces. Bob pondered that for a moment then smiled and told the ship to maintain stealth procedures but prepare for a noisy shutdown and a broadcast announcement over the entire network.

After that he went to every workstation, powered them up, and set them to making copies of the research as well as everything the ship had uncovered about the criminal network and its activities. While that was going on, he called up all the independent traders he knew to offer them a special courier opportunity. Most were free and eager to accept, especially when offered a holiday bonus. Bob told them to come to his office in an hour, no later, to pick up the packages and delivery instructions.

With that deadline, Bob went around to the workstations to replace the backups with fresh media—Core society used small data cubes instead of rods—and set them to repeating the process. While waiting, he prepared shipping forms ... the destinations were the police, armed forces, and governments of a dozen of the major worlds in the Core. For good measure he made forms for two dozen more. When the inevitable forensic analysis of the systems happened, he wanted to spread as much panic as possible among the criminal network. His minimal efforts on Avilont had caused a lot of problems, far in excess of what he'd expected. This information had the potential to be seriously damaging in and of itself, never mind the panic it would cause among the criminal elites.

Bob finished packing things up a couple of minutes before his hour was up. He'd managed to make sixteen full copies of the data, and another dozen minimal copies of records specific to a handful of specific worlds. That would, as Rhian had once said, put the cat among the pigeons.

The door announced the arrival of visitors, and Bob confirmed it was who he expected before opening the door. There were eighteen traders in all, so Bob split up the deliveries as evenly as he could. He even paid them in advance as incentive to lift ship as quickly as possible. They hurried away with promises to leave within the hour.

When that was done, he hurried back to the workstations and collected the next batch of copies. He bundled those up and arranged for couriers to deliver them to all the major police forces, news services, and libraries on the planet.

"It's a holiday, citizen," he was told. "We can pick them up but can't guarantee delivery until tomorrow at the earliest. Probably not until after the holiday."

"After the holiday will be fine," he told them. "Just so long as it's on their desks first thing when they arrive." That could be guaranteed, so Bob told them to come by as quickly as possible.

The sun was beginning to set by the time he had dispatched the last of the couriers. The holiday break was beginning in full force, which suited him just fine as there would be no-one to ask questions for the next several days. He'd be long gone by then.

The next step was to do something to help the victims. There was no time to set up anything fancy, so he used the handful of inactive corporate fronts he had on hand. Those, in themselves, were standard procedure on this planet. Many companies kept such shell fronts on hand to be activated and de-activated as contracts came and went. All that was required was to modify the terms of business. That normally entailed changing the name of the cargo or destination. In this case Bob changed them from business-oriented to more of an activist charity. One was set up specifically for Avilont, one for Pilfrom, and the others to deal with the rest of the Core Worlds. Their terms of reference were to offer rehabilitation and training for victims of crime. Several, however, were set up to investigate and publish information about the criminal network itself, with special focus on civic leaders who allowed the criminal organizations to flourish unchallenged.

To fund them, he drained his own accounts, after first transferring a year's salary into the accounts of each of his employees. After interrogating the ship regarding its investigations of the bank, he transferred the funds from a number of anonymous accounts into those of the new entities. The ship also uncovered some unused blank corporations which he purloined and set up to help people on planets badly infested by the criminal gangs. He saved one such account for use by the smaller security forces to help them deal with interstellar gangs who were far better financed. Again, he used illicit money to fund everything. It was nearly midnight by the time he finished that side of things, and he'd paused only to drink his cold tea. Now, however, he forced himself to eat something a little more substantial from the supplies in the common room. There was still a lot of work to be done.

The comms system alerted him to several incoming calls which he ignored. Then his personal comm-link alerted him that Noremac was calling. That meant he was out of time. Bob ran to his office and used the data pad to summon the skiff, ordering it to meet him on the roof. He stuffed the few necessary things, including several copies of the data he'd accumulated, into his knapsack. The combat belt, with knife and pistol, he buckled around his waist. It was time to go.

Before he went, though, he told the ship to clean up the bank. That entailed scrambling its data net and as many records as it could find, then detonating the sensor wands that Bob had secreted in the secure storage facility. The wands were destructive in their own right, but Bob's store of gems were designed to enhance those effects many-fold. That explosion was designed to send out a burst of energy that would fry any tech within range as well as inflict physical destruction. That would destroy, or at least severely damage, many a store of blackmail material, illicit funds, stolen materials, and physical records. It would also play havoc with the bank's own equipment, however shielded they might be.

Bob paused for a second just before he exited the offices. This had been a good place with many fine people that he'd enjoyed working with. Uttering a small sigh of regret, he turned and ran into the corridor. Reaching the emergency exit, he bounded up the stairs to the roof, putting on his gloves and flexible helmet as he went. There were several locked doors between him and roof, but they were opened easily enough by using the pistol to blast the locks. At this point he didn't care about setting off any alarms. In fact, the more the merrier.

On the roof the cool night air was a refreshing change, offering a promise of the freedom to come. The crackle and boom of holiday fireworks echoed throughout the city. Bob sent the command for the skiff to reveal itself ... the air shimmered as it appeared off to one side. He got on, re-activated the camouflage, and flew into the night sky.

His luxury apartment had nothing worth keeping, so first stop was the roof of the hotel that Crewman Vorpal stayed at. Bob directed the skiff to land on the roof. He hopped off, blasted the door open, and then ran inside down the stairs until he got to the floor his room was on. Another blast from the pistol opened the locked emergency door. He ran down the hallway to his room. Opening the door with his key, he recovered the hidden sensor wand, paused to toss a financial chit on the bed to pay for the damages, then ran back to the roof.

There was a continuous roar of noise from fireworks all around the city as the holiday celebrations continued. This time, though, there were joined by a blast from the commercial district as explosions ripped through the bank. The sound of emergency sirens blended with the sounds of celebration.

Bob hopped on the skiff and sailed into the air. As he headed for the outskirts of the city, he triggered the sensor wands he'd planted in the Drawde warehouses. Those facilities were used for much more than mere storage, offering a secure place for communications and data storage. That security was shredded as his ship and the explosions scrambled those records and expensive gear. As Bob sped through the night, he could see plumes of smoke and flame. The ship reported that the criminal organizations were swinging into motion, but were impeded by the absence of so many senior members due to the holidays.

Once past the city and its buildings, Bob steered the skiff to follow a nape-of-the-earth return to the ship. There was little chance of him being spotted in the night sky, but there was no sense in taking any chances. Besides, he was enjoying flying the skiff. It was an indulgence, but he felt that he'd earned it. It wasn't every day that he got to deliver a serious blow to an entrenched transtellar criminal syndicate. He hadn't had this much fun since he'd taken down his brother's organization.

He arrived at the ship with no problem. After stowing and securing the skiff and backpack, he headed to the control room. The first thing he did was to record a message and have the ship transmit it over the planetary data net. In it he said that the day of the criminal cartels was over, and that now was the time for all citizens of honour to toss off the yoke of oppression. It wasn't his best work, but he was in something of a rush. The ship's messy disentanglement from the data nets would set off fresh waves of panic among the criminals.

The ship was ready to go, so he eased it up with full stealth capabilities engaged. It was well that he did so, as his activities had caused a full planetary defence alert to be issued. Fighter craft swarmed the skies, but they were hampered by all the fireworks. Emergency crews had arrived at all the sites of explosions, with more on their way. Messages left on his comm-unit warned of dire tortures once he was caught.

After clearing the atmosphere Bob eased through the busy space lanes. Ships were being told conflicting things by different people on the ground, and orbital traffic control was becoming frantic in its attempt to restore order. Bob slipped through the chaos without any problem and headed out at right angles to the ecliptic to avoid the commercial traffic. There were a couple of military reconnaissance patrol vessels, but they didn't detect him. Once past those, he engaged his FTL drive. It would take ten days to reach his next destination. That was faster than any of the local vessels but far slower than the ansible communications which would be spreading news of this assault like a ripples from a rock thrown into the water. As usual, he had a lot to do and not much time to prepare for it ... just like old times.

CHAPTER TWELVE
Third Time Lucky?

As he sped to his next destination, Bob took advantage of the time to review the information he had. Some of it he knew, but the ship had acquired all sorts of data he'd not had time to review. One of the things he had tasked the ship to look into was the ansible network, with an eye to being able to tap into it. To his disappointment, what little there was consisted of general information intended for public consumption. It was a technology that had been developed some time after the Veil had been erected, and had been instrumental in allowing the human fleets to defeat the Enemy who had been trapped with them. The only fact that all the explanations agreed on was that it was something large, embedded deep within a planet.

That was an interesting piece of information, as it meant that FTL communications was limited to planet-to-planet. That was something he'd wondered about during his time on Pilfrom, but hadn't pursued for fear of betraying ignorance. Sometimes it was best to abide by the unspoken assumptions and conventions, the better to appear part of the crowd. He'd known that access to the ansible was strictly limited and was one of the few uncorrupted institutions on the planet. It also explained why so many of the independent traders specialized in courier runs. Bob had assumed it for security, but it now appeared that it was also because of limited access to the ansible.

That insight made some of the commentaries about the social setups on other planets make more sense. Bob delved into the historical records the ship had uncovered and found that on many planets the running of the ansible network was considered something akin to a holy calling. Failure to maintain the ansible led to a planet becoming totally isolated and easy prey. Sometimes the predators were human ... as was the case on Avilont, a planet that had lost its ansible during the last round of wars.

As usual there was more information that he could possibly scan through, much less read in depth. He keenly felt the loss of his analysis team and hoped that they would be safe from the backlash that was sure to follow. Still, he did what he could to get a sense of it all. With that background in mind, he began a detailed examination of his next target planet.

It was one of the original founding members of the Core Worlds, with an unbroken history stretching back millennia, almost to the time of the creation of the Veil itself. Originally founded as a military stronghold, it was now a centre of governance with a strong capability in advanced research and manufacturing. It also had a diverse economy that included broad support for the arts and education. Access to it was open but controlled. All in all, a very high tech planet that had honed its security over millennia of warfare and uneasy peace. Not his favourite type of society to visit. The flash and glamour of such places held a certain attraction when he was younger and wilder, but wisdom had come with age.

On the plus side, the criminal syndicates had only a minor presence there, having been thrown out some centuries ago. There was no love lost between the two factions, but things had been at a stalemate for some time. Bob grinned ... with luck that was about to change.

Still, that meant that infiltrating it, much less finding the information he required, was going to be difficult. One approach would be to go to one of the "clean" planets—those free of syndicate influence—and book passage on a passenger liner. That would mean abandoning his ship and supplies, something he was loath to do. One way around that would be to go to the clean planet and send the ship on ahead under automatic control. That was feasible but risky without knowing more about what security the ship would face.

The last option was to replicate what had worked in the past ... land and pose as a down-on-his-luck crew member. That had considerable risks of its own, of course, given their advanced tech and level of security. At the very least he would have to come up with a better way to disguise his own advanced tech—possibly building it into his clothing. The ship could do that easily enough, as such tricks were used during his own people's Great Wars.

After a bit of thought, he set the ship to duplicating his Pilfrom clothes with the addition of basic comm link and sensor wand capabilities. He dearly wanted to add some form of armour to the outfit, but decided that was a risk too far. Instead, he analyzed the original clothing material and enhanced it to the limits of Pilfrom tech. That would give him a certain amount of protection ... not as much as a skin-suit but better than nothing.

That left the question of identity. He decided to create several based on his Pilfrom credentials: Crewman Vorpal, Citizen Rellevart, plus a couple of others he never got around to using while there. Each had financial chits loaded with funds appropriate to their station in life. The danger here was that Pilfrom was a known to be a syndicate-friendly world, which his destination definitely was not. Still, once there he could no doubt start creating something more appropriate to the local conditions.

Bob passed the time in transit learning all he could about his target and its affiliated neighbours. His identity was non-local, but he wanted to know enough about interstellar history and politics to be able to ask intelligent questions. This was a mission that was going to call for subtlety, not a smash and grab. If nothing else, he didn't yet know where to begin smashing. The best option, of course, would be to pull off what he'd done on Pilfrom ... set up a research agency that could find out what he needed to know. Checking into that sort of thing would have to be one of his top priorities, he decided.

The days passed all too quickly, and he dropped the ship out of FTL well beyond the limits of the destination solar system. It was well that he did, for their defensive monitoring systems began not much further in. He told the ship to set its cloaking systems to their maximum as he monitored the situation. That the monitoring stations used passive scanners was a given, but they supplemented that with periodic bursts of electromagnetic energy to check if there were anything reflective. Bob had seen such tech used on many worlds and appreciated that it was capable of some impressive and subtle feats. For example, his ship couldn't simply neutralize the bursts ... the cosmic dust that surrounded any solar system would give a certain pattern of weak reflection. Anything blocking that would create, in effect, a shadow.

What was required was to refract both the energy bursts and resultant weak echoes from the dust around the ship, creating the illusion that it wasn't there. It wasn't a perfect illusion, of course, because the refraction process attenuated the signal somewhat. That meant that the dust echoes would be somewhat weaker than expected ... a faint shadow, but much weaker than it would otherwise be. Bob got around this by moving the ship between energy bursts.

The trick here was to move by random amounts so as to better mimic a natural phenomenon or glitch in their monitoring equipment. It helped that his ship used the alternate energies which were undetectable by this society, and which allowed him to move faster than any ships here. It took him the better part of two hours, but he managed to jink the ship past the monitoring stations and further into the solar system.

Once past, he lurked around the usual traffic lanes and watched for ship traffic. Over the course of a day, he tracked six merchant vessels and three military vessels either inbound or outbound. He didn't care about their direction so much as how traffic was monitored and controlled. The inbound traffic went to several of the inner planets, but four of the commercial vessels went to his destination. The comm chatter around those told him how to differentiate their destinations.

Much of the traffic control was automated, reverting to human interaction only when the ships got within range of a planetary orbital control. Even more interesting was that one of the military vessels and one of the merchants went to the natural satellite around his destination. That meant a well-developed space-based economy, not just a planetary one. Such societies were always more interesting, if harder to infiltrate.

Bob slipped the ship slowly towards the inner planets, taking care to watch for monitors and the occasional random patrol vessel. The more he observed, the more he realized that he was only going to get one shot at this. A day of waiting brought him an inbound commercial vessel that was heading to his destination. He slipped behind it and ghosted along behind it. Just before it arrived, he broke away and headed to the planet's satellite. It had a lot of industry on it, but that tended to cluster in pockets. He found and landed in a crater that hid the ship quite well, and he settled there for a day of well-earned rest.

He discovered that the satellite had a busy port, used both for passengers and cargo. The local industries generated a heavy traffic with the home planet, but often incoming vessels dropped off passengers with their cargo, requiring them to take the shuttles down to the planet's surface. This was common enough to generate a steady stream of out-of-system passengers. Assuming he could get inside the port and create the necessary documentation, that looked like a possible way to gain legitimate access. The only downside would be that the ship would have to stay on the satellite. On the other hand, in an emergency it could get to the planet in under an hour.

That scheme looked to be his best shot, so he decided to reconnoitre the port. He donned a skin-suit then flew the skiff over to look at the port close up. An active camouflage netting was draped over both him and the skiff to prevent detection. It wasn't as good as the ship's systems, but Bob hoped it would be good enough. All the active sensors he'd detected were aimed skyward.

He approached the port with care, using natural cover whenever possible, and stayed there for ten hours. Ships came and went, cargoes were loaded and unloaded, and Bob managed to map out the general layout of things. There were several areas that were seldom used that he wanted to check out in more detail. He moved the skiff to the first such area and probed with his active sensors at their lowest intensity. The scans suggested machinery of some sort in that area, so Bob moved on to the next. That appeared to be a storage area, possibly a warehouse. The third, and final, area proved to be similar. That left him two possible points of entry. The security system was rudimentary, at least from his point of view, and could be bypassed without any problem.

Bob returned to the ship to rest and ponder his next move. While he'd been away, the ship had been monitoring the port's communications and as much of the local data net as it could. It had managed to discover the documentation process for incoming passengers. There was a security check when a passenger arrived, but little was required after that when going down to the planet. The ship had even found out what documentation was required, as it was transmitted by incoming vessels. Once past that initial security check, there appeared to be nothing but a perfunctory inspection after arriving on the planet. The plan was do-able.

The next two days were busy ones as Bob prepared the final details for his infiltration. There was documentation to produce, equipment to finalize, routes inside the port to finalize, and detailed instructions to give to the ship. He had just settled down for a meal when the ship announced the imminent arrival of a commercial vessel with cargo and twenty-three passengers. This looked like the opportunity he was waiting for.

Bob suited up, loaded his gear onto the skiff, and flew to the warehouse area of the port. When he arrived there, he probed the inside and found it empty of people. It took only a few minutes to erect a small survival tent affixed to the structure and fill it with air from a tank on the skiff. When the pressure was equal to that inside the port, he cut a small opening taking care not to damage the slab of metal, tossed his gear inside, and then followed it in.

Doffing the skin-suit, he put it into a bag along with the pistol. He crawled out, attached the bag to the skiff, and re-entered the warehouse. Using a special paste, he resealed the slab to the main structure ... the seal would be stronger than the original metal.

That done, he used a cleaning cloth to scrub himself clean before donning his business attire. Checking that everything was in order, he walked to the door pausing only to dispose of the cleaning cloth and paste container in a garbage bin. He tapped a hidden control on his carry-all bag, and the soft buzz reassured him that the security systems inside the warehouse were still being spoofed. There was a small window in the door, allowing him to wait until the coast was clear before he exited.

Walking at a brisk pace suitable for a businessman with places to go, Bob navigated the maze of the tunnels and walkways as if he knew the way. Which he did, of course, after extensive study of the port's layout. It was gratifying that the actuality matched his scans. After several minutes he arrived at the main concourse level. This was past the security checkpoint and not far from the area where the planetary shuttles were boarded.

He checked one of the many displays scattered around and determined that the next shuttle was leaving on the hour. Bob headed towards the shuttle departure lounge. This was the only random part of the plan. No bookings were required for these shuttles, one simply took what was available. He was in luck as the shuttle was only half full when he arrived. The crew greeted him with professional courtesy, and helped him store the carry-all in a cargo closet. A steward showed him to a seat and reminded him to stow all loose items before takeoff.

The shuttle interior was pleasant enough. There was a single row of seats to either side of an aisle that ran the length of the interior. The seats were comfortable and had plenty of leg-room. Which, given that the flight was twenty hours, was a pleasant surprise. Bob was reminded of an aeroplane flight he'd had on Earth, from London to Romania. It had been a very uncomfortable experience, almost as if the craft had been designed to torture the passengers.

As the departure time approached, the shuttle filled until it was three-quarters full. The steward moved several people around, including Bob, to better balance the load. Finally, it was time for departure. The cabin crew checked that everyone was strapped down properly as the steward recited safety instructions and expressions of happiness that he and the cabin crew were able to serve them on this final leg of their journey. A chime sounded for several seconds, followed by a one-second burst of noise, then the shuttle began moving.

There were bumps and clanks as it was manoeuvred into position on the electromagnetic launch ramp.

"Passengers please prepare for acceleration," came the announcement. A second later the craft began to accelerate and Bob felt himself pressed into the seat. The data screen in front of him showed that the acceleration was one and a half times the force of planetary gravity. The acceleration increased bit by bit until it was twice the force of gravity. That continued for nearly a minute then cut out completely as the ship flew into space.

Although he'd flown around the galaxy, Bob was never happy as a mere passenger. This trip, however, did have its amusements. The ship accelerated at a fraction of gee, but that was close enough to null gravity to disturb some of the passengers. The cabin crew cleaned up the messes with practised ease and indifference. Meals and snacks were offered at regular intervals to those who wanted them. Bob had no problems with the fractional gravity, and made sure that he stayed hydrated and fuelled. He passed the time checking on the local news, listening to music, and napping. It was all in all a rather pleasant break after the frantic days spent preparing for this.

Just before the ship entered orbit around the planet, the cabin crew made sure that everyone was seated and strapped down. The ride down was bumpier than Bob would have preferred, but he told himself to make allowances for primitive tech. The data screen showed him a view from the front of the craft. It had been a long time since he'd ridden on a craft that used aerodynamic braking, and found it quite fascinating. They landed in due course and were escorted out of the shuttle and into the arrivals area.

The arrivals procedure was not at all what Bob had expected. All of the incoming passengers were directed into a series of lines, where they waited to be called forward one by one. A guard greeted them, looked at their identification, and then pointed them toward one of a long series of doors arranged in a large arc ahead of them. The exit assignments appeared to be random.

Bob heard the same refrain many times before it was his turn. Finally, he was called forward.

"Welcome, honoured visitor. Identification please? Thank you, Citizen Rellevart. Please exit via the door marked Number Twenty-three. Please enjoy your stay. Next."

Bob thanked him and walked toward the assigned door. It opened with a soft hiss as he approached to reveal a three-metre long enclosed walkway. The door at the other end was open, and he could see another busy concourse beyond. He walked inside without hesitation, but had only taken two steps when the front door closed with a hiss. A similar hiss from behind him let him know the entrance door had closed.

"Hello?" he called out but there was no answer. A second later everything went black as he lost consciousness.

CHAPTER THIRTEEN
Roll With the Punches

Bob opened his eyes to find himself sitting upright in a chair but unable to move. There was a table in front of him and he could make out what appeared to be all his belongings arrayed along its length. There were two empty chairs on the other side of the table.

He could breathe, blink, and swallow but had no other control over his body. There was no sense of numbness. In fact he was fully aware of the sensations of his body. The chair he was in seemed comfortable ... he could feel padding that had adapted to his shape to ensure comfort. The other disconcerting thing was that he seemed to be naked. At a guess, his brilliant plan was not going very well.

From behind him he heard a pair of knocks, as if from knuckles on a hard surface, and a soft male voice saying, "He's awake."

He heard a door open and footsteps approaching his position. The steps swung around and to either side of him. Two male figures appeared in his field of view and stood beside the chairs behind the table. Both wore uniforms and had the bearing of either military or security men.

The man on his left nodded and said, "Hello, Citizen Rellevart. Please excuse this intrusion. We will explain everything, hopefully to your satisfaction. You have been administered a drug which leaves you paralysed. It is not permanent, I promise you. Nor are there any aftereffects. We mean you no harm. I will explain further, but please allow me to introduce ourselves. I am Investigator Evad, and this is Investigator Yreffej." The other man nodded, after which they both sat down facing Bob. Evad sat with his hands folded on the table. Yreffj placed a data pad in front of him then sat with his hands resting in his lap.

Evad gave Bob a smile that seemed more friendly than professional. "The other man in the room is behind you. He is a guard assigned to watch over you to ensure your safety. He reports to an oversight group that monitors us during these interrogations. We try to respect your rights as much as possible." He cleared his throat. "Interrogations of this sort are carried out for a number of reasons. The primary one is that our Enemy sometimes employs human agents. We have learned, to our sorrow, that enhanced security is the only way we can survive. People are selected for interrogation for any number of reasons. Some are selected as part of a random spot-check. Some behave oddly. And some, like yourself, have strange gaps in their histories. For whatever the reason, we select individuals for these special interrogations."

He paused for a moment, as if to give Bob a chance to digest this information. "I assure you that it quite painless. In fact, I can say that with confidence since I've been subjected to it myself, as has everyone in this room. At the end of it, you will have no memory of it ever occurring, just of having a slight dizzy spell. No need to worry on that score."

He turned to his colleague. "I believe he is ready for the next stage."

Yreffej nodded and left his chair to stand next to Bob, out of direct sight. "I will now give you an injection," he said in a quiet voice. "You may feel a slight pressure and perhaps a puff of air. It will allow you to speak and answer our questions."

Bob felt a slight pressure on the inside of his left arm. Yreffej returned to his seat.

Evad leaned forward slightly in his seat, his hands still folded in front of him. "What is my name?"

"You told me it was Evad." Bob heard the words coming from his mouth without any conscious control.

"Very good. What name are you travelling under?"

"Rellevart."

"Is that your real name?"

"No." Bob had no control over the words he was speaking. Worse, he knew that he should be worried, but all he felt was a sense of calmness.

"What is your real name?"

"Bob."

"That is a very strange name. Your travel documents say you came from Pilfrom. Is that true?"

"Yes."

"Were you born on Pilfrom?"

"No."

"On what planet were you born?"

Bob's mouth worked but nothing came out.

"Why are you having trouble with the name?"

"It has no name. I only knew it as Home."

"Well, Bob, we have had reports about a man named Rellevart causing problems on Pilfrom. Did you do those things?"

Bob's mouth once again worked but nothing came out.

Yreffej interjected, "The question is too vague."

"We have reports of a bank being damaged due to an explosion. Did you cause that?"

"I caused an explosion at a bank."

"Did you cause explosions in the warehouse district?"

"Yes."

"Why did you do that?"

"To damage the criminal syndicates."

"Why do you wish to harm the criminal syndicates?"

"They harm good people and interfere with the ability of humanity to fight the Enemy."

"What else did you do to harm them?"

"I collected detailed information about their activities and sent it to many planets."

"How did you send it?"

"By courier ships."

"When did you leave Pilfrom?"

"After I dispatched the courier ships."

"And yet you are here before them. How is that possible?"

"My ship is very fast."

"How did you get to this planet?"

"By shuttle."

Bob heard a soft chirp coming from behind him. The guard made a quiet cough and said, "The protocols say he is allowed his first break very soon now. Also, I have just received an alert that your office called and there is important information waiting for you. You can use the office down the hall if you require privacy."

Evad nodded at the guard then returned his gaze to Bob. "Please rest here until I get back. You will answer no questions until I return."

With that he and Yreffej stood and exited the room. They walked down the hall and entered a small office containing a desk and three chairs. Dropping down into one of the chairs, Evad used his comm-unit to call his office. After a few seconds of agitated discussion, he said, "Wait. Yreffej is here with me." He pushed some controls then said, "Could you say that again, please?"

The voice was now loud enough for both men to hear. "I said, we just got a message via ansible. Our agents on Arorua report that a courier landed with a package of data cubes addressed to the security forces. The documentation says it's from someone called Rellevart on Pilfrom. Might be the same

Rellevart that's being talked about, I don't know. But get this ... those data cubes hold everything we need to know about syndicate activity. Names, planets, ships, cargoes, finances, everything. There's more, too, but our agents wanted to pass on the basics while they go through the rest."

"How reliable is this report?" asked Evad.

"Well, our agents heard about it a few hours after it arrived. Since then there's been an exodus of private yachts and merchant vessels. Nobody's seen anything like it. And a couple of top local politicians have committed suicide, or so the story goes. I'd say that information is worth taking seriously."

"Anything pertaining to us directly?"

"Some. Our agents are encrypting it for transmission, but given the limited ansible bandwidth that'll take a few hours even for a summary. A courier will take several weeks, though."

"Alright," said Evad, "Send me whatever you've got as soon as you get it. It might help me with the interrogation I'm doing."

"Yeah, speaking of which, you need to call Medical. They took another look at his tests and want to talk to you."

Evad and Yreffej exchanged glances as the latter rolled his eyes and shook his head in disgust.

"Alright, I'll call them right away. Now don't forget to send me whatever you get the instant you get it. Bye."

The two men looked at each other. "What do you make of that? I don't see how it's possible, but is our man ... Bob or whatever his name is ... responsible for that?" said Yreffej.

"Hmm," replied Evad. "Maybe. Or maybe he's part of an organization called 'Rellevart'. Certainly worth asking him about."

Yreffej's comm-unit buzzed and he answered it. After a short conversation he turned to his partner. "Medical wants to talk to us right away. Something's strange about this Bob's physiology. They want answers asked while he's under the influence."

"They're coming here?"

"Yep. Their expert is hopping over as fast as he can. Says he'll be here in fifteen or twenty minutes, max."

"Gah. Well, that's not long after the time protocol demands for the first break. I guess we can wait. How much time do we have left with him?"

"Oh, another two hours at least, possibly more."

"Okay, we can afford to wait. One thing we need to figure out is how exactly he got here before the courier. Check with traffic control and see if any ships have come in from Pilfrom directly or indirectly. I don't see how he could have beaten the courier here."

"If he's part of a group, maybe they had access to the ansible? Not likely, I'll grant you, but possible. We could waste a lot of time dancing around until we hit on correct question to ask him. The interrogation drugs are great but make the subjects interpret questions quite narrowly."

Several minutes later there was a knock at the door and it opened to reveal a guard being pushed aside by a pudgy middle-aged man who puffed his way into the room like a steam engine. He stood before Evad and Yreffej gasping for air.

"The representative from the Medical Wing," said the guard as he smiled. "Said you were expecting him. Flashed a high-security clearance. Oh, and the taxi driver is screaming to be paid. Claims he was promised alpha-level rates and immunity from prosecution. There's civic patrol guards here trying to ticket the vehicle. Hope you can figure out what's going on."

Evad looked at the puffing guest and nodded at the guard. "My office will honour the clearance as claimed. Pay the driver and tell the patrol crews to talk to my office tomorrow. Thanks."

The guard nodded and shut the door as he left.

Yreffej guided their guest to a chair, and the latter sat down with a thud. He pulled out a puffer from a pocket and took several hits from it, which calmed him down enough to talk. "There's something strange about your prisoner."

"That much we already know," said Yreffej in a dry voice.

The medical man shook his head. "No, you don't understand." He took a deep breath and exhaled slowly. "My name is Eltrab. I'm a diagnostician on loan to your department. The first-glance look at your subject's scans looked clean so that's what was reported. Then it was passed on to me for a routine confirmation and, well, there's something not quite right about your subject."

"Is he ill?"

"Ill? No, far from it. He's the most physically perfect person I've ever heard of. Wait, let me explain. His genome has no negative traits that we can detect ... none at all. Physically, as I said, he is in perfect health, but that doesn't properly describe him. Everything about him is at the high end of normal for a human plus a bit more. His muscles are denser and more powerful than normal, giving him amazing strength for his size. Not superhuman, but greater than the norm. Similarly for everything else: reflex times, brain function, immune system, healing, everything."

"So he's just an amazingly healthy human?" said Evad.

"Yes, his physical condition exceeds that of a top-end elite athlete or soldier, but it's more than that. He's a perfect human. No genetic flaws, no physical abnormalities, and everything works just a little bit better than it should. No-one is that perfect. Oh, except for one thing ... he's sterile."

"Fine, he's a perfect physical specimen. Maybe just good breeding?"

Eltrab shook his head. "There's more. He may be physically perfect, but he's been injured many times. We can see the faint signs of damage from our scans: broken bones, injured organs, injured muscles, and so forth. The problem is that the traces are faint, as if the healing has been nearly perfect."

He stared at the two interrogators with impatience. "Don't you understand? He's incurred deep and extensive injuries that should have left him crippled or dead. Yet here he is none the worse for wear with barely a sign that those traumas ever occurred. That sort of healing, from those sorts of injuries, is beyond our expertise. I want those medical techniques, gentlemen. I want them very badly."

Evad opened his mouth to respond but was interrupted by a chirp from his comm-unit. He set it for external audio and said, "This is Evad."

Everyone in the office heard the caller speaking. "This is Oversight Controller Yttik of the Border Guard. Your office passed on the request for anomalous events, and we might have something for you. One of our cadets was looking into the on-going problem of sensor ghosts and discovered a mystery. A few days ago the picket monitors detected some faint readings just outside the planetary plane. That isn't unusual in and of itself, but those readings jittered about in a random fashion for a while then disappeared. Some hours later, the in-system pickets began picking up faint readings. Everyone chalked that up to the usual sensor ghosts until my cadent started sniffing around. She found that the characteristics of the inner ghost matched the characteristics of the ghost spotted by the pickets. Checking the records, she found that same odd ghost working its way inward before it was lost just as a cargo ship from Ecnarf was passing through."

"Where was that cargo ship heading, Yttik?" said Yreffej.

"The military outpost on Sunev, currently on the other side of the Sun from you."

"Anything spotted near here?" asked Yreffej.

"Not that we can detect. Traffic Control may have something, but I doubt it. They don't look for anomalies like we do, and we caught this one only through luck."

"Oversight Controller Yttik," said Evad. "In your opinion is it possible that we are looking at an incursion by a stealthed ship?"

"Yes. What's more, that level of stealth is far beyond what we are capable of. You might want to check with your military contacts, but in my opinion it is beyond anything we could ever hope to do for a very long time."

Evad thanked Yttik and terminated the connection. "Well, I think we have some interesting lines of enquiry to explore with our guest. Eltrab, please stay here in case I need you later. Yreffej, with me."

No sooner had the two approached the doorway than Evad's comm-unit buzzed. "Ignore it," said Yreffej. Evad nodded but the comm-unit buzzed again, this time signalling a high-priority message from his office. He activated it with the external sound activated. "This is Evad."

"Evad, Selrach here. I just got off the comm with the Director of the Museum of Antiquities. Several of their devices dating back to the raising of the Veil appear to have become active. They've been inactive for eons, if not longer."

"Active how, exactly?"

"Faint glow emitting from one end of all of them. One also hums just loudly enough to be heard. They started acting up just over two days ago and have stayed that way ever since."

"What sort of devices are these?"

"Small rectangular slabs of varying sizes, ranging from the size of a credit chit to about the size of a modern data pad. No-one knows what they were used for or what they do."

Yreffej interjected, "Do you have exact times? We've just heard from the Border Guard about some anomalous sightings over the past few days. I'd like to see how the two correlate."

"Give me a sec," said Selrach. "There ... I've just sent you the details the Director supplied."

Evad's phone emitted a soft *beep*. "Got it," said Evad as he manipulated some controls. "Hmm, it appears that most of the artifacts began emitting shortly before the Guard lost track of the visitor. One activated some hours before our subject's shuttle began its run. Correlation isn't causation, of course, but there's a lot of strange things happening around our guest's arrival. The interrogation has been delayed long enough ... make sure I'm not interrupted for anything less than a crisis-level emergency. Evad, out." With that he terminated the call and slapped the unit onto his belt. "Now, let's resume our search for answers, shall we?" He began to walk towards the door.

Yreffej hung back and turned to face Eltrab. "I've got a question about our subject's physiology. Would it affect his response to the interrogation drugs?"

At that moment they heard a commotion coming from down the hall. There was shouting followed by a series of crashes, a second of silence, then the sound of something large landing just outside the door to the room. Evad tried to open the door, but its outward swing was blocked by something heavy.

"Give me a hand with this," he called out over his shoulder to the others. Both of his fellows walked towards him, but at that moment the lights went out.

"I believe that answers your question," murmured Evad as he grabbed his comm-unit and set the display at full intensity. The others followed his lead and in a moment the room was lit.

"The comm-units are dead," yelled Eltrab.

"Not dead, just re-booting," said Yreffej.

"While we're waiting for the comm-units let's see what we can do with this door, shall we?" said Evad. Holding their comm-units with one hand, they attacked the door. It took some concerted effort but they got the door open enough to squeeze out. The weight blocking it proved to be the guard that had been assigned to watch over their captive. Leaving

Eltrab to deal with the unconscious guard, Evad and Yreffej hurried to the interrogation room. The door was open and the room was empty. Not only was their subject gone, so were all of his belongings.

Evad shook his head and sighed. "We can't do any good here. Let's get to the Security Wing and see if they're doing any better."

They trotted off, pausing only to let Eltrab know that they'd send someone to assist him as quickly as possible. Using their phones to light their way, they got to the Security Wing without incident. There were portable emergency lights waving in the darkness, and the sounds of many people shouting to be heard. Finally one voice yelled out above the others for silence and within seconds the room was still.

"That's better. Remember your training and start acting like professionals or I'll have you all busted down so low you'll be cleaning toilets for the new recruits." Evad recognized the speaker as the Security Chief, Nodrog. The man saw Evad and said, "Why are you here, Evad? Shouldn't you be with your subject?"

"He's gone. Your guard is injured and unconscious just down the hall from the interrogation room. Medical Officer Eltrab is with him."

Nodrog pointed at two of his people and snapped out, "You and you ... take a medical kit and assist the medical officer. Go." The two nodded and left at a trot. "The rest of you, back to your stations and get me answers. Use your comm-units once they start working. Give me answers, people."

The lights flickered and came back on. Consoles began to come to life once more. "We were hit by a jamming pulse," called out one of the security officers. "The field is still active. Power is up, but video and data links are down. Repair crews have been dispatched to transfer data link connections to the backup links. Estimate fifteen minutes."

"Not good enough," yelled the Security Chief. "Faster, people, faster. We have a hostile incursion in progress. Combat teams to full alert status and stand by for deployment."

Evad's comm-unit warbled for attention. "Investigator Evad? This is Rewerb in Foreign Tech Analysis section. Those clothing samples you sent aren't as innocuous as we first thought. They look standard at first glance, so we passed them. Further analysis shows that it's not quite the standard polymer we initially thought. It's ... well, the only way to describe it is as being surreptitiously advanced. In summary, it's very much like a flexible armour. Not impossible tech, but as if someone had pushed current state of the art forward by a decade or three."

Evad rubbed at his head with his free hand. "Anything else? You sound as if there's more."

"Yes, sir, but this next part is more speculative. The fabric, advanced as it is, seems to be differentiated. That is, it isn't all quite the same but not in a decorative sense. There's, well, a hidden pattern running through it. If I had to guess, it's as if instrumentation of some sort has been incorporated into the fabric. We can't even speculate as to what its purpose might be, just that it's way beyond what we can do."

Evad's comm-unit warbled again. "I've got another call, Rewerb. Thanks for the update and keep on it. Hello? This is Evad."

"This is Namlessac at the Armoury Division. We got handed an artifact from your subject after your people detected high energy readings. It looks like a rectangular slab about the size of a hand, but there are fine grooves in it that we think indicate that it is meant to be unfolded in some fashion. We've not tried to do that, but it looks like it might unfold into something resembling a pistol. I must emphasize that we have no idea what its function is. Active probes indicate a high energy concentration, as if it contains a power cell of some sort with power densities beyond our capabilities. As per protocol it is being transferred to a secure military site."

Evad paused for a moment then spoke with such haste that his words almost tumbled over each other. "Bury it deep ... as deep as possible, as quickly as possible. Forget the military site, just get it into a mine or something similar, but do it now on my authority. We have a situation here and that artifact is associated with the subject causing the problems. Go go go." He terminated the call and turned to Yreffej. "This keeps getting better and better." He spent several minutes filling his colleague in on the new information.

"Jamming field getting weaker," called out a security officer. A minute later he called out, "Jamming field gone. All video feeds active. Security systems rebooting. Security systems fully restored."

The Security Chief waved Evad and Yreffej over. "An emergency meeting has been called. Video feeds from senior administrators are being set up so they can take part. It's in a conference room just down the hall ... follow me, please." He turned on his heel and trotted out without checking to see if the others were following.

The conference room was a maelstrom of people both physically present and on video screens. Both groups—humans and screens—were arranged around a large table, but there were many different conversations going on at the same time. It took the Security Chief several minutes to restore order. The expressions on the faces of the Highly Placed People on the video screens were less than happy at being ordered about by someone they considered to be an underling.

Nodrog was unperturbed by the disapproval emanating from his superiors. "The integrity of this facility has been restored. The threat appears to have left the building. Port and City security forces have been alerted."

The people on the video circuits began calling out. Cries of "How could you let this happen?" and "Who is responsible for this outrage," rang forth. The tumult of voices began to approach chaotic levels once more.

"Did anyone see him leave?"

The question cut through the babble and the noise level lessened.

Evad cleared his throat. "I said, did anyone actually see him leave?"

That got everyone's full attention and the room grew still. Nodrog barked questions at several of his officers. It turned out there was no evidence—eyewitness or video—that the subject had left the building, only a lessening of the jamming field and cessation of hostile activities.

"Any casualties?" asked Evad.

Nodrog shook his head, unhappy that someone else was taking control of his meeting. "Well, no. Your subject injured many of my people, but no-one was killed."

"What sort of injuries?" asked Evad.

"Bumps, bruises, concussions ... a couple people with broken bones. We're still evaluating the situation, you understand."

"So, nothing serious. What about the subject?"

"My people report a number of clean hits on him that had no effect. The guards had low-power weapons, though, to prevent collateral damage. High-power weapons have been issued."

Evad took care to look at everyone around the table, including the ones on video. "So what we've got is an extremely capable individual with advanced tech running loose. He takes care not to cause anyone serious harm—at some risk to himself from the sounds of it—and then just vanishes. Where is he now? Did he even leave the building?"

Security Chief Nodrog looked quite unhappy, but turned to his officers. "Have a strike force harden all exits on the ground floor and lower levels. The second strike force will start a room by room search of the facility, from the lower levels up. Keep people with tight-beam comm units in the stairs and on each floor as you move ... those will work whatever the jamming tech he's using. If he's in the building, we'll get him."

CHAPTER FOURTEEN
The Old Razzle Dazzle

Bob sat in front of a work station and stretched carefully. He ached all over but was otherwise unharmed. The lightly armoured clothing had worked well, although it was now somewhat scorched and battered. It was fortunate that his captors had left one change of clothing after taking the rest. The only real item of concern was that his gun was missing. It was a covert model, folding into an inconspicuous slab when quiescent. He'd have to remember to trigger the self-destruct before he left.

The ship had been summoned and would arrive in less than half an hour. He'd used the covert gear within his kit to allow it to tap into the local data net, albeit at a modest bandwidth. While it performed its methodical work, Bob poked around to see if human insight could find something of note.

* * *

In the security meeting the assembly was discussing tactics for finding their escaped subject. Security Chief Nodrog turned to Evad and asked, "If he were inside the building, where do you think he'd go? The roof? That'd be the best location for a pickup."

Evad shook his head. "I don't think so. He's here for something ... something that requires his physical presence."

"For a meeting?" piped up Yreffej. "Or, perhaps, his mission is to reconnoitre."

"Reconnoitre ... now there's a thought," mused Evad. "Rellevart—whether individual or organization—went after the criminal syndicates via their data trails. That takes a broad and deep set of skills. So, trapped on a hostile planet, what's the thing he needs first and foremost?" He looked at each individual in the room in turn. "Information. Security Chief Nodrog, I suggest that all personnel not in this room or under your direct control log off their work consoles right away. Anything active after that needs to be checked."

Nodrog nodded and with a predatory grin turned to bark out orders.

* * *

The ship alerted Bob to a change in the data patterns within the local net. He frowned as he realized what his hosts were up to.

"Clever," he muttered. "Guess I'm out of time for the subtle approach."

Checking its progress, Bob saw that the ship was at least fifteen minutes away. He ordered it to come at top speed regardless of how much that would limit its stealth capabilities. That left him seven or eight minutes to wrap things up. Next, he ordered the ship to begin downloading all the data it could, as quickly as it could despite the meagre bandwidth it currently had. As for himself, he called up a map of the city and examined it with care.

* * *

"Sir, we've detected a massive surge of activity in the building's data net. The source has been isolated to a mid-level office." The officer rattled off an identifier.

"Physically sever the building's data links to the outside right away," snapped Nodrog. Send Third Squad to the roof and have them work their way down. We'll catch our target in a pincer between them and Second Squad."

* * *

Bob flexed his hands in a losing attempt to keep them limber. Between the fighting and the typing they were in sorry shape. The ship would be here any minute, and he needed to be able to move quickly. A thought came to him and he grabbed a piece of paper and a pen, then began writing.

"*There are some times*," he thought to himself, "*when I have too much fun.*"

* * *

"Sir, Planetary Security reports an anomalous atmospheric disturbance moving our way. Sensors can't determine the source but can see the effects of its passage. Fighters have been dispatched to intercept."

Nodrog nodded to indicate he'd heard the report. "What's the word on the assault teams?"

"Just about in place, sir," responded one of the security force.

"Excellent. Give us a couple more minutes and we'll be ready for the final assault. It's payback time."

"NO," yelled Evad. "I want him taken alive. Alive, do you understand?"

Nodrog's face hardened as he turned to face Evad with a sneer on his face. "He attacked my guards and tried to disable this entire facility. We're going to take him down hard."

Evad faced the Security Chief with calm intensity. "He's used non-lethal force so far, Security Chief. And at considerable risk to himself, I'll point out. We want to constrain and restrain him, nothing more. Think, man, think. We don't know where he's from or who is behind him. For all we know he's from one of the Lost Worlds looking to make first contact."

"That hasn't happened in over a century, nearly two," spat out Nodrog.

"Yes, but look at the tech he's been using. Do you really think if someone with that level of tech wanted to do us serious harm we'd be able to stop him? And what of whomever sent him? Contain and restrain. I'll take full responsibility. Contain. And. Restrain."

The two men glared at each other for a moment until Nodrog lowered his eyes, growling softly under his breath. "Yes, sir. I'll make sure the teams understand." He turned away to give his teams their final orders. Just then they heard a series of explosions coming from above as sirens began to wail.

"Sir, we're under attack. Hostile forces attempting to breach the roof."

Nodrog paused for a moment then began barking out orders. "When Third Squad gets to the roof, they are to secure the area and wait for reinforcements. Second Squad hold position so our target can't sneak down to this level. Fourth Squad deploy to reinforce the Second and Third. Send a request to Planetary Security for air support. All squads are authorized to respond with maximum force to any attack."

* * *

Bob grinned as he donned the skin-suit the skiff had brought. The hole in the outside wall allowed a welcome drought of fresh air to waft through the office. The air had a clean smell with hints of trees and flowers in it, and the city twinkled as the sun set. It was quite lovely, and he regretted not being able to spend more time sightseeing.

He stuffed his business clothing and other sundries into the carry-all and attached it to the skiff. As he did so he noticed with some pleasure the small container the ship had managed to attach at the last minute. One of the items was a thick wallet which Bob put it on the desk with the note underneath it. The other item was a small medical kit containing a mild stimulant and analgesic, which served to dull the edges of fatigue and pain. Without a backward glance he mounted the skiff and few out into the twilight.

The ship urged him to hurry back—it had landed in a parkland outside the city, and was worried about detection. Bob smiled and replied that he'd be there in a few minutes after taking care of a little chore. The ship said nothing, but Bob could sense its disapproval.

Bob guided the skiff on an erratic course throughout the city. He flew at breathtaking speed, pausing every so often to attach a sensor wand to the side of a building. It was only after deploying the skiff's load of wands that he headed to the ship. As he did so he ordered the ship to begin grabbing all the data it could find, making no attempt to hide its activities.

Insomuch as the ship could feel joy, it was happy. It had tapped into dozens of local data nets, each with varying degrees of access to the planetary data net and various databases. The multiple points of attachment gave it access to a breadth of information—financial, historical, political, and military—that no single access point could have given. Information about the Nexus was its primary goal, but there was so much more to acquire while fulfilling its mission.

Bob arrived at the ship and stowed the skiff. On the way to the control room he stopped at the medical bay to grab some healing salve for his wounds and something for the pain. More extensive treatment would have to wait.

In the control room, he settled down to monitor the situation. The port where he'd arrived was in lock-down, with incoming vessels being diverted to military bases. The various defence force—planetary, orbital, and system-wide—were on high alert. Bob was pleased to see that calm professionalism had replaced the initial chaos. The biggest complaint he heard from individuals was that the current call-out wasn't anything like any of their drills.

The ship alerted him that it had managed to penetrate several military archives but required more time. Bob considered the situation and gave it fifteen more minutes. He managed to extend that deadline twice before he felt obliged to leave.

* * *

Evad awoke with the taste of stale cobwebs in his mouth.

"There's water on the table. Best drink some of it before trying to talk," came a deep male voice off to one side.

After rubbing his eyes to help them focus better, he grabbed the glass of water on the table in front of him. He tried to sip at it but ended up gulping it down so quickly that some of it ran down his chin. When he'd finished, he sighed, wiped his chin, and placed the glass on the table.

"Thanks, Boss. How long was I under?"

"Not long. You were in detention for only a day before I finally convinced them to interrogate you. That took less than an hour, but the Powers That Be insisted that you sit it out rather than have the antidote administered. Sorry."

"Not your fault, Boss. So, what have I missed?"

"Oh, not much. Let's see. You were detained just after your friend smashed his way of the security building, right?"

Evad gave a rueful grunt. "He's not my friend, you know."

His boss waved a hand to dismiss such inconsequential reality. "A mere detail. That's the way this fiasco has been tagged, I'm afraid. But we'll be getting to that in a moment. Your friend, Bob, busted out by slicing a hole in the wall. Not blasted, I'll note, but sliced. Then he flew off into the night. The videos we have of him leaving are blurred, as if he had some sort of active camouflage. Interesting point though ... there was little actual damage done aside from that one clean-

181

cut hole. The attacks on the roof that got everyone's attention were just smoke and noise. The real damage was caused by the security troops tromping around."

He shook his head but smiled as he did so. "They aren't happy at being made to look like fools, by the way. Many bruised egos."

"They deserved it," grumbled Evad.

"Won't argue with you. Anyway, this Bob of yours disappeared from view after that. There were, however, reports of a blurry something flitting about the city at high speed. It paused every so often to attach something to the side of several dozen buildings before vanishing."

"Excuse me, attached what?"

His boss chuckled. "We don't know. No-one investigated this because at the same time there was a massive security breach on private and public data nets throughout the city. We're still trying to work out exactly what was taken. All we know for certain is that it covered a range of topics including history, financial data, politics, and military records."

"As if a stranger were trying to understand us," mused Evad.

"That's one theory ... and one that I like, by the way. There are other more nefarious ones, of course. They focus on the fact that that those attached whatnots melted themselves into slag when he left, as did that folded-up slab of his. Oh, and so did those irreplaceable artifacts that activated upon his arrival."

"How long did it all last?"

"Just under an hour. Then came the big fuss when a ship was seen leaving the Eastern Parkland area. At least we think it was a ship. Left a depression large enough to fit a good-sized military courier vessel. That size, by the way, roughly matches the mysterious something that caused the atmospheric disturbances, both in and out."

"Out?"

"Indeed. Your friend even contacted traffic control—both atmospheric and orbital—in an attempt to prevent panic. At the speeds he was going, though, no-one would have had much time do much panicking. Still, it was very considerate of him."

Evad nodded. "From what little time I spent with him he seemed a decent sort. Why are you grinning like that, Boss?"

That worthy withdrew a folded piece of paper from within his jacket. "He left a note. This is a copy, of course."

Looking askance at his superior, Evad accepted the note and unfolded it. As he read it, he began chuckling, then laughing until tears came.

The note read: "Greetings. I must take my leave of you now. I'd thank you for your hospitality, but I think we can agree that is has been less than perfect. Still, I like to pay my debts whenever possible. I've left a financial chit with more than sufficient funds to pay for any repairs to people or buildings. Those are syndicate funds, by the way, so by spending them you are taking direct action against the syndicates. The bag contains data cubes holding the information I mentioned during our little chat. The courier should be arriving by and by, but now you can get started analyzing the data sooner. This is payment for the data I'm extracting from your systems. My most profound apologies for damages to property and persons incurred during my time here. I'd hoped for a more subtle visit. Just so you know, my purpose in coming here was to find the location of the Nexus. My plan is to attack and destroy it. You might want to place your fleets on alert. Whether I succeed or fail, the Machine Intelligences will be most unhappy. I wish you the best of luck in the battle against our common Enemy. Your recent guest, Bob."

Evad's laughter wound down and he wiped his eyes on the sleeve of his shirt.

"Do you believe him?"

"Oh, yes," said Evad still chuckling. "He went after the criminal syndicates, didn't he? And with what sounds like great success. But the Nexus itself? I can't see him succeeding, though I believe he will try." Then he became serious. "But I suspect I'm out of a job."

"Yes you are, Evad. Someone has to be blamed for this debacle. You've been chosen for that honour."

Evad shrugged. "Oh, well. I'm long overdue for a vacation. A nice long one, sitting beside a mountain lake drinking beer all day. Been a long time since I've had a chance to relax."

"You can have a week, no more. Preferably less."

"Excuse me?"

"You heard me. I've got a new job for you. Oh, close your mouth before something flies in. This Bob person came out of nowhere and you were the only person who grasped the implications of that. We need to start reaching out to the other worlds—here in the Core as well as the so-called Primitive Worlds. We've grown too insular and wrapped up with ourselves. Thanks to your friend, there's a groundswell of support for action against the criminal syndicates. A lot of the outer planets think we're behind it, and quite frankly we could gain a lot of good will by going along with that. The fleets have been placed on alert, but the actual deployments have yet to be decided. We need to start dispersing them instead of keeping them bunched up like we have. Perhaps we should clean things up a bit while we're waiting for the results of your friend's efforts."

Evad had been nodding while his boss had been speaking. Now he shook his head. "It's not that easy. The syndicates have set up whole planetary infrastructures to service their requirements. We can't dismantle those without offering something to replace them. It'll be the work of generations."

His boss nodded. "Between the chance to break the stranglehold of the syndicates and the threat of a new war against the Nexus, we've got a chance to become united and make changes quickly. Been a long time since that's happened. Dispersing the main fleets and organizing the smaller planetary ones will help keep things from falling apart as we reorganize. Besides, your friend Bob—or Rellevart—has already set up the basics of several such organizations we can use, financing them with syndicate money."

Evad sighed and shook his head. "Be careful of using those events as shortcuts. We tried taking shortcuts once before, and that resulted in the criminal syndicates getting established on an interstellar scale."

"Exactly right. That's why we need to start bringing in the other worlds, the ones we ignored in the past. Worse, we tended to look down on them. We need to find out what they know and look for new ways of doing things. Your friend Bob showed how hidebound we've allowed ourselves to become. But you're right on one point ... it needs to be done correctly. That's why I want you in on this. What do you say?"

"It all sounds quite lovely except for the promise of a new war against the Nexus."

"Well, one can't have everything."

CHAPTER FIFTEEN

Into the Fire

Bob immersed himself in the cornucopia of new data the ship had grabbed. It was a heady mixture of history, art, military intelligence, and commercial records. The ship required over a day to simply sort and catalogue it all.

Some of the time was spent dealing with the injuries he'd received—they weren't serious, but required some physiotherapy to augment the healing. The majority of the time, however, was spent in developing a plan to infiltrate Nexus-controlled space.

It was obvious from this latest trip that his skills and techniques needed improvement. Determining how the Core Worlds had detected him was added to the list of priority searches for the ship as it catalogued. According to the records from the scholars on the Terminus World and the criminal syndicates, Nexus-controlled space was at least a week away. Recent events, however, had impressed upon him the need for stealth and patience when there were so many unknowns.

To that end he decided to stop off in a solar system that by all accounts was reckoned to be uninhabited. The local sun was prone to periodic busts of energy at random intervals so it was marked on all charts as a dangerous place. Bob slipped in, taking the usual precautions, and detected nothing of note. There was an asteroid belt that served as a good hiding place, so he nestled the ship next to one of largest asteroids while he did his planning.

That turned out to be a fortuitous course of action. The purloined data showed that the volume of space controlled—or at least patrolled—by the Nexus was larger than expected, extending to less than four days away. The rough location he had for the ancient portal was well within enemy territory. That meant he needed to stay stealthy for longer than expected, which led him to the question of infiltration techniques.

The new records included a brief communication discussing anomalous sensor ghosts that appeared to be detection of his entry into that solar system. That level of sensor sophistication was unexpected and somewhat disturbing. On the one hand, Bob was impressed and pleased by the cleverness of the local humans—they were relatives of a sort, after all. On the other hand it meant that it was very likely that the Nexus had similar technology and capabilities.

There was nothing he could think of to improve the ship's stealth capabilities, but a search of the ancient training manuals uncovered a technique for randomizing the diffraction effect of those stealth technologies. Unfortunately it required a special piece of equipment. On a hunch, Bob checked the manifest and found it listed. When he checked, it was indeed present so he tied it into the ship's systems.

Taking a break for a meal, he pondered on that as he ate. Such a device was standard for some, but not all, missions. Whoever had stocked the pod had managed—somehow—to equip it with just what he required for his mission so far. Thinking along those lines made his hackles rise, so he decided to ignore that until the mission was completed. What was one more minor mystery among so many others?

As for the destination, he decided to get close to the volume of space where the ancient portal was located. Destroying it was his primary mission. It was just over a week away, so he had the ship fly towards there while he tried to locate the probable location of the Nexus itself.

It turned out that the new military records held only a vague location, although they did hint that there was more specific information available. The problem was that he didn't have those other records. After some head scratching, Bob decided to approach the problem from the other end. The historical records held information relating to the construction of the Nexus, and that allowed him to work out the actual location. To his shock it was within the volume of probability for the ancient portal.

The ship, by this time, had arrived just outside that volume of probability. He sent out a command pulse using the alternate energies and settled down to wait for a response. Almost a day later it arrived, giving him the location of the portal ... it was located on the Nexus planet.

* * *

Bob halted the ship in interstellar space just before entering the volume controlled by the Nexus. There were nearby planetary systems that were probably safe—at least according to the records he had—but now was not the time to take chances. He sat there for two days while the ship ran diagnostics as he prepared his gear. This was the final run of his mission, and there was no margin for error.

The Nexus planet itself was human-compatible, slightly smaller than Earth, and included two moderate-sized natural satellites. The initial construction teams had seeded it with off-world vegetation more suitable to their own requirements, but the current state of the ecosystem was unknown. The purloined records made mention of third-hand accounts that spoke of volcanoes, vast forests, and vast wastelands. The only part that matched the old construction records were the volcanoes—there were notes indicating that several had been used as energy sources.

All in all, it wasn't much to go on. About all Bob knew for certain was that he'd be facing an advanced, industrialized, space-faring enemy with eons of battle experience. Records of those battles spoke of vast screens of monitors scattered throughout the region. He would have to assume those still existed, which meant going in under full stealth and careful navigating. In the past he'd snuck into planetary systems, but this time he'd have to start sneaking over the course of many stellar systems before he even got to his destination planetary system.

Once there, he'd have to sneak in, survey the planet to find the portal, land, access the portal, destroy it, and then do whatever other damage he could. All the while evading a relentless Enemy who was determined to wipe out humanity in general, and any interlopers in particular.

"Easy peasy," Bob said to himself. "Done it countless times before." He looked at his image reflected in a shiny surface and grinned at it. The image blurred as his knees went weak, and he sank to his knees. He banged his head against the metal plating of the hull and shook his head. "But not like this," he whispered. "Not as a merely human."

Escaping from the Core Worlds had been a matter of luck tempered with preparation ... but mostly luck. His opponents there had been human, with human impulses, and capable of being reasoned with and understood. He could walk among them—even make friends with some. This time was different. Perhaps Rhian had been correct ... who was he, one man, to go against the Nexus?

One merely human man, without any of the enhancements he'd been born into as his birthright. With that enhanced body he had destroyed the empire his brother, Set, had tried to establish. Then gone on to make the galaxy safe from the others of his own kind. Then he'd died and been reborn— much lesser than before—and struggled to regain a fraction of what he'd had, what he'd been. Never-ending struggle and pain and sacrifice ... and all for what?

Bob looked around the hold of the ship and felt the chill of the deck in his hands as they rested on it. He remembered everything: the centuries of pain of his upbringing and training, the centuries of pain trying to forget what he'd done as the War Demon, and centuries of pain as he tried to atone by stopping others of his own kind from harming the merely human in the galaxy. His breathing by this point was reduced to laboured gasps, and his vision became increasingly blurred as memories assaulted him.

He grunted as he tried and failed to rise, as if straining against a great weight. His mind filled with the memories of broken bodies of those he'd failed to save. Memories of dead and broken planets, the victims of war or sometimes their own stupidity. His breathing was ragged and painful. Memories of those failures made his knees weak. Memories of his father enumerating his inadequacies after failing a test, memories of being taunted as a 'cripple' by his own kind, memories of torments as his healing factors tried to mend his broken body time after time after time.

Each memory was like knife-sharp cold steel twisting into his body. A consuming darkness made his thoughts slow and jumbled, with the jeering echoes of failures screaming at him. The weight of it all was too much, and he was too inadequate ... a failure ... a cripple. Less than a cripple, now. His mouth opened in a soundless scream. His body ached from the spasms that had been running through it.

Then, like flashes of light in the dark, there came other memories.

Memories of a promise made and kept to a friend to see her home safely despite the many obstacles and dangers.

Warming memories of kindness given to him by strangers and friends.

Bittersweet memories of loves long gone.

Fulfilling memories of helping strangers and watching them get on with their lives.

The memory of a promise made to accomplish this mission and what it meant to those whose ancestors had sacrificed so much.

Those flashes of light ignited a blaze of realization — the remembrance — of who he was, whatever the form he wore.

Bob's mind began to clear as the darkness that had consumed him lifted. He didn't know how long he'd been huddled on the deck, arms wrapped around himself, but he felt stiff and cold. He forced himself to stand upright, using the wall for support, the effort becoming easier the straighter he stood. As he wiped at his eyes, the weight of memories fell away. He knew with certainty and clarity who he was and why he was doing this. His breathing became less ragged and after a minute became almost even.

"One last time," Bob whispered to himself. "He said ... he promised ... one last mission and then I could rest."

Turning on his heels he limped towards the control room, gaining strength with every step. There was a mission to prepare and complete. Lives hung in the balance. There was little chance of success and even less for survival. It was just like old times. It was time to get to work.

CHAPTER SIXTEEN
Unexpected Complications

Landing on the planet turned out to be easier than expected. He matched the planet's rotation speed and drifted downward without leaving any tell-tale atmospheric disturbances to mark his passage. The slow descent gave him time to refine his scans of the structure that the portal was in. The closer he got, though, the more confusing the readings of the portal became. It responded to command queries, albeit slowly, but he couldn't get a fix on the device itself. Moreover, the room that contained it reacted to the scans as if it were some sort of device in and of itself.

Bob had no worries about his scans being detected—he was using only the alternate energies for the active scans—but the response of the room worried him. Those sorts of emanations could conceivably be detected by the Nexus. There was no sign of increased activity, though. In fact, the portal room appeared to be in a side-corridor in a part of the facility that was rarely used despite the fact that it was close to, but offset from, the centre. The facility itself covered an area about two hundred metres square, some twenty metres in height and about the same below ground. There was some activity within the structure but not a great deal. From what he could see it was a storage depot for various sorts of equipment. Overall, it had the look and feel of a seldom-used warehouse.

The scans indicated that despite its mundane function, the exterior of the building was constructed out of material that was an effective armour. The only weak points he could see were the several large doorways located around the perimeter. The interior of the building was constructed in different layers of material, from weaker to stronger, as if it had grown over the years. Again, the weakest points were the doorways.

As the ship drifted down, Bob ordered the ship to begin to search for areas where the portal might be hidden. He'd seen several potential spots from orbit but close-up scans were required to refine the selection. Landing was not his first option, but it looked as if it were going to be required. The location of the portal within the subterranean portion of the structure meant that it would take time for the ship's weapons to bore down and destroy it. More time than the Nexus defences were likely to allow him.

The other issue was the active nature of the room itself ... that indicated that there was something special about it, something that required a closer look. Doing that would require entering the structure, preferably surreptitiously.

Studying the layout, he saw that the fastest way to the portal room was via one of the external doorways. Each of the doorways had a road leading to it, suggesting a loading and unloading function. Such features were usually monitored and guarded, in Bob's experience. The resilience of the building material, though, would inhibit fast cutting or even safely blasting an opening. That left the doorways and a brute-force entrance. The real trick was going to be getting close enough to put that plan into effect.

By this time the ship had found a good nesting spot about three kilometres from the facility, so Bob commanded it to go there. While descending he had seen infrequent, periodic road traffic moving to and from the facility. The ship's sensors picked up chatter between the facility and the vehicles, and what it consisted of at different points as they approached.

With luck, duplicating that interaction would get him close enough to the doorway to force a breach.

Minutes later the ship was nestled in a hollow that was only just deep enough to hide in. However, it had the advantage of being hidden from the facility by a series of low hills. There was no indication that he'd been noticed, so Bob went down to the pod to gear up. For this mission he had chosen a skin-suit with a layer of flexible armour added over it. That would optimize flexibility and protection while on foot. Heavier armour would offer better protection and weapons, but at the expense of flexibility.

Getting to the facility with both speed and firepower was a tougher choice. An anti-grav pack offered moderate speed, but no protection or inherent firepower. The skiff offered the best speed, but had no protection and limited firepower for the task. That left the rover, a two-wheeled armoured motorcycle. It was the slowest option, but had lots of firepower and armour. It was, in essence, a small tank.

Knowing that the battle plan would be finalized on-site, Bob already had all three loaded up and ready to go. He put the skiff into standby mode, then climbed into the rover. A final systems check showed that it was at full power, weapons hot, and ready to go.

That left one last detail. Scout ships had often gone into situations such as this, and the inviolate rule had been to never let one be captured intact. In worst case, it could be used as a powerful bomb ... not as powerful as a portal set to overload, but quite effective, nonetheless. Bob calculated it would, at a minimum, shatter the portal and the room that contained it. At best it would obliterate the entire facility.

Bob took a deep breath and gave the ship its final commands: do not allow itself to be captured, self-destruct if he didn't return within one day, and no countermanding order allowed unless he was physically in the ship and gave his command authorization.

He closed his eyes, took several deep breaths, and forced himself to calmness. With a final exhalation, he activated the ship's exit ramp. The rover shot out and up onto the surrounding field. The sun was at his back as he headed to the road. The rover was nearly silent except for the sound of its tires on the ground, but he could feel the power than enveloped him. Finding the road, he raced along it, increasing his speed. Turning past the low hills he saw the facility up ahead and his equipment picked up the first of the broadcast challenges. He triggered the response and increased his speed. Further challenges came and he replied to them all with the duplicate responses he'd recorded.

That proved to be insufficient, and a series of unknown challenges were broadcast to him. In response he fired three missiles at the rapidly approaching doorway. Just before they hit he triggered a series of energy blasts that would hopefully soften the material before the missiles hit. The missiles hit, creating a fireball of plasma and debris. His sensors indicated a breach. Into that maelstrom he fired several more energy blasts as he flew through the breach and into the facility.

His maps indicated a hallway up ahead, and his energy blasts had broken through the less-robust door that led into it. Bob drove the rover through the shattered doorway, decelerating to a safer speed as he navigated through the maze of hallways to his destination. As he passed hallways, he fired grenades and mines down them to sow chaos and confusion. Some of the devices merely exploded, some sat and waited for something to pass by them, and others emitted signals designed to confuse sensors and communications.

It took only a handful of seconds for the facility to respond to the attack, far quicker than Bob had hoped. Hidden guns, which he had mistaken for mere conduits and infrastructure, spewed forth solid bullets and energy blasts. His sensors indicated swarms of powered equipment headed towards him along several routes. The walls and floor blackened and cracked as shots were deflected by the rover's armour.

He turned a corner in the final dash to the corridor down which the portal resided, to find his way blocked by mechanisms the size of the rover. They spat gouts of energy at the rover, sufficient to damage its armour and force it to slow down. Sensors showed many similar mechanisms racing towards his position.

As Bob triggered his own weapons, the hallway became ablaze with energies. Explosions ripped through the air and blew craters in the building and the rover. Pieces began flying off the rover as the ravenous energies struck it. One large piece went flying off with enough force to break through a door into another room. The rover wheeled around and roared back the way it had come, spitting deadly energies as it went. The facility's defensive mechanisms chased after it, firing their own weapons. In a matter of seconds, the sounds of violence receded. Lights in the hallway and the rooms flickered randomly and infrequently.

The large piece of debris within the room rattled and opened up. Bob stood up, and a check of his suit's sensors confirmed that the defensive mechanisms had followed the rover. He signalled the ship to have the skiff ready for a fast extraction. Out of the shadows of the dimly lit room, a figure walked towards him.

"Who are you and why are you here?" a deep male voice boomed out.

Bob touched a control and the faceplate of his helmet retracted.

"Hello, Set. I might ask you the same thing." Then he held up a hand. "Can we hold off on the reunion for just a second? I'd like to secure this doorway."

He picked up the broken doorway off the ground and held it upright in position. To secure it in position, he drew a pistol and attempted to tack-weld the door to the frame, but nothing happened. Puzzled, he examined the pistol but could see nothing wrong. Holstering it, he drew a second pistol, but it failed to work as well. He turned to his brother, only to see him sagging to his knees. Bob ran to him and put a supporting arm around his shoulders.

"What's wrong?"

"Gah. Not sure. Feel ... weak." He shrugged his shoulders and moved them around several times. "Everything itches. Wait ... what did you do?"

"I'm not doing this. Can you stand?" At Set's nod, Bob took one step away and examined his sensor readouts, only to find nothing working. "Jamming field," he said, turning towards his brother.

"Figured that much out myself. What's going on?"

Bob shook his head. "It's complicated. You OK?"

"Yeah, no thanks to you."

"Me?"

"I was doing fine until you showed up. Therefore, logic dictates that you're to blame for this."

Bob blew out a gust of air and made a disgusted sound. "Fine. I'm to blame. Just like always. So follow my lead ... we need to get out of here. My target's a room just down the hall. You alright to walk or do I need to carry you?"

Set made his own sound of disgust. "You? Carry me? Not going to happen. Let's go." He shook off Bob's arm and stood on his own. "Lead the way."

The two brothers left the room and trotted down the hall to the final corridor. There was a sealed door several steps in. Bob opened it with a breaching charge that blew out the locking mechanism but left the door intact. He motioned Set to enter, then turned and closed the door.

"Hold on." Bob attached several items from his belt along the door's perimeter. He ripped a patch from each item, then stepped back. Several seconds later there was a brief flash of light from each of them, revealing melted metal where the patches had been.

"That'll hold for bit, I think. You feeling better?"

"Yes, thanks. Not perfect, but a lot less woozy and itchy. What was that all about?"

"Not sure, to be honest. Hold on just a sec." Bob tapped at the controls of his suit but got no response from the ship. "Comms to my ship are down, too. Well, still active but filled with static of some sort."

"Yeah," said Set. "I heard your transmission this time." He looked around the room. "Whatever is happening, this room seems to be shielding it to a large extent."

"Interesting. Let me try my pistol again." Bob aimed the pistol at the doorway and managed to coax out a series of spot welds before it was drained. He used the other pistol to run another set of spot welds.

"That'll hold well enough that they'll have to use a serious breaching charge to get in" declared Bob. "Pistols are drained, though, and not recharging. That's very strange. What do your healing factors say?"

Set stood still and his eyes took on a faraway look. After several seconds he shook his head and looked at Bob. "My energy levels are low. Access to the alternate energies is severely restricted. Never felt anything like this. My sensorium says there's some sort of interference but can't pinpoint it. What about yours?" To Bob's surprise Set blushed and said, "Oh, I forgot. Sorry."

Bob was rattled by Set's apology but managed not to show it. He held up a sensor wand and said, "Getting the same sort of readings from this. Seems to be a strange sort of random effect."

The two men looked at other and in unison said, "Quantum jamming."

Both jerked their heads back as if embarrassed by the synchronicity of their thinking. "Uhm," said Bob. "Yeah. The

Nexus and the MI are based on quantum technology beyond anything we ever developed. If there's anything related to the alternate energies at the base of it, that might be generating the interference."

Set nodded. "Or maybe a strange quantum effect that generates harmonics into the region of the alternate energies. That's very interesting. Dangerous, to be sure, but interesting." He paused to glare at his younger brother. "Which brings us to why you're here, Bob. Why is this particular room so important?"

The two men looked around the room. It was nearly square, roughly ten metres on a side. A layer of dust covered everything. The only obvious markings were their own footprints in the dust.

"Not seeing anything," grumbled Set.

Instead of answering, Bob walked to the centre of the room, bent down, and swept away the dust in an ever-widening spiral. "Look at this," he said, pointing to a faint pattern etched in the floor. "What does that remind you of?"

Set frowned, then joined Bob at the task of wiping the floor clean. Several minutes later they stood up and brushed their hands against their legs. The pattern was a series of rectangles and circles, over an area of three by four metres.

Bob looked at his brother with a condescending smile. "Well?"

Set uttered a brief, low, growl of exasperation and examined the pattern while frowning. After a minute he turned to Bob and said, "If I had to guess, I'd say it looks like the outline of a portal of some sort. But why? Hey, what are you doing?"

While Set had been examining the pattern, Bob had been wandering along the walls and examining them with his sensor wand.

"I said, what are you doing?"

Bob pointed at the walls. "When I probed this structure from orbit and descent, this room stood out as something different.

Unlike anything else on this planet, it responds to the alternate energies."

Set uttered a thoughtful noise and his brow furrowed. "As far as I know, knowledge of those has been lost by everyone within the Veil. Why is this room so different? Oh stop looking so smug and just tell me."

"Sorry," said Bob with a small laugh. "It's very old tech. Think back to when the Veil was erected." He swept an arm to encompass the room. "This room is a phased stasis chamber."

"Like a sealed cache?"

"Sort of, but you've not got it quite right. This room doesn't put things into stasis, but rather shifts them out of phase with this space-time."

Set shook his head and looked puzzled. "You mean like hyperspace?"

"No, nothing like that. Look at the outline of the portal on the floor. That's the anchor point. The room itself is the mechanism that controls the phasing process. It was a technique used in times before the Veil, to hide important things."

"Like portals?"

Bob nodded. "Exactly. After that period, portals were stored in hyperspace and instantiated on demand. More secure and didn't require an external mechanism like this."

"Huh. So how did you learn about such things?"

"From Dad, actually. He mentioned it on one of our maintenance trips. That got me curious, so I went to Auntie Gertrude's library and found some mentions of this sort of portal tech. Very old, as I said, and only used in the early days of the Great Wars. An early form of portal security used in hardened bases."

"Alright, but what's it doing here? And why doesn't the Nexus know about it?"

"Been wondering that myself. Maybe it was used during the construction phase and got forgotten about in the fog of war. We've both come across stuff like that."

Set nodded. "That's true. But to forget about something like this on this particular planet is very strange. Don't forget that this facility got built around the room. Built by the Nexus, I'll point out."

Bob puffed out his cheeks as he exhaled. "Yep. It's a mystery, that's for sure. Doesn't seem to be any clues here, though."

"That might not be entirely accurate, you know."

"Excuse me?"

"Think about it, Bob. This room was meant to hide secrets, and probably not just the portal."

Bob gave his brother a questioning look. "You know something?"

Set shook his head and sighed. "Hints, nothing more. Anyway, we can discuss this later ... we need to catch up on things, too. But right now I think our first step should be to get the portal instantiated. Something this old can take hours to bring back up." He gave a wry grin as he added, "Assuming we can even access it. Do you see any controls?"

Bob shook his head. "Been looking, but can't see or detect anything. Your sensorium is more sensitive than my portable gear. The rover had the good gear, but it's gone."

"Hmm, I suppose. But won't the Nexus detect us?"

"Don't see how. This room's been undisturbed since it was built. We'll be using the alternate energies, and those can't be detected. The walls are pretty good shielding against anything else."

Set winced. "Good but not perfect. I can still feel the jamming. But let's give it a go." He extended his sensorium and turned in place as he scanned the room. "Nope, not sensing anything."

Bob took his sensor wand and made some adjustments to it. He walked over to the outline of the portal and placed the wand inside it before walking back to where Set stood. "Try it now."

Set looked puzzled for a moment then smiled. "Yep, I see. You want to set up a coherent interference region. Smart."

He extended his sensorium and moved his head slightly from side to side around the probe. After a couple of seconds the air shimmered for a moment then returned to normal.

"Something's there, alright," said Set. "Hidden. Now what?"

Bob sighed and thought for a couple seconds. Shaking his head as if making an unpleasant decision he said, "Copy this burst and modulate your scan with it." He touched a control on his wrist.

"What is *that*?" murmured Set.

"Just do what I said," replied Bob.

"Okay," said Set with a shrug. He scanned the area again, got the shimmer, and before it could fade he sent the new signal. The shimmering became something more solid, like a wisp of smoke.

"Keep sending the signal," urged Bob.

The wisp became a ghost-like outline of a low, squat structure. After nearly a minute of that it snapped into view and Set rocked back with a grunt. "That's hard work. Seems to have worked, though. What is it?"

The two brothers walked towards the structure and then around the perimeter. It was a low, thick, circular wall with three rods around it. The wall was about knee height, two hand widths wide. The rods were waist height and about one hand-width in diameter. Bob paused in front of one cylinder and tapped it at several point along its length. In response, it emitted a single short, sharp note. He repeated the process at the other two rods, with the same result. As the sound of the last tone was fading, a slab arose from within the centre of the walled section. It glowed a pearl white that faded when it stopped rising at about chest height.

"Doesn't look like any portal I've ever seen," grumbled Set.

"That's because this is the basic control panel. Not enough power for anything else. See those lights over there? The system is charging up."

"Any guesses on how long will that take?"

Bob shook his head. "Nope. But as you said earlier, probably several hours. Maybe as long as a day. We might as well make ourselves comfortable while we wait." Then he smiled. "And, as you said, we need to catch up on things."

The two brothers sat off to one side, their backs resting on a wall. Bob reached into a belt pouch and pulled out two meal bars. He offered one to Set who took it with a nod of thanks. They finished their snack in a silence that stretched on for several minutes.

It was Set who spoke first. "I'm sorry about the last time we met," he said in a low voice. "Stranding and attacking you, I mean."

"What? Excuse me?" replied Bob, not sure what to make of this.

Set took a deep breath then exhaled rapidly. "Look, we've always been at odds with each other. Poking at each other to get a reaction."

Bob grunted. "You were older. Your pokes hurt worse."

Set frowned and opened his mouth to make an angry retort. He paused, then grew thoughtful. "Yeah, I was. But you always managed to find a way to get under my skin and into my head. Made me defensive. Huh. Never thought of it that way before."

"So why think of it now?" Bob's tone was one of honest curiosity.

"Part of the Change process is to understand one's past. To accept it without judgement. To look at it with fresh eyes. Oh, don't look at me like that, Little Brother. I may not agree with the Philosophy of Change, but I'm not above seeing that some of its teachings are useful."

"Uh huh."

"Truly." Set's gaze became far away. "I understand where a lot of my anger came from and work to conquer it."

"Conquer? Isn't the goal of the Change to work towards understanding?"

Set's countenance became irritated, then he laughed. "Yes, indeed, Little Brother, it is. But what they do with that understanding is what set my teeth on edge."

"How so?"

"Well, for one they insist that one accept the mistakes, forsake the emotional turmoil they create, and move forward."

"Sounds not so bad, actually."

"Yeah, well, you haven't had an Eldest One yammering away at you, going on and on about your faults and failures and wrongness of thought." Set shuddered.

Bob laughed then said, "Well, you've got a large pool of mistakes to draw upon."

To his surprise, Set looked sad as he answered. "Yes. Yes, I do." Then his voice became firmer. "But at least I was trying to put together something larger than myself. Something that would last beyond me."

He held up his hands as he continued. "Yes, my methods were ... unnecessarily crude, even cruel at times. My path, and my visualization of the future, were faulty. That I will freely admit. But you never seemed to understand that I was sincere in my efforts. Oh sure, at first it was about self-gratification. But that paled after the first couple of temples filled with worshippers. Then I had an epiphany ... I could use what I'd learned to make something larger."

"That when the Ravens contacted you"

Set's face darkened for a moment, then he hung his head. "Yeah. I was struggling to improve my organization. Got a few of the Family involved, each trying to duplicate my setup on their own worlds. Tried to set up a ruling council to figure out how to run it all."

"Didn't work out so well?"

That got a large sigh from Set. "Not at all. Oh, we all meant well enough, but no-one had the experience to put together the sort of organization we needed. Or, if truth be told, a sufficiently detailed plan of what we wanted to accomplish. Then the Ravens contacted me. They had the organizational skills, the manpower, and ..." Set's voice trailed off as he looked away.

"And the means of ensuring obedience?" Bob finished the sentence.

"You don't understand," Set replied with some heat, his head snapping back to face Bob. "The whole organization was teetering, threatening to fall apart. Lives—many of them—were in peril. The Ravens offered a way to get obedience without a lot of time wasted in indoctrination and such."

"The mind gems and pure quill."

Set hung his head. "Yeah. Not one of my best decisions. Seemed like the best way forward at the time." His voice took on a pleading tone as he turned to look at Bob. "It seemed like the best way to bring the Family and the Refusers back together. To build a better future as a reunited humanity. To make alliances with a new species against potential foes."

"So how did that work out for you? For us all?" sneered Bob.

"Not so well," admitted Set. "On the other hand, it brought the Eldest Ones back into the thick of things. It got you nosing around. And then you found this." He waved at the room they were in. "Bob, you found a whole new offshoot of humanity from the time of the Great Wars. They're ... well, cousins I guess you'd call them. Our own kind. We aren't alone anymore."

A soft series of sounds came from the area around the portal, as several rods and a slab rose up from the floor to form a console.

"Send a low-level recall code," snapped Bob. "Don't try to instantiate it, just check on the power levels."

Set concentrated for a moment then turned to Bob with a smile. "Done. It's not ready for full control access, but it'll soon be. Well done, Bob."

Bob responded with a grunt of derision. "It'll be some hours yet, actually." He looked at Set for a few seconds, then leaned back and closed his eyes. "So, Set, what was it that made you think that creating an empire would be a good thing? Yes, yes, you said that you were trying to build something new and better. But what got you thinking along those lines in the first place?"

Set gave his younger brother a sharp look, then leaned back and closed his own eyes. After a moment, his features softened and a faint smile played on his lips. "You played a big part in it, to be honest."

That got Bob's attention, and he opened his eyes and turned towards Set. "Excuse me?"

Set's smile broadened. "Truly. Oh, sure, it was the sort of thing both Mom and Dad had gotten involved with in their younger days, but their generation never did anything about it. Nothing except talk endlessly about it for eons before settling down." His smile became a frown.

"So where do I come into this?"

Set opened his eyes to stare at Bob, his smile returning. "Someone had to clean up the messes you made after you left home and began sleazing around the galaxy." He shook his head and looked away. "Mom and I spent a lot of time visiting the families you hurt or offended. She soothed the ruffled feathers of the parents while I dealt with their offspring." He snorted a laugh and turned to look at Bob. "Managed to stop quite a few of them that wanted your skin."

It was Bob's turn to chuckle. "Not all of them, though. Made things interesting for a while, but none of them had our training."

That got a belly laugh out of both of them that lasted for some seconds before petering out.

"Ah, Bob, you don't really understand, do you? Except for those flings and fights, you left us all behind you to go your own wandering way. Me? Because of you, I got to talk to rather a lot of people, some of them quite important. Got pretty good at talking, too. That got me a reputation as someone who was good to know, someone who was willing to travel and work hard. I saw that people needed and wanted something to bring them together. Having a lot of people angry at you made me realize that even something as minor as that could bring them together, if only to a certain extent. That got me thinking a lot harder about creating something larger than ourselves that could bring us together."

"Sounds like something Mom would approve of. What about Dad?"

"Yep, it was just the sort of thing she could throw herself into, that's for sure. Travelling around, being socially active with all the right people, playing the part of the long-suffering mother of a wayward child. Oh, she dearly loved that. On the other hand, it hardened her opinions against you, I'm afraid. That rather coloured my own to some extent, but any positive feelings she might have had for you were burned out of her. As for Dad, he looked after our younger sister and gave a lot of training courses to the other families. You defeated and humiliated enough people to create something of a back-to-basics movement for a time."

"And you used that, no doubt, when forming your own organization."

"Yes, indeed. Some wanted sufficient training to get revenge on you, some wanted to return to the old ways of readiness for battle, and others wanted something to give their lives meaning. The nucleus of a movement was there, just waiting for something—someone—to bring them together. Talking to all those people gave me an idea of what sort of organization would appeal to the broadest base, and I came up with a way re-establish the old civilization of our ancestors."

"Because of me?" Bob was aghast at the revelation. His eyes were wide with shock.

Set looked at him and laughed. "Oh, not just because of you, Little Brother. But you and your carousing ways were certainly the catalyst."

They sat in silence for a time. Bob was obviously disturbed by the revelations, and Set was amused at his discomfiture.

CHAPTER SEVENTEEN
A Difference of Opinion

It was nearly ten minutes before either of them said anything.

"So how'd you get here?" asked Bob, breaking the silence.

"With difficulty," said Set with a chuckle and a grin.

"Hah hah. No, really, how'd you do it? And what made you come here in the first place?"

"I stumbled across a cache of records dealing with the Veil. It included why this place—the Veil, that is—was chosen, along with a detailed astrophysical analysis."

"Sounds interesting, but—"

Set raised a hand to stop Bob's question. "Attend me, Little Brother. This region of the galaxy wasn't chosen at random. There were a lot of interacting forces here creating tides, for lack of a better term, of energies. Those energies made it difficult to navigate through this region at the best of times. In was, in short, just the sort of place a desperate band of refugees would go to escape an Enemy who was poised on the brink of success."

Set's voice broke. "You know the story after that. How they set up a false shell of civilization. Except it wasn't just a shell, as it turns out. It really was set up as a last-chance bolt-hole. If the Enemy followed, the Veil would trap them inside to be fought. If the Enemy didn't take the bait, well, the Veil would act as a shield to protect a piece of humanity. That's the part the histories leave out—or forgot—but it makes sense."

Both men grew silent for a time. Then Set cleared his throat to continue. "Anyway. We'd picked up a few brief anomalous transmissions from within the Veil. Not much to go on, but they seemed to be generated by human-type equipment." After a moment's pause, he shrugged. "I wanted to investigate. The others didn't. We argued. I left and came here."

"Uh huh. Just left?"

Set laughed. "Well, took a few things. Like a cruiser."

Bob gawked at his brother. "Your group had a cruiser? What class?"

"Early-style light cruiser, Sharp Talon Mark Three," Set said with some pride. Then he made a wry face. "Pretty beaten up, though. Engines still worked well, but no heavy weapons and very few of any other type. Best of all, at least for my purposes, the controls were suitable for single-person operation."

"I'm impressed. Still, they just let you take it?"

"Heh," Set chuckled. "Not really. We were on a mission that Kydos had set up. Very mysterious about it, too, so only one other person knew the details besides her. We were to fly out, drop off a small shuttle, then loop back to the main base. I figured there was something close by that the shuttle was to investigate, but that's all anyone knew. Other than Kydos and her confidant, of course. Anyway, I made the drop, put the others into stasis, dropped them back at the main base, and then headed out to the Veil."

"So why'd you do it?"

"Kydos and the others wanted to set up a new empire. Never could understand why, since the old one didn't work out. Oh, yes, you had a hand in its destruction, but that only accelerated things. I can see now that it was doomed to failure by its nature and design. Poorly thought out, I'll admit. The others, though, couldn't see that. Still, I stuck around because they were my friends. Oh don't look at me like that ... they were my friends, some more so than others to be sure. Everyone else we knew were part of the Change and all we had were each other, so we stuck together. And it wasn't all work and planning, you know. We had some fun times."

Set paused for a moment and looked sad. "Then things changed. They got ... well, quite single-minded I guess you'd call it." After a short pause he chuckled. "And I guess I caught a touch of that wanderlust you always had."

They grinned at each other for a few seconds. Then Set continued, "Anyway, I wanted something more, and the mystery of those signals originating within the Veil caught my attention. The old records showed the energy tides at the time and how the Veil solidified them. We had some long-range scans of the area that gave hints of a lessening of the fields and possible new paths. Pretty sketchy stuff, but enough to get me interested. So I headed out."

Bob's eyebrows rose to their limit. "You took a capital ship—a damaged one at that—and picked your way through the energy fields? On a hunch? That's impressive, Set. Very impressive." Then he frowned. "But those energy fields ... weren't they supposed to be severely damaging to our kind? Interfering with our implanted tech?" Bob forgot for the moment that he was no longer physically like his brother.

Set nodded. "Just so. But those old warships have the very best shielding, and I beefed those up with some tricks I'd picked up over the years. My healing factors dealt with the worst of it. When things got too rough, I went into stasis."

He shrugged. "It wasn't too bad, all in all." Then he grinned as he added, "Not something I'd want to make a habit of doing, though."

Bob chuckled in agreement. "Then what? How'd you find this place?" He waved a hand around to indicate the Nexus.

"Once inside the Veil, I did standard sneaky recon stuff. You're not the only one who can do that, you know," Set said with a touch of indignation. "Found no sign of the ancient Enemy—no physical remains or transmissions or energy signatures. Instead, found a flourishing array of human-inhabited worlds. Didn't make contact with them, just observed. Saw that they were actively ready for battle with something or other, but it didn't seem to be among themselves. Then I picked up some transmissions from another area within the Veil. Did a basic signals analysis and tracing, figured out where their major base was, and here I am. Oh, and the cruiser's sensors picked up a hint of the alternate energies in this area and no-where else on the planet. Figured there must be an old base or weapons cache here ... I've gotten pretty good at sniffing those out, you know." He paused for a moment then looked at Bob with curiosity, "So how'd you get here?"

Bob thought furiously for a second before replying. "Similar to yourself. Picked up strange signals and other hints, so decided to investigate the mystery." He grinned as he added, "You know how I enjoy chasing down a good mystery."

Set rolled his eyes and let out a disgusted snort. "Stick your nose into other people's business, you mean." Then he grew serious. "Where's your ship now?"

"Just beyond the outskirts of this facility. Hidden from visual sight well enough, and the stealth systems are engaged. Well, as much as they can be within an atmosphere. Oh, don't give me that look. The failsafe is engaged ... it'll self-destruct if breached." Then he grimaced. "Or if I don't return within the allotted time. What about yours?"

"Hid it on one of the natural satellites of the next planet sunward. Fewer defences there, you see. Flitted over here in a pinnace." Set made a wry face. "Lost it while landing then apported down. That got the attention of the Nexus right away, since no-one within the Veil seems to know about the alternate energies or the effects they can be used to produce."

"You tell them about those?"

Set made a disgusted face as he snorted. "Seriously? Give me a little bit of credit, Bob."

Bob shrugged. "You seem awful friendly with them."

"Friendly, but only to the point of establishing the basics of a working relationship. It's called 'diplomacy', Little Brother. You should try it some time."

"Meh. Where's the fun in that?"

Set glared at him for a moment then chuckled. A moment later Bob joined him. The room soon echoed to the sound of brothers laughing as when they were young. After laughing themselves out, they sat in companionable silence for several minutes.

"The recharging looks to be about one-quarter done, judging by the indicator lights," said Bob. "If the old records I saw apply to this one, the main control panel should become active when it's half-charged. Then we can run some diagnostics and maybe get some answers."

Set nodded, a happy smile still on his face. Then he cleared his throat and looked embarrassed. "Uhm, mind if I ask you a personal question? You don't have to answer if you don't want to."

"Sure, ask away."

"Do you remember Snuffles? The stuffed toy that Mom and Dad made for you?"

Bob gave a short, happy laugh. "Oh, my, yes. We'd have long chats, he and I. Well, I'd talk and he'd listen. Haven't thought of him in many years."

Set gave an embarrassed chuckle. "I was always a bit jealous of you for that. Rather more than 'a bit' at the time, if I'm being honest."

That admission surprised Bob and he said so.

In response, Set shrugged and said, "It's how I felt, I'm ashamed to say. They stayed up all night, you know, making the silly thing. That was after your first experience with public school, as I recall."

Bob's expression became sad. "Yeah. Things didn't go well. We'd had outings to various public places, you'll recall, and those had ... mixed results. At school, though, all us kids were on our own and the vitriol came out in full force."

"I am sorry about that, Bob. I didn't understand how bad it was until much later. At first I convinced myself it was a foolish crutch, but later on just considered it childish nonsense if I thought of it at all."

Bob shrugged, his face impassive. "It was what it was. I survived. Snuffles helped a lot. When they gave it to me, they said he'd always be there for me, always be my friend. And he was. Made things a lot less lonely."

"A raggedy thing helped that much?"

Bob chuckled. "Surprisingly, yes. Of course when I got older, I saw it not so much a confidant as a reminder of happier times." He grinned and looked at Set. "And, yes, it really was a raggedy old thing, wasn't it? You know, for such talented and competent people, Mom and Dad were terrible at sewing." That got them both chuckling for a time.

"But that's not the question, is it?"

Still grinning, Set shook his head. "No. I was just wondering what happened to it."

Bob's grin reduced to a wan smile. "When I left after my Naming Day, I gave Snuffles to our youngest sister."

"Yeah, I thought so. Mom was angry when you left. Really angry ... furious, in fact. Destroyed everything in your quarters, then went looking for Snuffles. Never found it, though. No-one saw it again. Now that I think about it, that's about the time Dad began teaching Youngest Sister how to do sleight-of-hand magic tricks. Said it was to improve her hand-eye coordination." He gave Bob the barest beginnings of a smile. "She got quite good at it, actually."

A soft chime interrupted their remembrances. Turning towards the portal they saw another section appear. It consisted of three pillars, each a head taller than the men. The space between them was filled with a shimmering fog that began to coalesce into solidity as they watched.

"The main controls," said Bob as he rose to his feet. "Let's check it out."

By the time the brothers walked there, the newest addition to the portal had solidified. They spent several minutes examining the controls, taking care not to touch anything.

"Not sure that I recognize anything. How about you?" said Set.

Bob nodded. "Yeah, some of it." He pointed to the controls on the right. "Pretty sure that's a data console." Pointing to the left, he said, "Those are the portal controls ... I recognize them from the old records and Dad's tutorials."

"Can we transit out of here?" asked Set.

"Let me check. Nope. It's not seeing any beacon signals from other portals. Now that is very strange ... hold on." Bob tapped at the controls and examined the readouts. "Confirmed. It can't see any other portals. Hold on, let me check something." After several minutes of activity, he leaned back and shook his head. "Nope, nope, and nope. It's configured in a non-standard way."

"Meaning?"

"Meaning we can't transit to or from any standard portal. And, no, I don't know why." He moved to the other console and began a tentative tapping at the controls. "Ah, this is useful."

After several seconds of silence, Set cleared his throat. "Still waiting for a coherent answer, Bob."

"What? Oh, sorry. The portal is tuned for a closed link ... sort of like our private portals. Except there doesn't appear to be any others like it. No, I don't know why. Give me a few minutes to check these records."

Bob typed furiously at the controls, paused to read what was on the displays, then typed some more.

Set watched in silence for a time then blurted out, "I don't recognize the language. It looks similar to ours, but not quite the same. How is it that you're reading it?"

"Been here a while," said Bob absently. "Talked to people. Learned things." He turned to smile sweetly at his brother. "It's called 'diplomacy'. You should try it some time."

"Hah hah. Very droll. So what have you learned?"

Bob continued to type and read the results for several seconds before answering. "Working on it. Yes ... got it." He turned to face his brother. "This room was set up by the humans who created the Nexus, as a last-gasp effort to finish it in time to make a difference. But they didn't entirely trust the Nexus. This room was set up as sort of blind spot. That is, the Nexus would be aware of its existence but unable to enter or question it. That's why the facility was built around this room ... like an oyster creates a pearl around an irritant."

He continued to access the data records for several minutes. "And ... yeah, the portal was meant as both a back door and storage for records and equipment. You were right about that, Set. The human workers set this place up, exited through the portal, and that's all there is. No-one ever came back to finish the job. What we see is what we get."

Set stood there stroking his chin for a minute as he digested this new information. "So, what you're saying is that we've got a portal that goes nowhere and some limited data records that pertain to the building of this facility and the Nexus."

"Correct."

"So the question becomes: what do we do with this?"

"What do you mean? The only choice we have is to destroy it and the Nexus along with it."

"Oh, Bob, you idiot. This is a chance to bring peace—real peace—to the Veil. This can be a way to bring both sides together and end their foolish war."

Bob stared at his brother, a chill of horror running up his spine.

"In any case," Set continued, "the Nexus knows about this place, now. At the very least they realize that someone—that would be you, Bob—finds this place interesting enough to mount a reconnaissance in force against it. It will investigate. In force, I assure you. The question is, how do we respond?"

Bob looked down at the floor and tapped a foot for several seconds before replying. "How is it you know so much about the Nexus? You've left all that out of your explanations." He looked up to stare directly at his brother.

Set shrugged. "Not much to tell." Then he gave a brief chuckle. "Well, there is, but some of it is embarrassing, if truth be told. They detected me as I was descending, as I said, and managed to severely damage the pinnace. After I apported down they decided that I wasn't human, or at least not the kind they knew. So they, in essence, began a first contact scenario."

"They brought you here from the start?" interrupted Bob.

"No. This is just the last of several facilities I've been in, each less imposing than the last." Set held up a hand. "Let me explain. It all started out with full pomp and circumstance, or rather, what passes for that among the Machine Intelligences. They wanted to recruit me to their side. When I refused, citing a need to gather information, they transferred me to a smaller facility. It was a museum, of sorts, where they showed me how they had helped humanity to defeat the original Enemy. Humanity then turned against them. The MI and the Nexus simply wanted to live in peace, and so forth and so forth, and would I now help them?"

"You believed all that?"

"No," Set looked insulted by the suggestion. "But it did get me thinking. There was an opportunity here to help both sides, but I required more information. Requesting that got me sent to yet another facility, a library of sorts. There wasn't much there, to be honest, and I started to push for more information. That's when I got sent here. Suspect it's a dumping ground for all their unwanted stuff." He looked around the room. "Don't think they realized this was here. Which brings me back to my original question: when they come, how do we respond?"

"I take it you have something in mind?" Bob said as the hint of a sneer appeared on his face.

"Well, yes," said Set, rather puzzled by his brother's reaction. "I've had a lot of time to think about this. And, don't forget, I'm more experienced in such things than you."

In response, Bob snorted in disgust.

By this time, both brothers were glaring at each other, too angry for words.

CHAPTER EIGHTEEN
Last Words

It was Bob who broke the minutes of silence. "So what's this grand plan of yours, Set? You always have a grand plan." He had hoped to sound reasonable, but the words came out as a snarl.

His brother sighed, took a deep breath, and spoke in a quiet voice that was only slightly thickened with anger. "I'll begin by brokering an understanding between the Nexus and the humans in the Veil. Once hostilities have ceased, or at least a cease fire declared, I can begin the real work." Set gestured at the portal. "That represents the heritage of the humans within the Veil. With it, they can transform themselves into a true galactic civilization. In cooperation with the Nexus, that civilization could exceed even that of our ancestors. A prize like that will surely bring the two sides together, if you and I help them to see reason." By the end of his speech, his anger was gone, so sure was he of the correctness of his argument.

"Are you insane?" yelled Bob.

Set frowned as he struggled to contain his resurgent anger. "I'm quite aware that there's been a history of misunderstanding that has led to outbreaks of violence between both sides—"

"Excuse me? Misunderstandings? Set, the MI were developed by the humans after the Veil was erected. The

Nexus was created to coordinate their actions. Did you even know that?"

Set's head jerked back in surprise. After a moment's pause he cleared his throat before responding. "Uhm, I was unaware of the details of their origin. I was under the impression that they ... well, all I really knew was that they were trapped here. Along with the humans and the Enemy, of course. After they combined forces with the humans to defeat the Enemy, animosities grew between them that led to conflict."

Bob glared at his brother, his face twisted with anger and frustration. "Idiot. What did Dad teach us about doing a proper recon of an existing conflict? Remember his prime rule for that? Huh?"

"Well, ah, of course." Set was taken aback. "It, ah, was to stay out of long-term conflicts. They're always insanely complicated."

"And the second?" demanded Bob.

"If it can't be avoided, tread very lightly until you figure out who is actually fighting whom, and why."

"Exactly. So tell me, Elder Brother who is so very clever, what is this fight about? How did it start, *exactly*?"

Set's face assumed a neutral expression. "Well...that is...I'm not exactly sure. However—"

Bob brought his brother's dissembling to an end when he huffed out a lungful of air, hung his head, and looked away.

The silence between them stretched on for nearly a minute. When Set spoke again, it was in a soft voice as if they hadn't been arguing. "So why are you here?"

"Excuse me?" snapped Bob.

"If I'm here for the wrong reasons, then why are you here? Seriously."

"Long version or short?"

"Let's try the short version to start with. Not sure how much more private time we're going to have."

"As I said earlier, The MI were created to fight the Enemy. When the Enemy was defeated, the MI refused to stand down. The Nexus here," Bob waved his hand, "was the coordination centre for the MI. Created to help in defeating the original Enemy, and assumed lost during battle. When the war was over, it decided that humans were a threat to its existence. Then it began a campaign to exterminate them."

"But it's a stalemate, isn't it, Bob? Has been for a very long time from what I've gathered."

"Not quite, but close. Enough human worlds had sufficient tech to maintain the balance. When they fell, others took their place. A rough, unstable sort of stalemate."

"Again, Bob, why are you here?"

Bob sighed in an attempt to rein in his anger. "The Nexus is on the ascendant once more. The main human alliance is in the wane with nothing to replace it. It had to happen sometime, and that time is now. Worse, now the Nexus knows there's something special on this planet. And, as you've pointed out, will very likely trace that down to this room."

"But isn't the portal protected here?"

"Not all that well, actually." Bob pointed at the floor and the walls. "Remember what's special about this room ... it's a mechanism for a phased stasis field. Like an encrypted message, it requires a special passkey to bring it back into phase. But any passkey can be broken, in time. You know that."

Set gave him a puzzled look. "So where did you get that passkey in the first place?"

"Uncle Lou."

Set's head jerked back. "He talked to you? He hasn't talked to anyone in, I don't know, centuries."

"Yeah, we talked. He told me there was something dangerous within the Veil, gave me the passkey, and then he died."

"Oh, no. I'm ... I don't know what to say, Bob. I only met him a couple of times, but he was never unkind. Strange, but not unkind." Set shook his head. "He was the last of the eldest ones, I think. The last not among the Changed, that is." Once again he shook his head. "It's the passing of an era."

"Yeah. I'll admit to not knowing quite how to feel about it myself."

"So, what now?" said Set after a brief pause. "You say Uncle Lou died giving you the ability to access this. Not getting anything more out of it since we activated its controls. No sense of power or use of any energies." Then he frowned. "Wonder if the Nexus picked up on its arrival. That might be awkward."

"Which brings us back to the question of what to do with it," replied Bob in a soft voice.

Set looked at his feet for several seconds before looking back up. "Humanity within the Veil has lost all knowledge of the alternate energies, correct?"

Bob nodded.

"As I said earlier, this room and the portal are part of their rightful heritage." Set gave his head a thoughtful shake. "In a very real sense, they're all that's left of our people. The alternate energies were the highest achievement of our race, Bob. What right do we have to deny them their birthright?"

Bob shook his head. "The risk is too great. The MI and the Nexus are set on a genocidal war against the humans here, and there is no reason to suspect that it will stop. Or even if it is capable of stopping, at this point. That portal is the key to the alternate energies. With control of those, the Nexus will overrun humanity within the Veil, and after that the galaxy at large. The portal must be destroyed."

"What, without even trying to broker a peace?"

"You want to play peacemaker? Fine. But the portal must be destroyed. I might be persuaded to initiate a minimal overload that will just turn it into slag, but destroy it I will."

* * *

Their argument carried on for nearly half an hour, becoming more acrimonious by the minute.

"Argh! Stop and think," yelled Set. "Once done, this cannot be undone. Just for once, think. Please."

There was a note of pleading in his voice that Bob had never before heard from his brother.

In response, Bob glared at Set, too furious to even speak. Tight-lipped, he turned and walked to the control console. Once there, he concentrated on setting the controls to the appropriate sequence. Appropriate for his purposes, that is. Set's hand fell onto Bob's left shoulder and began to squeeze, the armour groaning and cracking under the strain. Bob winced then kicked back and down to his attacker's instep, then a knee. That was followed by a hard elbow thrust into Set's solar plexus. The attack elicited a grunt of pain and a removal of Set's hand as he was forced to take a step back.

In a strained voice Set said, "That's enough, Little Brother. You know very well that armoured or no, your current body can't harm mine to any great extent. I have no wish to harm you, but you must cease these intemperate actions."

Set was forced to stop talking and concentrate on blocking a flurry of blows. His step back had given Bob the opening he needed to spin around and attack Set face to face. After several seconds of being on the defensive, Set lashed out with a sweeping blow from an arm that knocked Bob to one side. Bob, in turn, used the momentum of the blow to sweep a foot across Set's face with enough speed to catch his nose. That blow, glancing as it was, caused Set to take several steps back, his nose bleeding and looking somewhat off kilter. Bob's trajectory had sent him flying, but he landed with a controlled tumble that ended with him back on his feet and ready for battle.

"Fine," growled Set. "If that's the way you want it."

He launched himself forward towards his younger brother, but the coarse dust on the floor prevented him from achieving the blindingly fast speeds that better footing would have allowed. Bob was quite aware of the floor's condition and had used the brief respite to sweep a small clear area around each of his feet. That secure footing allowed Bob to meet and halt Set's rush, as well as to block or evade every blow Set threw at him. This went on for a handful of seconds before Bob managed to land a strike to one of Set's elbows and another to a knee. Each strike was forceful enough to evoke a snapping sound where it struck and gasps of pain from Set, who stepped back and stumbled backwards into a sitting position.

"Just sit there for a moment and listen to me," Bob said, embarrassed that he was puffing from exertion and hating that his brother could see how much effort the battle had cost him. Set, on the other hand, was puffing only slightly, and that from the pain. His nose had stopped bleeding and the blood was disappearing into his skin. The injured joints were being carefully worked to assess the damage, then oriented into a neutral pose to allow for healing.

"We had the same teacher, Set. Besides, your constant bullying when I was younger forced me to learn counters to all your moves. Not to mention that I've had considerable experience dealing with opponents stronger and faster than myself. Now shut up and let me work. We can talk all you want after I'm done."

He turned and walked back to the control panel, the tightness of his expression a reflection of pain as much as from anger. His own injuries, although only deep bruises, were causing his muscles to throb as they tightened up.

A grunt of effort from behind caused Bob to spin and dance to one side. That allowed him to avoid the worst of the blow that now merely glanced across his shoulder. That blow, though cushioned by armour, hurt enough to cause his muscles to spasm from the impact.

Set's rush carried him past Bob and his attempt to stop was thwarted by a not-quite-healed knee, causing him to stumble and bend forward to right himself with his arms. The damaged elbow, however, could not take the strain so Set tumbled to the ground and skidded to a halt. His breath puffed the dust on the ground into small clouds as he bounced to his feet, favouring his injured leg.

Taking advantage of his brother's tumble, Bob hurried to the controls and began to complete the self-destruct sequence. He kept track of Set's progress by the noise the other made. All he needed was a few more seconds but it seemed that Set was not going to give him that time. With one hand typing on the controls, Bob used the other to loosen the few weapons he had left. They weren't much, but all he needed was to gain a few seconds.

Bob spun and tossed a knife towards Set, who used a blast from his sensorium to destroy it before it could hit. That gave Bob time to tumble to one side and toss a small piece of debris from off the floor. Set dashed towards Bob, and didn't even wince as the debris hit his head and opened up a deep gash. He whipped past Bob and used the momentum of his passage to slam a rock-hard fist into Bob's left shoulder, eliciting a satisfying *crack* as both armour and shoulder joint shattered. He skidded to a halt, but the condition of the floor and his damaged knee forced him to shift focus to deal with that.

That shifting of focus gave Bob time to take his last knife and slash at Set's head with a downward stroke. That blow finished up with the knife embedded in Set's right hand, severing several tendons in the process. Set's left hand, though, came up and slashed several times across Bob's left side. The flurry of blows first tore off armour, then through unprotected flesh. The final blow not only shattered ribs but ripped open a gash deep into the torso. The force of that blow sent Bob reeling as he fell to the floor. Set was unable to follow up his attack, as the momentum of his leap had once again unbalanced him and he stumbled to the floor himself.

Bob blinked rapidly several times in an attempt to stop his vision from flickering as he wiped his eyes with his undamaged right hand. He heaved himself to his feet, not caring if Set heard the anguished gasps that effort caused. Nothing mattered now except to finish the mission. Nothing.

He fumbled at his belt and took hold of the case with the monomolecular bolo. Not bothering to remove the device, he crumpled the case and twisted it as best he could. The amount of twisting affected the final explosive effect, but even a small explosion would be sufficient. He heard Set moving behind him. Bob took a couple of rapid, deep breaths and spun around to face his attacker.

Set was slow in getting to his feet and turning towards Bob, who took advantage of that slowness to snap the case forward. Set by this time was beginning to run at his brother without bothering to deal with the case, as if it were just another piece of debris.

The effort of turning then tossing the weapon caused Bob to sink to his knees, moaning as gurgling sounds came from within his chest. The explosion knocked him onto his back. When he was able to raise his head, he saw that Set was no longer a threat. As small as the explosion had been, it had been sufficient to rip off part of his face and chest. The tendrils of his sensorium lay limp. Bob could see no indications of breathing.

Rolling onto his right side, Bob forced himself to stand. He staggered to the control panel, leaving a trail of blood behind him. At the control panel he finished setting the self-destruct sequence and slumped to the floor. There was nothing else he could do but hope that the sequence activated before the Enemy breached the door. He tried to keep his eyes open to meet the end, but his injuries were too great. He tumbled onto his left side and lay on the floor, his breath ragged and irregular as a pool of blood formed around him.

CHAPTER NINETEEN
Bittersweet Reunion

Outside the room came faint sounds of battle that grew ever closer. The door began to glow as if a great heat were being applied ... first red, then yellow, and finally white just before it evaporated. A glowing, pearl-white ovoid came into the room, dashing towards the portal. It hesitated for a moment over Set's inert form, then Bob's, stopping finally at the controls.

A sound at the ruined doorway preceded the entrance of a small device that rolled in. Once past the frame it exploded, filling the room with shrapnel and bursts of energy aimed at the ovoid. The ovoid flared as its shields blocked the assault, extending them to protect both of the prostate forms. More devices appeared, and the ovoid fired a series of energy bursts that made short work of the intruders before they could explode.

The ovoid rushed to the doorway and fired several long and intense energy blasts down the hallway to either side. Several seconds later answering blasts came, but they were aimed to hit no further into the room than the doorway. Both sides wanted to destroy the other, but not at the expense of damaging the room's contents. That kept the intensity of battle below that which both sides were capable. Still, the ovoid was struck several times as it moved to shield the men inside from stray blasts, to its own detriment. Then came the sound it had been dreading—the sound of a portal building up to an overload and explosive self-destruction.

At that sound, the intensity of the attacks upon the ovoid increased and gave it no time for further matters. Without warning, a series of energy blasts from within the room shot past it and savaged the ranks of the attackers. The ovoid followed up with blasts of its on that finished the current wave of attacks and created a moment of calm.

"Thank you for the assistance, Set," said the ovoid in a strong female voice that was tinged with pain. "How much time do we have before the overload reaches critical?"

"Not much," he answered, his own voice ragged with pain. "Our brother's gotten quite good at this, unfortunately."

"Set—"

"Shut up. No time." He examined the controls and gave several of them tentative pokes. The intensity of the sound from the portal diminished but did not cease. "Can you apport? The Nexus had some sort of inhibitor field earlier but I can't tell if it is working or not."

"The field is still there. I had to fight my way in using rather more energy than I expected."

"Fine, we do this the hard way." He examined the controls for a few seconds. "I can use the portal to create a bubble of energy to counter the inhibitor field. Not a large one, but I think it'll be enough to get you to Bob's ship. Or pretty close, at least. You know where it is?"

"Yes, I detected it on my way in." Then her voice became soft. "But what about you?"

Set shook his head. "You'll need all your remaining energies to fight through to the ship, so you'll only be able to apport one of us there. My own injuries haven't healed enough to allow me to apport."

"I can carry us all," she insisted.

"No, you can't. You're injured and not at full strength." He turned to face her and gave a crooked smile. "I'm the eldest

229

and it's my duty to make sure you get out of here. To keep you both safe. Haven't been doing a very good job of that these past few centuries. Besides, someone has to stay here to hold off the self-destruct long enough to allow you to escape."

He turned to the controls, then paused and went to Bob's prostrate form. Set examined his brother for a moment before removing the few remaining weapons. "I'll need these. Let him know I took them, would you? He hates it when anyone touches his things." His ruined face flashed a grin that made her think of happier times that were long ago and far away.

Returning to the control panel, he made some adjustments. To the portal's moaning was added a sharp note.

"Ready? The bubble will only hold for a few seconds before it collapses. After that you'll have a couple of minutes at most before the overload. That's all I can give you."

"Thank you, Set. You are a credit to your ancestors."

"Thank you, Ashira. Give my love to everyone." He paused for a moment, then his ruined face smiled in an embarrassed way. "Tell Bob that he was right. Just this once, he was right."

The sound from the portal became sharper. "Get ready. Bubble forming ... now."

A ripple burst out of the portal and expanded outward at a speed almost too fast to follow.

"Go!"

Ashira hovered over Bob. There was a soft *plop* as they both vanished from the room, and another as they re-appeared on a deserted plain. She quickly scanned the area and determined that they were just outside the valley where Bob's ship lay. The sound of mechanized attack units approaching their position indicated that they'd been detected. Extending tendrils of energy that enveloped and lifted Bob, she floated towards the ship.

She could see the ship some distance away, but it was surrounded by a handful of combat units that began firing at her. She was able to shield both herself and Bob, then destroy the attackers, but the effort all but depleted her energy reserves. They would replenish, of course, but that would take several minutes. Those were minutes she did not have, as the sounds of approaching attackers indicated.

Several seconds later the attackers burst into view, firing as they came. Ashira fired back, but her blasts were feeble imitations of her previous efforts and could be produced less frequently. She concentrated on shielding herself and her brother. After a handful of seconds she ceased firing and concentrated on shielding Bob while blasts rippled around them and into her. Her body became criss-crossed with a fine network of dull white lines.

"I'm sorry, Bob," she whispered. "I tried, but—"

She was interrupted by a flash of light that seared away all her attackers. Through failing senses she saw a pair of ovoids nearby.

"Hello, aunties," she murmured. "I—"

"No time, child. Hold still and let us get you out of here."

The universe seemed to swirl around her as she lost consciousness.

* * *

When Ashira regained awareness, she was in deep space between stars.

"About time you woke up, young lady," came a contralto female voice in prim, no-nonsense tones.

"Uhm, hello Auntie Gertrude. How long was I unconscious? I didn't think that was even possible for one of the Changed. And I *hurt*." She extended her perception to examine herself and was shocked to see a network of pale ragged lines throughout her form.

"Well, no-one has pushed the limits of these new forms like you have," Gertrude said. Then her voice softened. "You were very badly injured, Ashira. Still are, in fact. It will take quite some time before you are fully healed, I think. Once again, you are breaking new ground for our kind." The last was said in wry tones.

"What about Bob and Set?"

"Set perished in the blast, I'm afraid. We arrived seconds before the portal went critical. We had a choice of saving you or him. He was in the midst of battle and gravely wounded. His last words were to save the two of you. For what comfort it may bring you, he sounded content. Whatever mistakes he made in the past, he was a credit to his ancestors."

Ashira was silent for a moment. "And Bob?"

"Alive. Freida saw to that. She should be back any time. Oh, hello dear."

Another ovoid appeared next to them.

"Hello, Gertie. Hello, Ashira. You're looking better, child. How do you feel?"

"I'm fine, Auntie Freida. How is Bob?"

Freida harrumphed for a moment before answering. "He'll live. That artificial body of his is so primitive. Hardly better than a standard human form."

"Auntie Freida," Ashira said in a horrified voice. "Forbidden technology or no, that body is the equivalent of our ancestors."

"Oh, piffle, Ashira. Our ancestors were as merely human as any of them. Nothing more, nothing less. Bob knew that even before his new aspect."

"So he's healed?"

"Nearly. I improved his auto-medic sufficiently to deal with the remaining injuries after I fixed the major ones. Such primitive equipment. It's a wonder our ancestors survived, quite frankly."

"But he'll be as good as new, won't he?"

"Oh, better."

Both of the aunts cackled as if sharing a private joke.

Ashira looked from one to the other and frowned. "What. Did. You. Do?"

Both of the older women managed to contain their amusement with great effort.

"Well," said Freida, "It was Gertie's idea, really." That was followed by a barely-contained chortle.

"Oh, you're too modest, Freida. I simply mused about the possibility." Her subsequent guffaw threatened to set the pair of them off again.

"Aunties." Ashira's sharp tone stopped the sounds of amusement right away.

Gertrude calmed herself, looked at Ashira, and said in a soft voice, "In a very real sense he is the last of us. The last of how we used to be."

"And those artificial bodies were designed to be sterile," added Freida.

"Wait. You didn't ..."

"Oh, yes. Quite simple, really," said Freida with a trace of pride in her voice. "He is now able to father children."

"With the DNA of your family," added Gertrude.

"So, how does Bob feel about this?"

The silence of the aunties spoke volumes.

"Wait. He doesn't know about this? You did this to him without his express permission?"

The two aunties looked at her without any shame whatsoever.

"Oh, my dear, it would have interfered with the healing process to awaken him. And given your brother's history I don't expect it will be a secret from him for very long," said Gertrude.

That got both aunts cackling once more.

Ashira let out an exasperated sigh. "You two are horrible, and I love you both very, very much. But the Conclave forbade any interaction with him. Won't you get into serious trouble for this?"

"What interaction?" asked Freida in an innocent tone. "We never spoke to him. In fact, neither did you."

"All that remains," said Gertrude, "is to make a report to the Conclave."

"The Conclave," spat out Ashira. "They kept Bob's resurrection from me. Then somehow arranged with Uncle Lou to send him on this suicide mission so they wouldn't have to risk their own lives."

Freida sighed. "It's not that simple and you know it, child. Lou acted on his own, as he always did, and caught the Conclave quite by surprise. Set and his associates had learned how to stay out of sight. Besides, there are factions and schemes forming within the Conclave about which you know nothing."

"Even so, Auntie, it was cruel to use Bob in such a way. I found out about it nearly too late to help him. And I never even had a chance to talk with him." She paused for a moment then said in a soft, sad voice, "He doesn't even know me. Doesn't know who I am...not as an adult, at any rate. It's cruel to the both of us."

Gertrude piped up. "I'm very sorry that circumstances have caused you pain, my dear. But your brother has always seen himself as a guardian of humanity. He even named himself after one of the ancient guardians of legend. It was the path he chose, however imperfectly he followed it, and was prepared to pay whatever the cost."

"With a bit of help along the way, I suspect," said Ashira, regaining her normal good spirits, at least in part.

Both of the aunts tried their best to look innocent—a neat trick for glowing ovoids of coherent energies.

Finally Gertrude snorted. "As if I'd be bound by any geas of the Conclave. Oh, I went along with them to keep the peace. But there's no geas made that'll bind Freida or myself, much less allow them to track our activities."

"Can you teach me how to do that, Auntie Gertrude? I can block the geas to a certain extent, but not that well. Oh, and I hadn't thought about them tracking me."

"We took care to block their trackers, never fear. As for the other, well, all in good time. First you need to heal and rebuild your strength. After that we'll look at getting you some advanced training that only a few of us know about. But for now, it is time for us to go. We'll be taking Set's ship home. Slow as it is, it has the necessary shielding and you need the time to heal before facing the Conclave again."

There was a brief flare of brightness. When it subsided, they were gone.

CHAPTER TWENTY

Expectations and Consequences

Bob awoke within the embrace of the auto-medic, stiff and sore. Worse, he had no idea how he'd gotten there, much less onto the ship. His last memories were of fighting Set and setting the portal to overload and self-destruct. He climbed off the table and examined the displays. According to them he'd had very severe injuries—all but fatal, in fact. Looking around he could see a bloody trail leading into the compartment and bloody smears on the controls.

Without bothering to get dressed, he followed the trail of gore out of the compartment, to and from the control room, and back to the airlock. He took a careful look around, but it all indicated the passage of a single, badly-wounded person. It seemed possible, but he remembered none of it. Not surprising, perhaps, given the extent of the injuries described by the auto-medic.

In any event, the ship was heading somewhere under FTL drive. It was a measure of his grogginess that he hadn't thought to check the destination while he'd been in the control room. To gain a better focus and chase away the mental cobwebs, he took several deep breaths and focused on his breathing for a few seconds. When he felt able to think, at least a little, he walked back to the control room and peered in without entering.

The control systems showed no indications of anything untoward. There were bloody smears on the controls, as if a badly wounded person had set them. Without bothering to look at the destination, he turned and walked back to his quarters. The ship was fine, if off to parts unknown, and he was in no condition to deal with mysteries or problems at the moment.

Upon reaching his quarters he washed up and put on some clothes. After that he headed to the galley for a light meal. The rituals of normalcy helped to settle his nerves and clear his head, so long as he ignored the images of Set's broken body that kept appearing in his mind. He firmly pushed those images and associated negative thoughts to the background to better focus on the here and now.

With a clear, or at least not so foggy, mind he returned to the control room. He was still within the Veil, and en route to the transit tube terminus, with an expected arrival in just over a day. A quick diagnostics check showed that the ship was in good condition, if a bit singed as if from battle or a titanic explosion. He examined the logs and determined that the ship had, indeed, outrun a large explosion. The coordinates coincided with the planet of the Nexus. Delving deeper into the sensor logs showed readings of a large explosion on the planet, consistent with that caused by a portal self-destructing. The initial explosion had thrown a blast of energy and debris into space, and it was that which had damaged the ship's hull. As for the planet, it appeared that the explosion had fractured several subduction zones, causing severe planet-wide earthquakes and rampant volcanism. In addition, the energy burst of the blast had been powerful enough to fry any advanced technology within that solar system, including Set's own ship. It would appear that the Nexus was destroyed and his own escape had been a near thing.

Bob sat back in the chair and contemplated what he'd discovered. After a few seconds he set up the control system to do a deep diagnostic and integrity scan of all systems. Everything seemed fine, but it couldn't hurt to confirm that his ship hadn't been tampered with. There was probably something in the Precepts of Survival to that effect, but he couldn't be bothered trying to remember it.

He sat there staring at the controls without really seeing them. There were so many mysteries here. Not least of which was his battle with Set. At the memory of that he shuddered as he covered his face with his hands. They had been at each other's throats for so long, but at the last it had seemed like they had reconnected as brothers—if only for a moment. Almost, but not quite enough.

With his eyes closed, Bob could picture Set's body lying on the floor next to the portal. The damage to his head and torso looked very bad, so far as Bob could remember. Quite possibly fatal. Or hopefully at least severe enough to keep him unconscious until that final explosion.

It was just one more death among uncounted legions who had died by his hands. Yet this one weighed on his soul more heavily than any other. He lowered his hands, uttered a weary sigh, and examined the control systems. The diagnostic was still in progress and would be for some hours, but early indications showed nothing amiss. Given his physical condition, perhaps a nap was in order. Things often seemed not so bleak after a good sleep, though Bob suspected that his sleep would be troubled for some time to come.

* * *

Bob landed his ship on the outskirts of Leap, the town he'd left Rhian in. He couldn't be sure she'd be there, of course, but it was a good place to begin looking. It had been several months—the better part of a year—since he'd left and there'd been changes. To his surprise there was a clearly marked, if rudely laid out, space port with several landing areas sketched out with furrows and flagpoles. Out of respect for their efforts, he landed in the area defined by colourful flags and signal fires on the edges. He guided his ship to the exact centre and allowed it to settle as gently as possible. It sank significantly less than expected. Sensors indicated that the area had been overlain with a layer of stones. Not quite sufficient to bear the weight of his ship, but a very good first try he thought.

There were several buildings on the edge of the landing field and one of them began raising a rapid sequence of signal flags. Despite his weariness he was intrigued by the procedures. A minute later, a rider on a horse-like creature came galloping towards him. That, he figured, was his cue to get ready to receive official visitors.

His clothing was a standard ship uniform. He decided to add a warm jacket to the ensemble ... it was part of the uniform, and it would help with the chill that the sensors had warned him about. It was also resistant to kinetic and energy weapons. Along the way to the airlock, he stopped off at the medical room and took a pain killer along with his other scheduled medications. Once again he bemoaned the loss of his healing factors, but this time he was successful in tamping those feelings down below the conscious level.

Bob reached the airlock and saw that the rider had reached the ship, dismounted, and was waiting just outside. For just a moment he allowed a trickle of self-pity to surface ... official pomp and ceremony was the last thing he needed. Then he squared his shoulders and prepared to meet his fate. He tapped the controls to open the airlock and stepped outside.

The rider was a young man, obviously thrilled to be the official greeter and trying very hard to be nonchalant about it.

"Greetings, star walker. On behalf of the Council of Academics I welcome you to our world. Please follow me to Port Control that we may process your arrival." After delivering his short speech, he stood braced at attention.

With great effort Bob kept a straight face. He gave a short bow and said, "Thank you for the welcome. I come in peace as a traveller looking for rest." That was close enough to the societal norms here, he thought.

"Follow me, if you will, Traveller," said the young man with a flourish, indicating that Bob should follow him. The two walked side by side, with the youth leading the horse by its reins.

After a minute of silence the young man asked, "Sir. If I may ask ... were you successful? There have been only rumours."

Successful? Bob thought of his reception on the various Core Worlds, his battles with the Nexus, and the killing of his elder brother. Successful?

Something of the coolness of Bob's attitude must have been obvious to the young man. He blushed and said, "I meant no disrespect, sir. It's just ..."

"Never mind," said Bob. "I take no offence." He paused for a moment. "The Nexus was destroyed along with its planet. The Core Worlds were alerted before that, so they should be prepared to defend themselves."

"Oh, that is wonderful news," burbled the youth. "It must have been an amazing adventure. So exciting. So glorious ..."

Bob opened his mouth to disabuse this callow youth of his illusions, then shook his head. "Yes," he said. "It was quite the adventure. Fearsome battles against terrible foes."

The youth yammered on about the glory of adventure, but Bob tuned him out. It was just before they reached the buildings that the young man said something that penetrated Bob's consciousness.

"Excuse me? I missed that last bit."

"I said that Senior Academician Faernsworth is waiting for you in the Council chambers once you are done here."

Bob nodded and thanked him, keeping his face calm. Inside, though, he grinned at the thought of his friend being named to a senior position in such a short period of time. As expected, the formalities of landing were brief and cursory. The customs officer, a middle-aged man, grinned broadly and asked few questions. Bob surmised that the success of his mission was somehow already known.

Over the course of the next half-hour, Bob was handed over from one official to the other. More than once he was tempted to turn around and head back to his ship, but each time the cheerfulness and delight of the officials extinguished that thought. Finally, though, he was brought to the Council of Academics. Or, rather, an anteroom outside of the council chambers. There, at least, he was offered refreshments and a chance to sit in blessed silence and solitude for a few minutes. All good things came to an end, though, as an orderly arrived to suggest that he come to address the council in his own good time. Bob recognized an official summons when he heard it, and followed the orderly to the Council chambers.

By this time his tolerance for official foofarah was pretty much at its limit. The orderly brought him into the chamber, bowed, and left. Bob faced an arc of a dozen robed figures hidden in shadows.

"Greetings, Traveller," came a stentorian voice from one of the Council.

Bob stood there for a moment before answering. "Greetings and salutations. I have returned from battle and so forth and so forth." He sighed with a great gust that blew out his cheeks. "Just ask me your questions, I'll ask mine, then I'll be on my way. That agreeable to you?"

The silence was palpable. Several seconds later, a female voice said in dry tones, "Might I suggest that we forgo the formalities and get to the essentials?" Bob recognized the speaker as Rhian.

One of the Council leaned forward and said, "That's all very well, but there is a proper way to do things. A report must be made so that we may enter it into the records."

Bob closed his eyes and took measured breaths as the Council debated the appropriate protocols for several minutes.

"Enough." Rhian's voice rang out. "Our guest deserves better." She paused and leaned forward enough that Bob could see her features in the dim chambers. "You have questions. Perhaps I can start by telling you what we know?"

Bob nodded.

"The ansible network is awash in stories and rumours about the destruction of the Nexus. The Core Worlds have launched a series of successful attacks on the outposts of the Machine Intelligences. For the first time in many centuries, the tide of battle appears to have turned, thanks to you."

Bob nodded again, then said, "I take it you've decided to stop hiding."

"Yes. I counselled caution, but there's been such a dearth of hope for so long that it was impossible to stop it. The Core Worlds have contacted us, and we expect a diplomatic envoy at any time. Plus trading vessels." She grinned. "Quite an exciting time, all in all."

"I see. So no reason for me to stick around then."

At that, the room grew silent.

Rhian chuckled. "Bob isn't one to stick around after the mission is done. Perhaps we could call a recess, and I could speak to him privately?"

After a brief discussion a vote was taken and a recess was declared. Bob was escorted to a well-appointed office. Rhian shut the door, removed her official robes with a sigh of relief, and then motioned him to a comfortable-looking chair as she sat behind a desk.

"Would you care for some refreshments?"

"No, thank you. Had some just before that last meeting." He shook his head. "Haven't seen them in full pomp mode before. Not a big fan of such things."

Rhian laughed. "Well, to be fair, they can usually manage to forgo most formalities when the circumstances call for it. But they're brushing off their company's-coming manners and you're the first chance they've had to put them into practise."

Then she leaned forward, a happy smile on her face. "I'm so glad that you made it back, Bob. From the way you were talking when you left, I wasn't expecting that." A sad look replaced the smile as she said, "I'd almost lost hope."

"It was a near thing, to be honest. But here I am. Sorry it took so long." He paused for a moment as he looked around the well-appointed office. "You seem to be doing well by yourself."

"Oh, yes. It's not been easy, but they want to break their isolation and join with the rest of humanity within the Veil." She chuckled and gave her head a small shake. "Their social system is quite similar to the universities back on Earth. Similar sorts of internal politics, too. I'm familiar with both, and managed to make myself useful."

Rhian shrugged and leaned back into her chair. "They know that change is coming and want to be able to survive it. I might be an old academic, but I've seen more of the galaxy than they have. Figured they'd want me as an adviser, but they put me on the Council itself. It's a shrewd bit of politics, you see. They get advice on what's outside the Veil, they're the only planet with someone with that experience, and having someone not from around here on the Council makes them look cosmopolitan rather than a backwater."

Bob nodded, smiling at his friend's good fortune. Then he caught her looking askance at him. "More to it than that, I gather," he said with a wry grin.

"Yeah, well, you helped." At Bob's raised eyebrows she snorted a short laugh. "While you were here, you rubbed some people the wrong way and stepped on a lot of toes. Oh, stop grinning, you fool. Anyway, soothing ruffled feathers allowed me to know, and be known to, a lot of people, some of them well-placed in the social hierarchy. That, combined with my other experience, allowed me the opportunity to present some ideas I had to improve things." She waved a hand around her office. "And here I am."

She paused for a moment then gave a short laugh, missing the flash of pained embarrassment on Bob's face. "Then there's my ability to work with the old tech. Me, of all people, being considered a technical expert. The tech on your ship is close enough in function, if not operation, to the stuff they've got squirrelled away. What I can't figure out, I can at least give hints on, and their experts do the rest while giving me the credit."

Rhian's face took on an annoyed look. "The Core Worlds look down on places like this, you see, as being too primitive to be of any use. But now that we have access to old tech—and those old records you helped us access—suddenly we're someone worth talking to. Or, perhaps, exploiting before being cast aside once again." Rhian fell silent after snorting her disgust.

"Couldn't the primitive worlds band together somehow?" asked Bob.

"Already done. The Council has decided to freely share what we know with the other primitive worlds via the ansible network. Most of them will have something the Core Worlds covet, to a greater or lesser extent. Anyway, freely sharing that information has given the Council a lot of prestige and influence. There's talk of banding together to form an alliance to force the Core Worlds to deal with all or none on an equal basis."

"What about the weapons I left with you?"

Rhian nodded. "We've offered to share those freely with everyone, of course. That's another reason why the Core Worlds want to establish diplomatic and trade relations with us." She grinned. "Lots of things happening in a short time, but things seem to be working out." Then her face grew serious. "Wasn't supposed to mention this to you, but I think you need to know about this. The ansible network is awash with reports of a mysterious group ripping apart criminal gangs on multiple worlds. We knew that there were criminals, of course, but had no idea of their extent or power. Anyway, the reports are a mixed lot, too. Some praise this group for freeing slaves and financing rehabilitation programs for them, and some condemn them as terrorists and anarchists that blew up vital commercial holdings. There's been quite a shakeup in the Core Worlds security forces, too, with multi-world anti-corruption efforts growing rapidly. You wouldn't know anything about that would you?" Her eyes twinkled with amusement.

"Who me?" said Bob in his most innocent voice. Then he chuckled. "Yeah, I'm responsible for some of that. Oh, that reminds me ... along the way I created a detailed geo-political analysis of nearly all the worlds within the Core's influence and details of their trading patterns. Was told it was the first time in a generation or more it had been done."

He handed over a pair of fat wallets. "The Core Worlds use data cubes, so I included a set of those. Also duplicated the information on data rods you should be able to read. This'll put you on a more even footing with the advanced worlds."

Rhian's eyebrows threatened to rise above her head as she stared open-mouthed at the gift. "How did you ever get this information?" she whispered. She lifted her head to stare at Bob. "How? It can't be all of it public knowledge?"

Bob laughed. It felt good talking with Rhian again. "I set up a research group on one of the Core worlds that was deep in the influence of the criminal syndicates. Lots of criminals there, but also plenty of good people. You need to keep that in mind, Rhian, you really do. Anyway, my original intent was to hop around the worlds and grab whatever I could to figure out how things worked. This was so much easier and did a much better job. The trading corporations found it useful enough that they began sharing some of what they knew with me. Then the small-time traders and financiers wanted in, and shared still more. It snowballed beyond my expectations, to be honest. And it really was a lot of fun."

"And then you blew it all up. Or so it would appear."

"No, not really. Well, I blew up some warehouses used by the major criminal syndicates. Destroyed the facilities they used to harvest slaves on another world. Oh, and a bank. Aside from that, the bulk of what I did was to scramble the financial records of those criminal syndicates ... but not before sending copies of those records to the authorities throughout the Core Words. You have no idea how much people despise those syndicates, Rhian. I didn't destroy any criminal organizations, but I did paralyse them for a time. With luck, that will buy enough time to cripple them once and for all."

"How did they get so powerful in the first place, Bob? We never heard anything about transtellar criminal syndicates until recently."

"It happened at the end of the last round of wars here. The governments decided to make a deal with the Devil, as you might say. At the end of it, the criminals were so entrenched on so many worlds that it wasn't news any more. Besides, so much of the criminal activity was handled by ship rather than ansible to keep things quiet. It's all there for you to read at your leisure."

"Wow. Uhm, that seems an inadequate response, but ... wow. We've been trying to figure out what's going on out there and how to respond, and this will help us more that you realize."

"I figured it would. They've been lucky to have you here to help them. Anyway, I've decided to return to the greater galaxy outside the Veil. There's still some cleanup work to do ... old weapons caches and such." He paused and looked carefully at her. "So what about you?"

Rhian fiddled with some items on her desk for nearly a minute. She looked up at him and said, "I'm staying. It's a good place, Bob, with lots of good people. I think I can make a home here, a fresh start doing something that really matters.

I can make a difference. Feels like a home even after this relatively short time."

Bob nodded and grinned. "It seems to suit you." Then he became serious. "Anything else I should know about? Everyone in the governing council seems to be on edge about something. Been giving me sidelong glances when they think I'm not looking. Not picking up anything threatening, just bad news that no-one wants to tell me about."

"Not much gets by you, does it?" she said with a grin. After a moment, though, she became serious. "Just one thing, but it's a biggie. Something or someone arrived at the terminus a couple months after you left. I didn't see it, but the description matches that of the Changed, except somewhat larger than your descriptions. Perhaps two or three times larger. It said you were in great danger and needed assistance, then demanded to know where you were."

Rhian shook her head slightly. "The Senior Chancellor was at the terminus facility at the time and spoke with it. He's no fool but was absolutely convinced of the thing's good intentions. Told all he knew, which wasn't much, and the whatever-it-was raced up into the sky and vanished. You meet anyone like that during your mission?"

Bob simply said, "No." The look on his face let Rhian know not to push the issue.

"As I said, the Senior Chancellor is no fool," she continued. "Met with psychological specialists to see if he'd been influenced in some way. He claimed—and still does, by the way—that whatever it was emanated a purity of spirit that touched his cynical old soul."

She paused to look at him straight in the eyes. "Was he influenced, do you think?"

Bob considered the question for a few seconds, then shook his head. "Impossible to say. There's tech to do such things, but it'll leave traces that should be detectable even by this lot. There are a few—very few—among my people who have had that gift of purity of spirit over the years." He inhaled and exhaled sharply. "Not many like that currently around, though. All I can suggest is that if any of them show up, to let them pass." His tone grew somewhat bitter. "There's not much we can do to stop them, in any event."

Then his tone became lighter with a touch of humour. "Besides, whoever it was probably just wanted to warn me to be careful not to injury anyone's feelings. That's what they've been mostly telling me recently. Or at least before I died that one time."

Rhian considered that for a moment then nodded. "Possibly. Except there was a second visit several days after the first. This time, though, there was no attempt to communicate. It came through then shot up into space. Observers just saw a luminous blob that was so bright that no-one was able get a good look at it. Consensus is that it was perhaps twice the size of the first, but that's about it."

Bob shrugged and shook his head. "Again, I have no idea what that was about. Whomever they were, I didn't meet them."

Rhian peered at her friend's face and said in a soft voice, "But you did meet someone, didn't you?"

Bob turned away to look out the window. He said nothing for nearly a minute then whispered, "Set. I met Set."

The look on his face told Rhian that something very bad had happened, but she said nothing. A few seconds later Bob turned to her and said, "On the Nexus planet."

"What happened? It might help you to talk about it."

He inhaled deeply then exhaled with a whoosh. "Yeah, alright. I found an old, old portal on the Nexus world. A small one of ancient design that hadn't been used in a very long time. Set showed up and wanted to pass it along to the humans here, as part of their heritage. We share ancestors, after all, and they'd suffered so much for so long."

"But the Nexus controlled it?"

248

"No. They didn't even know it existed until I showed up. It was apparently set up by the humans who built the Nexus as some sort of fail-safe. It appeared as a blind spot to the Nexus, who built another facility around it. Much like an oyster builds a pearl around an irritant. Why it was never used, I don't know. Anyway, the portal was on the planet. That meant that there was a good chance that eventually they'd find it and figure it out. And that would give them not just portal technology, but access to the alternate energies. Humanity— even the Changed—wouldn't stand a chance. So I figured the only solution was to destroy it and the Nexus with it."

"And what did Set think about that?"

"Didn't agree. Believed the risks could be managed. Thought the Nexus could be reasoned with. He didn't know the history here, of how the Nexus came to be and how it had been struggling to destroy humanity. He saw them as just another alien species that could be reasoned with or at least managed. He was wrong, but there wasn't time to convince him of that." Bob shrugged. "So we fought. He lost. I set the portal to self-destruct and managed to get back to my ship and set it to return here."

"Ah. And Set?"

Once again Bob's gaze went to the window. Rhian pretended not to see him take a quick wipe at his eyes.

She gave him a minute before asking, "So, you're going back to continue your work? Think you'll ever come back here? You'd be of enormous use. The Nexus is gone, but there's still lots of MI out there. The threat is certainly not finished."

Bob shook his head. "No. The struggle and the victory belongs to the people here. I will not take that away from them." A crooked smile appeared on his face, but to Rhian's eyes it had a touch of sadness to it. "Besides, Rhian, I'm so very tired. Been doing little except fighting for a long, long time. Need a break. Think I mentioned that to Celcilia more than once."

"Yes, you did. Which leads me something I need to ask you about that. Great-gran Celcilia's book, I mean. I've showed a bit of it—not much, just a bit—to a couple of trustworthy souls here. They and I agree that it's an important piece of history. If nothing else, it helps the people here understand a bit about the life of their kind—your kind—outside the Veil. It means a lot to them, Bob." She took a deep breath before continuing. "Do I have your permission to publish it? I could make sure that distribution is restricted to senior academics ... there's a history of doing that sort of thing for sensitive materials."

Bob closed his eyes, made putt-putt sounds as he puffed out his cheeks, and then exhaled loudly. "Can't say I'm happy about it, but that's just my pride. Not everything that happened during my time with her reflects well on me."

After a moment he laughed. "Sure. Publish it. Distribute it as broadly as you see fit. The people here are my family, I suppose. Distant cousins, at any rate. They deserve to know about what happened after the Veil was created and that their sacrifices have not been in vain."

Then he became serious. "But make sure they know about our mistakes, too. That's important. The Veil won't stay up forever and they need to think about how to deal with the greater galaxy. The regular humans, I mean."

Rhian swallowed a lump in her throat and nodded.

They sat in companionable silence for several minutes, each lost in their own thoughts. Finally Rhian asked, "Will you ever come back here? If the galactic energy patterns allow it, that is?"

Bob shook his head. "Can't say. Would like to, if only to drop in and see how you are doing. But I've learned the hard way not to make promises like that."

Rhian smiled. "True enough, but then you do tend to get caught up in saving the galaxy." They both shared a laugh at that.

"Still, now that you're planning to retire, or at least slow down, perhaps you'll find the time to travel for its own sake. Great-gran said you used to do that sort of thing. And your Uncle Th'or hinted at it."

Bob grunted a laugh. "Not for a long time but, yeah, perhaps it's time to wander for fun once more. And there is no time like the present to start. I think I'll take my leave and head back."

Rhian clutched at her chest with her right hand in feigned horror. "But, Bob, there are official dinners and receptions and celebrations. Detailed reports to be made. You simply *must* stay." That got them both laughing so hard that her secretary knocked on the door and enquired if they were both quite alright. Through her giggles Rhian managed to gasp out that all was well. The secretary left, shaking his head.

Finally they both wound down and sat calmly wiping their eyes.

"Whew. I'm going to miss having you around, Bob. Oh, you'd better take the back way out. I'll have one of my assistants escort you to the port. Oh, and have the ship grab a copy of everything we've managed to dig up since you left ... lots of interesting tidbits you'll want to know about. Those two control systems you left us keep links with each other as well as for our other stuff, so your ship should be able to gain access easily enough. I kept your credentials active."

"You look like you've found something exciting. Care to give me a hint?"

Rhian grinned at him. "Remember that ancient race who built the transit tube? The researchers on that base found indications they had also done some seeding of humans across the galaxy. That might explain how some of the human worlds got started. But hold on, there's more. After the humans in the Veil defeated the original Enemy, there were attempts made to get out of it. There are very old, fragmentary records of transmissions claiming to be from at least two of those attempts. Most of the attempts failed, of course, but if true might explain some of the other human worlds."

Bob's eyes opened wide at the news and his head rocked back. "Really? That's amazing." A happy grin split his face. "As usual, finding answers to one mystery opens up a dozen more mysteries to take its place."

Rhian nodded. "It's the work of a lifetime ... many lifetimes. There's been so much change here since we arrived, and all sorts of new information, that there's something of a social upheaval. That's my main purpose, actually—to organize the efforts to begin to analyze and categorize all that information. So many old theories and beliefs rendered moot. So many important noses put out of joint. But for all the problems, there's a growing sense of vitality and purpose here that's just amazing. That new information you brought about the Core Worlds will help us more than you can know, I think."

She gave him a wry grin. "Unless you care to stay? It's a good life, here, Bob."

Bob chuckled. "Me, a scholar? Oh, that's an interesting thought, isn't it?" Then his face became sad. "Thank you, but, no. If there's one thing I've learned over the centuries, it's when to leave."

Rhian nodded. "I think understand. Is there anything I can do before you go? Did you want me to arrange for food?"

Bob nodded. "Some fresh fruit would be nice, thank you. That's one thing the food replicators can't do very well, you know. Oh, and a selection of some of the teas and beers would be most welcome."

He stood up and smiled at her. "Celcilia would be proud of you, you know. Very proud. You do her honour." He gave a formal bow.

Rhian returned the bow, then wiped at her eyes. "Thank you, Bob. That means an awful lot to me." Then she became once more the efficient administrator. "Now, let's see about arranging for transportation for your escape from official functions."

CHAPTER TWENTY-ONE
Home is the Hunter

Bob arrived back at the base without incident. He'd spent much of the transit time engaged in physiotherapy and resting. There were a lot of records that needed looking at, but he only gave them the most cursory of examinations. The records he did examine in detail, though, were of the base that was his destination. He discovered several interesting items that would bear looking into.

Upon arrival, the first thing he did was to ensure that his ship was fully secured and locked down. Before exiting, though, he donned a skin-suit and helmet. Although not as resistant to weapons as powered armour, it offered better flexibility. He also strapped on a small toolkit, supplies, and several hand weapons. Suitably equipped to fight a battle in a hostile environment, including vacuum, and survive for several days, he went to the main control room.

Bob was reassured to discover that the security system appeared to be functioning within normal parameters. Regardless of appearances, he ran a complete diagnostics check supervised by the ship. Only after the check found no traces of the rogue sentience or any other outside influences did he relax and remove his suit. He did, however, keep the toolkit and one of the pistols attached to his belt.

His next task was to see if any ships had been seen, but the records indicated that none had. Perhaps Set's boast that he'd stolen his group's only long-range craft had been true. But true or not, Bob spent several hours ensuring that the monitoring and defensive protocols were as tight as they could be. It was vital that this station, and its transit tube terminus, be protected.

The check of the records did show two instances of the transit tube being activated. Both were instances of passages out of the base after his departure. There was no indication of how the intruders got to the terminus area. Given that the intruders were in all probability members of the Changed, stopping that sort of thing would take some serious thought.

With the essentials taken care of, Bob decided to take a break. Rather than eating in the mess hall, he munched on field rations. After that, he set out on a thorough exploration of the base, something he and Rhian had done only to a limited extent before being sidetracked with saving the galaxy. The records he'd studied on the trip here indicated several storage areas that were in use but were unclear what was being stored. That sounded interesting, and was the sort of minor mystery that he wanted.

His first stop brought him to a locked door. He queried the security system and determined that whatever lay on the other side was in a normal atmosphere with no discernible dangers. He confirmed that the area was logged as in use, but the records were silent on what lay inside. Smiling at the thought of a new mystery, he ordered the door to be unlocked. Alert for danger, he walked in and was delighted to find that it contained a half-dozen portable portals. It would take some work to get them operational, but that was a minor consideration. The base portal had been severely damaged by the rogue sentience, so these gave him a way to set up another. If nothing else, he could transit back to his home base. Bob gave a cursory examination of one of the portals, then instructed the base to begin the pre-activation diagnostics. That would take at least a day to complete, and he left the room in high spirits.

His next stop brought him to another mystery storage area that proved to be full of construction equipment of various sorts. Much of it was too large to be handled by a portable portal or his ship, but the remainder would be useful if he ever needed to build anything up to the size of a house. The cabin constructed by Uncle Sid on the home planet of Rhian and Celcilia came to mind.

The third storage area proved to hold a selection of art, from paintings to sculptures to things he'd never seen before. It was a strange collection to find on a military base, and Bob figured the explanation of how it got there might be an interesting story.

The fourth storage area held three shipping containers. An examination of their associated records indicated that these were part of an in-transit shipment that never got forwarded before the base was closed down. Two of the containers held pre-packaged weapons caches on their way to be dropped off for deployment elsewhere. The third held spare parts for ships of various classes. There was nothing there suitable for his own ship, but one never knew what the future might hold.

By now, Bob was beginning to feel quite tired. It had been a long day, and he wasn't fully recovered from his injuries. He decided to head back to his ship and rest there. It was small and cramped, but it felt more like a home than did the base.

The next day, feeling rather more refreshed, Bob got down to serious work. His ship was convinced that the base's control system was free of external interference, which was a great relief. The base's portal was, as expected, beyond repair. It was—or, rather, had been—a full-fledged permanent portal that had a lot of capabilities that the portable units lacked. With a limited tech base and a workforce of one, repairing or replacing it was going to be a long-term project—if it was even possible at all. Not for the first time Bob felt a deep sense of sadness and guilt at the passing of an era.

Still, there was that cache of portable portals to examine. The one he'd left being checked out was still undergoing diagnostics, but everything was looking good so far. The defence systems were all clear and ready. He added some extra sensors in the transit tube terminus room and tied them into the defence network. Anything accessing the transit tube—either coming or going—would cause an alert to be sent to both Bob's ship and home base. As an afterthought, he had the base's defence systems also send notices of any alerts.

After a brief lunch, Bob discovered that the base's control systems had managed to complete their task of breaking into the captured shuttle's control system and records. That meant that he now had a second fully functional FTL-capable ship, albeit a lesser one than his scout craft. If nothing else, he could send it out with a portable portal that would activate when it reached its destination. The trip itself might take a long time, but at least he wouldn't be shut up in a small ship for the duration.

Interested to find out who his opponent had been, he ordered the ship's records to be transferred to the terminal in his office. While waiting for the data to be transferred, Bob spent the time thinking about what had led him to this point and what he wanted to do in the future. Neither held any great appeal to him.

The recent past held too many painful memories. The future seemed bleak and ill-defined. He'd been tempted to stay behind the Veil. Rhian had been correct to say that he could be of great use ... but he'd already spent too much time in endless battles. Still, his adventures with her and others had awakened in him a sense that perhaps he should be spending more time with people. Bob smiled as he pondered that strange new development in his life.

He'd spent centuries on his own and enjoyed it. Of course, he hadn't ever been truly alone. His healing factors had kept up a constant buzz of low-level conversation, and his sensorium gave him a broader and deeper view of the universe. Bob sighed. Sometimes it felt like he'd been struck blind and numb. After a short time wallowing in self-pity, his terminal alerted him to the arrival of the requested data. With a wry smile, he snagged his cup of tea and began wading through the volume of data in hopes of finding some insights into Set's organization.

After several hours of digging, he found the insights he'd been hoping for. For one, Set's boast that his group had a capital ship appeared to be true. They'd been using it to seed portable portals that, combined with some private portals, had created a small network to replace the larger one Bob had destroyed. In addition, the capital ship had been used to transport the smaller craft to a nearby stellar system, and it was from there it made its approach. The capital ship was crewed by Set and a few others, and was supposed to head back to their main base.

Bob couldn't tell exactly what that main base was used for, but he could see that the two ships had done considerable ferrying of equipment to there, with little coming out. From the sketchy manifests, the bulk of the cargo was being used to set up a manufacturing base for, among other things, portable portals. A bit of further digging revealed that the group was fairly small, perhaps a dozen people. Bob's frown grew the more he dug into the records.

It appeared that this gang was, indeed, trying to set up the core of a new empire. They had another two small ships— both armed freighters—and were setting up an industrial base. Their plans included the manufacture of heavy weapons, portable portals, and eventually ships. He sat back with a grunt. This was a clear and immediate danger and would need looking into sooner than later.

Bob spent the rest of the day digging into the captured records and cross-correlating them with the ones stored on his ship. He only emerged from the hunt when the pangs of hunger and pains of stiff muscles forced him back to reality. It took a bit of effort to rise to his feet and several steps before his muscles loosened up enough to make walking not too uncomfortable. His stride gradually changed from a hobble to his regular long-legged march as he headed towards the mess hall. By the time he got there, he was whistling under his breath. After a leisurely supper he opted to head to bed.

He awoke several hours later feeling better than he had in some time. His many aches and pains were still there but seemed to be not so important any more. His mind felt clearer than it had for a long, long time, and he refused to be burdened by the deep sadness buried deep within him. The physical ailments would, he knew, fade in a relatively short time. The mental trauma would take considerably longer, but he had long experience in dealing with such things. He would heal.

The first thing he checked after getting dressed was the status of the portable portal. To his delight it was fit for duty and fully charged, so he ordered the base to bring it up to full operational status. After a quick breakfast, he gathered together a small kit (never again would he be without caught without the basics on his person) and marched to the base's control centre. Once there he set up the controls for unattended operation and informed it that he should be back before too long.

With the security of the base ensured, Bob headed to the storage area where the new portal was located. As he gazed at the dark forms of the other portals, he considered the wisdom of prepping the rest of them for use. He pondered the question for a couple of minutes, then decided that the risks outweighed the benefits. In addition to Virgil, whom Kydos had mentioned, a couple of names on the list of Set's gang were portal experts. All had more experience using portable units than he had, so perhaps caution was called for.

With that decided, Bob activated the portal and set it to link up with the one in his home base. It took nearly a minute to work through the security handshaking his home's portal demanded. As annoying as that was, Bob didn't begrudge the time. He was, after all, alone in a galaxy with a newly-discovered group that had every reason to do him harm. A little paranoia under those conditions was a good thing, he figured.

Finally the link was established, and he walked through to emerge back at his home base. He took a deep breath and let it out slowly. It felt good to be somewhere that felt like home. Stepping to the controls, he dismissed the transit film but kept the two units in a security lock. That meant nothing could contact either of them until he terminated the lock.

He felt a wave of weariness and realized that his injuries were still in the process of healing, requiring him to take frequent breaks. The old thoughts of the nearly unbearable weakness of his merely human body threatened to destroy his newly-acquired sense of purpose until he beat them back. He reminded himself that there was work to be done, with no time for self-pity. Besides, he had some very nice tea that Rhian had given to him and perhaps this would be a good time to try some.

Bob walked to the mess hall with a gait that had become somewhat stiff. He gathered a pot, tossed in some of the tea, added some near-boiling water, and sat down to let the tea steep for a few minutes. After a few seconds he stretched out in a chair, leaned his head back and closed his eyes, trying very hard not to think of anything—especially nothing related to his latest adventures. Despite that, an inner bleakness lapped at and eroded his sense of well-being.

The soft *ping* of the timer brought him back to the here and now. He sat up, not bothering to stifle a groan, and poured himself a cup of tea. Bob blew on the tea to cool it, then took a small sip. That sat so well that he took a mouthful and swallowed, feeling the nearly-too-hot warmth slide down his throat and warm his insides. It was a small note of comfort against a cold universe.

Holding the mug of tea in his left hand, he used his right to scrub at his scalp taking care not to press on the scars with much force. More scars on the outside to match those on his soul. He wrapped the hot mug with both hands and shook his head. Bob tried to shake his feelings of despair and isolation, but only managed to refrain from burying his head in his hands.

Barely.

He settled for leaning back and closing his eyes.

For a moment, a wave of bleakness threatened to overwhelm him, and he scrubbed at his eyes to wipe away the moisture that had appeared. Putting down the mug, he grabbed a napkin and blew his nose into it. He gulped several deep lungfuls of air and managed to regain his equilibrium. Blowing out his cheeks, he held his head in his hands. It had been a long while since he'd had to deal with mental trauma of this magnitude, and he was out of practise. Not to mention that his new body reacted in new and different ways to stress. He was in dire need of some rest, that much was certain. Once he'd dealt with this new threat, a bit of harmless wandering was very much in order.

Bob felt a stirring of air that ruffled his hair. Ignoring it as a transient in the environmental system, another stirring of air tickling his nose caused his eyes to open as he sprang to his feet. The chair shot out behind him propelled by the rapidity of his standing. There was nothing in the room that shouldn't have been there, but a slight sigh caused him to look down at the table. On the end of the table was a ragged, multi-limbed lump of a stuffed toy. He felt a wisp of air caress his cheek, then saw a hint of shimmer in the air that vanished as quickly as it had appeared.

He looked at the object for a moment, then chuckled.

"Hey, Snuffles. It's been a long time."

He lifted the creature and saw a folded piece of paper beneath it. Holding onto Snuffles with one hand, he unfolded the paper with the other. It turned out to be a note.

"Dear Bob. Thanks for the loan of Snuffles, but I think you need him back once more. Remember that he's not the only one who loves you. Please try to stay out of trouble for a while. Even better, stay out of sight for at least a decade or two. You've managed to stir things up and any contact with you is now absolutely forbidden, so it'll be some time before I can contact you again. Love, your youngest sister, Ashira."

As soon as he'd finished reading it, the note turned into a fine dust that vanished into the air.

Bob stood motionless for the space of a few heartbeats. This was something only the Changed could do, but he didn't know who this 'Ashira' person was. Claimed to be his younger sister whom he hadn't seen since he left home centuries ago. He examined the toy. It was very much as he remembered it, if a bit more worn and with a few inexpertly-done repairs.

He chuckled and gave a wave with the creature. "Thanks for returning Snuffles. Wish I knew who you are, though."

The only answer he got was silence.

Bob stared at the figure for a few seconds, then sat back down. Soon enough, Snuffles was sitting on the table across from him with his own cup of tea. After a few false starts, Bob began telling his old friend about his travels and adventures.

* * *

As the hours and days of research and planning dragged on, Bob's initial enthusiasm waned and the dark feelings returned. It wasn't just the death of Set that had dragged at his spirits. Uncle Lou had led him to believe that his merely human body combined with his training and experience made him special ... one of a kind. Supposedly the only one who could enter the Veil. As it turned out, not only could Set enter it (albeit at the cost of time and pain) but so could the Changed.

In truth, he'd been just a useful tool for others that thought themselves better than him. Just like always. Oh, the task was needful—that much was true—but to lie and manipulate him was what hurt. That and the fact that he'd fallen for it. He'd begun to ask questions but circumstances kept pushing him and forcing him into action without much time to analyze the situation.

To help combat the bleakness, he made a point of doing mundane tasks and put off making plans for the future. To begin with, he downloaded the data acquired from his sojourn behind the Veil into the base's records. He also focused on healing his body, spending hours each day in physiotherapy and exercises. Whatever the future held, he'd need to be at peak physical condition to meet it. The activity also helped to take the edge off the blackness that threatened to engulf him.

His mental condition, however, was a problem of a different sort. The inner darkness was a constant threat that required purposeful effort to contain. Experience had taught him that after-action reactions could linger for some time, so he did not begrudge the breathing space he required. Failure to do so was folly, at best.

One morning he woke up with the urge to do a bit more, so he did a general cleanup of the base. Every day after that brought greater strength and clarity. That gave him the strength to sit down and write down everything he could recall about what had happened to him after he'd left to investigate the new base and the subsequent adventures behind the Veil of Tears.

More than once he had to stop as the tears flowed. The process eased his mind, but there remained a weight on his soul. He came to realize that it had begun with his trial on the

Hell Planet, and had come to a head when he fought and defeated Set. They'd been sparring for centuries, but to have it all come to such a nasty end was unsettling and created an immense feeling of loss.

One day he put on a skin-suit and went outside to the airless surface. There, next to the monument to his ancestors who'd died at the base, he built a cairn in Set's memory. As each stone was placed, he paused to remember something positive about his brother. To his great surprise there were enough of those to build a cairn that rose to his waist. Once finished he stood back to examine his handiwork. The suit's systems hummed with the effort of dealing with the hours of exertion.

"You did what you thought was right, Eldest Brother. I may not have agreed with you, but you stayed true to your chosen path."

He stood silently for a few moments, then turned and went back inside with a lighter heart. There were plans to make and schemes to smash. Kydos and her small group were still out there, a menace to everyone. It was time to get back to work.

CHAPTER TWENTY-TWO
A Wanderer Once Again

Bob sat alone in the busy tavern. He was taking up a table in an otherwise crowded establishment, but the clientele had learned to leave him alone. A pitcher of quite good ale sat in front of him to keep his mug full. A plate of cooked meats, cheese, and biscuits sufficed for his meal. He was feeling rather pleased with life at the moment. The planet was advanced enough to offer good hygiene and excellent food, and had yet to be spoiled by excessive technology and the blandness it too frequently brought.

The door opened for long enough to let in a blast of the cold evening air. Bob observed the newcomer with care before turning the bulk of his attention to his meal. The newcomer was an old man, scarred of face and limping slightly with a motion that spoke of long practise. There were no available seats, so the barkeep made to grab the old man and force him outside. The newcomer dodged the extended hand and hurried over to Bob's table.

"It's a cold night, esteemed sir. Might an old soldier tarry a minute to warm up?"

The barkeep hurried up and apologized for the intrusion, promising to evict the old man immediately.

"Let him sit," Bob said. "And bring a mug." He turned to the old man. "If you would honour me with your company, sir?"

The old man nodded his thanks, and after glaring at the barkeep, settled down across the table from Bob. They regarded each other for a moment as Bob pushed his full mug towards the newcomer. "This will take the edge off the cold, I think." He pushed the plate of food forward. "And this will take the edge off your hunger."

With a nod of thanks, the old man quaffed half the contents of the mug in a single gulp, then turned his attention to the food. The barkeep came up to hand Bob another mug. He looked at the old man, then Bob, and quirked an eyebrow. Bob smiled and nodded, sending the barkeep back to his station.

Bob studied the newcomer. His face was lined with age and scars, and had been baked into leather by a life spent outdoors. The outfit was dirty and consisted of layers. After a moment Bob revised his opinion. The clothes were old, battered, and dusty ... worn but well cared for. The greatcoat was long, had a short cape and wide lapels, and was a style favoured by soldiers of a certain age on this planet. As the man's arms moved to grab more food, Bob caught a glimpse of a dagger with an ornate hilt with a military design.

"Have you seen service, old sir?" he asked.

"Aye. Spent my life in service to the Queen and her family. Got too old and stiff so they discharged me last year." He drained the mug and put it on the table, sighing happily. "Seen most of this continent and many of the islands."

Bob filled both mugs and took a sip from his own. "Any family?"

"Aye. A wife, two daughters, two sons." A look of pain flashed across his face. "All living except for my youngest son."

"I'm sorry to hear that. The others are well, I trust?"

The old man shrugged. "Well enough. Everyone is busy with their own lives and we don't talk much these days. Haven't seen the eldest boy in quite some time." He gave a rueful chuckle. "A soldier's life will do that to a family. And since I retired, well, old habits get too ingrained to change much."

266

They drank in silence for a minute until the old man said, "It's hard for a father to bury a child. Not the way it's supposed to be. Feels like I failed him somehow."

"How so? Did you ignore him as a child?"

"No, nothing like that. Taught him everything I could. Taught them all, of course, but him most of all."

Bob raised an eyebrow.

The old man smiled. "Parents aren't supposed to play favourites, but I had a soft spot for him."

"Your best pupil, then?"

That got a snort from the old man. "Hardly. Caused me more trouble than all the others put together. Not of malice, mind. Just very enquiring and always questioning. Disrespectful of authority, too."

Bob smiled. "Did he become a soldier like you?"

"Nah. My eldest son did, but it wasn't for the younger one. A questioning soul like his is destined to be a wanderer. That's one of the toughest and most dangerous paths anyone can take. So I made sure he could take care of himself."

A haunted look came into the old man's eyes and he took a large drink to steady his nerves. "Taught him the only way I knew how. T'was the wrong way for him, but I was so certain that it was what he needed."

"And then?"

The old man shrugged and took a pull of his beer before replying. "It ended badly. Angry words on both sides. Hateful words that could never be withdrawn or made right. He left home. Last I saw of him until I visited his grave."

He stared down at the tabletop for the space of several heartbeats. "But he did me proud. A credit to his family, for all that we fought each other. He'd found a cause, you see. An evil too large to let go by unchallenged. Saved many souls but paid the ultimate price."

Bob raised his mug in salute. "To the memory of your son."

The old man nodded and returned the salute. Both of them drained their mugs and slammed them down on the tabletop.

"Another?" asked Bob.

"Thank you, esteemed sir, but I cannot tarry. The family is no doubt waiting for me at home."

The tavern door opened again to reveal a half-dozen soldiers clothed in a variety of modern, off-world uniforms. They scowled at the crowd and enough of the locals scampered out that the newcomers found room at the bar.

The old man sneered. "Off-world mercenaries with their fancy uniforms and fancier machines. The Queen—long may she reign—should never have signed a trade agreement with that transtellar mining outfit. Especially after they brought in their own mercenaries for 'protection'." He spat out the last word.

The newcomers saw the old man looking at them and responded with their own blood-curdling snarls. The old man smiled broadly, opened his greatcoat to expose the dagger, and tapped its hilt. His mouth smiled but his eyes promised swift death to any that dared to cross him. The newcomers looked away and grumbled into their drinks.

"They seem to know that style of dagger," said Bob in a soft voice that did not carry far.

The old man responded in kind. "Aye, they do. More than one of them has learned the price of disrespecting our people." After a moment he growled, "And more than one of my old comrades paid the price for teaching them that lesson."

"Weren't there two lots of off-world mercenaries?"

"Aye. The Queen hired a protection detail to train our troops and provide enough show of force to create a stalemate. Tensions ratcheted up until a few days ago. Lots of noise and yelling and then nothing." The old man grinned. "Rumour has it that their fancy machines aren't working so well any more. Honest negotiations have started. Very mysterious, but most welcome. Well, I must be off. "

He rose and limped towards the door. As he passed the off-world mercenaries, they began to snarl at him, but turned away from the intensity of his glare. Jackals cowering before an old wolf.

Bob grinned and signalled the barkeep for another jug of beer. The barkeep was about to carry it over when one of the mercenaries grabbed it out of his hands, carried it over to Bob's table, and slammed it down with enough force that some of its contents slopped onto the table.

The mercenary, a young woman, glared at Bob with undisguised anger. Not a violent anger, but rather that of one who has been greatly inconvenienced and made to look foolish.

"You," she growled. "What did you do?"

Bob opened his mouth to answer but closed it with a snap when she gave a dismissive wave of her hand.

"Don't bother to deny it." Her eyes narrowed. "No-one saw you or you'd be in chains. Or dead." Her expression grew thoughtful. "Chains. Chains would definitely be better."

Her expression hardened. "That way we'd be able to beat the cost of replacing all that equipment out of your worthless hide. Do you realize how much that gear was worth?"

"Not worth the lives of any of the innocents that stood between your two armies," said Bob in a mild voice.

The woman's head snapped back as if slapped. "We're here to provide security and training, nothing more. It was the other battalion who are here as aggressors."

Bob examined her carefully. She was a half-head shorter than himself, sturdily built of solid muscle without being chunky, and pleasing of face but not a conventional beauty. Her insignia showed her to be an intelligence officer of earned rank. All in all, an impressive woman who should not be taken lightly.

"Signals officer?" he asked.

"Battle-Captain, Signals Intelligence speciality. Not that it's any of your business."

Bob sighed. "The fact that your two forces were about to engage in combat made it my business. And with weapons and armour—including powered armour—that were far beyond what the locals have or could defend against. I've seen what powered armour does to civilian populations."

His face was grim, and his eyes held a faraway look that the Signals Officer had seen before ... sometimes in the mirror. Then he shook his head and his mood lightened. "I was just passing through, but couldn't let that happen. Would you care to sit down and discuss it?"

He indicated a chair opposite him and gave her his most charming smile.

She sneered at him.

Bob shook his head in mock sadness, but continued to grin. "No-one came to harm, aside from some bruises. Equipment can be replaced, people cannot."

She glared at him, snorted, sat down, and poured herself a drink into the mug the old man had used. "Cuts. Severe bruising. Broken bones. Concussions. Oh, nothing major I'll grant you. Well, except for all that very expensive equipment. Including that powered armour our opposition had—thank you for that, by the way. Though I've no idea how you managed it all, and so quickly. Oh, stop grinning. You seem to think this all fun and games. Well, it's not."

She leaned forward and shook a finger at him. "There are serious economic and political issues at stake here that go far beyond this one planet."

"Oh, I'm well aware of that," said Bob, topping up his own mug. "The Queen made a bad decision going with the Sirob Nosnhoj Cartel. Not surprising given how little contact she's had within the local stellar group, but there are better choices. As for politics, well, I'm sure we can agree that there are several excellent trading blocks that would make much better

270

partners. This planet has some unique resources that could alter the balance of power in small but significant ways. Its location also makes it a potential trading port when those settlements farther out begin to prosper."

The officer's eyebrows raised. She was obviously not expecting this level of discussion from a random stranger in a backwater bar. Especially from one who had single-handedly just stopped a small war by incapacitating both sides—and without fatalities. She took a small sip from her beer as the man across the table from her smiled in a disarming manner.

"Perhaps we could start by introducing ourselves?" he said. "My name is Bob."

She sneered again, but not so broadly as before as she answered, "Herja."

Her visage softened to a wry smile as she leaned back into the seat. "So, Bob, what's a guy like you doing in a place like this?"

CHAPTER TWENTY-THREE
An Unexpected Visit

It was a pleasantly warm afternoon and Bob was fixing the fence around his property. His neighbour's herd was getting rowdy, as it always did at this time of year. The adolescents had a tendency to check out the edges of their territory and test the boundaries. Fixing the fencing was a tedious chore, but one that Bob didn't mind. It gave him a chance to tramp around on his own, the work wasn't difficult, and the neighbour repaid his efforts with meat at the end of the season.

Bob twisted the last link of the barbed wire fence and stepped back wearing a satisfied smile. There were many high-tech solutions for fencing, but barbed wire was cheap and easy to put up. Over the years he'd replaced much of it with stone fencing and thick hedges, but wire fencing had its place. He doffed his wide-brimmed hat and wiped the sweat from his forehead, pausing a moment to fan himself before donning it once more. Reaching behind him, he pulled out a container from the well-worn combat belt and took a long drink. The cold, sweet tea tasted marvellous after the afternoon's efforts.

He felt a faint tingling along the hairs on the back of his neck, a feeling he'd not experienced for many years. Whirling around, he saw a large ovoid that shone with a mother-of-pearl radiance standing several metres away from him. Bob made an annoyed sound as he examined it more closely.

Unlike the ones he remembered, this one had a network of fine white lines throughout its surface.

"Haven't seen one of you for quite a while. Is this a social call or are you here on Conclave business?"

The ovoid spoke. It had a woman's voice, warm and friendly. "Hello, Bob. Yes, it has been a long time. May I be permitted to visit?"

"Is this a social call, then?"

The ovoid chuckled. "Oh, very much so."

Bob shrugged. "Do I have a choice?" Without waiting for an answer, he waved a hand. "Fine. Sure. Put your feet up and stay a while."

"I thank you for the offer of hospitality," said the orb in formal tones. It shimmered and transformed into the form of a young woman. She was a half head shorter than Bob, slim built but not skinny, and the fine lines were no longer evident.

"My name is Ashira." She paused for the space of a heartbeat. "I don't think you remember me, do you?"

Bob shook his head. After a couple of heartbeats, his eyes widened slightly. "Wait. Did you leave me Snuffles all those years ago? After I returned from the Veil?"

She nodded and smiled. "Yes, I did. But you don't seem very happy to see me. May I ask why?"

Bob shrugged. "One glowing ovoid looks much like another, and you lot can take on pretty much any shape you wish. Or any name, for that matter."

"We don't lie, Bob."

"Uh huh. But that doesn't mean that you tell the whole truth, either."

Ashira's smile became sad. "I can't say that I blame you for being suspicious, given what you've gone through." Her hands were folded in front of her and she radiated a sense of calm serenity. "Along with Snuffles there was a note signed by 'Ashira'. I swear to you that I am that person, and that it was I who left you Snuffles and that note. It was designed to disintegrate after you'd read it."

"In the note, you claimed to be my youngest sister," said Bob in quiet tones. "I left home years before her Naming Day and wasn't able to return. I know nothing of her name or her auric signature" He winced and looked away for a moment. "Not that I'd be able to sense it anymore."

"I know about your ... transformation. If you like, I could prove myself by telling your things that only you and I know. How you protected me from Set. How you taught me to protect myself." She smiled broadly. "You even took me to our training planet and showed me that hidden room along the ledge. I made tea and snacks for us, and we sat and talked for hours."

She laughed at the memory. "Looking back, neither the tea nor the snacks were very good, but you acted as though they were the finest you'd ever had. You always made me laugh and feel loved and safe." Her face became serious. "You made me feel strong and capable."

Throughout this, Bob stood quietly, his face showing no emotion. As she spoke, his hands curled into fists, the knuckles white.

"I knew her. I don't know you," he whispered, his voice harsh. He gave her a hard stare. "Memories can be shared or stolen."

Ashira looked away for several seconds before turning back to face him. "That's correct, Bob, they can. All I can offer you is my word that I am who I say I am."

It was Bob's turn to be silent and look away. When he turned to face her once more, his hands were still clenched. "I missed your Naming Day. I promised you that I'd be there, and I failed." He hung his head.

"Bob, it's alright. I understand, and I promise you that I understood then as well. You got caught up in events larger than ourselves."

"I should have made the attempt."

"No." The sharpness of her tone caused him to look at her in surprise. "No," she said in a calmer voice. "That would have been ... bad."

Ashira surprised him by giggling. "Your name was mentioned more than once, though, and by many important people. Ruined Mom's plans to pretend that you didn't exist anymore."

She spread her hands, a large smile on her face. "She was forced to speak of you more that day than she had in years. Hearing your name again, and hearing stories of what you were up to, made me very happy that day."

"Except I wasn't there," came the forlorn response.

Her own reply was firm. "You were there in spirit and people knew it. For the first time in years, our parents were forced to acknowledge you. They'd used the dawn boats to send the announcement of the ceremony rather than posting via the portals, just so you'd not know about it."

She grinned once again. "If it makes you feel any better, Set was late. Almost missed the ceremony, in fact." She waggled a finger at him. "That was your doing, as I recall. Oh, the tongues were wagging about that."

That got them both laughing for nearly a minute before they settled down.

"So how'd you track me down?" he asked. "Thought I'd covered my tracks well."

Ashira laughed. "You did. Took me a lot of effort and time to do it, too. I see you figured out the energy-tracking trick with the ship's engines ... your shielding is very good. How'd you figure that out?"

Bob shrugged. "Kind of obvious." He paused for a moment before continuing in a somewhat embarrassed tone. "Well, obvious once I got back from behind the Veil and had time to think. After that, I bummed around to places where I didn't care if I got tracked or not. When I wanted secrecy, I used a portal." He grinned at her. "I know how to harden those very well." After a second he frowned. "So, seriously, how did you track me here?"

She shook a finger at him as her face assumed an expression of mock seriousness. "I know you, Bob. And I'm no longer the little girl you used to tease and play tricks on. Learned some tricks of my own, I did." Her manner lost the air of playfulness but remained smiling as she shrugged. "Took a long time, as I said. Had a few locations based on your ship's travels until you stopped using it. Made some guesses, followed up leads ... stuff that you taught me to do."

Then she frowned. "Took longer than it should have, though. Had to do it on the sly, when no-one else was watching me. No-one else seemed to know where you were, and I wanted to keep it that way."

"Thanks for that," he said with a nod. "I've worked hard to stay out of sight of the Conclave."

"And that's for the best," she agreed.

Bob pondered that for a moment before replying. "Thanks for leaving Snuffles and that note for me."

"You're welcome. The Conclave had loosened the rules just a bit after Uncle Lou contacted you. They tried to keep that terrible task he'd put on you from me — from *me* who'd been grieving your death for so long. That was the first time I found out that you hadn't actually died. I wanted to contact you but was told not to. *Forced* not to."

Bob felt a momentary pulse of heat from her as her visage darkened with anger, then an instant later she had herself under control once more. He waited until her good humour returned before speaking. "Yes, well, Snuffles helped. More than I think you can know."

"He helped me after you left. He's a good listener," she replied.

He flashed a smile at her, which she returned. They stood in comfortable silence for a minute.

"I need to ask you something. As my sister. Not a member of the Conclave."

"Ask me anything, Bob."

"This isn't the first time we've met, is it?"

She stopped dead in her tracks and turned to face him. Her form softened into a glowing ovoid before snapping back into a human aspect once more. "No," she whispered.

Bob nodded and his voice softened. "The first time was when I died, wasn't it?"

"Yes." The pain she felt was plain to see, and she made no attempt to hide it. "You saved a planet from a portal overload. You'd been chasing your target and got him to leave, but he fiddled the controls before he left. It wasn't a maximum overload, but almost." She closed her eyes for a moment and swayed as the memory of that time overwhelmed her. Then she opened her eyes. "You reset the controls to diminish the energy release and channel it upward."

"Mostly," he said.

"Mostly," she agreed.

A smile tugged at the corners of his mouth. "Ah. Re-channelling an energy release is rather tricky at the best of times. Not surprised that I got it not quite right."

She glared at him.

He laughed for a moment before becoming serious once again. "But the planet ... it survived?"

Ashira nodded. "Yes. Muddled the weather patterns for a few weeks, but that's all. You saved the planet and the sentients living there."

"Then it was worth it," Bob said in a firm voice that brooked no argument.

She opened her mouth to speak, then closed it and instead just nodded.

They walked in silence for a minute, enjoying the sounds of nature around them. Bob stopped and turned to look at Ashira. "There's more, I think. My friends within the Veil spoke of a single ovoid, followed several days later by a larger one that was twice the size of the first. The first emitted a sense of purity as it spoke. That was you, wasn't it?"

Ashira nodded, not trusting herself to speak.

Bob smiled and said, "Not sure who the other was." Then he became serious. "Did we meet there? Within the Veil, I mean." When she didn't answer, he pleaded, "Please, I need to know what happened. I lost so much there. That's where ... where ... I killed Set." He sagged as if being crushed by a great weight.

"No, Bob, you didn't."

His head snapped up. "What? I saw it. I ... we ... fought. He hit me and I hit him and he ... died. Then I set the portal to overload and collapsed. Next thing I knew I was on the ship and safe. How did that happen? Was that you?"

Ashira gave a long, heavy sigh and looked away for a moment. Returning her gaze to him she said, "I arrived on the planet and fought my way to the room you were in. I found both of you laying there badly injured. Set revived enough to help me fight off an attack. Then he neutralized their jamming field long enough for me to apport out to your ship."

She paused as a look of infinite sadness came over her. "I only had enough energy left to apport one of you. Set said that he'd stay behind ... said it was his duty to protect us." Ashira gave a wan smile. "Also said to tell you that you were right. Just that once, you were right."

Bob's hand was over his mouth as tears began to flow. Ashira placed a gentle hand on his arm and allowed him his grief.

"All this time ... all this time I thought ... thought I'd ..." His voice trailed off into a series of strangled gasps.

"No." Her voice was firm. "He died fighting to buy us enough time to escape. Our brother died with honour, Bob." Then her hand fell off his arm to hang limply at her side as she looked away. "It wasn't enough, though. I failed him and you."

Bob regained control of himself and wiped his eyes. "Those marks on your energy form ... those are scars, aren't they? You were badly wounded."

"Yes. Almost died. There were too many of them. Would have died except ..." she looked away and hung her head.

"The other or others came in time."

Ashira nodded. "Two of them, in fact. They showed up as I was on the verge of death, just outside your ship."

Bob's eyes were wide. "I didn't think the Changed could be seriously harmed."

She turned to him, her lips quirked into a wry smile. "Neither did we. Live and learn, I guess."

"So what happened?"

"Aunties Gertrude and Freida showed up seconds before the portal exploded. They grabbed us and your ship, then apported out of range of the blast. Then they healed us both."

"Ah. So why the charade with making it look as if I'd crawled back to the ship on my own? Oh, wait ... the Conclave's edict. None of you were supposed to be there."

Ashira shrugged and tried to look innocent. "Strictly speaking, I was looking for Set and they came looking for me. Not entirely true, but close enough that the Conclave had to accept it. It's complicated."

"Ah. Well, thank you for saving me. And please thank the Aunties for everything. Even the little surprise they added to their repairs."

"Uhm, about that. They did it without your consent, I know."

Bob laughed. "One of the best gifts ever, I assure you." He turned to look back at the house, then back at her. "I have a family now, and they mean the universe to me."

"I'm so glad. Really. Would it be possible for me to meet them?"

He hesitated for a moment then nodded. "They'd like that. I'd like that. It's about a fifteen minute hike to the house. Do you need to change your form for that?"

"Of course I can walk that far," came the indignant response. Then she grew thoughtful. "At least, I think I can. Haven't actually walked much for a long time." With a grin she added, "Let's give a try and see what happens, shall we?"

They began walking, gradually increasing their pace until striding along at Bob's usual military clip.

"You doing OK?"

"Yep. Just have to remember to let the local gravity interact with my feet. Heh, last time I walked with you I was quite a bit shorter. Feels strange to see you at this height."

Bob laughed. "As I remember it, you would complain about being tired and convince me to carry you on my shoulders."

"I was doing you a favour by helping you with your strength training. It was good for you," she sniffed. "It is the duty of every younger sister to help her brother with such things."

They both chuckled, reducing much of the remaining tension between them.

They walked in silence for a time. After a minute Bob said, "I built a memorial to him. To Set, that is. On my home base."

"He'd have appreciated that, I think."

"Yeah." Bob grunted a strained laugh. "First time in ... well, ever ... that we had a proper conversation as adults. Felt good while it lasted." A pained look came to his face. "Didn't last, though."

They continued to walk in silence for several minutes.

"So how'd you get out of the Veil, Ashira? There's been no reports of anyone using the transit tube to get back here other than myself."

"Set's ship. The Aunties got it safely away, and we used it's shielding to pass through the Veil and other energy fields. I needed the time to heal."

"So how'd you get back in time to drop off Snuffles?"

Ashira smiled. "Thanks to Set, the Aunties knew the best way out. They also managed to get the ship to go much faster than designed. Not sure how they managed it ... I wasn't fully myself for much of the trip."

They walked in silence for a time, each lost in their own thoughts. They were interrupted by a soft *bleep* from Bob's belt.

"Ah, that would be my wife," said Bob, as he reached for the communicator. He listened for a moment then said, "Home soon. Bringing a guest. No, it's a surprise. Yes, to me as well. See you soon." After listening for a moment, he tapped at it and returned the device to his belt.

"What's her name?" asked Ashira, a large grin on her face.

"Herja. Eldest boy is Belinus, his younger brother is Balder, and our daughter, the youngest, is Celcilia."

"You named your eldest after our grandfather?"

Bob nodded. "And his brother after Herja's grandfather." He paused for a moment. "Celcilia is named after a good friend who stood by me during a bad time. Anyway, we need to get moving. We're about halfway there."

They continued to walk with Bob guiding the way. Ashira kept glancing over to her brother, smiling in a way Bob had never seen from her.

"What?" he finally asked.

"You ... married with a family. Not something anyone would have expected."

"Oh, really?"

They bickered in a friendly way until they came into sight of the house. Without warning, Ashira stopped. Bob took a couple of steps before coming to a halt, then turned to face her.

"Something wrong?"

Ashira shook her head, paused, and then said, "Yes."

Bob gave her the universal elder brother look of 'what are you talking about?', but said nothing.

She sighed. "You don't understand. Just look at me." Ashira motioned with her hands from her head to her feet. "I don't look human. Not like you. I don't want to frighten them."

Bob opened his mouth to speak then closed it. He looked at his younger sister critically. "Well, you're a little glowy, I'll admit. And a bit floaty. Didn't notice it until you mentioned it."

Ashira snorted and rolled her eyes. "You're my brother ... you don't notice these things." She chuckled as she added, "Look at me, centuries old and nervous as a young girl of a hundred. Me, who brokered a truce with the True Dragons."

Bob's eyebrows raised. "You did what, now? When did that happen?"

She waved a hand. "Not important. Focus, Bob. I don't want to frighten them."

Bob laughed. "I was afraid of them frightening you, to be honest. My kids can be a handful."

At her stern look, Bob held up his hands. "OK, when we get to the porch, you wait outside and I'll let them know what to expect. You'll be fine, I promise."

In a soft voice devoid of humour, he muttered, "Don't say I didn't warn you."

That mollified her, and they continued to the house. Mounting the steps, they paused just outside the door.

"Ready?" said Bob, hands on the door handle.

Ashira took a deep breath and nodded. Just then there was a *thud* as something on the other side hit the door, forcing it open a crack. Through that crack ran three children, yelling at their father as they asked why he was in the way. They skidded to a stop when they spied Ashira, whose concentration broke enough that she floated slightly above the floor of the porch. She glanced down, muttered an apology, and drifted back down. The mouths of the children were open.

"Wow how did you do that who is she she's beautiful why is she glowing where did you find her float up again how high can you go ..." the stream of questions came fast and furious as the children surrounded her. Ashira was taken aback until she saw her brother roll his eyes, and mouth, "I told you so."

A woman's head poked outside. "Don't just stand there, you oaf, get out of the way." The laughter in her voice took the sting out of her words.

Bob stood to one side as the woman slipped out. She surveyed the scene for a moment then clapped her hands twice. The children fell silent, looked at her, looked at Bob, and then back to Ashira. The woman bowed, and said, "Hello. You must be the guest my husband told us about. My name is Herja." She shot a stern glance at her spouse.

"Uhm, yes," said Bob. "Herja, this is my youngest sister, Ashira. Ashira, this is my wife."

His visage darkened as he glared at his children, who took no notice of him. "And these are my unruly children: Belinus, Balder, and Celcilia. Children, this is your Auntie Ashira. She's come a very long way to visit us. I want you to be on your very best behaviour."

In response the children turned as one to look at their mother. Herja nodded, and the children all sighed. "Yes dad if you say so dad yes father," came the chorus of replies.

Herja smiled warmly at her sister-in-law and held out her hand. "I'm in the middle of making supper. Would you care to join us?"

Ashira grasped the welcoming hand and nodded, relief plain on her face. Bob herded his children into the house, and they ran in with shrieks of joy. Herja led Ashira to the kitchen, saying, "Why don't you help me prepare the meal? You look as if you need some time to acclimatize."

In the kitchen, Herja began peeling vegetables while Ashira stood there looking uncomfortable.

"I understand you're one of the Changed," said Herja, not missing a stroke. Ashira noted that she was using what appeared to be a large combat knife.

Ashira nodded. "Bob told you about us?"

"Some. Even after all these years, he's still a hard one to pry information out of." The two women grinned at each other.

"Yes. I don't know how much he told you about us. About me." Ashira paused for a moment. "Is there something I can do to help? I'm not used to just standing around."

Herja pointed at a cupboard with her chin. "Could you get me the medium pot out of the bottom drawer, please? No, the next size up. Great, now fill it half full with water and bring it over."

When it came, Herja dumped the peeled vegetables into the pot. "They stay fresher after peeling when you put them in water right away," she explained. "There's more in the bin over there, if you wouldn't mind fetching them."

From the next room they could hear the children laughing and shrieking. Ashira glanced in and saw Bob tossing the children about as if he were juggling them. His face had a large smile on it, but she could see the effort the exertion was causing him.

"Is that safe?" she asked Herja.

"They're getting too big for that," Herja said with a grin. "He's going to hurt himself one of these days, I'm afraid. But the children love it so, and he'd do anything for them."

"Ah. Uhm, mind if I ask some personal questions? I'm his sister and, well, I worry about him."

Herja chuckled. "I'd be shocked if you weren't curious and caring enough to ask me questions. Pretty sure I know what they'll be, but ask away. As Bob likes to say, ask me anything."

"Thank you, Herja. You're taking my appearance very calmly. As much as I appreciate that, I'll admit to being surprised."

Herja laughed. "I've been hanging around with your brother from some years now. He's told me stories, and I've read the records of quite a few more. There's very little he's hidden from me, I assure you."

Ashira sighed and looked down, her hands still. "He's had some dark times."

Herja stopped her work and looked at Ashira. "I know. Trust me, I know. Just so you know, I've got my own share of dark times as well. Did he tell you how we met? No? Well, I used to be a mercenary, with all that implies. Came from a planet where society had collapsed. The other worlds had all but abandoned us except for a single port they kept open by force of arms. Our only export was fighters. Anyone who survived was a potential recruit." Her eyes took on a faraway look for a moment, then she shook her head. She paused in her work and looked at Ashira. "I worked my way up to the rank of intelligence officer. That's when I met Bob."

"Uhm, not to be nosey, but I'm nosey when it comes to my brother."

Herja chuckled. "I take no offence. My platoon was on a security contract. No fighting, as such, just training and surveillance. We were there to counteract another platoon of mercenaries hired by a transtellar mining outfit. Anyway, tempers were running high. Between us and them, between them and the locals ... you know how it goes. Things were getting to the point of outright conflict when Bob wandered by the planet. One night, just before the situation was about to explode, everyone's high-tech gadgets stopped working. Not just stopped working, in fact, but rendered inoperable in some mysterious manner. There were no fatalities, but a number of guards got beaten up by a mysterious someone who raced through both camps. With all the outworld mercenaries disarmed, the local government decided to take advantage of their formerly weak position to begin serious negotiations. It all worked out well, more or less. I encountered Bob in a bar. We exchanged heated words, and then reasoned arguments, and then ... well, here we are."

Ashira tilted back her head and laughed uproariously for several seconds before regaining control of herself. That caused Bob and the children to pause in their play and stare. Ashira grinned and waved a hand at them. With that, the children continued the harassment of their father.

The two woman talked as they continued to prepare the meal. After a while, with the meal cooking in the oven, Ashira joined the children in the other room. Bob took advantage of the break to go off and clean up. She noticed them playing with a stuffed animal of some sort. On closer examination she saw it was Snuffles. It had new patches from when she'd last seen it, but it was the same old Snuffles. She asked the children about it, and they said they've had it for as long as any of them could remember.

Ashira knelt down and grinned at the children. "Snuffles used to be mine, you know. And your father's before that."

"Really?" said Celcilia, her eyes wide as she stared at Ashira.

"We've had it since forever," added Balder.

"Where did it come from?" enquired Belinus.

She paused a moment before answering. "Our parents made it for your father. I think it was when he was about your age," she said pointing to the middle child, Balder.

"Where are they now? Are they dead? Why does Father never talk much about them?" came the torrent of questions from the children.

Ashira was taken aback by all the questions. This was not something she had experience in dealing with. From the corner of her eye she saw Herja smiling then nodding at her. Ashira took a deep breath before answering. "My parents— your grandparents—are both alive and well. But they are very far away and can no longer make the journey. As for your father, well, he never got along with our parents as he grew up. Ours was not the happiest of families, I'm afraid." Which was close enough to the truth, if a bit simplified.

"It's complicated," stated Belinus in a firm voice. "That's what Dad always says about things he doesn't want to talk about."

It took considerable effort, but Ashira managed to hide the smile that threatened to burst forth.

Celcilia looked up at Ashira and asked, "Why is everything so complicated?"

"Uhm ..." began Ashira, unsure of how to answer.

"That's enough, all of you. Go set the table. No whining, now. Go." Herja clapped her hands twice to enforce her command. With a great show of reluctance the children rose to their feet and headed off to the dining area.

Herja turned to Ashira, a large smile on her face. "They can be a handful. Always asking questions." Then her face became serious. "Bob and I each have parts of our lives that they aren't ready to hear about. They've gotten used to the blank spots in our histories, but keep trying to find out more." She shrugged. "Can't blame them, of course, but it's for their own good." She paused for a moment then added, "You about ready to eat? The children will start without us if we don't get there soon, I'm afraid."

As they sat down to eat, the children noticed that Ashira didn't take any food.

"What's wrong, Auntie Ashira?" asked Celcilia.

Bob cleared his throat. "Auntie Ashira is an energy being, and can't handle food like we can."

That generated a barrage of questions that was halted only when Ashira rapped her knuckles on the table. All eyes turned to her as she took a bit of every dish onto her plate. She lifted some onto her fork, put it into her mouth, chewed, and swallowed. A brief flash of light emitted from her stomach, to the astonishment and delight of the children. They demanded that she do it again, so she obliged them. After that, Herja demanded that they finish their own meals. Each child grimaced as they swallowed, obviously trying to duplicate the flash of light. Ashira smiled and duplicated the feat several times.

"Please stop encouraging them," Bob sighed. Ashira responded with a knowing smile at her brother that made him roll his eyes and bend down to his own meal.

Eventually the meal was finished and the dishes cleared. Everyone gathered in the living room, and Bob lit a fire in the fireplace. The children peppered Ashira with questions until Bob called a halt to it. For once they obeyed in a timely manner. They looked so despondent that Ashira offered to sing them a song their father had taught her. That brightened their mood, and they listened in rapt silence for several minutes as she sang. When it was done, Herja clapped her hands and demanded that the children go and do their homework. They clomped off with minimal grumbling.

"That was lovely, Ashira," said Herja. "Bob taught that to you?"

"Yes, when I was very young." She turned to her brother. "Remember that?"

Bob grunted a chuckle as he leaned forward to give the fire a poke. "Yep. As I recall, you'd stubbed your toe or some such, and thought the world was ending."

Ashira grinned at him. "I heard that tune years later, but not with those words."

This time Bob laughed. "It was a song Auntie Gertrude taught me. A very old song ... old even in the time of our ancestors, as I was given to understand." He shrugged. "I changed some of the words to suit the situation."

"I don't recognize the language," said Herja. "What is the song about?"

Ashira grinned. "As Bob said, it's very old. It's a story about a warrior who changes his ways to become a guardian. Except Bob changed the words to make the story about a young girl who learns to be brave and conquer fear."

Her grin faded to a look of affection as she looked at her brother. "I never forgot it. Always sang it to myself whenever I felt alone or afraid."

A distracted look flashed on her face, vanishing as quickly as it came. She turned to Herja. "May I borrow my brother for a few minutes? This is important."

Herja nodded.

"Bob, can we take a walk? Outside?"

CHAPTER TWENTY-FOUR
The Final Sacrifice

They left the house and walked down the driveway, Ashira setting a brisk pace. They walked in silence for nearly a minute before Ashira stopped and turned to face Bob.

"There's so much we need to talk about but so little time. Thought it best to do this in private."

"What—?"

"We're leaving. All of us."

"Ah. And by 'all' I assume you mean the Changed?"

"Not just the Changed, all the remaining ones as well." She stopped and hung her head.

"Except me," he said in a soft, kind voice.

Ashira said nothing, but only nodded, unable to look at him.

"I'm sorry to see you leave, but not sorry to be left behind with my family. I'm fine with that. More than fine, if truth be told. Wouldn't leave them for anything or anyone."

They both looked away into the distance for the space of a few heartbeats. Bob turned to Ashira with a wry smile. "I think I've got just the going-away gift for you. It's in the ship. Care to walk with me?"

"No time. Hold my hand."

He did as he was told. The air around him blazed with heatless glory for a second. When the glow faded, they were in the interior of his ship.

"Hmph. Nice trick. Follow me." He led her to the room he normally used as his cabin. She looked around with obvious fascination.

"Thought you'd seen all this before," he said.

"No. Well, not when I was fully conscious at any rate. This is amazing, Bob. Like something out of the histories."

"Well, it is something out of the histories. Literally. Anyway, this is what I wanted to give you."

He fiddled with a set of decorations and a section of the wall vanished to reveal a cavity. He reached in and withdrew a dull black cube. Each side was roughly the size of his hand. He turned and handed it to her. She examined it with care then looked at him and said, "It's lovely, but what is it?"

"An old-style data storage unit. It's got pretty much everything I've ever accumulated from every ship or base I've encountered. Set's bases and ships, my own ships and bases, my diaries, everything. Pretty sure some of those are places only I've seen since the Great Wars. It'd be a shame if all that history of our ancestors was lost."

Her eyes went wide. "Thank you, Bob. But we've got no tech that'll read these, you know."

"So it'll be a hobby to pass the time along your big journey," he said with a grin. "Help teach you to master the fine control of your energy manipulations. The older folks will have seen things like this and be able to assist you."

"It's encrypted?"

"Of course. The keyword is the name of the toy we shared."

They grinned at each other at the memories that invoked.

Bob cleared his throat. "Anyway, you'll notice that it is actually two units contained in a single box. They're duplicates, so you have one to practise with."

"Heh. You sound like Dad."

"Oh thanks ever so much for that," said Bob with exaggerated nonchalance. "There's some fascinating ancient histories of what happened behind the Veil, too. Helps to explain some of those mysterious human worlds scattered across the galaxy."

Her eyes widened at this.

Bob's face became neutral as he added, "And evidence of a pre-human precursor race. Predates all the other races we ran into, as well."

"Excuse me? A precursor race?" Ashira's form wavered for a moment before re-solidifying.

Bob laughed at the shocked expression on her face. "Oh, not something you overly-evolved types knew about? Humans aren't the first galaxy-wide species with portal tech."

Then his features softened to a grin. "Sorry, that was a bit mean. Truly, there's data about them. Not much, but everything I have is there."

"Your innate talent for understatement has deepened over the years, brother dear. Any still around?"

"Not that I can determine. They appear to have left a long, long time ago. I suspect it was to leave a clean slate for those that were to come after. That'd be us and the other races that tried to wipe us out."

"I look forward to reading about all that. And your diaries. I appreciate that ... more than you realize, I think."

"I wish there were more time," said Bob.

"As do I," said Ashira with a sigh. "Which reminds me ..."

The air about them glowed for a moment as they returned to the field where they had originally been standing.

Ashira once more mentioned how much Bob now reminded her of their father.

"I am not my father," Bob said with some heat. "I am nothing like him. Nothing at all."

"Ah. Well. Uhm, mind if I ask what became of Kydos and her friends? We can't seem to find them ever since you got back from behind the Veil. Did you kill them?"

"Only the one. But he was trying to kill me." Bob's face turned grim as he added, "And had slaughtered some innocents who got in his way."

"Oh. I am sorry for that. Who was it?"

"Mordad, I think. He never gave his name, but I found the ship he was using and got into the control system. That gave me enough information to go after the others."

"I see. So you went after them with the intent to kill them?"

"Nope," said Bob with a large grin. "Did you know that they were trying to re-establish the portal network with old wartime portable portals?"

Ashira's eyes widened as she shook her head.

"Yep. That and re-establish a tech base to start up yet another little game of empires. After all I'd been through to knock down Set's scheme, I wasn't about to let that happen." His smile faded as he thought about his dead brother.

"And?"

His grin returned, but with a touch of sadness. "Was tempted to put a permanent end to them and their schemes. In the end, decided that it wasn't my place to do that." His grin returned in full humour. "Decided instead that they needed more time to contemplate the lessons of the Philosophy of Change."

"Oh, dear." She tried to look stern, but hints of a smile kept plucking at the corners of her mouth. "What did you do?"

"Put each of them on their own planet. No portals, no tech of any kind. Oh, and a planetary jangle field to keep their enhancements in check to help focus their minds on the important things in life. I figured you lot would hear from them when they reached a sufficient level of enlightenment. If and when."

Ashira laughed and clapped her hands, a grin on her face. "Care to share those locations?"

"Well, you know how forgetful us old folks are." He evaded a playful punch with ease as he added, "Figured a century or three of isolation will do them a world of good."

Her smile vanished as she bowed her head for a moment before raising it to look at her brother.

"We don't have centuries any more. We're leaving. And I mean right now."

"Excuse me?"

"It was decided that we need to leave. All of us. For the sake of the younger races as well as ourselves. Most have already begun the journey."

"Ah," said Bob. "Well, the planets are all located within the Tancel Sector. The jangle field generators can be located with a standard command interrogation burst, and that'll give you the exact locations. The data cube has the information, too."

The faint sounds of shrieks and laughter coming from the house caused them both to turn and look into the distance.

Ashira smiled and waved at them. "They seem happy. You seem happy. Happier than I've seen you in so very long. I've never seen you so contented, either. You've got a wonderful family."

"Yep. Heh. Can't help but notice the kids have an uncanny resemblance to our family."

At the sudden guilty look on her face he laughed. "Oh, I'm not complaining. Quite the contrary, in fact. Just curious how you did it. Didn't think you had that level of knowledge."

"Uhm, I don't. Look, this isn't something the Conclave knows about or needs to know about. Understand?"

Bob just stared at her with the stern look of an older brother. "What did you do?"

Ashira giggled. "Oh, that tone of voice brings back memories." Then she cleared her throat and became serious. "When the aunties reversed your sterility, they decided that our family's genome should be preserved."

"Oh. Well, it ended up for the best. Say, uhm, maybe it'd be best not to mention it to Herja."

"Oh, she knows. We've already talked about that."

"Ah. Just out of curiosity and a sense of self-preservation, what else did you tell her?"

"Everything she needed to know about you."

The look on her face and the tone of her voice caused Bob to grunt as if hit in the solar plexus.

Ashira smiled sweetly at him. "It's a sister's duty."

"Gah." Bob rubbed his temples for a moment before turning to face his sister once again. "Well, alright. I guess. Anyway, how long are you staying? Seriously, we'd all of us love to have you around for a while. A long while, to be honest."

She shook her head. "Just another minute or so, I'm afraid."

"Oh no. That's ... wait. Is the geas against interacting with me still in effect? After all these years?"

She nodded, her face serious.

"Ah. So this little visit is also unsanctioned?"

Ashira grinned. "Indeed, my brother. But there was no way I'd leave without saying goodbye. But I can't keep blocking them for much longer."

Bob laughed. "I'm surprised you can do it at all. How'd you learn that little trick?"

"Auntie Gertrude gave me quite a bit of advanced training. Uncle Th'or taught me a few tricks, too."

"Uncle Th'or, eh? My, my, imagine that." He paused for a moment. "So where are you going?"

"Far away. Too far for another visit within your lifetime, I'm afraid."

"Thank you for dropping by. I'm very glad that you met my family."

A sound from the direction of the house caused them both to turn and look. Herja and the children were standing outside, waving. Bob and Ashira waved back. Then she glanced at the sky. "Gotta go. My minders have tracked me down and are very cross with me."

"You have minders?"

She snorted a laugh. "Oh, yes. They arrived with a long and serious lecture about not following in your footsteps, bad example that you are."

Bob's eyebrows rose to their limit.

She cleared her throat and looked embarrassed. "Uhm, well, after you ... died, that is. I ... uhm ... finished your chore. Of closing down the last of the portals."

He bit his lips in an effort not to laugh. After a few seconds he managed to choke out, "And ... ah ... encouraged them to seek counselling?"

"For their own good, yes. And, uhm, made sure to tell them that you had sent me."

Bob burst out laughing. After a few seconds he managed to get his humour under control. "I'm sure that went over well."

She grinned. "Yes, and—" Her face clouded as she winced. "They're yelling at me now. I really do have to go."

Bob grinned. "Give 'em hell, little sister."

"I learned from the best. That's why they assigned me those minders." With a happy smile on her face she turned her face towards the sky and muttered, "Don't get your knickers in a twist, I'm coming."

Her form began to glow with a heatless light that outshone the sun for a second. When it faded, she was gone.

"Say goodbye to Mom and Dad and Elder Sister for me," Bob whispered as he looked skyward. He wiped at his eyes, then turned to re-join his family.

CHAPTER TWENTY-FIVE
Family Past and Future

Bob was enjoying a day alone with his youngest son. His wife and other two children had gone to the local town to do some shopping. Bob was using the time to do some baking, an activity that he'd learned to quite enjoy.

"Father, father," yelled the son as he ran down the stairs. "The perimeter sensors have picked up an intruder."

Bob sighed. "You sure it isn't just a large animal. Remember last time you thought there was an intruder? Is it moving?"

The boy blushed. "Not this time. I'm sure of it. You need to see this. Whatever it is has stopped at the fence, right where the cameras can't see it very well."

Bob frowned. This was going to interfere with his baking and probably ruin it. If it was an animal, he'd turn it into a meal. If human, he'd make sure to teach him or her a lesson they wouldn't soon forget—a man's baking was too important to be interrupted for trivialities.

He trotted to the security room, wiping his hands on his apron as he went. When he got there, it was obvious that the boy had been correct. There was, indeed, something there. A human-sized something. A look the detailed sensor logs showed a number of strange readings, though. Bob grunted in annoyance and triggered a full sensor pulse towards the intruder. The displays showed a blur as the target disappeared then re-appeared at the main gate, within range of a camera, but still outside the fence.

As he gazed at the figure, he frowned in concentration then inhaled sharply. Without turning he said, "Call your mother. She—"

"She's on her way, Father. Just got a message from her. Says she's coming weapons hot."

Bob sighed heavily. "Tell her that weapons aren't needed. In fact, tell her to be sure to disable them. Don't want any misunderstandings."

"You know him?" asked the boy, pointed at the display. The image was of an aged, rather scarred, old man.

"Yeah. Unfortunately. Wait here. I'll deal with this."

"But, Father..."

"Stay here." The ice in Bob's voice put an end to any argument. "Monitor and record. You know the drill." He forced himself to smile and soften his tone as he ruffled the boy's hair. "It's alright. It's just someone I need to talk to."

He turned and left the room, picking up a light-duty combat belt as he left. It was an old habit, and one that he'd worked hard at keeping.

It took several minutes of brisk walking to reach the gate. He could have taken a vehicle, but he needed the extra time to calm himself for what lay ahead. Despite his training and centuries of experience at keeping calm in the face of peril, his nerves were still on edge as he approached the figure.

"Hi, Dad. Been a long time."

"Hello, son. Yes, too long."

"Gonna disagree with you on that."

"We managed to have a nice chat in that pub."

"Didn't know it was you."

They stared at each other for a few moments, then each looked away. The old man cleared his throat a few times but didn't speak. Bob's face was a study in stone. After several heartbeats, Bob puffed out his cheeks as he exhaled and looked at his feet.

"Ashira came by a few days ago. Said all of you were leaving. Sounded like a big rush." He kicked at the ground with a toe, still not looking at his father.

"Yes, well, the Conclave has its own schedule. I have mine."

Despite himself, Bob smiled. "Ah," was all he said. Then he turned his head to look at his father.

"Dad..." he began.

The old man held up a hand as he looked at Bob. "It's alright, son. We can't pretend that there's no issues between us. Serious issues. I'm here for two reasons." He paused, a look of pain on his face.

"Uh huh. Go on."

The old man stood ramrod straight as he looked at Bob. "To say goodbye. Whatever has passed between us, we'll never meet again." His face spasmed for a moment as he regained control of his emotions. "And I'd like your permission to see your wife and my grandchildren."

"And if I refuse?"

"This is your home. I would, of course, leave immediately," the old man said in formal tones.

The two men stood staring at each other. A minute passed in silence, then another.

"Please, Bob. I'm begging you. Just a few minutes. To see them and to say goodbye." The words came out of the old man as if torn from his soul.

Bob just stared into the distance for a moment before speaking. The words came out clipped and harsh. "You trained me to be a soldier. You trained me to not care about the feelings of others. Then you sent me into Hell, to survive or die."

The old man stood silent for a moment before replying. "It wasn't like that, Bob. There was more to it than that. It—"

"It's complicated. Yes, Dad, it's complicated. It always has been." Bob exhaled sharply and looked towards the horizon for the space of several heartbeats before turning back to his father. Then he gave a shuddering sigh as if a great weight had been released from his soul but not before tearing its way out.

"Yes. I'd like you to meet my family. My wife and two of my children aren't here right now."

"I can sense their vehicle approaching at speed," said the old man with eagerness in his voice. "We have a few minutes before they arrive. But you have a third child, I believe?"

Bob smiled, a proud look on his face. "My second son. He's monitoring at the security console and relaying events to his mother."

"Ah. Should we switch to another language, then? One they can understand?"

"No, this will do for the moment. We need to talk, Dad. A private talk for now."

The old man nodded. "Probably for the best. I take it you have questions?"

Bob snorted. "About a million or so. As do you, I suspect. You go first."

"Bob ... are you alright with Set's death? He died well. With honour. But I'm worried about how you are dealing with it."

Bob's head jerked back. This was not going at all the way he expected. "Uhm, always thought I'd killed him. Then Ashira showed up and told me what really happened. Tough to process, but took a weight off me."

"But you're dealing with it? No guilt?"

The look of concern on his father's face caused Bob to laugh. "Excuse me? When did you get so worried about my feelings?" Then he blushed and apologized.

"No, son, you've a right to laugh. But it's all part of the Philosophy of Change, you see. To understand ourselves and how we've affected others by our actions." He paused and his voice grew soft. "I did the best I could. Did what I thought was right."

Bob glared for a moment, then gave a heartfelt chuckle. "I know, Dad. Didn't really understand until I had children of my own. But to answer your question, yes, I'm alright. Set and I talked a lot ... at the end." He got a faraway look in his eyes. "Connected in a way that we never did before." Bob paused. "Then we ran out of time, and circumstances forced us to choose." He shrugged as he added, "It was what had to be, I guess. Wish it could have been different, but don't see how."

His father nodded. "Set achieved his peace at the end. I'm glad to hear that you've achieved yours. But you have questions of your own, I think."

Bob nodded. "The Conclave forbade interaction with me, yet you met me at the pub. In this guise ..." Bob waved at the figure before him.

His father laughed. "Oh, yes, the Conclave. I go along with them as it suits me. Which it mostly does, I might add. But when you got sent to back to the Testing Planet ..." the old man paused and looked down at his feet for a moment before looking back at Bob. "I am so very sorry about that. More sorry than you can possibly know. It wasn't supposed to happen that way."

"But it did, Dad," Bob said in a soft voice. "Then thanks to Kydos and her crew, I was sent back to be punished for surviving your testing."

The old man snorted. "As if I'd let that happen."

Bob's head snapped up and he stared at his father. "The ship. You arranged for the ship to be sent there, didn't you?"

The old man laughed. "Of course it was me. I knew you'd find some way to drag things out ... out of pure cussedness if nothing else. I tweaked the control systems of the base and ship to get the ship sent there."

"Tweaked? How? There was no record of tampering."

"Oh, please, son. I've been twiddling security systems for centuries before you were even born."

"Hmm. Speaking of which, Ashira said the aunties taught her how to bypass the Conclave's minders."

"Heh. And who do you think taught them?"

The two men shared a laugh about that. Then the sound of a horn beeping from the direction of the house caused them both to turn towards it. Herja waved and stood expectantly.

"She's back, Bob. May I meet her and your children?"

Bob's face hardened for a moment, then he sighed sharply. "Yeah, why not. Let's go meet them." He signalled her to stay where she was.

They walked toward the house in silence. Just before they got there, Bob's father muttered, "I should have brought gifts."

"It's fine, Dad. They'll be thrilled just to see you," Bob whispered back. He'd never seen his father act so nervous.

Then they were at the house. The children stood in the doorway, in a state of motionless silence that was foreign to their nature.

"Honey, this is my father. Dad, this is Herja. Those little ones in the doorway are Belinus, Balder, and Celcilia."

The old man greeted Herja warmly then knelt on one knee and faced the children. Celcilia approached him and touched his scarred face. The scars melted and his face became smooth.

"You have the touch of a healer, little one," he said softly.

The young girl gave a shy smile, then moved to her mother's side and hugged her legs.

The old man turned to the boys. "I'm pleased to make your acquaintance, young sirs."

"Auntie Ashira said you and Father never got along. Is that why you've never come before?"

Herja turned to rebuke her son, but the old man waved her to silence. "Your father and I stopped speaking long ago, it is true. That was a failure on my part. I cannot change the past, as much as I wish I could. But it's never too late to start."

That broke the ice, and the children began chattering away at the old man. He listened with grave attention to their words and answered as required. To Bob's amazement, his father was quite at ease being surrounded by the conflicting demands of a group of small children. For their part, the children were quite taken by their new-found grandfather.

Herja smiled and whispered to Bob as she squeezed his hand, "He seems very nice." Bob grunted noncommittally.

After several minutes the old man rose to his feet. "I'm afraid that I must take my leave of you. As your Auntie Ashira no doubt told you, we are taking a long journey."

"But you just got here," whined one of the children.

"Auntie Ashira stayed for supper," said another.

The old man gave a serene nod. "She had the gift of time that I do not."

Bob interjected, "Ashira got here before the great journey. My father is running a bit late, and will be getting into trouble for that."

"But you said he was the greatest warrior ever," said Belinus.

"Yeah," said Balder. "Who's going to mess with him?"

"Thank you for the votes of confidence," said the old man as he quirked an eyebrow at his own son. "Still, it is the wise warrior who chooses his battles. In this your father is correct, and I must abide by the decision of the Conclave. One must obey authority." Then he paused and added with a twinkle in his eye, "But it is up to each of us to decide in what form that obedience will take."

With that he turned to Herja and said, "It has been my deepest pleasure to make your acquaintance. To see my son happily married and with family is my greatest joy, I assure you. Thank you."

He turned to the children. "Honour and obey your father and mother. They love you with all their hearts. Never doubt that."

Finally, he turned to Bob and said, "Walk with me for a few moments, son, before I have to go."

The two men walked away from the house. When out of earshot of the others, the old man said, "Thank you for that, Bob. It means a lot to me."

"And Mom? And Elder Sister?" asked Bob. There was a hint of pain in his voice.

The old man shrugged. "That's more complicated than you know. Both feel the loss of Set very keenly. I thought it best not to expose your children to that."

Bob nodded. "Probably for the best." He paused for a moment. "So what happens now?"

The old man smiled. "We leave. You stay and raise your children. Be happy. Live well."

"Thanks, Dad. We will."

"Oh, one last thing. I dropped by our private training planet a while back and noticed that you'd started building a cabin."

Bob nodded. "Yeah. We had our honeymoon there."

"Ah. Fine for that, I suppose, but a bit ... primitive."

"Yeah, well, I've been meaning to fix it up. Hard to find the time."

"Oh, I know how that is, trust me," the old man said with a nod. "Well, we've fixed it up a bit."

"Excuse me? Who is this 'we'?"

"Oh, Th'or and Sid and I. Sort of a wedding present. Figured you could take your family there for vacations."

"I'm not sure the kids ..."

"Oh, I planted a thick hedge to create a safe area for the children. Sid selected a good variety of plants, including several different types for the orchard. The house—did I mention we enlarged it—has several different power sources. And a fantastic library, much of it donated by Gertrude with additions by Sid. Oh, and he left a strange glass sculpture there ... said you'd know what it was. The place will be a wonderful learning opportunity for the kids, you know. Has a proper security system, of course."

"Dad ..."

"We installed food synthesizers as well as a few stasis units stocked with enough food to feed an army. Speaking of which, I moved those weapons caches you left so the kids can't get at them. Can't be too careful, you know. Marked the locations on maps left in the cabin."

"Dad ..."

"I made sure to neutralize all the traps, by the way. In all the training levels. Still lots of dangerous areas, of course, but no sense in ..."

"Dad ..."

"Oh, and I tuned up all the portals on the planet. Those small ones need re-calibration every few centuries. Been longer than that since I last did it, so they were overdue. My bad."

"Dad ..."

"Speaking of which, I took the liberty of re-calibrating the portable portal you set up on this planet's moon. Good spot for it, by the way. But those things need to be looked at least once every couple of decades. Just so you know."

"Dad ..."

"Th'or set up a private portal on the planet he was using when you last met him, with yourself as the only authorized user. You can modify that if you like. It'll make a nice change of scene for the kids. Be good for them to see more of the galaxy than just a couple of planets."

"Dad ..."

"Oh, and I tuned up that private portal of mine above the volcano." His voice took on a note of pride. "Left it as is ... I'm quite proud of that one. No-one else ever managed to make a stable aerial portal like that, though quite a few tried. You'll need anti-grav packs to access it, of course, but that'll be a good place for the kids to go after their basic training. Oh, and Freida made me promise to ask you to look in on those pets of hers once in a while. Not sure I'd allow the kids near them, myself, but she swears they'll be fine. Not sure if she was referring to the creatures or your children, though."

"Dad," Bob said in a firm voice that brooked no argument. He took a deep breath and let it out slowly. "Thank you. And thank Uncles Th'or and Sid for me, if you would. And Auntie Gertrude for the library." Then he paused for a moment as he face took on a puzzled look. "How long have you been working on this?"

"Oh, a few years on and off. You stopped going there after your honeymoon, and the gang and I got to talking about how it'd be a shame to let a nice planet like that go to waste. It's been in our family a very long time, you know. Hate to think of it not being used. By family, that is." His voice turned quite wistful at the end. After a short pause he asked, "We had some good times there, didn't we, Bob? It wasn't all training, you know."

Bob hung his head for a moment then raised it to look at his father. A slight smile tugged at the edges of his mouth. "Yeah, some good times for sure. Lots of happy memories associated with that place."

The old man relaxed as if a great weight had been lifted from him. He smiled and nodded at his son. The two were silent for the space of a few heartbeats, then the old man said, "Mind if I ask you a question?"

"Eh? Sure."

"I went to those two bases of yours and tried to get in to re-tune those old portals but got stopped by a new barrier. You've improved the defences, haven't you?"

"Yep. Those are my private places, and I've learned a few tricks. Including how to block the Changed."

"Well done, son. Though you might want to step up the power and check the phasing of those new barriers. They can hurt us, but won't stop a determined attacker who is willing to accept pain and damage. I, uh, left some suggestions for improvements in that new cabin. Oh, and be sure to check the tuning of those old portals on the bases. They can get cranky."

Bob laughed. "Yes, sir. I'll put that on my to-do list. And thanks for the tip on the barrier."

"Yes, you need to protect the transit tube. Speaking of which, did you ever go back to the Veil?"

"Just a couple of times. Took Herja to meet an old friend of mine who lives there. A few years later I got an urgent request for assistance, so popped over. The MI had been trying to build a new Nexus and were putting up a good fight. I took it out, then came home."

"Hmm, more to it than that, I suspect. Were you ever tempted to stay there?"

"Nope. Would have gotten sucked into years of warfare. Then, of course, the subsequent rebuilding and trying to create an alliance among all those factions who would no longer have a common enemy or cause to unite them. Well, some of them are fixated on me as an enemy, so there's that."

He shuddered. "Not sure which would have been worse ... brutal warfare or political intrigues."

His father snorted. "Can't dodge your responsibilities, son. You could have been a big help."

Bob shook his head. "Not really. You don't know the politics and sociological history of the region like I do. To set up a proper foundation for the future, it had to be their battles, their successes, done their way. Stepping in as the living embodiment of our common ancestors would have set up a toxic social dynamic. That's not my analysis, by the way, but that of some brilliant scholars who have spent their lives there."

"Ah. Well, I guess you know the local situation best." He heaved a large sigh. "Would have liked to go there. So much history. So much ancient loss."

"I gave Ashira a copy of all my notes and data records. Everything I learned is in them." His eyes twinkled. "There's also some interesting new mysteries for you to ponder on your journey."

"Not going to give me a hint?"

Bob laughed. "What, and spoil the surprise? Just remember that it is her gift to share however she wishes."

"Heh. Well, in that case I suppose there's nothing for it but to be extra nice to her."

They both chuckled for a few seconds then grew silent. This time, though, the silence was a companionable one. Finally, Bob spoke in a soft voice, "Thank you for dropping by. You were right ... it's been too long."

They stopped and looked at each other.

"Yes, it has, son. What's that old saying, 'too soon old, too late wise'? Pretty much every culture I've ever visited has a variant of that."

Bob nodded. "A universal piece of wisdom." He paused for a second before continuing. "Thanks for teaching me how to survive, Dad."

The old man nodded, not trusting himself to speak. His form blurred then became a luminous ovoid. "Three grandchildren. And they know their grandfather. Oh, that is riches beyond measure, my son. You have blessed me."

He glowed with a heatless light for a moment, then was gone.

Later, when the children had been put to bed, Bob and Herja sat on the porch as they sipped their wine and stared up at the stars.

"So, that's your father. He seemed nice."

"I suppose so."

She gave his arm a playful punch that had a bit of sting to it. "He's your father, Bob. Be nice."

They sat in companionable silence for a minute. "So what did you two talk about? Just before he left, that is."

"Nothing much. He and a couple of uncles fixed up that old cabin we honeymooned in. Made the area more kid friendly, he said."

Herja brightened. "Oh, that'll be a great spot to take the kids."

Bob turned to her in surprise. "When we were there you said it was a great military training area."

"I also said it was one of the most beautiful planets I'd ever seen. So tell me about these improvements."

Bob shrugged. "He didn't say much. Seemed quite proud of it, though."

"Uh huh. I may not be the linguistic expert that you and Rhian are, but I picked up something about orchards and a library. And a bigger house."

Bob shrugged, not looking at her as he took a sip of his wine. "So why ask me what he said when you already know? And when did you learn that particular language?"

It was Herja's turn to shrug. "I used to be an intelligence officer, you may remember," she said with a sniff. She took a sip of her wine. "Rhian gave me her language notes when we saw her. And a copy of her ancestor's book, given that we were hoping to name a girl-child after her. Interesting reading, that. Rhian suggested I not mention it until the proper moment. You pick up the most interesting women."

Bob wisely remained silent, choosing instead to take a large sip of wine.

"We should go," she continued. "To your training planet. With the kids."

"I dunno. Not sure if I want to expose the kids to the sort of training I was forced to endure."

"Yeah, yeah, you're not your father. Heard that before, my love. Still, it is part of their inheritance. And probably a lot of fun for them. Well, the first level area at any rate. The others are military-grade, I agree."

She looked at her husband with a no-nonsense look. "I think it would be good for them. And you. It'll give them a link to their family history. Mine's nothing they need to know about, at least not for a good many years. Yours has some rough edges, sure, but they'd get a real thrill out of a visit. Especially now that they've met Ashira and your father. And didn't your father mention something about other planets?"

Bob rolled his eyes. "It'll mean a trip in the ship to get the portal."

"Oh, the kids will love that!"

This time he turned to look directly at her. "Our kids. In that small scout craft."

She nodded.

"Our hyperactive kids who get into everything. In a very small craft with limited space."

She threw a gentle punch to his shoulder. "They're ready for this, and you know it, my love. Besides, it'll only be for a few hours even allowing for a bit of sightseeing. Then through the portal and to a new planet. You've been drilling them on ship routines and disciplines for a couple years now. It's time to reward them." She sighed and waved a hand around. "I love our home, but could use a good wander. We've been so busy here with the kids and all. It'll be a good family adventure."

Bob thought about it for a few seconds then laughed. "Sure. Why not? What could go wrong?"

Author's Afterword

Although authors are to blame for the final product, none of us are an island when it comes to inspiration and assistance.

The original inspiration came from pictures posted on Twitter as writing prompts ("write a story based on this picture"). I started making up strange and silly responses around a character named "Bob". I'd especially like to thank @DougWallace1973. He not only posted interesting pictures, he encouraged my silly micro-stories and jokes.

Many thanks to my beta readers: Janice, Lynn, and Trit. Your encouragement helped keep me going.

The cover image is based on a 1905 advertising poster created by Adolf Hohenstein (1854-1928) entitled "Fiammiferi senza fosforo del Dottor Craveri" (Doctor Craveri's Matches without Phosphorus). The background astronomical image is emission nebula SH2-114, credited to T.A. Rector (University of Alaska Anchorage) and H. Schweiker (WIYN and NOAO/AURA/NSF)

About The Author

Brian retired from the software development rat race to take up the carefree life of an author. He lives with his wife and two cats in Ontario, Canada.

For the latest news about this and forthcoming books, the occasional commentary on life, or to leave a comment (we love feedback), check out Brian's blog at

www.BrianGreiner.ca

Books by Brian Greiner

All books are available as e-books and paperbacks
from:

kobobooks.com

amazon.ca

amazon.com

overdrive.com

The Ascending Darkness series
#1 Darkness Creeps Forth
#2 Darkness Comes Reaping

The Accursed North series
#1 The Werewolves of Winter
#2 The Final Doom

The Saga of Bob series
#1 Ancestors and Descendants
#2 Dagger of Eons
#3 Burden of Consequences
#4 Barrier of Tears

Ancestors and Descendants

Bob has spent much of his life crisscrossing the galaxy trying to protect people from the ancient evils, horrors, and demons that lurk among the stars; fearsome creatures that consider humans as mere nothings, if they bother with humans at all.

Some call them monsters.

Bob calls them family.

Now he has discovered evidence of an insidious and corrupting influence spreading across the galaxy, threatening his family and all of humanity. Unsure of who he can trust, Bob must fight to uncover the truth and find a way to save everyone. He will discover there are no perfect solutions, and all come with a price.

Dagger of Eons

There are horrors and evils that lurk among the stars. Bob has spent centuries trying to protect humanity from the worst of them, especially from the schemes of his older brother.

Now humanity's ancient enemies are rising once more to exert an insidious and corrupting influence. On the run and with time running out, Bob must sift through the layers of mysteries and find a way to stop the destruction of all he holds dear.

Desperate times call for desperate measures; measures that will demand a high price.

Burden of Consequences

Actions have consequences.

Bob has always been willing to accept responsibility for his own, but now he's being forced to assume the burden of others. Reduced to being merely human, he's being pursued across the galaxy by a rogue AI, a planet of fanatics out for his blood, and his own people. His many enemies think he's now weak, vulnerable, and ripe for exploitation. They've forgotten that Bob has spent centuries learning how to deal with opponents more powerful than himself.

It's time for Bob to remind them who they're dealing with as he investigates a mystery that threatens humanity.

Barrier of Tears

Bob has saved humanity throughout the galaxy on numerous occasions, and successfully battled against fearsome opponents.

For his efforts, he was forced to be reborn as merely human. Despite his greatly diminished powers, a new challenge has been thrust upon him. An ancient refuge has been turned into a prison, and a force that once protected humanity is poised to destroy it.

Once again, Bob must dive into mysteries that span the galaxy, uncovering and decoding clues. Once again, he is opposed by secretive and powerful forces, some human and some not. The chances of success are low and his chances of survival even lower.

There are many types of barriers. Bob will discover that the least substantial can be the most deadly.

Darkness Creeps Forth

A terrorist attack that leaves Toronto's financial district in shambles and the country's economy vulnerable. An investigative reporter who uncovers a major national scandal and then dies of apparent natural causes before his story can be published. Investigating these seemingly unrelated events draws small-time private investigator Yancey Franklin and his friends into a century-old web of corruption and deceit that threatens the security and independence of Canada. In a desperate race against time, Yancey and his friends rush to prevent an attack by a ruthless opponent on an ageing secret military facility in northern Ontario that holds a deadly secret.

Darkness Comes Reaping

Small-time investigator Yancey Franklin has thwarted the plans of a ruthless enemy to unleash biochemical weapons in Northern Ontario. Now he is on the run and trying to uncover the secrets behind a century-old web of corruption and deceit that strives to eliminate Canada as an independent nation. In a desperate race against time, Yancey and his friends struggle to stay alive as they rush to stop their enemy's latest plan – the deadly "Harvest of Souls".

The Werewolves of Winter

The werewolves were created by the Change Plague—the result of ill-considered biotechnology. It was only their annual winter die-off that saved humanity. But every spring the Change Plague returned to create a new and more deadly crop of werewolves.

People adapted and managed to carry on despite the increasingly precarious situation.

One man, trapped on his farm north of Toronto, began to piece together hints of a deeper and more dangerous threat. With werewolves closing in, time was running out in a desperate race to uncover answers.

A novel of modern horrors, ancient prophesies, data analysis, and nerds who save the world.

The Final Doom

Felix Kurtsius discovered that the Change Plague was being dispersed as part of a deliberate attack. Toronto appeared to be the epicentre for the infection, which targeted Canada preferentially. He escaped to Toronto after werewolves began purging the rural areas of humans, only to discover insidious forces at work. In a race against the clock, Felix and his friends must use all their skills to unravel the forces behind the werewolves, and prevent the destruction of humanity.

A novel of modern horrors, ancient prophesies, data analysis, and nerds who save the world.

www.ingramcontent.com/pod-product-compliance
Lightning Source LLC
Chambersburg PA
CBHW020909200626
46814CB00001BA/249